"Excuse Me?"

Tannim jumped in startlement, and turned to face the barn door.

And froze as he saw who was standing there behind Joe, his mind lodged on a single thought, unable to get past it.

It's her—it's her—it's her—

And it was: the woman who had haunted and hunted him through his dreams for the last decade and more. The woman he'd dreamed of this morning. *Her.* And she stood there, nonplussedly taking in his look of complete and utter shock.

There was absolutely no doubt of it; she matched his dreams in every detail. Gently curved raven-wing hair swept down past her shoulders and framed a face that he knew as well as he knew his own. Amused emerald-green eyes gazed at him from beneath strong brows that arched as delicately as a bit of Japanese brushwork.

"Excuse me," she said again, in that throaty contralto, " . . . but I understood that I could find someone here who works on Mustangs."

He looked past her and spotted her black Mustang standing in the midst of the tall grass outside the barn door.

"Not—for a long time," he said dazedly.

"Ah," she replied.

Then her eyes widened as she looked past his shoulder, and she stepped back in alarm.

Fear lanced him. He whirled to look. There was nothing there.

He turned back, and she was already gone. And so was her car.

Only *then* did his ~~~~~~~~~ ~~~~ into gear, as he sprinted past the broken-d~~~~~ ~~~~~~ ~~~~ ~~~~~ ~~~ had been. There was th~~~ ~~~~~~~~~~~~~~~~~~~~~ ~t no track-marks leadin~~~ ~~~~~~~~~~~~~~~~~~ ~t the car had actually b~~~~~ ~~~~~~~~~~~~~~ ~ that spot, and there ha~~ ~~~~~~~~~~~~~

She was haunting him still, ~~~~ ~~

CHROME CIRCLE

A NOVEL OF THE SERRATED EDGE

MERCEDES LACKEY
LARRY DIXON

BAEN

CHROME CIRCLE

Copyright © 1994 by Mercedes Lackey & Larry Dixon

A Baen Books Original

Baen Publishing Enterprises
P.O. Box 1403
Riverdale, NY 10471

ISBN: 0-671-87615-5

Cover art by Barclay Shaw
End piece by Larry Dixon

First printing, August 1994

Distributed by
SIMON & SCHUSTER
1230 Avenue of the Americas
New York, NY 10020

Typeset by Windhaven Press, Auburn, N.H.
Printed in the United States of America

● CHAPTER ONE

Gently bending the speed limit, eh? Turnpikes were fine things, out here in the Southwest; long stretches of arrow-straight macadam where you could really burn up some hydrocarbons. With one eye on the radar/laser detector and one ear on the CB radio, Tannim was confident there weren't too many Smokies, plain brown wrapper or otherwise, that he wouldn't know about long before he had to back down.

Heat waves distorted the landscape on either side of the Mustang, and made false-puddles on the asphalt ahead. Tannim had forgotten how hot it was in Oklahoma at the end of May, and how intense the sun-glare got by mid-morning. Despite the protection of his ultra-dark Wayfarers, he still squinted against road-shimmers, the glare of sunlight off the metal and glass of other vehicles, and the occasional flash from reflective debris beside the road. In Savannah, Georgia, it was still spring; here it was already summer, and the long grass in the median showed the first signs of sun-scorch. Not as much as there would be by the end of June, but enough to make the ends of the cut stems noticeably brown, even at the speed he was moving.

One good thing about traveling by day. No ghosts. Usually. He wouldn't have been entirely surprised to have seen a weary spirit trudging along the shoulder, equally weary ox beside it, pulling a wagon that would not have been much larger than the Mach One Mustang he drove now, laden with all the worldly goods the long-dead pioneer owned. *Or an Osage or Cherokee, trying to defend the last corner of the homelands he'd been promised.*

He chuckled at his overactive imagination. In all the times he'd driven this stretch of the turnpike, he had yet to see a ghost, and he wasn't likely to this time, either. Not unless there was another Ross Canfield somewhere down the road, existing in an endless loop of time and replaying the mistake that got him killed, over and over again—until Tannim or someone like him happened by to free him.

Shoot, by now, Deke Kestrel's cleaned up every highway ghost between here and Austin.

The Mach One's air-conditioning worked overtime against the heat outside the car. This morning in the motel outside Little Rock, the weatherman on CNN had predicted temperatures in the upper 90s for all of Oklahoma. Tannim suspected it was closer to 110 than 90, at least out here on the open road with no shade. He recalled working on his first cars in heat like this, spending every free moment during the school year and most of his summers out in his old barn, with no a/c and scarcely a breeze to dry his sweat. He'd come a long way from that barn, and the kid with all the dreams. Never had the dreams included anything *like* what had really happened.

Funny, when I was a kid, I'd thought the things I "saw" were nothing more than oddball hallucinations, entertaining as hell, but no big deal. Like an imaginary friend, only better, some a lot sexier than any imaginary friend a high school kid would imagine. I just chalked it up to puberty, but they're still on my mind. Hell, back then I even thought Chinthliss was an "imaginary friend," and I figured that still seeing him just meant I had a better imagination than everyone else. Until the spring dance, I never knew it was all real.

How old had he been? Young enough to think he knew everything; old enough to impress that visiting writer playing chaperone with his "maturity." *Then things at the dance got ugly. Somebody there was using the emotions as a power source. I noticed, and so did that lady writer— Tregarde? Was that her name? She not only saw what I saw, but knew it was trouble. An adult, seeing it as sure as I did. It wasn't my own little fantasy anymore. Showed me I'd have to stop playing around with magic, or it'd eat my lunch.* He'd had a long talk with Chinthliss that sleepless night. Given how things looked on the surface, intensive psychotherapy seemed like a fine option until his not-so-imaginary friend had confirmed it all. The magic he'd been playing with was real; the things he'd been seeing were real. In pilot parlance, it was time to get out of the simulators and take a real stick, or give it up. *I grew up on heroes; I opted for taking a shot at becoming one and doing something about the bad guys. Clever me, I thought that just having magic would let me take care of everything. Always happened that way in the comics.*

Since then, he'd seen things no "rational" person believed in anymore; he'd been shot at and beaten up and chewed on—as his often-aching left leg reminded him— by creatures nobody'd ever heard of outside of myths and horror movies. The magic had brought him good times, too, but plenty of moments when he wished he'd never taken the particular path his life was on. Sometimes he wondered if it had been worth it. If the green-eyed kid had known what was going to happen to him, would he still have gone for it? Or would he have sold off every piece of chrome, burned his little notebooks, and gone into accounting?

Well, maybe not accounting. Maybe art, like my folks thought I would.

His eyes itched, and he groped reflexively for the package of antihistamines on the seat beside him, popping one out of the foil and into his cupped hand without taking his eyes off the road. This was the time of day when people suffered highway hypnosis, especially people in cars with no a/c; more than once he'd had someone in front of him start to swerve into his path as they dozed off. And there were always the "Aunt Bee" and "Uncle Josh" types, who thought forty-five was *way* too fast to be driving; you could come over one of the deceptively gentle rises and be right on top of them before you knew it. Especially out here. But the double-nickel was just too slow, and the sixty-five limit wasn't much better.

He washed the bitter pill down with lukewarm Gatorade, and tossed the now-empty foil packet in the back seat with its crumpled brethren. Hopefully the pill would kick in before his nose started again.

Right. Your Majesty, may I present the Incredible Hero Mage with the dribble-nose. He'd learned pretty quickly that magic was like any other ability—you needed to be aware of it to use it, and not only did it not solve everything, it didn't solve *most* things. It was about as miraculous as a lug wrench. Hell, he couldn't even cure his own allergies with it!

He never had any trouble remembering why he'd left Oklahoma; his allergies never failed to remind him, usually long before he crossed the state line. He sighed and downed another mouthful of his drink. *The planet must dump every substance I'm allergic to on the state when I head this way.* The only good thing about his allergies was that by the time he graduated from high school, they were so bad that he needed no excuse to leave the family farm. *Not when I can't get within twenty feet of a cow without my eyes swelling shut.* Never mind that the antipathy between Tannim and farm animals seemed to be mutual. Cattle took a perverse pleasure in chasing him, geese hated him on sight, chickens went out of their way to shed feathers on him, and as for horses—

The only horses that don't try to flatten me come under sheet metal hoods.

That was most of the reason for his sinking feeling of dread as he approached the outskirts of Tulsa, headed ultimately southward toward Bixby. His father's last several letters and phone calls for the past year had all been about the changes he was making. Since he had resigned himself to his son's career-track in car testing and racing and Tannim was not expected to take over the family farm, his father had decided to turn the farm into something more lucrative. Not incidentally, it was also now more likely to sell when he retired. The old homestead was no longer a farm, it was a ranch. A horse ranch. Doing well, too, it seemed.

Quarter horses. Just what I need. They're going to take one look at me, and I know what they'll do. Tannim had never once gotten within a foot of a horse without it stepping on him, kicking him, biting him, or attempting other assorted mayhem on his person. Dad would expect some help, even if it meant that Tannim had to take allergy pills until he was stoney. *Well, Al told me that Joe likes horses. Maybe I can talk him into helping Dad out, and getting me off the hook, at least until we can head back to North Carolina and Georgia.*

Young Joe was the other reason for this trip, besides the Obligatory Familial Visit, though the connection between the young man who now called himself "Joe Brown" and Tannim was a convoluted one.

Yeah. Once upon a time.

It all started with Hallet Racetrack.

Hallet International, the small and slightly silly monument to the desire of men and women to hurl their bodies as quickly as possible around a loop was not all that far from Tulsa, or more importantly, Bixby, where the old family farm stood. And last summer, Hallet was where two Fairgrove Industries mechanics had been sent to help out in track-testing the first Fairgrove foamed-aluminum engine block to leave their hands.

Fairgrove also "employed" Tannim as a test-driver, mechanic, public relations, and general "outside" man. Or, as Rob had called him, a "gentleman flunkie." He also drove for their SCCA team, but he'd have done that without the pay.

So far, so good. Ordinary enough; plenty of racing concerns had a guy who was that kind of jack-of-all-trades. And plenty of racing concerns hoped to become big enough one day to field engines or parts of them to other teams. But that was where the ordinary took a sharp right and snapped at the apex.

One of those two Fairgrove mechs that had found themselves out in the heart of Oklahoma just happened to be a Seleighe-Court Sidhe.

In other words, Alinor Peredon, "Al Norris" to the real world, was a genuine, pointy-eared, long-haired, green-eyed, too-pretty elf-guy, just like the kind that clogged sci-fi bookstore shelves and played Tonto in the comic books. So, too, was the head of Fairgrove, one Keighvin Silverhair, Tannim's long-time friend and employer.

The other mech, a laconic fellow by the name of Bob Ferrel, was human enough—but *he* just happened to be a wizard. A minor wizard, whose magics mostly had to do with making engines purr like kittens, but a wizard nonetheless.

Not that he's in my league, but he isn't bad in his own area. Al's better, of course, but you don't dare send an elf out into the Land of the Mundane without a human helper to keep him from blowing his cover. They may be competent enough Underhill, but out here in the wild world, they're rubes.

Perhaps if Tannim had been sent along on that little junket, things would have turned out differently.

Then again, maybe not. Some way or other, though, I'd have wound up with severe bodily injury. I always do. Why is that?

Somehow Alinor had gotten himself mixed up with a desperate mother, her kidnapped and mediumistic child, and a looney-tune preacher. The preacher called himself "Brother Joseph," and manufactured bargain-rate zealots that made skinheads look like cupcakes, and called his little social club the "Sacred Heart of the Chosen Ones". . .

. . . *add in a Salamander from the era of the Crusades, the ghost of a murdered child, and a bigger bunch of incendiaries than the Branch Davidians. Naw, I don't think anything would have been any different if I'd been there, aside from my hospital bills. The situation was too unstable. The Feds would still have moved in, and the Salamander would still have blown things sky-high. Nasty creatures.*

Alinor and Bob had to handle the whole mess on their own; Keighvin Silverhair and Tannim had their own fish to fry at the time. A spiteful bunch of Unseleighe Court creatures had made themselves nuisances over a crucial period out at Roebling Road Racetrack in Georgia. They'd almost cracked up the Victor GT prototype, and they'd managed to cream Tannim's *good* knee while they were at it. Coincidence? Maybe; maybe not. The Unseleighe had ears and eyes everywhere; like Murphy's Law, they always chose the worst possible time to act.

For the most part, Al and Bob had handled it all very well. Alinor had been rather sloppy towards the end, though; he'd had to play fast and loose with the memories of several of the humans involved, and he'd had to do a quick identity switch on himself. But by and large, there hadn't been too many loose ends to deal with, and most of those had been taken care of within a month.

All except one: young Joe, the teenage son of the lunatic preacher Brother Joseph, a boy who had taken his own life in his hands to expose the crimes going on in his father's compound. He'd turned informer partly out of a revolted conscience, but mostly hoping to save the little boy Al had been looking for—Jamie Chase, the kid who'd been kidnapped to the cult by his own father.

When everything was over, Al had forgotten there would be one person around who still knew something about the supernatural goings-on. He couldn't really be blamed for that. He was a mechanic, not a military strategist or superhero. Young Joe still had unclouded memories, and he had no relatives, nowhere to go. For the short-term, the Pawnee County Deputy Sheriff, Frank Casey, had been willing to take the boy in. Joe was eighteen—barely—but did not have a high school diploma and was not particularly well socialized. Frank felt the young man deserved that much help.

Young Joe had seen a little too much for his own peace of mind, and not enough to keep him from getting curious once most of the furor had died down.

Turned out that he was both curious and methodical. It wasn't hard for him to find out *some* of what had gone on, not when his little friend Jamie Chase and Jamie's mother Cindy were spending a lot of time with Bob at the track. Between one thing and another, he'd managed to ingratiate himself with Alinor and Bob before the test runs ended, and that was when they discovered that the kid was a potential wizard himself. He was telepathic and also had that peculiar knack with human machines that Bob, Al, and Tannim shared.

Now, there were several options open to them at that point, including shutting his newly awakened powers down. But while he was not quite a child, he was still close enough to that state to qualify for elven assistance, at least so far as Alinor was concerned.

Alinor had an amazingly strong streak of conscience, and was quite a persuasive master of argument when he put his mind to it.

He had stated his case, articulately and passionately, to his liege lord, Keighvin Silverhair. In the short form, Al wanted "Joe Brown" brought into the Fairgrove fold, as many other humans had been in the past. Bob backed him up. They both felt the kid had earned his way in; certainly Jamie would have been dead two or three times over if Joe hadn't protected him.

Joe sure was emotionally and spiritually abused by his old man, which qualifies him for help as far as my vote goes. Poor kid. I wouldn't have wanted to go through what he did for anything. Then you figure out what he must have felt when they told him that the compound went up and that the Feds shot it out with his dad and killed him. Poor Joe; everything and everyone he knew either went up in smoke or is rotting in a federal pen. And rescuing that little Jamie kid by going public and turning his nut dad in—that took some real guts. From all Al said, the cult played for keeps; people like that usually find ways to deal with "traitors." Permanently.

Keighvin listened and Keighvin agreed, allowing Al and Bob time enough in Oklahoma to reveal something of their true natures to the boy. If he accepted them, he could be invited to join the human mages, human Sensitives, and elves of Fairgrove Industries. That organization was loosely affiliated with SERRA—the South Eastern Road Racing Association, which itself had more than a few non-mortals and magic-wielders in its ranks. And if he freaked, they would wipe his memory clean, shut his powers down, and let him go join the normal world.

Joe didn't freak; in fact, he was relieved to find *some* kind of explanation for what had happened at his father's compound. Either the kid was very resilient, or this was a side effect of being taught so many half-baked, conflicting notions that nothing really seemed impossible anymore. Bob was convinced that the kid would make a first-class Sensitive and a fine assistant to Sarge Austin back at the Fairgrove compound. Sarge would make a good role model and father figure for young Joe; a true rock of stability, with honest, simple values. The one place where Joe had actually been happy was military school—working under Sarge should do wonders for him. The only pot-holes in the road were the facts that the kid was barely eighteen, being watchdogged by the Feds, under the temporary guardianship of the local sheriff, and they couldn't just kidnap him.

So they reached a compromise, worked out with Frank Casey: Joe would finish his last year of high school in Oklahoma, so that he had a genuine diploma. When he graduated, someone would come from Fairgrove to pick him up with a "job offer." And meanwhile, Al and Bob would keep in touch with him through letters, phone calls, and occasional visits, by means both mundane and arcane.

Enter Tannim, who hadn't been back home in more than a year. The elves felt very strongly about the ties of kith and kin, and took a dim view of people who treated such things carelessly. Around about March, Keighvin had begun to hint that it would be a good idea for Tannim to "spend some time with his family." By the end of March, the hints had turned about as subtle as a ten-pound sledgehammer upside his head.

In April, Tannim thought he *might* get off the hook; a major disaster Underhill and in the more mundane lands of North Carolina had left Elfhame Outremer in ruins and all of the Seleighe Court in shock. Virtually everyone on the East Coast was needed to help put the pieces back together again. But by the middle of May, with Joe about to graduate, Keighvin's hints turned into an order. Tannim *would* go visit his family, and while he was there, he would pick up young Joe and bring him back to Fairgrove. But not until he had spent *at least* two weeks in the family bosom.

Go rest, he says. Spend time with your family. They miss you; they need to know you're all right. Relax, he says. Like I'm going to be able to relax around my parents! I can't tell them more than a tenth of what I really do! And good old Chinthliss—if he gets wind of the fact that I'm not busy, he'll want to show up, and the last time he showed up—

"Hiya, boss!"

Tannim yipped in startlement and rose straight up in his seat, narrowly avoiding running off the road. He was no longer alone in the Mach One.

Lounging at his ease in the bucket seat next to him was James Dean, famous boyish good looks, Wayfarer sunglasses, red leather jacket, and all. There was just one small addition: in fancy chrome over the right breast of the jacket was a tiny logo composed of two letters.

FX.

"Mind if I come along for the ride?" Foxtrot X-ray asked with a lopsided smile.

Tannim calmed his heart and his temper with an effort. There was no point in getting mad at Fox; the Japanese *kitsune*-spirit operated by his own rules. There was no point in complaining. Fox wouldn't understand why Tannim was upset. And Fox was good-hearted. He'd done Tannim plenty of favors since they'd met.

"Can anyone see you but me?" Tannim demanded, his attention torn between his sudden passenger and the road. Having a James Dean lookalike along was going to complicate an already complex situation. . . .

Why couldn't I just be gay? It would be a lot easier to come out of the closet than to explain any of this to my parents. . . .

"Of course not!" Fox replied. "Why? Do you want to show me off? That could be fun—"

"*No!*" Tannim shouted. "No, I do *not* want anyone else to see you! *Not* my parents, *not* the neighbors, *not* the people in the next car—"

"Oh, they won't be able to see me," Fox said, shrugging dismissively. "I don't know whether your parents have the Sight, but even if they do, I can keep them from seeing me if you really want. They won't think I'm real, and that's half the battle. Half the fun, too!" Fox cracked a vulpine grin. "But what about that kid you're supposed to pick up? He could probably see me even if I shield from him, unless I made a point of not coming around while he's with you. That could be fun, too. I could make it a game. You sure you want me to stay hidden?"

Tannim paused a moment before saying anything, thinking hard. It could be useful to have Fox appear to Joe—could it cause problems as well?

"I don't know," he said finally. "Just do me a favor and stay out of sight until I get a feel for the situation, all right?" It was useless to ask Fox to just go away; there wasn't a chance in the world that he would if he thought Tannim was going to be doing anything really interesting. Fox had more curiousity than a zoo of raccoons, and every resource imaginable to indulge that curiousity. There was no place here, Underhill, or in any plane known to Tannim, that the charming and often annoying fox could not go. He was not a powerful spirit, as power was measured among such beings, but what he had, he used cleverly.

Fox sighed and shrugged his leather-clad shoulders. "I 'spose so," he said with some reluctance. "It won't be as much fun, but I 'spose so. Hey, how 'bout some tunes?"

Glad for something to distract his uninvited passenger, Tannim fumbled for the still-unfamiliar controls of the CD player in the dashboard. Not exactly stock equipment for a '69 Mach One, but then, neither were the in-dash radar-detector, the cassette player, the CB, the police-repeater scanner. Tannim had never been one to let authenticity get in the way of gadgetry.

Even if he had been, *this* CD player, gift of a friend, would still have become the crown jewel in his dashboard.

Donal, my friend, I never jack up the volume without honoring your memory. Miss you, pointy-ears.

He'd forgotten what he'd left in the player, but the first bars told him. *Icehouse. "Great Southern Land." Appropriate.* Fox certainly appreciated it; he slouched down in his seat with every appearance of pleasure, propped his black fox-feet on the dash, and surveyed the rolling hills beyond the window. An Australian "digger" hat appeared from nowhere to cover Fox's head.

"So, where are we going?" the *kitsune* asked innocently. "For that matter, where are we?"

"Oklahoma," Tannim said in answer to both questions. Fox's brow wrinkled in puzzlement.

"Isn't it supposed to be—like—flat?" he asked. "No trees? Covered in dust?"

Since that was what virtually everyone said, Tannim only sighed. Fox wasn't stupid; he had perfectly good eyes. "If you want flat and treeless, I'll take you to West Texas," he said. "Not everything's the way you see it in the movies. Most things about Oklahoma are filmed out in California anyway." He had no idea if that was really true or not, but it probably was.

"Except *UHF*," Fox reminded him with glee. "Supplies!"

Trust a Japanese kitsune *to remember an obscure Asian joke from a Wierd Al Yankovic film,* Tannim thought, grinning in spite of himself. "Okay, you're one up on me. How about sitting back and enjoying the ride while I get us through Tulsa rush hour?"

"Tulsa rush hour? Both cars and a mule?"

Tannim smirked. "Just you wait, silly fox."

They survived rush hour, although Tannim had never been able to get used to the schizophrenic traffic patterns even when he still lived here. The mix of granny drivers too timid to merge, urban cowboys determined to prove their macho behind the wheel of their pickups, guys who'd stopped off for "one for the road" before heading home after work, midwest Yuppies in Range Rovers, and people who just plain shouldn't have been allowed in the driver's seat all made for some white-knuckle manuevering. By the time they escaped the stream of traffic headed out of the city toward Broken Arrow and outlying bedroom communities, Tannim's tangled hair was sweat-damp and he had to force the muscles in his hands to relax.

No way am I going to go through this on the way back. I'll wait until after dark and start the drive at night. I'm a racecar driver, I don't need commuter craziness. It's too damned dangerous.

Fox wasn't the least bit perturbed, which was aggravating. Then again, if there was an accident, Fox wouldn't have to stick around and suffer the consequences of someone else's stupid driving. *I've been in fights that were more relaxing.*

Never mind. The last of it was behind him now. In a few more minutes, he'd have an entirely new set of problems to worry about.

"Don't try to talk to me when my folks are around, okay?" he said to Fox. "Don't try to crack me up, don't make faces at me, don't play practical jokes. Don't try to distract me. Whatever you think about doing while they're there, *don't.*"

"Would I do that to you?" Fox replied, all injured innocence.

"Yes," Tannim said shortly, and left it at that.

Fox pouted. Tannim ignored it.

Hi, Mom. Hi, Dad. Look what I brought home. Oh God, all I need now is for Chinthliss to show up.

He resolutely put the thought away, because sometimes simply thinking about Chinthliss would conjure him up.

No. I do not need that.

Finally, with a mixture of anticipation and dread, he turned down a county section-line road running between two windbreaks of trees. Beyond the trees were fields that hadn't seen the touch of a plow in decades, dotted with the fat brown backs of grazing cattle. The road itself was bumpy and pitted; they didn't exactly pave roads out in the county, they just laid asphalt over what ruts and holes were already there, and hoped it wouldn't wash out too soon. As long as it stayed flat enough that VW-swallowing valleys didn't form, it would usually do.

He crossed two more section-line roads, ignoring the rough ride. Not a lot of money in the county budget for fixing these roads. Well heck, a few years ago they hadn't even been paved, just graveled, and wasn't *that* hell to drive on? The blackened remains of an old barn loomed up on his right out of a sea of uncut grass, and he averted his eyes. *That*, if anywhere, was the place where his current odyssey had begun, in the ruins of that barn, and his budding "business" of restoring cars. If the barn hadn't burned, would he be the person he was now?

Rhetorical question. One that did not need answering. One thing led to another, and if one path was not taken, who was to say that another would not have brought him to the same end?

One more section-line road, and then a bright red, oversized mailbox with "Drake" in reflective letters on the side, and "RT 4 Box 451" appeared on the left. It was his father's little surprise for mailbox-bashers; it was really two mailboxes, a smaller one inside a larger, with a layer of concrete poured between them. Anyone who hit that with a bat was going to regret it, and anyone who tried to run it over with a truck was going to be a *very* unhappy camper.

Depending on whether they were driving a tall truck or a short one, it would end up in their radiator or in their laps.

He signaled, and turned into the gravel drive. There were changes evident immediately.

He replaced the fences! That was an expensive proposition, especially since the post-and-barbed-wire had all been replaced with welded pipe. *He must've dug out my old welding rig—I didn't know he knew how to weld!* Behind the fences, instead of cattle, horses looked at him with interest, while foals sparred with each other.

The house looked a little more prosperous, too. And— *I don't believe it. I do not believe it. He put in a satellite dish!*

The mesh dish presided over a front yard patrolled by guinea hens, birds which were noisy as a Lollapalooza tour, but the only sure-fire means of getting rid of ticks without spraying. Tannim pulled up in front of the garage, beside a pair of shiny aluminum four-horse trailers.

Altogether it looked as if the quarter-horse business was doing well.

"Vanish," he growled out of the corner of his mouth, as the front door opened and two middle-aged, slim people in jeans and work shirts came out to greet him.

Fox vanished, eyes wide, obeying the warning in Tannim's voice. Parents. Now things were going to get scary.

Tannim had always known that his father loved techie-toys as much as Tannim did. He just hadn't realized that Trevor Drake *knew* as much about techie-toys as his son did.

" . . . so we've got a LAN hooking up the office, the stable, and the kitchen, since your mom has to access the database if we get a call from a customer and I'm out in the fields," Dad said, as Tannim's head spun under the burden of all the computer neepery. "We're using dBase for our data, and I've got a record not only of full pedigrees but everything I've ever done with every field. Got a plat of the property in a CAD program, can keep track of where every buried line and fencepost is to the tenth of an inch." Trevor's voice filled with pride. "We're doing as much without spraying and chemicals as we can, and we let the horses free-range all year except for foaling and really bad storms. The file-server's a 486 with a 2-gig read-write optical drive—it's in the closet in your old room so don't kick it or drop something on it."

There was no doubt that Trevor was Tannim's father; the two had the same slim build, although Trevor's hair was lighter as well as laced with gray and cut as short as a Marine's. Their faces had some superficial similarities in the shape of the jaw and the high cheekbones; Trevor's was tanned to a leathery toughness by years in the fields in all weathers. But there the resemblence ceased; Trevor was as muscular as a body-builder from all those years of hauling hay and wrestling calves, and if he looked like anyone, it was Will Rogers. For all his strength, Tannim really didn't look as if he could defend himself in a fight against a wily garden hose, and he looked more as if he belonged on MTV than behind the wheel of sophisticated racers. Unlike his father's buzz-cut, he'd had his hair styled short in front and on top, but let it grow long in the back, where it formed a tangle of unruly curls. That changed due to the couple of months he usually went between haircuts, though. He was expecting to hear something about the length of his hair, but so far the only comment had been from his mother, a compliment on the style. Peace flag up and accepted.

Trevor cocked an eyebrow at his son, a signal that Tannim knew meant he was waiting for a reply.

"It's very cool, Dad," Tannim replied dazedly. "I didn't know you'd been doing all this—"

What he was thinking was, *Where did he get the cash? The beef market hasn't exactly been booming. Even if he liquidated the whole herd, he wouldn't have had enough for all those horses, let alone computers, software, satellite dishes, renovations. . . .* There were a number of ways he could *think* of where his father could have gotten a bankroll, but none of them were on the Light Side of the Force, so to speak. It worried him. *If I'd known he really wanted all of this so badly, I could have found a way to make it happen, somehow.*

"Well, I wouldn't have been able to, if it hadn't been for that boss of yours," Trevor Drake said, with a certain fond satisfaction. "You signed on with a good firm, there. Remember when you had that pile-up a couple of years ago that landed you in the hospital, and he sent you off for some rest?"

When that mess with the Unseleighe against the Underhill side of Fairgrove happened, and I creamed my knee the first time, yeah. He nodded cautiously. *Dad had been talking about wanting to convert to quarter horses, but he didn't have the bread.* A certain suspicion dawned, hardening into certainty when he dredged up a vague memory of drugged hallucinations while healing. Yeah, he'd been babbling something in a dream about his parents' money troubles, how he was worried about who'd take care of them if something happened to him, and how it would take a big load off his mind if only he could do something about it.

"You wouldn't believe how well he has you insured," Dad continued. Tannim nodded cautiously again. "Turns out he's got a basic load of policies on you, with us as beneficiaries on some of 'em. And when you tore up your knee, once the fuss all died down, they sent us a check. A *really* big check. I thought it was a mistake, so I called Fairgrove, but your Mister Silver said no, it was right, and I was supposed to keep the money, and then he asked if the herd was still for sale. Paid me top dollar for 'em. Between that and the insurance money, we had enough for some top stock and all the rest of this."

That pointy-eared— Tannim bent down to adjust his pant-cuff as an excuse to keep his father from seeing his face flush. He throttled his reactions and simply shook his head, expressing mild appreciation of "Mister Silver's" generosity. Actually, he wasn't quite sure how to feel. Not that he wasn't pleased that his folks had been taken care of, but—

It felt like a cheat.

You've got no right to feel that way, he scolded himself, as his father led the way to his old room and showed him where the file server lurked in the back of the closet, humming to itself. *Dad's worked hard all his life. He earned all this, it wasn't just given to him! Yeah, Keighvin was making sure that Mom and Dad were going to be okay. That's the way he operates. No matter how modern he acts on the surface, underneath it all he's still a medieval feudal lord, and medieval feudal lords take care of their people and the relatives of their people. It comes with the territory.*

Put that way, he felt a little better about it all. But it would have been nice if Keighvin had *asked* first.

Medieval feudal lords don't ask, they dictate. It's just— dammit, he took it all out of my hands, and they're my parents! I thought I was doing all right by them, and then Keighvin comes in and trumps me! I feel like he took me right out of the loop, and he eavesdropped on my dreams to do it. I suppose I ought to be grateful he didn't send them a bag of gold or something.

"It was pretty funny, son—Mister Silver had the check for the cattle sent over in a Wells Fargo bag marked 'gold bullion.' I thought I was gonna bust a gut laughing!"

That does it. Silverhair Stew when I get back to Georgia.

"When you're ready, come on down to the stables," his dad was saying while Tannim brooded over the file server as if it was personally responsible for all this. "I've got some stuff down there that I have to take care of right now, and a lot more I can't wait to show you."

"Great—" Tannim began, but his Dad was already gone.

He turned around slowly, and shut the door. The Ferrari poster he'd hung on the back of the door when he was ten was still there; so were all the models he'd built, although *he* had never arranged them quite so neatly on the shelves. And he didn't remember all those shelves being there, either.

The plain wooden desk was empty, except for a clean blotter, a phone, and a single pen next to a cube of notepaper. It had never been that empty when he'd lived here, not even on the rare occasions that he'd actually cleaned the room. It was always piled with car magazines, comics, rock rags, books about art, and paperback science fiction books. His autographed picture of Richard Petty had been neatly framed and now hung right over the desk, but the holes where he'd thumbtacked it to the wall still showed near the edge of the mat. The drawers of the desk and the matching bureau beside it were empty, but all of his paperbacks were in a new bookcase on the other side of the desk, with a set of magazine-holders taking care of the magazines. There was a metal Route 66 sign hanging on the wall opposite the Petty photo, and his tattered Rush 2112 banner.

Someone had refinished the desk, and done it well enough that all the stains from oil and WD-40 he'd made when he rebuilt carburetors on it were gone. He ran his fingers slowly across the edges and surface. It felt as if someone had erased part of his life with the stains, even though he had tried to remove those stains himself a hundred times.

The room had been repainted and there were new curtains, but the carpet was the same, and the bedspread. But in place of his old clock-radio on the stand beside the bed there was a new digital clock-radio that included a CD player. Replacing the old black-and-white TV he'd rescued from the junkyard and repaired with Deke Kestrel's help, there was a new color portable. No cracked case, no channel knob that had to be turned with vise-grips; this television had an auto-tuner. It could effortlessly lock in a vivid image, just like he had tuned in those strong images in that very bed, so long ago, of the dragons and magic and *her*. All she had done with him—and to him—had seemed so rich and real, erotic and more. But only a few of those images of dragons and adventure had come true, and his ethereal lover had yet to appear in the real world.

This, the real world, where he stood like an artist who has walked into a gallery to see his life's work re-framed while he was away for lunch.

The room felt both familiar and alien at once. *This is surreal. Very, very surreal.* He just wasn't certain of anything at the moment; he felt unbalanced, uncomfortable, as if he had tried on clothing that was too tight.

This is why I don't come back. Because you can't come back. I can't be what I used to be, I can only try to fake what my folks remember. If I just act . . . no . . . if I'm just myself, they'd never be able to handle that. They'll wonder what they did wrong. Parents are as fallible as anyone else, and they made mistakes with me. They want to know what they did right—but like anyone else, they have rigid ideas of exactly what's right. It doesn't take a rocket scientist to figure out that a boy-genius grease monkey isn't what a farmer wants or expects.

As he stared down at the worn red ribcord bedspread, Fox materialized on the bed. He looked a little less like James Dean now, and a little more like the lead singer of the Stray Cats.

"Hey," he said cheerfully. "Nice place! You seen the stables yet?"

"No," Tannim replied cautiously. "Why?"

Fox just snickered. "You're in for a big surprise."

Tannim stared at the horse. The horse stared back and laid its ears down in an unmistakable expression of threat. "Just hold the reins, son," Trevor repeated patiently. "He won't hurt you."

"Dad—that's a *stallion*. Stallions are aggressive, even I know that much. And he doesn't like me." Fluorescent lighting hanging from the metal rafters of the ceiling showed every nuance of the stallion's expression, and it was not a friendly one. Tannim would have backed off another pace, but there was a cinder-block wall in the way.

The horse bared its teeth at him and stamped its foot on the rubber mat covering the cement floor.

Trevor sighed. "That horse is a kitten. Tannim, your *mother* can hold that horse."

"Then why isn't she here instead of me?" he asked, as the stallion stamped his foot a second time—possibly indicating what he wanted to do if Tannim's feet got within his reach.

"He's not interested in you," Trevor replied, patiently. "He has other things on his mind right now."

"I'll bet," Tannim muttered, trying to inch away.

Trevor stood beside something that vaguely resembled the gym apparatus known as a pommel-horse, holding an object like a cross between a large hot water bottle and an elephant's trunk, he referred to as an "AV." He *said* he was going to "collect" the stallion, and he wanted Tannim's help. Tannim did not want to know what an "AV" was, and he certainly did not want to help in what he *thought* his father was going to do.

"Dad, that horse is going to kill me." He said this slowly and carefully, so there could be no mistake. The horse confirmed his words with a neigh, a snort, and another exhibition of teeth. "That horse *wants* to kill me. I did not drive all the way from Savannah to be killed by a horse, *or* to assist you in giving one a good time!"

Trevor shook his head, whether in denial or in disgust, his son wasn't entirely certain. But at that moment, Tannim's allergies realized that he was standing in *straw*, in a stable full of *hay*, *dust*, and *powdered grain*, and not more than ten feet away from a large, sweaty, dander-laden *animal*.

He exploded into a volley of violent sneezing. The horse lost all interest in killing him, and backed away from him in alarm as far as the lead on the halter would permit. The horse's eyes rolled alarmingly, and it uttered a pitiful whine as it danced around and jerked on the rope holding it to the side of the stall. Trevor swore under his breath, put the "AV" down, and worked his way hand-over-hand up the rope to the stallion's head to try and calm it. Tannim took this as permission to escape.

He retreated immediately, eyes streaming, nose running, only to meet his mother at the kitchen door. "Dad deeds you, Bomb," he got out between sneezes. "Dable. Wid da dallion."

Correctly interpreting this as a message that Trevor needed help with his champion stallion, Tannim's mother thrust a box of tissues at him and trotted across the backyard in the direction of the stables. He continued his retreat to the bathroom across from his room, where he had prudently stashed everything he was afraid he might need.

He turned on the shower as high as it would go, and steam poured over the top of the curtain-rod, giving him a little relief. As he popped pills out of their plastic-and-foil bubbles and gulped them down, he heard the shower-radio come on all by itself.

It can't be heat- or water-activated. So— He stripped off his clothing and ducked into the shower, putting his head under the hot water to ease his aching sinuses. *It's him. Maybe if I ignore him—*

"Hey! It's Fox-on-the-Radio, taking the third caller who can tell me Elvis Costello's favorite flavor of chewing gum, or answer the Super Mondo Nifty Keen-o Boffo Kewl Bonus Question: Just what is Tannim, the most eligible bachelor mage in southern Bixby Oklahoma, listening to?!" came an all-too-familiar voice from the waterproof speaker.

Tannim took his head out from under the stream of hot water long enough to look blearily at the white plastic radio. "Fox," he said at last, "you are *weird.*"

"Hey! That's the *right* answer, caller number three! And you win—*a bar of soap!*" A bar of soap popped out of the bottom of the radio, forcing Tannim to grab for it before it got under his feet, only to discover that it was an illusion. "That's right, it's WYRD, *weird radio!*"

"WYRD is in North Carolina," Tannim corrected automatically. "In Haven's Reach. This is Oklahoma."

"So how *'bout* that reception?" Fox replied gaily. "It must be something in the pipes. Yes, it's WYRD, all-talk-talking, all day, all night, all the—"

Tannim reached over and turned off the radio with a firm *click*.

One super-hot shower with lots of steam, half a bottle of eyedrops, two antihistamines and a few squirts of lilac-scented "prescription stuff" up his nose later, he felt as if he might survive until suppertime, at least. Even if he *was* groggy now, it was better than being unable to see or breathe.

Maybe I can just stay in the bathroom for the whole visit?

No, that would be the coward's way out. Besides, Fox would DJ him to death. Or worse. The fox was shameless.

He ventured out into the hallway, hearing voices from the kitchen, and decided he might just as well face the music. The kitchen had been redone, too, but he *knew* that he had paid for that, at least—it had been his Mother's Day gift about three years ago. Right now, that made it the one place in the house he felt the most comfortable in.

His father was sitting at a stool at the wood-and-tile breakfast bar while his mother did something arcane with a piece of raw meat. Both of them looked up as he came in, and to his relief, both of them were smiling.

"I was beginning to think I'd failed my Test of Manhood," he began, and his mother giggled. She still looked a lot like her old high school pictures from the late '50s; a little grayer, a little older, but still remarkably like a Gidget-clone.

"I'm sorry, son," Trevor said, with real apology in his voice. "I keep forgetting about your allergies—that is, I *remember* them, but I keep forgetting how bad they really are. I shouldn't have even asked you to go out there with me."

This, of course, immediately made Tannim feel even more guilty than he already did. *Didn't live up to their expectations, again.* "Look, I should have known better," he interrupted. "I brought a respirator, like we use for painting cars. It's in the trunk. I could wear that and—"

His mother shook her head, still giggling. "Oh no—dear heaven, no, don't do that! The horses would be terrified!"

Well, that'll be a first. Usually they terrify me.

"It's all right," his father said hastily. "Your mother can help me, it'll be fine. She's the best hand with a stallion I've ever seen, anyway."

Tannim bit his tongue to keep from saying anything really crude, and managed to dilute all the things that sprang immediately to mind down to a mild, "Well, she *did* rope you, didn't she?"

That made his father roar with laughter, and his mother blush and giggle, and eased at least a little of the tension among them.

He managed to keep the conversation on safe subjects up to and through dinner—mostly on what those few of his classmates who were still in the Tulsa area were doing. He didn't really *care,* if the truth were to be told, but it gave his parents something to talk about, and when they were talking, they weren't asking him questions he couldn't answer.

In a way, it was rather sad. The stars of the high school athletic teams had all, to a man, washed out in college or in the minor leagues and were now selling cars, or working oil field or construction jobs. Most of the girls that were still in the area were married, and on either their third kids or second divorces. Tannim hadn't kept in touch with any of them, for good reason. He'd had nothing in common with them in high school, and had even less now.

The only kid he *had* kept in constant touch with was Deke Kestrel, and he knew right where Deke was. Down in Austin Texas, working as a studio musician, and doing a damn fine job of it. Deke was sitting in with Eric Johnson and the other local heroes of the Oasis of Texas. He was also training *his* more "esoteric" skills, but once again, that was something he couldn't talk to his parents about.

"What ever happened to that girl you used to date, honey?" his mother asked, breaking into his thoughts. "The one who was so into science? Trisha, Trixie—"

"Trina," he corrected without thinking. "She finished her doctorate. She's at Johns Hopkins, doing research into viral proteins."

"Oh." From the rather stunned look on both his parents' faces, this was not something they had ever anticipated hearing over the dinner table. *How nice—and you drive cars for a living, dear? Congratulations Tannim, you certainly killed that subject dead in its tracks.* But his mother was persistent, he had to give her that. "Well, what about that friend of yours that went into musicals—"

"I don't know," he lied. "I lost touch with him after he went to New York." *I lost touch with him after he died of AIDS, Mom.* This was turning into the most depressing dinner conversation he had ever had. *I'd better talk about something cheerful, quick.* "I heard from Deke Kestrel just a couple of days ago, though—he's doing backup work for a really incredible guitarist in Austin. It's the guy's fourth CD, and Deke says the guy might do a guest shot on his first solo project."

That revived the conversation again, and he managed to keep it on Deke and how well Deke was doing until the dishes were safely cleared and in the dishwasher.

Then he pleaded fatigue and fled to his room. At least he could call Joe and get that much accomplished. Set up the meeting, feel the kid out, make sure he wanted to go through with this. Try and tell him what the pros and cons of the job were. That was one thing Chinthliss had never been able to get through *his* head, but Joe already had a taste of the "cons." And at least with Joe, he would not have to hold anything back.

It wasn't very comforting to think that he had more in common with Joe, someone he didn't even know, than he did with his own family.

He moved the phone over to the bedside stand, called directory assistance for Frank Casey's number in Pawnee, then took a deep breath to steady himself and dialed.

"I'd like to talk to Joe Brown, please," he said carefully. "This is Tannim, from Fairgrove Industries. . . . "

• CHAPTER TWO

Joe nodded as he spoke, forgetting that the man from Fairgrove couldn't see him. The window-unit a/c in the living room came to life with a shudder. The banter of a news-show anchor harmonized oddly with the hum. A drift of cold wafted down the hallway at ankle-height from the direction of the living room. "Yes, sir," he said. "I can do that, sir. I'll be ready."

Joe hung up the old hall phone with a feeling of anticipation mixed with trepidation. So, it was finally going to happen. This whole strange year was finally over. "That was the man from Fairgrove," he called into the living room. "He's in Bixby. He says he'll meet me tomorrow for lunch."

His guardian, the sheriff of Pawnee County, Frank Casey, got up out of his chair with a creak of wood and leather audible over the television and the air conditioner. He turned down the volume on the television and came out into the hallway of the tiny house he shared with Joe, blocking off most of the light from the living room. Frank was a big man, one who truly filled the doorway, and his Native American ancestors would have identified him immediately as a warrior, even without paint, honor-feathers, or any other traditional signs. It was the ambient radiation of *warrior*, a halo of not-quite-there colors that Joe was able to see now, after some coaching and training from Alinor and Bob. There were other colors in that aura, colors that told

27

Joe that his guardian was just as hopeful, and anxious, as he himself was, despite Frank's impassive expression.

"You don't have to go through with this if you don't want to," Frank said solemnly, while the a/c shuddered into silence and the sound of cicadas outside the front door behind Joe grew louder. "I don't care what you promised that fellow from Fairgrove. If you aren't comfortable with this, we can find somewhere else for you. Maybe you should consider college again?"

Joe shook his head as the cicadas wound down for a breather. "No, thanks," he said awkwardly. "Sir, I appreciate your thinking about it and all, but this is going to be for the best. You know I won't ever fit in around here. These Fairgrove people, they know about people like me. I don't think college is the right thing for me now. I'm not ready for it, and I really don't think any college is ready for me. Besides, Fairgrove promised me a full ride if I want to go to college later."

Frank grunted, and the wooden floor creaked beneath him as he shifted his weight. "Sounds too good to be true, like the things recruiters promise you to get you to sign up."

It was Joe's turn to shrug. How could he ever explain to his guardian *why* he trusted these people to keep their promises? Frank would never believe him. Even though he'd been right there to see the worst that the Salamander could do, he no longer believed in the creature's existence. Somehow he'd managed to convince himself that more than half of what had happened during the raid had been optical illusions and the rest was delusion. He'd even forgotten how the Salamander had warned the cult followers about police raids and the like.

That happens to people, Al said. When something happens that just doesn't fit with their idea of reality, they'll chip away at it and twist it until they make it fit. I guess that's what happened to Frank.

"They have a good reputation, sir," he replied. "You checked them out yourself."

His guardian nodded slowly. "I did, and I admit

they came out clean on all counts. And you are old enough to make up your own mind. Still—you're also old enough to change it if you want, and if you do, well, you've got a place here."

Joe flushed, but with pleasure as well as embarassment. He knew there were more things that Frank could not bring himself to say. The lawman was nothing if not stoic. "Thank you, sir," he replied awkwardly. "I—ah—I probably ought to get some sleep. Good night, sir."

"Good night, son," Frank said softly, as Joe retreated to the little guest room that had been his home over the past year and more. "Pleasant dreams."

The ten-by-ten room was tiny, especially in comparison with the luxurious suite his father had bestowed on him just before he had defected from the cult. The walls, with their faded floral wallpaper, sometimes leaked cold air in the winter, but it was nothing compared to the cold fear he'd always endured around his father. The ancient window air conditioner wheezed every time it came on, and it vibrated so hard that it rattled the windows in their frames, but the machinery that kept the underground complex of his youth running had been just as loud. The only furniture was a single bureau, a tiny corner-desk where he did his homework, and an equally tiny nightstand with a gooseneck lamp from K-Mart on it. Joe's own belongings all fit in that bureau with room to spare. But this was a more comfortable room than anything in the mansion in Atlanta or the Chosen Ones' compound could ever have been. He felt welcome here, as he had not there.

For one thing, he didn't need to worry about hidden cameras watching his every move. He didn't have to worry about his father breaking the door down in a psychotic rage, destroying everything in his path in the name of his own holiness.

Joe piled up pillows at the head of the iron-framed bed and leaned back into them, contemplating the poster Bob had given him, now framed on the otherwise empty wall. It was an artist's rendering of the Victor GT prototype,

over the Victor logo and the logo of Fairgrove Industries
itself. The latter was a strange piece; at first glance it was
simply a pair of trees against the sky, but when you looked
closer, you saw that the trees formed the face of a lovely
woman, wearing an enigmatic smile. Then you looked
again, and it was only two trees.

Which was the reality and which the illusion?

Bob would have shrugged and said it didn't matter. Al
would say, "Both. Neither."

But it *did* matter. So much of what he had thought was
true turned out to be deception. Just one illusion after
another.

Everything my father told me was a lie. He thought
about that for a moment, then realized that he actually
had more of a start than he'd thought. *If everything he
told me was a lie, then the truth would be the opposite of
what he told me, wouldn't it?* That made sense—and what
was more, a lot of what Al and Bob had told him *was* the
very opposite of what his father would have said.

That meant he could trust what the two Fairgrove men
had told him. He had no reason to doubt them, and every
reason to believe them. But this—it was jumping off a cliff
into a sea of fog and no way of knowing if what lay below
him was the warm, friendly pool he'd been promised, or
rocks he would be shattered upon.

Would it be better to change his mind, and see what
Frank could find for him? He could still do that.

Could he, though? He'd spent a whole year here, and
every moment of it had been as an outsider. His father
had done one thing for him that was decent—he'd had a
better education than most of the kids here. Even if half
of it had been laced with the manifesto of a lunatic. At
least what he'd gotten in the military academy had been
sound. He'd tested out of just about everything, and he
was able to go straight into his senior year with no trouble.

That was one thing that Frank, Al, Bob, and Mister
Keighvin who ran Fairgrove had all been adamant about.
Joe *had* to get his high school diploma. "It may not seem

like it's worth much," Bob had drawled, "but without it, if for some reason something happens to us, you'll never get anything better than a fast-food job. You won't even be able to get into the Army. That diploma is your safety net."

He'd breezed through his classes with no academic trouble—and despite the doubts of the principal and many of the teachers, no other kind of overt trouble, either. He knew what they thought—or feared. There were those who were certain he would take up where his father had left off, corrupting the other students with the poisonous doctrines his father had taught. Others expected him to bully the other students, start fights. A few simply expected fights to find *him,* whether he wanted them or not.

They were all wrong. The other students were afraid of him, most of them, but even the worst bully in the school was too cautious after the first time he disrobed in gym class to try to pick a fight with him.

Just as well, since I could have wiped the floor with his face. No boast, just fact; the cult of the Sacred Heart of the Chosen Ones had emphasized that there would be battles, and the faithful would be in the thick of them. Every child, Joe included, was trained in self-defense from the moment they entered the compound. Joe had the added advantage of years of training in military school. When he walked into Pawnee High School in the fall, he knew that he had no intention of starting fights—but if they started, he knew that he would be the only one left standing afterward.

There were no fights; no one even *said* anything to his face. But they whispered behind his back and watched him with wary eyes, as if they expected that at any moment he might pull out an assault weapon and start shooting. Despite his powerful build, none of the coaches asked if he wanted to be on a team. Despite his looks, the few girls he'd asked out were not interested.

He really couldn't blame them, not after what had happened at the cult compound. People were still talking about it, and a year later, the FBI and ATF still had the place cordoned off. Joe wouldn't go anywhere near the place; the very idea made him sick. But how were the ordinary people of Pawnee going to know that? For all they knew, he was just like his father. He didn't blame them for being scared of him. In fact, it was probably only the fact that Frank Casey was his guardian that kept them from running him out of town.

From time to time someone in a car with darkened windows would pull up to Frank's house after school and ask to talk to Joe. It was always a different person, but the questions were always the same: Do you remember any more bunkers, or places where there might be weapons or ammunition stored? Whoever the person was, he would always bring a new map of the compound, and there was generally one more tunnel or bunker drawn on it than there had been before. It was hard for Joe to picture where things might be, since he was always working from the memories of having walked through the compound and not from any recall of a map, but with the aid of the ever-growing layout the Feds were building, he could at least say things like, "I think there's another tunnel there—I wasn't allowed down that way."

They may never find it all. Only his father had known where everything was. He'd told one of the men that once. "Why does this not surprise me?" the man had answered—and in the voice used by that parrot in the Walt Disney movie. It had kind of surprised him, that a supposedly grim FBI guy would have seen the movie, and delighted him more that the guy would have enough of a sense of humor to do that. In its own small way, it reaffirmed to Joe that he was dealing with human beings and not faceless chesspieces.

But strange cars pulling up to Frank's house did not add anything to Joe's popularity at school. Would it be any better in college, where he'd turn into the subject of every psych major's term paper and master's thesis?

The cicadas started droning again, right outside his window, loud enough to carry over the sound of the a/c unit. He didn't mind—in fact, he kind of liked it. In the bunkers you never heard anything but the drip of water in the tunnels, and the hum and clank of machinery.

And sometimes, the marching boots on concrete. That sound haunted his dreams—sometimes in the dreams, the marching men were coming to get him, sometimes he was leading them. Both were horrible.

Frank thought that college would be easier for him, and better than high school, but Joe wasn't so sure. *How long before everyone found out who I was?* Even if they didn't, he *still* wouldn't fit in, not unless he went to some other military school. He was just too—too—

Too straight-edge. It didn't seem to matter that he liked trucks and cars, the way a lot of the guys did, that he liked the same kind of music and listened to Edge of Insanity after midnight when he could. He got rid of that swastika tattoo right off, before he ever set foot in school. That had to go before he grew his hair or tried to. None of it mattered. The differences were bone-deep. They slouched; he stood and sat at rigid attention. They wore grunge, or cowboy-chic; he wore carefully laundered blue jeans and spotless t-shirts or slacks and button-downs. He said "sir" and "ma'am" reflexively. Even the nerds looked more normal than he did.

But with Al and Bob, now—he had felt comfortable for perhaps the first time in his life. However strange he was, they were stranger, they had far more secrets to hide.

And they understood this knack he had for seeing into peoples' minds, for knowing something about what was going to happen, for seeing *things.* Things like ghosts. . . .

Bob said that this Tannim guy could see ghosts. Said he could do a lot of other things, too.

The a/c went off, leaving only the drone of cicadas and the chirp of crickets. This Tannim guy—he sounded interesting on the phone. Easy to talk to. He'd mentioned that Joe's first job would be as assistant to a "Sarge" Phil Austin, running Fairgrove security, a man who had some of the same knacks as Joe. So he was going to get picked up by a guy who talked to ghosts, and he was going to be errandboy to a guy who ran security for a place where they built racecars with magic.

Sounded like the kind of place where one Joseph Brown just might seem ordinary.

Right now, that didn't sound too bad. At least these people wouldn't be staring at him all the time, waiting for him to go off the deep end, and whispering about him at PTA meetings.

Funny thing; every time he looked at the Fairgrove logo, the lady seemed to be smiling a little more.

Tannim didn't have too much trouble finding Pawnee, even though he'd never actually been to the county seat. The address and the directions Joe had given him were perfectly clear; it was equally clear that there wasn't much of a town to get lost in. Like the rest of the area around Tulsa, this was not a place that had suffered in the Dust Bowl; the trees here were probably as old as the town itself and lined the streets on both sides, giving shade and the illusion of cool. To Tannim's amazement, the streets surrounding the courthouse were cobblestone. Hell to drive on, like River Street in Savannah, but very picturesque. The town itself probably hadn't changed much since the 1920s.

The tiny house belonging to Deputy Sheriff Frank Casey could have been built any time in the last seventy-five years: a white-painted, single-storied frame house with a native rock foundation. It was trimmed with just a little bit of "gingerbread," sporting a huge front porch with a cement floor and a pair of porch swings. Tannim pulled up into the vacant driveway, which was two overgrown and cracked parallel strips of concrete. Before he could get out of the Mustang, two men emerged from the house and stood waiting for him on the porch itself.

The older man of the pair would have dwarfed most people; he made Tannim feel like a midget. He was huge, copper-skinned, hawk-nosed, with intelligent dark eyes, wearing a dark brown uniform shirt and tan pants. He wasn't wearing his badge at the moment, but he didn't have to. This could only be Joe's court-appointed guardian, Sheriff's Deputy Frank Casey.

But Joe was big enough not to be dwarfed even by his guardian. He looked as if he'd been pumping iron since he was a fetus; blond and blue-eyed, he'd have been a perfect model for a Nazi recruiting poster, except that his blond hair had been done in a fairly stylish cut that looked a lot like Tannim's, only shorter. There was a pale patch on his upper arm that made Tannim suspect he'd had a tattoo there, once.

Tannim got out of the car and went around the nose to meet them. There was no breeze under the trees, and he was glad of their shade. It was probably close to 90 out in the sunlight.

Frank Casey stepped forward to intercept Tannim. "I'm Deputy Frank Casey, Joe's guardian," he said, in a carefully neutral voice, holding out an immense paw of a hand.

Tannim met his firm handshake with a clasp that was just as firm. "I'm Tannim, from Fairgrove Industries in Savannah," he said, looking straight into Frank's eyes. "My folks are from around here, though—the Drakes, over in Bixby. They used to have cattle, but they're running quarter horses, now."

He had figured that invoking local ties would relax Casey, and he was right. The man's tension ebbed visibly. "Bixby, hmm? Good horse country," he replied.

Tannim shrugged and grinned.

"Couldn't prove it by me," he answered cheerfully. "The last thing I know is horse-stuff. Well, I'm supposed to bring Joe Brown here over to my folks' place; they want to meet him. Fact is, they insisted on it." He turned to Joe. "I'm not going to inflict them on you until we've had lunch, though. Dad wants to show off his stallions. I wouldn't do that to anyone on an empty stomach."

Frank chuckled, as Tannim had hoped he would. Joe probably thought he was managing a pretty good poker-face, but Tannim read any number of conflicting emotions there.

"Well, *my* lunch hour is about over, so I'd better get back to the office and find out what disasters came up while I was gone." Frank shook Tannim's hand again and clapped Joe on the shoulder. "Enjoy yourselves."

He strode off down the street under the ancient trees, heading in the direction of the aged county courthouse only three blocks away.

Well, looks like I passed inspection. Now let's see what Joe has to say. Tannim waited until he was out of earshot before speaking again.

"Okay, just so you know, Bob Ferrel is a pretty good friend of mine, and Alinor is some kind of cousin of my boss, Keighvin Silverhair. I've been working for Fairgrove for a good few years now, and I was told pretty much the whole story." He quirked an eyebrow at the youngster, who looked a bit uncomfortable. "I'm sure this is going to sound unlikely, but I promise you, I've seen things weirder than snake shoes and Mets pennants. I've had stuff straight out of Tim Burton films happen to me before breakfast. So don't worry about my thinking you're crazy if you let something slip. You're more likely to think that about me."

A faint hint of skepticism crept over the young man's handsome face, but he didn't say anything.

"So, how about that lunch?" Tannim continued. "I wasn't kidding about Dad and the horses. He's doing something kinky with them. 'Collecting them,' he said. Whatever that is, I don't want to know." He shuddered. "They hate me, I'm allergic to them. Seems to *me* those are pretty good reasons to keep a decent distance between us."

Joe finally smiled. "I like horses," he offered. "There were horses at the military school I went to, and I learned how to ride and take care of them. I'd have been able to get on the horse-drill team, but Father pulled me out—"

His face darkened momentarily, and Tannim nodded sympathetically. "Look, from here on, no one is going to tell you what to do with your life, all right? If you decide to back out of this before we leave, that's okay; if you want to leave Fairgrove after you've been there a while, that's okay, too. Keighvin'll cut you a ticket to anywhere you want to go. Hell, he might even be able to get you into West Point or Annapolis, if that's what you want."

Joe blinked, as if the idea of an elven lord having the ability to influence people in the normal world had never occurred to him. "He can do that?" he asked.

Tannim allowed a hint of cynicism to enter his expression. "Keighvin has money. Politicians need money. Senators are the ones who make recommendations to West Point. Got it?"

Joe nodded. "I'd like to make sure I gave Fairgrove my best shot, though," he replied a little shyly. "I mean, it's only right."

I like this kid. How in the name of all that's holy he turned out this good with that fruitcake for a father— "You about ready for that lunch?" he said by way of a reply, and waved Joe over to the Mustang.

Joe's eyes widened at the sight of the Mach One, and widened even further when he got into the passenger's seat and saw all the electronic gadgetry in the dashboard. He didn't say anything though, until Tannim asked him if he had any preferences in music.

He shrugged. "Rock, I guess. Anything but country." There was something behind that simple statement; something dark. Was there someone in Joe's past who *had* preferred country and western? His father, maybe?

Tannim's fingers closed on the Rush CD, *Roll the Bones*. He took that as an omen, and put it in the player before pulling out into traffic.

God, Donal would have loved this album.

One advantage of the CD player was the extraordinary clarity of lyrics; the title track began, and Joe seemed more than a little startled by the chorus, then began paying attention. Very close attention.

Though Tannim was not one for placing life-guiding meaning into most rock lyrics, Rush was a pretty darned articulate band. And Joe could do worse than get a dose of "hey kid, sometimes things happen just because they happen—for no other reason, not your fault, not anybody's fault." He left it on.

He wasn't in the mood for franchise food, so he picked the first good-looking roadside diner that came along and pulled into the parking lot. GRANNY'S DINER, the sign said, painted on a cracked wall that looked as old as any "granny." The place was crowded, which argued for decent food, and the interior could have come right out of any movie from the fifties. So could the waitress, from her B-52 hairdo to a pink uniform with "Peggy" embroidered over her right pocket. *Fox would love this place. Thank God he isn't here; he'd be freaking out Joe by now and giggling about it.* Kitsune. *I'll never understand'em. As bad as dragons, I swear. Thank God I don't have to deal with them too often. Well—except for Fox and Chinthliss.*

Joe's tastes were simple: big, juicy hamburgers, a large salad instead of fries, milk . . . just amazing quantities of all of it. Unlike Tannim, he didn't talk while he ate, so Tannim kept up a one-sided ramble about the more mundane side of Fairgrove between bites.

"What do you do?" Joe asked, when the waitress came to take their orders for dessert. "Al and Bob never really told me." His brow wrinkled a little. "I hope you don't mind my saying this, but you don't seem very old."

"I seem too young to be doing anything important, right?" Tannim chuckled. "I guess I started kind of young; a lot of people in racing did. As for what I do—I'm a test-driver and a mechanic, I drive on the Fairgrove SCCA team—"

"SCCA?" Joe interrupted.

"Sports Car Club of America," Tannim explained. "We have three teams: GTP, SERRA and SCCA. The ah—people like Al drive the GTP and SERRA cars; I handle most of the SCCA driving, since SCCA doesn't allow modifications like aluminum engine blocks and frames. It's a racing club, but for regular people with regular budgets."

Joe nodded, then accepted his apple pie à la mode from the waitress with a smile and a polite "thank you." He spooned up a mouthful, and looked at Tannim expectantly. "That can't be all you do," he said.

Tannim chuckled. "You don't miss much, do you? No, the people like Al and Keighvin can't go out much, so I do a lot of outside contact work—Sarge Austin will probably have you doing the same, before too long. We can always use someone who's smart enough to know their way around, and straight-edge enough to make the suits comfortable. I'm afraid a lot of the folks at Fairgrove look kind of like a cross between a rock group and a Renaissance Faire."

Once again, Joe nodded—but then he knew all about needing people for "outside" work. From what Tannim had heard and guessed, Brother Joseph hadn't let too many folks outside the barbed-wire walls of his compound, once they got inside.

The rest would have to remain unsaid, at least until they were safely inside the Mustang again. Joe evidently realized this, for he remained silent until the meal was finished and Tannim had paid for it, with a generous tip for the smiling "Peggy." They walked out into the midday heat, the air so full of dust that there was a golden haze over everything. Tannim thumbed the remote on his keychain; the doors of the Mach One unlocked and popped open, and the engine started. Joe looked startled, then grinned his appreciation as they both got in.

Joe buckled up, fumbling a little, as he had the first time, with the unfamiliar belts. Not too many people put on a four-point harness like it was second nature, after all.

"So," Joe said, with a tension in his shoulders that told Tannim he was bracing himself for the answer to his question, "just what comes along besides the ordinary stuff in this job?"

"How about me?" said a voice from the backseat.

Tannim looked into the rearview mirror. His jaw dropped.

Oh, it was Foxtrot all right. But he was a five-foot tall *fox*, a cartoon-style fox, only one with three tails and a little collar with "FX" on the gold tag dangling down in front.

But just as startling as Fox was Joe's reaction. His eyes were wide with surprise, but also with recognition.

"Long time, no see, Joey," Fox said genially. "If I'd known it was *you* they were talking about, I'd have come for a visit months ago!"

Tannim said the only thing he *could* say under the circumstances. He pointed to the back and locked onto Joe's eyes. "You know this lunatic?" he asked calmly.

Joe's mouth was still wide open, his eyes dazed. "I—uh—he was my imaginary friend," the young man managed, weakly. "When I was a kid."

"Not so imaginary, Joey," Fox replied. "Of course, I'd much rather look like this—"

The whole figure shivered, blurred, and changed back into a leather-jacketed James Dean lookalike. "Hard to pick up chicks when you look like a stuffed toy," Fox offered, leaning back in the seat. "Well, most places. By the way, what *are* you doing here? You were supposed to be in Georgia."

"It's a long story, Fox," Tannim interjected, and sighed. "Well, at least now I don't have to worry about you freaking Joe out by showing up out of nowhere."

"Yeah," Joe said faintly. "He already started years ago."

Tannim decided that he might as well seize the moment and use it for a short lesson. "I told you weird things show up around me. This is one of them," he told the young man as he pulled the Mustang out onto the highway. *Thank God he didn't materialize while I was actually driving.* "Fox isn't human, never was, never will be."

"Hey!" Fox exclaimed, feigning injured pride. "I resemble that remark! I *happen* to come from a very distinguished pedigree!"

"Pedigree is right." Tannim nailed the throttle for a quick pass around a slow-moving haywagon. "He's just what you saw as a kid: a fox-spirit, a shape-changer. Take a good look at him. No, *really* look at him, the way Alinor taught you."

Joe turned around and stared at Fox, who posed for his edification, magicking a white sparkling gleam off his teeth as he grinned. As Tannim had hoped, the order to look at Fox steadied Joe considerably. Having your imaginary friend from childhood suddenly pop up as real was enough to take the starch out of anyone. "Well, he's just a little see-through," Joe said slowly. "That means that he's a spirit, using everything he's got to make people like us *see* him. And there's a kind of an outline around him, and it isn't like a human aura."

"Good," Tannim said with satisfaction. "Right. He's a *kitsune*—to be precise, a Japanese fox-spirit—and *don't* ask me how he ended up in Georgia, 'cause I don't know."

Fox smirked. "I'll never tell. My lips are sealed."

"I wish," Tannim muttered. "Anyway, he's tricky—that's what he enjoys doing, seeing new things and playing tricks on people. He has absolutely no ability to change anything in the real world, unlike a human ghost, but he's pretty hot stuff Underhill or in the spirit plane. The reason you can see and hear him is because you *can* see into the spirit plane and he is making the effort to be visible. He's kind of half here and half there—and again, that's unlike a human ghost, who can choose to be all here and affect the material world in a limited sense."

Joe nodded, his forehead wrinkled with concentration as he tallied this with whatever Bob and Alinor had already taught him. "So there's things like ghosts that can be *here*, and things like Fox who can't, really?"

"Pre-cisely," Fox replied for Tannim. "I can make you *think* I can affect the real world, though." He snickered. "Like I did to you, hotshot, with the soap."

"Yeah, well I'd like to know how you did that trick with the radio, though," Tannim grumbled.

"Hey! It's Fox-on-the-radio!" The *kitsune*'s voice came from the four speakers, even though the radio was off.

"Betcha caller number three can't guess how I'm doing this!"

Fox put his hands behind his head, leaning back, looking unbearably smug. His mouth had not moved at all.

"I know!" Joe said suddenly, looking pleased. "It's because since he's really talking with his mind, he's just making us *think* his voice is coming from the speakers instead of his mouth, which it isn't doing either."

A bit tangled, but Tannim got the gist of it, and muttered imprecations under his breath. Fox looked crestfallen.

"Awww," he said. "You *guessed!* That's not fair!"

"Life's like that," Joe and Tannim said in chorus and complete synchronization. They exchanged a startled glance, then both broke up in laughter. Fox pouted for a moment, then joined them.

Either he's handling this really well, or he's so blitzed by Fox and all that he only seems to be. I think my bet's on the kid. "Well now that Fox has joined us, I was wondering if you wanted to tool around Tulsa for a while." Tannim looked at the young man out of the corner of his eye. "Keighvin told me to outfit you while we were here, and I can put it all on the company card. I kind of figured you didn't have a lot of stuff."

"Take him up on it, Joe," Fox advised from the backseat. "Tannim's a Fashion God."

Tannim flashed the *kitsune* a withering look. "I'm supposed to get Nomex for you—that's fireproof underwear, basically, real popular back at Fairgrove. Some jeans and boots, too, and a few other things. And—" He paused. This was a delicate subject. "And personal gear. It can't be a lot, since the Mustang will hold only so much, but Keighvin seemed to think you ought to get yourself the same kind of things you'd be furnishing a dorm room with. You know, CD player, clock-radio, that kind of thing. And clothes."

Joe's face darkened. "I don't take handouts," he said stubbornly.

Tannim sighed. "Look, it isn't a handout, all right?

You're going to be meeting people, some of them important. If you're gonna be Sarge's assistant, you'll have to escort Big Guns from places like Goodyear and March and STP all over the plant. You can't do that wearing jeans and a t-shirt. And as for the rest of it, well, if you had anything to move, Fairgrove would be paying moving expenses, right? But you don't, so you're getting it in gear."

Now Joe looked confused. "I don't know," he said uneasily. "I never knew anyone who got a job with a place like Fairgrove. I don't know what's right."

And until you get to Fairgrove, you won't *ever meet anyone who's gotten a job like this.* "Trust me," he said persuasively. "It's perfectly normal."

For Fairgrove.

"If you say so, sir," Joe replied, looking very young and uncertain.

"I say so," Tannim said firmly, taking the Mach One onto the on-ramp for the interstate. And in his head, though he was certain it was only in *his* head, he heard Fox snickering.

"That's right, he says so! Now how much would you pay?" the radio blared in Fox's voice. "But wait, there's more if you order by midnight tonight! You get two free neuroses, a fixation, and your choice of—"

Click.

There weren't a lot of bags in the back of the Mustang, and not just because Joe had balked at purchasing too much. It had occurred to Tannim that "shopping for Joe" could be the way out of the house that he had been looking for. In fact, "shopping for Joe" might become his salvation. He could use it as an excuse to flee the house even when Joe *wasn't* with him.

So, Joe was now wearing a good pair of Bugle Boy pants and a snappy shirt ("You want to impress my folks, don't you?"); and there was a bag of Nomex jumpsuits in red and black in the trunk of the car, and a box containing a clock-radio. It was *not* the one Joe had selected; Tannim had switched it on him for a pricier model with a CD player in it. But since it was going to remain in the trunk of the Mach One until they reached Savannah, Joe wasn't going to find that out.

Fox was gone; he'd lost interest in the proceedings early on and simply vanished. He'd claimed he had a karaoke tournament to judge. It hadn't been easy persuading Joe that clothing could look good *and* be comfortable, but Tannim had managed.

The kid looked really good, actually. He was probably going to cut a wide swath through the secretaries at Fairgrove. Tannim guided the Mach One through the traffic of south Memorial on the way to Bixby, feeling relaxed and pleased with himself. *Modest, polite, and a hunk. And he has round ears. Uh huh. They aren't gonna know what hit them. He isn't going to know what hit him. Oh, things are going to be interesting around there.*

Well, heck, why limit the mayhem to the secretaries? There weren't too many unattached female mechanics and engineers, but there were a few—and the elven ladies would probably be just as intrigued with the polite young human.

Tannim grinned, but only to himself, and freed a hand just long enough to pull his hair away from the back of his neck to let the sweat dry. Joe's mere presence would get some of the ladies, human and elven, off *his* back. Not that they weren't charming, but they tended to get possessive, and there just wasn't a one of them that Tannim found—right.

Yeah, throw Joe into the pool and see all the lady-fish go into display, ignoring me. *Good plan!* Keighvin would see to it that they didn't eat him alive or get him into any trouble, physical or emotional. And if he didn't, Bob, Al and Sarge would. *Do the lad some good. Loosen him up.*

With those thoughts to elevate his mood, he pulled into the driveway and into his "spot" beside the horse trailers, reflexively checking his watch as he turned off the engine.

Right on time for dinner, just like Mom asked. Perfect. The folks always said, "tardiness is the height of conceit, punctuality the height of respect."

His parents came out to meet them, both obviously very curious about Joe. They climbed out, and Joe waited diffidently beside the passenger's door while Tannim made introductions. He charmed Tannim's mother immediately with his politeness, and impressed Trevor Drake with his soft-spoken attitude. Supper was waiting for them, and it went *much* more smoothly tonight, since Trevor could not say enough good things about Keighvin Silverhair and Fairgrove, and Joe could not say enough good things about the food. He completely won over Tannim's mother by volunteering to do the dishes afterward, and by insisting that he help clear the table. Tannim vetoed the former, and helped with the latter. "You and Dad can go enjoy the horses," he said. "I'll give Mom a hand. I'm *not* allergic to dishwashing."

So Joe changed back into his jeans and t-shirt for a trip to the stables to inspect the horses, leaving Tannim alone with his mother.

"I was a little worried about this Joe," she told him, as she stacked the dishes he rinsed in the dishwasher. "We saw so much about those awful people on the news, and I was afraid he'd be—oh, I don't know—just someone I wouldn't feel comfortable around. But he's a really *nice* boy, honey." She paused to fix him with a look he knew only too well. "He's so polite, and he looks respectable."

She did not say "why can't *you* be more like him?" but Tannim knew that was what she was thinking.

"Well, Mom, when your father puts a gun in your mouth to discipline you, you learn to be polite pretty quick," he said, off-handedly.

"He *didn't!*" she exclaimed, eyes round. At her son's nod of confirmation, she turned just a little pale. "Well, the poor boy," was all she said, but Tannim sensed the thoughts running around in her head. Joe had just gone from "that nice boy" to "that sweet, mistreated boy" in her mind, and he had an idea what might come next. Actually, he was all in favor of it.

Joe and Trevor came in then, talking horses. Tannim joined them at the breakfast bar, letting them do all the talking, just observing. Joe had relaxed a good bit; Tannim knew his dad probably wasn't like anyone the young man had ever met in his short life, and that was all to the good. *Expose him to something normal, and let that show him how abnormal his own parents were.*

"Listen, Joe, you don't have much to pack up now, do you?" Trevor asked, finally.

"No, sir," Joe replied, looking faintly puzzled. Tannim held his peace; this was what he thought might be on his parents' minds.

"Well, it's a long way out to Pawnee—if your guardian doesn't mind losing you a little early, why don't you come move into our guest room until you and Tannim leave?" Trevor asked, making it very clear that he meant the invitation. "That way you and my son can talk whatever business you need to, and he won't be spending a lot of time driving around in the heat."

"I think that's a great idea, Joe, if you'd like it," Tannim seconded enthusiastically. "A *really* good idea, in fact."

It means I can continue some of those magic lessons without worrying about interruptions. I know every good place around here to go where we won't be disturbed. And maybe if my folks feel like they've got a replacement son, they won't look at me as if I'm not really what they wanted.

Some of the same might be going through Joe's mind. "I can call and ask him," he said tentatively. "If he says it's okay, I can pack up tonight and be ready in the morning."

"Go call," Tannim's mother urged, adding her vote to Tannim and her husband's. "I'd love to have you here. Tannim doesn't eat enough to keep a bird alive, and I love seeing someone who appreciates food."

Joe blushed and excused himself. Tannim grinned at his folks. "Thanks, Dad, Mom," he said sincerely. "Joe is going to need a lot of help getting used to the way things are in this world. I think we can help him out quite a bit in two weeks."

Absolutely true, complete truth, but not the way they think.

"I kind of figured that, son," Trevor said warmly. "Boy's been sheltered in a pretty peculiar sense. He knows everything there is to know about the way lunatics think, and nothing about the way normal folk tick. And we raised you, so we know how to talk to lunatics. We can translate for him."

Tannim mock-threatened his father with a hand and then said, "Well, you have a point, actually." Tannim patted his mother's hand. "And he could use seeing a lady who stands up for herself, too. Where he comes from, women are supposed to go hide themselves in the kitchen and let their men do all the thinking for them."

"Well, he won't get that here," she replied, forthrightly. "I think he's lonely, honey. It would be nice if we could make him feel as if he had a home to come back to, if he wants."

Well, it sounds like they've adopted him! Heh. He could sure do worse.

"Thanks, folks," was all he said, but he put feeling into it.

At that point Joe returned. "Frank said to make sure I wasn't making a nuisance of myself," he reported, looking anxiously at all three of them. "And if this is going to be an inconvenience to you—"

"Well, if you're worried that much about it, you can give me a hand with the horses," Trevor said comfortably. "Tannim can't; boy takes one look at 'em and starts sneezing. Help me run some of the friskier ones on the lunge, maybe saddle up a couple of the mares and give them some exercise in the mornings. Some of those ladies are getting a little pudgy."

"Could I?" Joe's face lit up. "You have beautiful horses, sir. They're so great, are you sure you can trust me with them?"

Hoo boy, wait until the kid gets a look at the elven-steeds. Did Al ever show him Andur and Nineve in their true forms? He thought back over what Alinor had told him in his briefing. *No, I don't think he did. Didn't want to put the kid into overdrive. A Sidhe was bad enough. Heh. He and Rosaleen Dhu are going to get along just fine, and that'll make him one of Keighvin's favorite "sons."*

"If I didn't think I could trust you with them, I wouldn't have asked you to help," Trevor said, invoking logic. "That's a lot of cash tied up in horseflesh, son, and I know you'll be as careful with them as I am. I saw for myself you can handle them fine, and you know your way around a barn. So, can you move in tomorrow morning?"

Tannim sighed. The way his father said "morning," he knew that Trevor meant it. That meant rising at seven A.M., no excuses.

"Sure thing, sir!" Joe was eager now. His blue eyes were alight with anticipation. "If I can tell Mr. Casey that you want me to help out, he'll know I'm not imposing on you."

"Good, it's settled then." Tannim's mother nodded firmly. Her curly hair bounced with the nods. "I'll have the guest room ready for you, and we'll expect you tomorrow morning."

Joe looked at his watch. "In that case, Mr. Drake, Mrs. Drake, I'd better be getting back. I don't want to wake up Mr. Casey coming in."

Tannim rose, stretching. "Right. Mom, Dad, I'll get Joe here back to Pawnee, and I'll probably take the long way home. It's a nice night for a drive."

He watched his mother's face twitch as she repressed the automatic response of "don't stay out too late."

He winked at his father and led the way out for Joe. The sun had set while Joe and his dad had been out in the stables; now it was full dark, with no moon. Their feet crunched on the gravel on the driveway, and off in the distance, the whisper of a distant highway beckoned. It really *was* a good night for a drive, and Tannim intended to take full advantage of the solitude. He'd been promised some rest, and he was, by God, going to *get* some. He found driving restful, particularly when he had no place to go and no time he had to be there.

They climbed into the Mustang, and Tannim joined the stream of traffic on Memorial. Joe was far more talkative on the way back; for a wonder, Fox did not appear. Joe was a lot more relaxed now than he had been when they first drove out here. Tannim took that as a good sign; *he* already liked young Joe, and it seemed that Joe was far more comfortable with Tannim than the boy had expected to be.

"So, how are we shaping up?" Tannim asked, as he took the turnoff to Pawnee, headlights cutting twin cones of light through the darkness. "Me and Fairgrove, I mean. Are we anything like you thought?"

"I—" Joe faltered for the first time during the drive. "Sir, you're not at all what I expected. You're not like Al or Bob, I mean."

Tannim threw back his head and laughed. "Yeah, I can imagine! Sieur Alinor Peredon would probably be *horribly* offended if you thought he was like me! No, I'm not like anybody at Fairgrove, and neither is anyone else. That's the beauty of the place. You're supposed to be yourself, and no one else."

Joe's face was in darkness, but Tannim sensed his sudden uncertainty. "What if—what if you don't know who you are, sir?" the young man asked hesitantly.

"Well, wherever you are is a good place to find out. And Fairgrove is a good place to be," Tannim said firmly. "And quit with the 'sir' stuff. I'm not a knight like Alinor, and I'm not your guardian. I'm just Tannim, nothing more, and heaven knows that's enough for anyone. Okay?"

They entered the outskirts of Pawnee, and a few street lights dimly illuminated the cobblestones. Leaves made dappled, constantly moving shadows between each light.

"Okay," Joe said, although he didn't sound very sure. "Uh, if you don't mind my asking, what kind of a name is 'Tannim'? I never heard anyone by that name before. And why don't you use your last name?"

Tannim chuckled. "I use it, because one of my teachers gave it to me. 'Tannim' isn't the name my folks gave me, but I guess it must suit me since they started calling me by that right after I started using it. And I don't use my last name because I don't really need it." He shrugged. "People remember a guy who only goes by one name, and in this business sometimes you need people to remember you."

I'm not gonna bring Chinthliss up unless I have to, and that is the only way I can tell him where the name came from. Kid's got enough to cope with already. He's got Fox; he sure as heck doesn't need Chinthliss.

He pulled up into the Casey driveway at the stroke of ten; the lights were still on, and the flickering blue in the living room windows showed that the television was also going. Good. That meant they wouldn't be waking the deputy up.

"I'll pick you up in the morning, Joe," Tannim said, unlocking the doors from his console. "Some time between eight and nine, all right?"

"Great!" Joe said with an enthusiasm that made Tannim wince inwardly. *Terrific. The kid's a lark. Ah, well, he and Dad can mess around with the horses while it's still cool, and I can sleep in with a clear conscience.*

The young man slid out of the car, shutting the door carefully, waved a cheerful farewell, and trotted up the porch steps into the house. Tannim backed the Mustang carefully down the drive, and headed out of Pawnee.

He stopped under a streetlight to make a selection from his CD box, since there were no other cars in sight. *Driving to relax, let's see. Kate Bush, Rush, Icehouse, Midnight Oil, a-ha, Billy Idol . . . there. Cocteau Twins. That'll do just fine.*

He slipped the CD into the player, and turned the nose of the Mustang out into the darkness. No fear of getting lost; he knew the area around Tulsa like the back of his hand, every section-line road, every main drag. All he had to do was look for the glow of Tulsa on the horizon to orient himself.

He thought about checking out Hallet Racetrack, but thought better of the idea. It was probably locked up, and although he could get around just about any lock ever made, you just didn't trespass on a racetrack. Right now, when it came down to it, he just wanted the night, the tunes, and the road.

A brief tingling of energies warned him of a "friendly" coming in; Fox materialized in the seat next to him, but uncharacteristically didn't say a thing. Tannim let the Mach One set her own speed, and rolled the windows down to let in the night and the air. Music surrounded them both in a gentle cocoon of sound as the Mustang rolled on through the darkness, and the wind from the open windows whipped Tannim's hair and cooled his face.

Night, stars, and sound, and the open road. He felt muscles relaxing that hadn't unknotted for a long time. Fox leaned back in the passenger's seat, resting one long arm on the window-frame, graceful fingers tapping in rhythm to the song.

Stars blazed overhead. The headlights reflected from the bright eyes of small animals in the grass beside the road; once a rabbit dashed across in front of the car, and he braked instinctively to avoid hitting the owl following her. The owl was hardly more than a flash of wings and a glimpse of talons. *Barred owl? Looked like it. Be a little more careful, lady; the next guy might not know you were going to be on that bunny's tail.*

"I'll warn her," Fox said quietly, picking up Tannim's thoughts so easily that Tannim realized he must have relaxed enough to drop his shields. Well, that was safe enough in the Mach One; there were shields layered on top of shields, magics integrated with every part of this car, and the only reason Fox could get in and out so easily was because Tannim had made those shields selectively transparent to him.

The music ended, and Tannim reached for the CDs, trusting to his instincts to pick something appropriate. For the first time, he regretted the fact that Fox couldn't interact with the physical world; it would be nice to have someone in the passenger's side to change the CDs for him. This wasn't quite like changing a cassette; still, he managed with a minimum of fumbling.

A great rush of strings flowed from the speakers, and he relaxed still further. *Alan Hovanhess, "Mysterious Mountain." Good old instincts.* Not a lot of mountains in Oklahoma, but right now, with only the stars and the swaths of headlights, the hills seemed mysterious enough.

"This is good," Fox said quietly, his voice full of approval. "Really good."

Tannim made an ironic little bow in his direction, but did not reply; he didn't need to. Fox was so rock-obsessed, he probably didn't realize that any other kind of music existed. The music spoke for itself, sweeping through the Mach One like the night breeze, cutting brilliant streaks across the sky like the occasional meteor. He gave a sigh of regret when it finished; *someday* he was going to find a store that stocked enough obscure records that he'd be able to pick up more from this particular composer. He'd heard another piece on the radio once, "And God Created Great Whales," that he'd snap up in a heartbeat if he ever found it.

But when his hand sought the CD box for the third time, and the first notes screamed from the speakers, he was startled at what his instincts had chosen. *Billy Idol? Not very relaxing—*

Just as he thought that, Fox sat bolt upright in his seat, glancing to the rear in alarm. "Oh-oh," the *kitsune* said.

And vanished.

What the—

He glanced in the rearview mirror, to see a pair of headlights coming up on him from behind. Fast. Too fast for him to do more than react.

He winced away from the mirror in pain, squinting. Whoever this was, he had his brights on, and he was not going to drop them. The headlights filled his mirror, glaring into his eyes, as Billy Idol snarled over the speakers.

Some hot rodder? Got to be, but why alone and why out here? This is a lousy road for dragging.

He edged over to the side, a clear invitation to pass. The unknown didn't take it, moving up to hang right behind his rear bumper, engine growling.

Trying to pick me? Out here? Who is this jerk?

And why had Fox vanished like that?

He edged over further, until his right-hand wheels were actually in the grass, and waved his hand out the window. He wanted to flash the guy the finger, but the idiot was probably drunk and Tannim was not in the mood for a fight.

This time the answer was clear and unmistakable.

The car behind surged forward to hit the rear bumper. Not so hard that it knocked the Mach One off the road— or his hands off the wheel—but hard enough to jar Tannim back in his seat and bang his head and neck against the headrest.

"You *sonuvabitch!*" Pain blossomed in his neck. Savagely he jammed the pedal to the floor, spinning the wheels for a moment before he jarred into acceleration. The Mustang's engine thundered in his ears, drowning out Billy Idol, vibrating through him, a cross between a growl and a howl. For a moment, the headlights receded behind him.

But only for a moment.

The headlights grew again. The car behind caught up as if it had kicked in a jet engine. He had only a moment's warning, and then the vehicle pursuing him swerved to the left, accelerated again—

—and passed him, not quite forcing him off the road.

He got only a glimpse of the driver, just enough to see that it was either a very long-haired guy, or a woman. The car itself was clear enough; a late-model Mustang, '90 or '91. It was either black, or some other very dark color.

Then it was past him, accelerating into the night, impossibly fast unless the driver had a nitrous-rig under that hood. All he saw was the tail, red louvered lights winking mockingly at him, then disappearing.

You arrogant bastard!

His jaw clenched painfully tight, an ache in his neck and the base of his spine. He forced himself not to pursue his tormenter. He slowed, then stopped, right in the middle of the road, turning off the engine.

The license plate had been from no state. And he had not been able to read it. *Could not.* His eyes had blurred around the letters and numbers, although everything else about the car had been crystal-clear.

His hand reached out of itself and turned off the CD player. In the absence of the music, the singing of crickets and rustling of grass in the breeze seemed as distant as the farthest stars.

He reached under the seat for a flashlight, opened the door and got out. Heat rose from the asphalt as he went to the rear to see what the damages were.

He kicked rocks aside savagely as he took the few steps neccessary to reach the rear of the car, certain he was going to find a taillight out at least, and a crumpled bumper at worst. He moved slowly, played the beam of the flashlight over the rear of the car, and couldn't see even a scratch.

What the hey——? If I didn't get hit, then what did happen?

Then he turned, and froze, as movement toward the front of the car caught his attention.

There was something on the driver's side door.

He approached it, slowly, cautiously, playing the light over the door, and felt anger burning up inside him, hot bile rising in his throat.

There in the circle of light from his flashlight, pop-riveted to the door-panel, was a fingerless black leather driving glove.

With a growl of pure rage, he grabbed it and tore it off, the thin leather ripping away and leaving the rivet in the middle of his otherwise pristine door-panel.

I'm going to find him. And I'm going to kill him.

Something rustled inside the glove, and a strip of white paper peeked out at him impudently. He had the uncanny feeling it was moving in there on its own.

He pulled it out and unrolled it. His hand trembled as he held it in the light from the flashlight.

It was a thin strip of antique parchment, with a quotation written on it in black ink in a clear, if spidery, hand.

> *I have now found thee; when I lose thee again,*
> *I care not.*
>
> All's Well That Ends Well
> Act II, Sc 3

He stared down the black ribbon of asphalt under the stars. There was no way that driver could have done this.

No way on Earth.

● CHAPTER THREE

The warmth from the asphalt road seeped through his boots and the cool breeze whipped the ends of his hair around his face as his rage ebbed, and the fear began. Not fear for himself—any setup this obvious wouldn't make him fearful for himself—but for his parents, for Joe. *They* were vulnerable, and only because they were related to him, or connected to him. His first impulse was to get in the Mustang and start driving and not stop until he was back in Savannah, at Fairgrove. But that was no more than a momentary impulse, and he preferred not to act on impulse alone. Impulsive decisions were for when he had less than ten seconds to think before he acted.

Besides, that might be exactly what this challenger wants me to do: take off for help and leave them all unprotected. He throttled down every emotion with a fierce determination to leave his reasoning unclouded. *I have to think this one through before I do anything.*

He opened the Mach One's door and slid into the driver's seat, throwing the glove down on the passenger's seat. His mind hummed. *Music. I think better with music.* He started the engine and put the Mach One gently into motion, then punched the radio on. It was after midnight; time for the alternative rock program, Edge of Insanity, that took over the midnight-to-six slot from the classical station. With *real* luck, the program would work for him the way WYRD did, the play-list acting as a goad to his thoughts.

He tuned in right in the middle of a techno-trance piece; excellent. That was good, logical, thinking music. *Okay, I need to analyze the heck out of this. There's a reason why they talk about "throwing down the glove," and using a glove can't have been an accident. This was a gauntlet, a direct challenge. Not just the glove, though, all of it was meant to impress me so that it couldn't be igonored. Who- ever this was, she managed to produce enough of a magical shove to the back of my car that I thought she'd rammed my bumper. And she slammed that glove and rivet into my door, also magically, and in such a way that I didn't even know she'd done it.* He realized he had already come to think of his adversary as a woman; well, it was a reasonable assumption, given the silhouette, the small size of the long-fingered glove, and—the finesse. Not a bit of wasted energy; when males issued a challenge, they generally over-did it. Testosterone poisoning, clouding the brain.

Right. That's what she did. *Now, what she* didn't *do. She didn't shove the left bumper, although she made me think she had; if she'd done that, she would have sent me off the road, and I could have been seriously hurt. She didn't damage the rear of the car.* The damage to the pristine door panel was enough to send him into a rage all over again. *Don't be an idiot; you have enough equipment to make that hole disappear. Borrow Alinor or Keighvin, and they might even be able to stand the touch of Death Metal enough to ken the hole out of existence. No, the point is she didn't do anything at all that would really have harmed me or the Mach One. All she did was make me mad. And she did it with style. This was very carefully calculated. She could easily have done me some serious hurt if she'd tried.*

This also had the feel of something planned to enrage him, put him off balance, make him stop thinking.

But if she knows anything about me, she has to know that I've got pretty good control of my temper, and I think quickly. So if her ploy didn't make him act on anger or fearful impulse—what did that mean? Maybe this wasn't something planned to make him act impulsively. It was supposed to make him angry, there was no doubt of that. *If she can send a pop-rivet into my door, she could have sent something else through it. An iron spike. A crossbow bolt. Hell, a bullet. All right, rethink everything. Let me assume she's as brilliant and complicated as anyone I've ever seen. In that case, she'd do something that could have* multiple *outcomes. It might make me angry enough to chase after her, or afraid enough to run, but that wouldn't be her primary objective.*

And her primary objective must have been—

The challenge. An invitation to single combat.

Yeah. Everything she did points to the conclusion that this was a formal challenge, properly issued, artistically issued. Executed to show me clearly that I was dealing with a certain level of finesse and power, without giving anything else away. And done by the rules.

The road passed over a creek; a gust of damp, green-scented air wafted over him, and he thought he heard frogs. If this was a challenge, that meant a great deal; challenges were only meant for the person to whom they were issued. She who flung down the gauntlet would allow him time enough to *realize* that it was a formal challenge, and further time to think about it. Even the worst of the Unseleighe played challenges by the book.

There weren't supposed to be any Unseleighe living out here, though; that was one problem. So the questions of *who* and *why* still remained.

And a new question arose: *what next?*

If he turned and ran, he might very well make things worse. Creatures who played the game of "challenge-response" often took the refusal to accept the challenge as the signal for a no-holds-barred attack, for the once-honorable opponent made himself into "prey" by fleeing. A worthy foe would not act on impulse. An unworthy foe should be disposed of as quickly as possible, for it not only hinted at treachery by breach of format, but also threatened the system of honorable challenge itself.

Easier to be the honorable opponent. When you know the rules, you know the pattern. Thrust and parry.

The parents and the associates of the honorable opponent were not part of the challenge. The parents and associates of prey were—

More prey. No, I'll have to play this one clean until I know the answers to my questions.

He found himself headed toward Bixby and shrugged. *All right. I shield and armor the farm right up to the limit. Joe's going to be a lot safer there than at Frank Casey's. His education is just going to start a whole lot earlier than either of us thought. Damn. Now there's something else. He might be the ultimate "prize" in this little contest if I'm not careful. I have to keep that in mind. He might be what she's really after, and she's challenged me to get me out of the way, or to set things up so that he becomes, literally, the bone of contention. Winner take all.*

He vaguely recognized something by the McGarrigles playing in the background—"Mother, Mother," perhaps— and he turned the radio down until it was a mere whisper of sound. Good omen or bad? Good, if it was meant for Joe, as a warning to protect the young man; but maybe bad, very bad, if it was meant for him.

Another impulse was to call Conal or Keighvin at Fairgrove, but that was likely to be another mistake. First of all, calling in help might be a bad move at this early point. Secondly, this was not the sort of thing you could do much about over the phone. His associates at Fairgrove were not going to be able to help at long distance, and it had not yet come to the point where he could legitimately ask for help, reinforcements. The dance of "liege lord and equal ally" that he and Keighvin trod had its own patterns and measures. If he was to retain Keighvin's respect, he would have to deal with this quickly and appropriately.

But he had another source of help available to him; one with a different set of liabilities attached, but one for which the accounting was definitely on *his* side. Chinthliss owed him at the moment. Time to ask—politely—for a little payback.

One did not skimp on protocols and propriety when talking to dragons.

Tomorrow, he decided. *Tonight, just in case this lady doesn't play fair and I'm misreading everything, I put up the defenses.* That certainly matched the last song: the "house of stone" and the "cage of iron."

The house was dark by the time he pulled into the driveway; only the porch light left on, and a solitary lamp in his room still burning. He used his key and let himself in, and moved to his room, shadow-silent on the carpeted hallway.

He stripped out of everything, including his body-armor; donned a clean bikini-brief, and slipped into bed, turning the light off as he did so. But he was not going to sleep, not yet anyway.

All the old protections and shields he had put in place around this room as a kid were still here; dormant, but ready to be brought up at any time. That, at least, felt like "home." He closed his eyes, stretched in the comfortable and comforting embrace of mattress, clean sheets, and blankets, letting his body relax itself, feeling shoulders and neck pop and release their tension.

He chanted under his breath, old song lyrics invoking all the familiar energies he had learned when he first began his mage-training here. As the chant harmonized with the hum of the machinery within the house, his physical eyes drifted shut, and his body went rigid.

So far, so good.

He opened another set of eyes; everything around him glowed softly, each object clearly delineated in its own faintly-luminescent aura. It could have been dusk in this room, rather than fully dark, so far as the Othersight was concerned. A bit more concentration, and he could have lit up every item that he had cared for or spent time with, according to emotional attachment.

He "sat up," although his physical body remained lying

in the bed; his spirit-self rose from the bed, went to the exact center of the room, and took a fighter's stance. As he had when he was a teenager, he readied his magics and sent a spell of deeper sleep into his parents' minds. Not just because this would be a very bad time for him to be interrupted; if, for some reason, one of them walked in on him at the moment, they'd have the scat scared out of them. They'd be sure that he was dead—and certainly, his heartbeat and breathing were so faint at the moment that they would have every reason to believe just that. He was just short of death, connected to his body by the thinnest of willed tethers. Few people dared to go out-of-body this way, but the advantages were worth the risk.

Oddly enough, he had never used that power to keep his parents sleeping when he was a kid and had wanted to sneak out and raise some hell. Only when he had to meet with Chinthliss, or practice some of what he'd been taught.

Ah, I was just too lazy. I had to be in trance to make them sleep, so there was no point in doing all that work just to keep them from catching me. By the time I went into trance, mucked with their sleep, and came out again, half the night would be gone. Time's already burning away.

The old patterns of shield and armor were still in place; he examined them with a critical eye. He'd based his old constructs on the smooth dome-shapes of the silly, bad-effect "force-fields" of his favorite old science fiction books and movies. The basic *shape* was still good, but he knew a lot more now than he had then; he tore the structure down and began rebuilding it from within, constructing a crystalline structure after the pattern of a geodesic sphere, with his room as the center. Bucky Fuller, mage of logic that he was, would have been proud. He knew better, now, than to assume that because his room stood on solid ground, the earth afforded as much protection as a shield. No, now his shields extended below ground as well as above. The geodesic structure was a lot more stable than a smooth dome, able to bear a great deal more pressure. Once the initial structure was in place, he really went to work. Over that, he layered shields and shunts to drain off excess energies, and not a few traps for the unwary: magical deadfalls and power-sinks.

When he was finished, he sat within a beautiful, radiant construction that could have been a work of computer-generated art. Multicolored energies iridesced over the surface of his basic shield. Satisfied with what he had done at last, he repeated the patterns on a larger scale, weaving a web of energies and barriers around the house and stables, around the entire farm. Layer on layer on layer—it would take someone who *knew* what he had done to untangle it, and he would be warned and ready to deal with the intruder himself long before an enemy actually penetrated those protections.

He worked feverishly, right up until dawn. Then, and only then, he turned his trance into a true sleep and let weariness take him into a light slumber.

As Tannim drifted into the deeper realms of sleep, the dreams started again.

Warm gray mists surrounded his body, evaporating the clothing he wore. The tiny scales of his body armor whisked away, falling in a rain of silent sparkles. As he turned, the shadows from his lower body coalesced into a bedroom of night-black satin. Flames without candles lit the room, atop hundreds of fluted golden rods.

And when he turned around completely, she was there, indescribably beautiful, irresistibly seductive, waiting for him on a bed of silver satin, imploring . . . please . . . now. . . .

The alarm clock went off *far* too early, even though he was more or less ready for it. He opened one eye and blearily looked at the display.

Oh God, six in the morning. No choice, though; the sooner he got Joe under a safe roof, the happier he'd be. He dragged himself out of bed, picked out clothing, grabbed his armor with it, and slipped across the hall to the bathroom.

What was it about mothers and waterfowl? This *had* been a perfectly ordinary, plain bathroom when it had been his, but now that it was the "guest bathroom," his mother had gone berserk with decorating. Ducks. There were ducks *everywhere*. Wooden ducks with dried weeds in them on the vanity, duck plaques on the wall, a duck-bordered, pseudo-early-American wallpaper, ducks carved on the tissue-holder, even a matching potpourri warmer.

"Ducks," he wondered aloud. "Why did it have to be *ducks?*"

"What, dear?" his mother said, and opened the door to the bathroom before he could stop her.

"Oh!" she exclaimed faintly, as he flushed with embarassment at being caught by his *mother* in his underwear. Even if it did cover more than a pair of Speedos.

But then she paled. "Oh, dear," she whispered, even more faintly, her eyes running with horrified fascination over the scars crisscrossing her son's body.

Thank God none of them are new—

But there was no denying the fact that his entire body was interlaced with a fine network of scars, from the first, a knife-wound in the forearm, to the latest, four talon slashes running from the right nipple to the left hip. Not exactly the way a loving mother likes to see her child. Especially since he couldn't explain most of them.

She was staring at those talon-slashes at the moment, and he knew what she was going to ask.

"It looks worse than it was, Mom. They're just scratches. I was shopping at K-Mart," he improvised hastily, "And I got knocked through a plate-glass window during a blue-light special."

"A blue-light special?" she replied, recovering her poise a little, one eyebrow rising.

"I'm telling you, Mom, those women were *crazy*. There were almost knife-fights over those Barney dolls." *Sure. It could happen. . . .*

But her eyes were already traveling to the teethmarks that crossed his left leg from hip to ankle. "That—ah—was the wreck," he reminded her. "Remember? They had to cut me out of it."

"Aren't those bites?" she asked, in horrified fascination.

"Jaws of Life," he lied frantically. "They slipped. *Mom, please!* I'm in my *skivvies!*"

"And I changed your diapers, young man," she responded automatically, but at least she closed the door.

And at least she hadn't seen the glittering body-armor under the pile of clothing on the floor.

He locked the door to prevent any further incursions and turned on the shower. There were a few things he could do to recharge his body and make up for the lack of sleep, and the shower was the best place to do them. *Writing an IOU to my body. Oh, well. It won't be the first time.* Chinthliss was always on his case about doing things like this, but— *But sometimes there's no choice. If I get a choice, I'll catch a nap after I get Joe over here.*

He stood under the shower and let it literally wash the fatigue from his body as he drew upon his reserves. There was more in those reserve stores than there usually was, thanks in no small part to some payback on Keighvin's part, and a healer-friend of Chinthliss'. By the time he turned the hot water off, he felt better than he expected to. Almost human, in fact.

Certainly alert enough to deal with his mysterious lady in *her* Mustang.

Ersatz Mustang. Boy-racer fiberglass and recycled pop cans. Might as well have a plastic model. Nothing more than the sum of its parts, any of which you can pick up at Pep Boys off the shelf. Heh. If you can't have the real thing, why bother?

Maybe that was why she'd put a hole in his Mach One; pure jealousy.

Sure. It could happen. And Carroll Shelby will join the Hare Krishnas. But if she can have anything she wants, why pick a Mustang at all?

He reached under his clothing for the armor; glad now that he never, ever went anywhere without it, even if it *did* mean he had to wear long-sleeved shirts in the hottest weather. He and Chinthliss had worked on it together for three solid months, and no few of the scars on his body were the result of being in a situation where he *couldn't* wear it. It had saved his life more than once, and was worth all the trouble it posed. If the mysterious lady *had* fired a crossbow bolt, a bullet, or a spike through the door, she would have gotten a rude surprise. He might have gotten broken ribs, but she probably wouldn't have killed him. Not unless she *knew* about it, and how to get past it.

He squirmed into it, like a dancer getting into a unitard, and that was what it most resembled. Made of thousands of tiny hexagonal scales, enameled in emerald green, it was better than Kevlar because it offered as much protection from magic as it did from bullets or knives. The cool scales slipped under his hands as smoothly as silk; the entire suit of body-armor weighed about as much as a garment of knitted silk, and moved with him as easily and naturally as a second skin.

He crooked his finger and ran the nail up the split down the front to close it up again. There were no seams, for every scale was linked magically to every other scale, so it could be opened anyplace that he wished.

It wasn't perfect—he could, quite easily, be *clubbed* to death while wearing it. He could be injured *through* it, by impact. And it didn't protect his head, neck, or hands. But it gave him a lot of edge over someone expecting to do his arguing with a bullet, knife or elfshot.

His clothing slipped on easily over the armor, and he made sure that none of the green scales showed before he opened the door to the bathroom to let the steam out.

When he'd finished with hair and teeth, he sprinted to the kitchen just long enough to grab a banana and down a glass of orange juice, kissing his mother quickly in passing. "Gotta go pick up Joe," he said as he ran for the door. "I'll have a real breakfast when I get back."

Her protests were lost in his wake.

Personal shields were up before he left the static shields of his room and the farm, and he activated every protection he had on the Mustang once he was inside it. With every sense, normal and magical, alert, he drove the entire distance to Pawnee in a familiar state of controlled paranoia.

Nothing happened.

Once or twice he thought he saw a late-model Mustang that *might* have been hers, but it always drifted away in the traffic. There were no attacks, no probes, not even a whisker of power brushed up against his. The attack—or challenge—of last night might never have happened.

Except that there was still a pop-rivet in the driver's-side door, and a black leather glove on the seat beside him.

It taunted him; in no small part because he had been able to learn so little from it. It simply lay there on the black vinyl seat, a palpable presence. Finally he couldn't stand it any longer; at a stoplight he grabbed it and shoved it into the glovebox.

Good God, I just put a glove in the glovebox. That'll be a first.

Well, if she thought she was going to be able to winkle any of her magics into the Mach One via that glove, odds were she was wrong. The glovebox had its own little set of diamond-hard shields, and they worked *both* ways, shielding what was in the box from outside influence, and keeping what was in the box from getting any influences out. This wasn't the first time he'd had to carry something small and potentially dangerous. And for things large and potentially dangerous, there was the trunk.

Heh. Big enough for a body or two, if need be.

Jeez, his thoughts were bloody this morning!

He shook his head. This woman and her little "present" were affecting him in ways he didn't like, turning him savage. A single steel pop-rivet in the door panel and a stiff neck should *not* be doing this to him.

Whoa! Back up! A steel pop-rivet?

He pulled the glove out of the box for a moment and examined it with one eye still on the traffic before shoving it back in. *Why didn't I notice this last night? And steel eyelets on the back of the glove. Whoever, whatever this broad is, she's not Unseleighe. That glove's been worn; there's scuff marks and creases in the leather. No Unseleighe would be able to tolerate steel on a glove, and no Unseleighe would be able to use his magics to manipulate a steel pop-rivet. I don't think even Al or Keighvin could, and they have the most tolerance to Cold Iron of any Sidhe I know.*

That didn't mean, however, that she might not be in the hire of the Unseleighe, or an ally of some kind. They even had human allies and servants. But if she was that good, why would she be working on behalf of someone else?

He sighed, and mentally shrugged, as he took the turn-off to Pawnee. Maybe the pay was extraordinary. Maybe she wasn't with the Unseleighe at all. Maybe she was the local hotshot, somebody who'd moved in after he left, and she was pulling the equivalent of the young gun going after the old gunfighter.

She obviously knew a great deal about him; she had a distinct edge over him in that department. He *had* to learn more about her, and fast!

Joe came bounding out of the house before he even came to a full stop in the driveway, full of energy and enthusiasm, with a pair of duffel bags and a couple of boxes waiting on the porch to be loaded into the trunk. His guardian was right behind him. Tannim helped the young man stow his gear in the trunk, trying to sound and look as normal as possible, all the while reassuring Frank Casey that this was no imposition. Somehow he managed to smile and act as if everything was exactly the same as it had been when he'd dropped Joe off last night. Somehow he remembered to mention that Joe would be helping Trevor with the horses; evidently that was what finally convinced the deputy that Joe would indeed be pulling his own weight.

Being out here made Tannim nervous; he had to consciously force himself not to look over his shoulder. The last place he wanted to bring trouble to was the sleepy little town of Pawnee; they'd already had enough trouble to last them well into the next century, and Casey was obviously able to take care of anything normal that arose.

When Joe was buckled into the passenger's seat, and they pulled out of Pawnee with nothing sinister manifesting, Tannim heaved a sigh of relief.

"Is something wrong?" Joe asked immediately. "Did your parents change their minds or something?"

"Yes," Tannim replied. "No. Yes, there's something wrong, but it doesn't have anything to do with my folks, and they don't know anything about it. They still want you out there. Dad's making his famous omelettes and Mom is doing pancakes so we get 'proper breakfasts' when we get back. No, the problem's with what's in the glove compartment."

He nodded at the glovebox, and Joe opened it, pulling out both glove and quotation.

"A glove?"

"Yeah, weird, huh? After I dropped you off last night, someone in a late-model Mustang rammed the back of the Mach One and left that pop-riveted to the door. Except that she *didn't* ram me, she used magic to shove me forward hard enough to make me *think* she'd rammed me, and she whanged that into my driver-side door with magic, too, so that I didn't notice it until after she'd passed me and was gone."

Joe was quick; he cut right to the chase. "Why?" he asked.

"I think it's a challenge." He chose his next words carefully. "The trouble is, I don't know for sure. I don't know what the stakes are. And I don't know who or what she's going to drag into this."

"Like me, maybe?" Joe hazarded, turning just a little pale. "Tannim, I hope you don't mind me saying so, but I could have gone a long time without hearing that. I was hoping I wasn't gonna have to deal personally with this magic stuff for the next couple of years."

Tannim could only shrug. "Sorry. Sometimes stuff just shows up and bites you in the ass. Look, I've got major protections on the farm, you, my folks. I'm going to try to keep you out of this. *Maybe* this is as harmless as a drag race; she could be the local hotshot trying to pick on me. The main problem I've got is that all I know about her is that she planted *that* on me with magic. The rest is speculation. Except for one thing: she can't be Sidhe. Pop-rivet and the fasteners on that glove are Cold Iron, and that glove's been worn."

"So what are you going to do?" Joe asked, apprehensive, but covering it fairly well. Tannim negotiated a tricky bit of passing before he answered, using the traffic to buy him time to think of what he was going to tell the kid.

Everything. Teenage sidekicks notwithstanding, he's got guts and he's got combat experience.

"Use that glove to try and find something more about her," Tannim replied grimly. "Right now, I'm at a major disadvantage, since she obviously knows something about me, maybe a lot. And for the rest—besides being *very* careful, we're going to act as if this was all business as usual. We'll leave here on schedule for Fairgrove, unless there's a good reason not to. If we let her think she's disrupting our lives, she wins a moral victory, if nothing else."

Joe nodded slowly. "Just tell me what to do, and I will, sir," he said bravely.

Tannim smiled crookedly. "Besides putting that glove back, the best thing you can do is give my mom someone to fuss over, and someone for my dad to show off his horses to. Occupy their time. That'll keep them from wondering what I'm up to, and maybe keep them out of danger. I'm still thinking this through. Unless you really *want* to stay out of everything, I'm going to at least keep you informed."

"Right." Joe accepted that, and stowed the glove back in the box. "Ah—where's Fox?"

"That—" Tannim replied quietly "—is a darned good question." And one he hadn't considered until now.

He saw her coming. No—he sensed her coming. He looked back over his shoulder before I knew anything was up, said, "Uh oh," and vanished. And he hasn't been back.

Fox knew something. He had to. There was no other explanation for the way he'd acted.

Did he recognize her? There had to be something there that he knew, or sensed—something that slipped right by me, because I thought she was just some hot-rodder, or an obnoxious drunk, right up until she rammed the rear of the Mach One. I had no clue she'd done anything with magic until after she was gone. So what does Fox know about all this?

"You're thinking about something," Joe observed, watching his face alertly. "Something to do with that woman and Fox."

"Yeah." He ran his tongue over dry lips. "He was with me right up until the moment she showed up, then he just blinked out, and hasn't been back."

"Can you make him show up?" Joe asked hopefully. "It sounds like he might know something."

But Tannim had to shake his head with regret. "No. Not without violating a lot of trusts, as well as protocols. My friends—the ones like Fox—wouldn't ever really trust me again if I *forced* him to show up. That's part of the reason they like me. He knows I'm thinking about him, I'm sure. He'll only show up if he wants to."

Joe shook his head sadly. "Sometimes it's really *frustrating* to be the good guy, you know? The bad guys never have to think of things like this."

Despite the tension, Tannim had to chuckle at that. "'Fraid so, Joe," he replied. "I'm afraid so."

They reached the ranch without any kind of incident, but Tannim was not about to be lulled into lowering his defenses. If this was a challenge, that would be precisely the sort of thing she would be looking for. No, if anything, he had to redouble his efforts.

But before he did that, he was going to have to refuel and get some real rest. He'd done everything he *could* do to protect the innocent bystanders without having specific information on his opponent. Now was the time to get himself back up to top shape.

Joe had already gotten breakfast with his guardian, but he showed no reluctance to eat when presented with a second breakfast. Tannim marveled yet again at the way the young man could dispose of food, as he munched his way dutifully through as much of the "farmhouse meal" as he could handle at one time. *One thing for sure, he's solved our leftover problem for awhile.*

After breakfast, when his mother and father *both* mentioned work in the stables, he seized on the excuse to get a little more sleep. "You guys go right ahead," he said, trying to sound relaxed. "I have a ton of books with me I haven't had time to get to. I'll go read in my room, if you guys don't mind, and I'll catch up with you at lunch."

That gives me another three hours to sleep. I can pack six hours worth into those three, with a little hard magesleep. That should put me back up to par. Or at least as close to par as I've been in the last couple of months.

After the exhibition of allergic reactions Tannim had shown the last time he'd entered the barn, neither of his parents were eager to have him along. They accepted his statement with a minimum of fuss and ushered Joe out the kitchen door, all three of them looking eager. The proprietary way his parents flanked the young man made Tannim smile. They had definitely "adopted" him.

He shoved the dishes into the dishwasher, cleaned up the kitchen hastily, and practically ran into his room. He spread a book open on the nightstand, to make it look as if he really had been reading, but—

But if they happen to come in and find me asleep, it's not that big a deal. They know I need rest, they'll just think I'm actually getting it.

He thought, given the tension that he was under, that he just might have to will himself to sleep. He had not reckoned with the exhaustion, long- and short-term, he'd been enduring for the past couple of months. He laid himself down on the bedspread, closed his eyes, and fell asleep even as he was preparing the first stages of willing himself into that state.

He woke to the sounds of voices in the house; Joe and his dad. He lay motionless for a moment, with the memories of vivid dreams in his mind.

Dreams of *her*.

He'd dreamt of her, at least once a week, since he'd first encountered Chinthliss. Nightly, sometimes. And interestingly enough, she had aged at approximately the same rate that he had; when he'd been an adolescent, so had she, and now she was a full adult, although it was no longer possible to tell exactly how old she was. She could have been twenty or forty; showing nothing that pointed to chronology, only that she was no longer an adolescent and not yet showing any signs of middle age.

With raven hair that cascaded down below her shoulders, enigmatic green eyes, and beauty that was both cultured and wildly untamed, *she* was, in a sense, the perfect lover he'd never been able to find in anyone else.

Not that he hadn't looked.

For a long time he'd been certain that he would find her. He'd assumed, as most young romantics full of hormones do, that the dreams meant the two of them were destined to meet and become lovers. But as the years passed, and he never found anyone remotely like her, he became convinced she was nothing more than an unconscious expression of his wish for that "perfect" lover. Not that she was slavishly devoted to him in those dreams; far from it. *That* would not have interested him, once he was past the macho cockiness of every adolescent that demanded absolute devotion, or worse, ownership. Luckily, that unflattering phase of his development had been brief.

No, she was very clearly herself in those dreams, perfectly capable, perfectly competent, and quite able to take him on in a game of wits, in a game of intellect, of purely physical challenge, and in any other games as well. That was what made her so perfect. And so damned impossible.

He wondered why he'd dreamed of her now, though. And *that* kind of dream: erotic so far past what he thought were his ordinary fantasies. He'd been entangled to the point where he'd awakened in a state of sexual tension that was as demanding as the state of nervous tension he'd been in when he started this little nap. His undershorts felt two sizes too tight. And he was in his *parents'* house, for God's sake. Not in a position to do anything about it.

Oh, she was something special, though. She was just the kind of otherworldly succubus that would make all the sacrifices to get her worth it. He wouldn't *care* if she was going to eat him alive, if there was a chance he could win her heart. But, instead of *her*, he had some crazy woman in a hot-rod Mustang forcibly planting leatherwear on him.

The voices in the hall drew nearer, and Tannim hastily put his dreamy musings out of his mind. He grabbed simultaneously for the paperback on the nightstand and a throw-blanket to cover himself with, then assumed a posture of reading. When his mother tapped on the door and opened it, he was able to greet her with a reasonably calm demeanor.

"Ready for some lunch?" she asked.

"Sure," he told her, putting the book down and stalling a bit for his blood to cool. "I hope you three had a good time out there. I already know it was work."

That kept her busy, chatting about what she and her husband and Joe had accomplished; while she was talking, she wasn't asking him any questions. Joe had clearly enjoyed the morning's workout. A few minutes later, while they all ate, Trevor couldn't say enough about how well Joe had handled the horses.

"Well, if you haven't got anything planned for him this

afternoon, I'd like to borrow him," Tannim interjected. "There's quite a bit of outfitting we still need to do."

Joe paused in mid-bite and raised a single eyebrow at Tannim in inquiry. Tannim nodded, ever so slightly.

"There's not much for him to do in the afternoon," Trevor replied, "not in this heat. Remember, we were counting on that. I know you two have a lot of business to take care of, and I figured you were going to take afternoons and evenings to do it. And maybe just spend some time driving around together; if you're going to be working together, you ought to get to know each other."

Tannim smiled; if he hadn't had these current worries, that's precisely what he *would* be doing. Sometimes his folks showed some amazing insight. They always *had* seemed to get smarter the older he got.

"In that case, we'll take off," he said. "As soon as you're ready, Joe."

Joe made the last of his third sandwich and glass of milk vanish with a speed that meant he *had* to be either magical, ravenous or enlisted-Army, then pronounced himself ready to go. Tannim stayed only long enough to clear their own dishes away, leaving his parents lingering over coffee, before leading the way back out to the Mustang.

Which had, unfortunately, been sitting in the hot sun all morning.

He popped the doors open with the electronic gadget on his keyring and started the engine the same way, but waved Joe away from the car. He opened the driver's side long enough to start the a/c, then stood with the door closed beside it for a moment while the interior cooled a trifle. He tried *not* to think about that shiny pop-rivet in the door panel, but it seemed to be winking at him, mockingly.

Heck, I ought to at least hit it with a dab of touch-up paint so it isn't so blatant.

He finally couldn't stand it any longer and waved Joe inside, pulling open his own door and sliding gingerly over the hot black vinyl. The steering wheel was almost too hot to touch, and he made a vow to find some shade, somewhere, that would cover the car in the mornings. Joe winced away from the hot seat, sitting forward a bit to keep his back away from it. *He* didn't have the protection of the armor; all he had were jeans and a white t-shirt.

"Where to?" Joe asked expectantly. "I figured you didn't have shopping on the brain."

"Wish I did." He eased the Mustang around in the graveled half-circle in front of the house, pulled up to the end of the drive, and headed down the way he had first arrived. No more backing down the drive; not when that put him in a vulnerable position so far as a getaway was concerned. "No, I told you I needed to get more information on this woman; I'm going to a place where it's safe to work some magic to see if I can't get hold of—well, he's an old friend, and he's something of an expert on challenges."

When his encounters with Chinthliss had gone beyond *real* dreams and into situations he had originally thought were "waking dreams" or entertaining hallucinations, the old barn he'd rented for his Mustang restoration business had been the place where he'd first encountered his mentor. That would be the safest place to try to contact him again, even though there wasn't much left of the building. No one would bother them there, and the shield-frames Chinthliss had put in place were still there.

He hadn't intended to come back, but now he had no choice.

The track leading up to the place was long overgrown, visible only as two places where the grass was a little shorter and a little paler than the rest. He turned off through the broken gate in the fence that no one had ever bothered to mend, and pulled the Mach One up through the waving tall grass. If he hadn't known exactly where the safe track was, he would never have dared this with a car that was *not* an off-road vehicle. But the earth was packed down here, and there shouldn't be anything lurking to slash tires or foul the undercarriage. Still, he kept the car at a walking pace, just in case, bringing it up to what was left of the east side of the barn, pulling it into his old parking place in the shade of a blackjack oak.

He retrieved the glove from the glovebox and stuck it into his pocket. He climbed out of the car, and waded through the weeds and grass to where half of the barn door hung from one hinge, the other half lying in the grass. Joe followed, diffidently.

He stepped across the threshold. "You know," he said, conversationally, as he stared into the empty, weed-filled space that had once held his workshop and all his beloved Mustangs in their various states of repair, "I had a dream about this place, before I ever set foot in it. I dreamed that I came up to this door, opened it, and looked around. The place was mostly empty, full of shadows. And right there—" he pointed to the west corner "—there was a tarp with something under it. In my dream I would come up to that tarp, and pull it off, and there was an engine under there. Not just any engine, but a 428 CobraJet, in absolutely perfect condition. Mint, like the day it had come off the line. And it had just been waiting for me to find it."

He contemplated the corner for a moment; there was no sign now that there had ever been anything there. Somewhere under the weeds, there probably lurked all the bits of junk the guy he'd sold salvage rights to hadn't carted off, but you wouldn't know that from here. "Anyway, that was what convinced me to rent this barn; to begin my Mustang restoration business, to go ahead with the whole plan. I did just that, rented it sight unseen; walked up to the place with the key in my hand and unlocked the door and swung it open. And sure enough, in that corner, there *was* a tarp, with something under it. I walked up to it; my heart was pounding, let me tell you. I grabbed the end of the tarp, and I pulled it away—"

"And the engine was there!" Joe exclaimed when he paused.

Tannim shook his head, smiling. "Nope. Nothing but a pile of musty old lumber and some odd bits of farm equipment. And just at first, I was horribly disappointed. I felt like the dream had let me down, somehow."

He let his gaze drift upward to what was left of the walls, to the blue sky above where the roof had been. And he realized that coming here did *not* hurt, as he had feared it would. He'd given up the limited dreams this place meant a long time ago—outgrown them, so to speak. He might just as readily have felt pain at seeing his old tricycle, or his playpen.

"But then," he continued, "I had this revelation. The dream hadn't let me down at all, because it had spurred me to make the commitment to try the business. I might not otherwise have done it. And I knew at that moment that the things I would build here would be so much *better* than that phantom engine, there'd be no comparison. Everyone wants to hit it big and have something great just happen, like winning a lottery. But—the things I would create here would be all *mine,* built out of the work of my own hands and my own sweat, and not just thrown into my lap."

"Yeah . . ." Joe said, and nodded. "Yeah, I see what you mean." And although not everyone *would* have understood, Tannim had the sense that Joe did.

He took another step or two into the barn, and felt all the protective energies of Chinthliss' magics close around him. The blackened walls took on a peculiar golden haze as he reactivated those magics; gaps in the walls closed up, and a glowing golden field arched upward, between him and the open sky.

Joe stared, wide-eyed, open-mouthed. Tannim grinned, gazing right along with him. He still loved this place.

"Well, there it is, Joe. Real magic. Don't know how much Al and Bob showed you, but this is it: two-hundred proof."

"They never showed me anything like *this,*" Joe replied, still ogling around with unabashed astonishment.

Tannim permitted himself a chuckle. "Well," he said, "there's more where that came from."

Joe hadn't imagined why Tannim had brought them to this burned-out hulk of a barn, except out of nostalgia. He *did* understand what Tannim meant with his story about the dream-engine, though. He'd had more than enough experience with how gifts out of the blue could backfire on you, or have strings attached you didn't even know about until you began your puppet-dance. No, it was better to earn what you got, that was for sure.

Still—the place was not exactly prepossessing. The roof was gone, and although the remains of the four walls lifted ragged and blackened timbers to the sky, he couldn't imagine what Tannim could find here that he couldn't get in—say—a brush-filled ravine, or a tree-packed ridge, both of which would offer the same amount of privacy that this barn would.

Then Tannim had done—something—and as his skin tingled with the feeling of a lightning storm building, the walls came alive and rose unbroken to the sky in solid sheets of power.

More than that, a kind of roof appeared overhead—a roof of glowing golden light.

All of it was rather ghostlike, since he could see right through it, but it *felt* powerful, and he had no doubt that it would protect them in its way as well as armor plating.

That left him with a lump in his throat. Witnessing magic like this was an electrifying and bewildering experience.

Al and Bob had shown him a few things, including something they'd called "personal shields," but it had all been small stuff compared with this. Was this the kind of thing Tannim did all the time? Would he be expected to work with this kind of stuff on a regular basis? And what about the other people at Fairgrove? Were they all as—well—as powerful as this?

"What do you want me to do, sir?" he asked, pleased that his voice shook only a little.

"Just watch," Tannim replied, taking a relaxed pose in the center of the barn, legs spread apart almost like a pistol-shooting stance, arms raised over his head. "Nothing else."

Well, that was easy enough to do. . . .

He watched, and for awhile nothing much seemed to happen. Then he felt that funny tingling along his skin that he had learned meant something magical was going on, and a faintly glowing ball of green-and-gold light formed in front of Tannim, hovering in the air at about chest height. Soon it was quite solid, as if someone had hung a light bulb right in midair. He could not imagine what this thing was, but he watched it with wide eyes. This wasn't the sort of thing he saw every day.

Tannim stared into the ball, and Joe had the sensation that he was somehow talking to it. He dropped his right hand long enough to pull the black driving-glove out of one pocket, and held it up to the globe for a long time.

Then he tucked the glove away again, raised his hand back over his head, and stared at the globe for a moment longer.

This was as creepy as anything Brother Joseph had ever done, and only the sense that this was *not* anything evil or even harmful kept Joe standing where he was. He knew what evil felt like; whatever it was, this wasn't evil.

But he almost lost it when the ball suddenly brightened until it rivaled the sunshine and cast a tall shadow of Tannim against the wall behind him. And he *did* yelp when it vanished in a clap of thunder.

But Tannim only dropped his hands, dusted them off against his jeans, and stared at the walls for a moment. Abruptly, the glow disappeared, leaving only the fire-blackened timbers again.

"I love that effect!" Tannim laughed.

"What was that?" Joe blurted. "What did you do?"

"Call it—a magical version of a fax machine," Tannim replied after a moment, his green eyes luminous in the bright sunshine, as if there was some power making them shine. "I have a friend named Chinthliss who's like a more powerful version of Foxtrot, though he'd choke if you ever said it to him. I want him to help me, and that little glow-ball is how I told him pretty much everything we know." He grinned then, and pulled his Wayfarers out of his pocket, putting them on. "Now, we just wait."

A magical version of a fax? Joe shook his head; this was way beyond anything Al and Bob had ever showed him. Even though he knew that when they came to visit they hadn't ever come by airplane much less driven across the country, they hadn't once explained how they *did* manage to cross the miles between Pawnee and Savannah whenever they chose. They certainly hadn't *shown* him things like this. Tannim turned away from him for a moment and bent his head down to peer at something in the grass growing up through the barn floor.

Joe might have asked more questions, except that at that precise moment, someone coughed delicately behind him.

"Excuse me?" said a low, sexy, female voice.

Tannim thought he saw something give off a bit of mage-sparkle in the grass at his feet, and he peered down for a moment.

"Excuse me?" said a voice that was *not* Joe's.

Tannim jumped in startlement, and turned to face the barn door.

And froze as he saw who was standing there behind Joe, his mind lodged on a single thought, unable to get past it.

It's her—it's her—it's her—

And it was: the woman who had haunted him and hunted him down through his dreams for the last decade and more. The woman he'd dreamed of this morning. *Her.* And she stood there, nonplussedly taking in his look of complete and utter shock.

There was absolutely no doubt of it; she matched his dreams in every detail. Gently curved, raven-wing hair swept down past her shoulders and framed a face that he knew as well as he knew his own. Amused, emerald-green eyes gazed at him from beneath strong brows that arched

as delicately as a bit of Japanese brushwork. The regal
nose was just short of being hawklike, and gave strength to
the prominent cheekbones. The sensual mouth hinted at a
hundred secrets. And the body, the perfect, slim, small-
breasted body . . . did more than hint.

She stood as he remembered her standing; poised, and
not posed, graceful movement arrested for the briefest of
moments. She wore silk and leather; a red silk jumpsuit
that flowed in an exotic cut that spoke of expensive
designers, tooled and riveted black leather belt and boots.
She wore them beautifully, flawlessly, unselfconsciously, as
if they were the stuff of her everyday attire.

"Excuse me," she said again, in a throaty contralto that
he remembered whispering intimacies into his ear, " . . .
but I understood that I could find someone here who
works on Mustangs."

He took one step toward her; another. At the third step,
he looked past her and spotted her black Mustang standing in the midst of the tall grass outside the barn door.
The grasses waved gently around it, like something out of
a commercial. Joe simply stood frozen in place, staring at
her. She waited, calmly. She looked as if she would be perfectly ready to wait all day.

Tannim started to speak, and had to cough to clear his
throat before his voice would work.

"Not—for a long time," he said dazedly.

"Ah," she replied, with a smile tinged with something
he could not read.

But then her eyes widened as she looked past his shoulder, and she stepped back in alarm.

Fear lanced him. He whirled to look.

There was nothing there.

Quickly, realizing that she had pulled the oldest trick in
the book on him, he turned back.

She was already gone. And so was her car.

Only *then* did his mind click back into gear, as he sprinted
past the broken-down door, and stood where the car had
been. There was the imprint of four tires in the grass—but

no track-marks leading up to them. There was no sign that the car had actually been driven through the grass to reach that spot, and there had been no sound of a motor.

Belatedly, recognition. The car that had stood there had been the same Mustang that had shadowed him last night.

The grasses waved and parted; he looked down when his subconscious recognized that the shadow there was not a shadow. There was a second black, fingerless driving glove in the grass at his feet.

He picked it up, and immediately banished the thought that he might have dropped last night's glove and not have noticed. *That* glove had been torn where it had been riveted to the door and he'd ripped it off. *This* glove, also for the right hand, was intact.

And it, too, contained a small strip of parchment.

He took it out, and there was another quotation handwritten there, in the same spidery hand.

> *The painful warrior famoused for fight,*
> *After a thousand victories, once foiled,*
> *Is from the books of honour razed quite,*
> *And all the rest forgot for which he toil'd.*
> Sonnet 25

He stared at it, the meaning burning arc-light bright in his mind. *The challenge has been made. Chicken out of this one—or be defeated—and everything you are and ever were will be erased, and everything you ever did will be forgotten.*

• CHAPTER FOUR

Tannim tucked the slip of parchment back into the glove with special care. The sun burned down on his head, as the quotation burned in his mind. Of all the ways he'd ever imagined of meeting *her*, this had never once crossed his mind. He'd pictured himself simply running into her in some exotic place, imagined finding her on his side in a desperate combat, wondered if some day she might simply appear at Fairgrove as a new "employee" even as he had. He had fantasized rescuing her, fighting by her side, having *her* rescue *him*, even. It had never once entered his mind that she could be an enemy.

No—not an enemy. Have to call it like it is; I don't know that yet. An opponent, but I can't put her in the "enemy" column yet. Maybe that was wishful thinking, but he couldn't get all those dreams out of his head. Surely they meant *something*.

Grass swished and crackled behind him, and young Joe moved out of the barn to stand next to him. "There was a lady there a minute ago, wasn't there?" he said, his voice remarkably steady, given the circumstances. "And a car?" In the brilliant sun, his hair looked almost white, and his vividly blue eyes mirrored the Oklahoma sky.

"Uh-huh," Tannim confirmed. "I'm beginning to feel like Prince Charming. She left me another glove."

Joe regarded the glove in Tannim's hand with a dubious expression and made no move to touch it. "I don't think

85

you're gonna have too much luck going around Tulsa getting women to try those on to see if they fit."

Tannim smiled faintly. *Not bad; the kid's keeping his sense of humor.* "Not as reliable as a glass slipper."

No maker's mark in these gloves, though. No tag, and no sign that one had been cut or taken out. No identifying marks at all. Wasn't that a little odd?

Come to think of it, they didn't really look mass-produced. Huh. Custom work? If so, they might be as good as a glass slipper if I can find out where they came from.

He was just about ready to take the gloves apart, stitch by stitch, when a warning tingle along his personal shields alerted him. *Something* was manifesting in the barn!

He tested the energies, and recognized one he had not really expected to encounter quite so soon. But it was more than welcome, especially in light of this second challenge.

He sprinted back to the barn and reinvoked all the protections; the golden walls of power came up around him, enclosing him in a safe zone that only he, Chinthliss, or their sendings would be able to pass. He held his hands out at chest height, preparing the space in front of him to receive whatever Chinthliss' answer would be.

A thunderclap announced its arrival in his hands, and a flash of golden light that lit up the inside of the protective dome as it passed through the shields.

It came in the form of the same green and gold message-globe he himself had sent out, which confirmed his surprised and delighted guess that Chinthliss had answered him *immediately*, interrupting whatever else he was doing to do so. There *were* times when the dragon came through for him.

The globe settled in his hands, weightlessly, and pulsed for a moment, as it confirmed his identity. Then it deepened in color, turning from golden green to a deep bronze, and he felt a familiar touch on his mind. He relaxed and let the message flow into his thoughts.

:*I have heard, and am intrigued, Son of Dragons.*: The deep bass, purely mental voice tolled sonorously in his head. *:I will arrive at the usual place at the hour the sun has vanished. And in case you have forgotten, the "usual place" is the building in which you once kept all your machines.:*

The globe spun on its axis then whirled and changed, fading as it discharged its energies into the air, the shields, and anything else that was able to absorb a little extra power.

Including Tannim, who was not too proud to get a little of the charge he'd put into the thing back again.

Once again, he brought the protections down, and took a quick glance at Joe. The young man was not watching him; instead, he had taken up a "guard" position at the doorframe, and his alert stance told Tannim that his erstwhile protégé was perfectly prepared to fight anything that tried to cause trouble. Obviously Joe had not made the assumption that because the challenger was a woman, she could be dismissed.

Good. At least that's one lesson he won't have to learn the hard way.

"Joe?" he said quietly. The young man turned and nodded.

"Nothing out there that I can see," he said. "Nobody watching us as far as I can tell. Did your friend send you a return fax?"

Tannim had to smile at the ease with which Joe had accepted his own offhanded terminology. "As a matter of fact, he did," Tannim replied. "He's going to be here tonight. We'll have to come out here to meet him."

"And until then?" Joe asked, his expression stolid, only his eyes showing his nervous tension as he continually glanced from side to side, making certain nothing could creep up on them.

"First I need to make a phone call, and I want to do that from a private phone, not from home," Tannim told him. "My friend's going to need a hotel room, so why don't we go arrange that for him, and I can use the phone in the room."

Joe nodded, and Tannim reflected that it was really useful having someone like Joe around, a young man who was used to taking orders without question. Questions like, how was this friend going to get out here, and why couldn't he arrange his own room, or stay with Tannim's folks?

Setting aside the fact that Joe was in the only other guest room besides Tannim's old room—Joe could, after all, return to Frank Casey's house. No, Joe simply accepted that Tannim knew what he was doing, and waited for explanations instead of demanding them. Sometimes repressed curiosity was a lot easier to deal with than open curiosity.

Well, there was no point in standing around here in the hot sun; already his scalp was damp with sweat, and only the armor kept him relatively cool. Joe must be ready to drop; there was sweat trickling down his forehead, and his t-shirt was damp. "Let's get out of here before anything else happens."

"Right." Joe turned and strode to the barn door.

And there he stopped, crouched over, scanning quickly from side to side. Tannim watched in amazement; he had never seen anyone so young with such moves! These kinds of tactics had apparently become second nature to Joe. *Jeez, another good reason to have him around.*

He waited until Joe waved an "all clear" to him before joining him at the door, crouching beside him with one hand on the rough wood. "I can't spot anything out there, sir," Joe said in a soft voice. "The birds aren't disturbed, either, so I don't think there's anybody hiding in the grass."

"You can work point any time, Joe," Tannim told him quite seriously.

Joe flashed him a shy grin before returning his gaze to the field beyond the barn. "I'll go first."

"Go," Tannim said, and pulled out his keychain, pushing the button for the radio-transmitter that controlled the doors and the engine. On the other side of the wall, the Mustang rumbled into life. "There. The doors are unlocked."

Joe nodded and was gone in a flash, scuttling through the weeds in a bent-over run, rather than crawling. There wasn't a real reason to crawl, unless bullets or other projectiles started flying, and a formidable reason in the form of ticks and chiggers *not* to crawl. Tannim followed in the same way as soon as he got around the corner of the barn and out of sight.

He felt a little foolish as he crouched beside his car door, listening intently. But better to feel foolish than not feel at all. "Dead" was a hard condition to cure.

He slipped into the Mustang and punched up the a/c, backed into position so that he could drive straight out, and waited. Nothing rushed at them from the weeds, and there were no vehicles in sight in either direction once they reached the road. It looked exactly as it should: a sleepy section-line road that seldom saw much in the way of traffic.

Tannim did not drop even a fraction of his watchful caution, however, and it was easy to see by Joe's tense posture that he felt the same. Out here it would be easy enough for someone to perch in a tall tree and watch their progress. Not that he could really picture *her*, in that flame-red silk jumpsuit, clambering up a tree.

But if she can make herself and her Mustang vanish, she can certainly change her wardrobe as easily, he reminded himself. *Or, for all I know, she has flunkies out here keeping an eye on us.*

For that matter, she was a mage, and she *could* be using any of the birds around here as "eyes." There was nothing he could do about that—not without endangering himself and his passenger. Anything he did to make the Mach One less visible to birds would make it less visible to other human drivers. The drivers around here were bad enough without complicating the situation by tricking their minds into thinking he wasn't there.

He passed both gloves to Joe, who locked them in the glovebox without a word. There was one thing he could do; birds had distinct territories, and in the summer they didn't tend to venture out of them. Right now, the best thing he could do, if she was using birds as her scouts, was to drive some distance before stopping at a motel. With luck, she'd lose him and not find him again.

Unless, of course, she's using something like a bald eagle. Well, there was only so much he could do without his precautions hedging his actions so much that he couldn't move.

He drove around in circles for about an hour, stopping once at a convenience store for Gatorade for the two of them, before finally seeking out a motel for Chinthliss.

The south side of Tulsa was a lot more upscale than Bixby; it was where the Yuppies collected in expansive, milling herds, and was thick with condo-complexes with gates and expensive, fenced-in houses set on quarter-acre lots. The blight crept farther south with every year. Tannim figured that he'd be able to find something to suit Chinthliss out here. Nothing less than a palace would make the dragon happy, but at least he wouldn't complain as much as he had the time he shared a room at the Holiday Inn with Tannim and FX.

High and mighty dragon couldn't unwrap the little soaps by himself. Poor baby.

With a little bit of searching, he found exactly what he was looking for: one of those high-end "suite motels." If it became too dangerous to stay with his folks any longer, he and Joe could just move in with Chinthliss. He pulled up to the office, and left Joe in the car with the motor running and the a/c on while he took care of throwing money at the clerk.

He returned with a grin on his face and slid into the seat. "Amazing what a paid-up Gold Card will do, even in this neighborhood. I got a two-bedroom with a parking slot guaranteed to be in the shade all day," he said, and tossed Joe a key. "That's for us, if we need someplace else to go. Hang onto it for me."

"Sure," Joe said obediently, pocketing the key.

"Now, let's go see what kind of digs poor Chinthliss will

have to stoop to." He pulled the Mustang around to the side of the complex and found the slot assigned to Chinthliss' suite. As promised, it was in the shade. They locked the car and ventured into the depths of the complex. The suite was supposed to be like a townhouse: two-story, with two bedrooms upstairs and living area and kitchen down. The door wasn't more than a few feet from the parking slot, and when he opened it, cool air rushed to meet them, faintly perfumed with disinfectant.

It was as advertised, and would probably suit His Draconic Majesty just fine. Joe went immediately to the living room and turned on the TV. Tannim let the a/c blow through his hair for a moment, then went to the kitchen. As the clerk had instructed, he filled out the grocery list with things he knew Chinthliss liked. Someone from the staff would be around in the next couple of hours to stock the refrigerator; an extra service invoked by the Gold Card's near-bottomless cornucopia effect. After this, the maids would keep the fridge stocked the same way. This was going to make life much easier for him, even if he was in for over a grand already. *I'll have to put the old lizard up in places like this more often. He can prowl around and poke into things to his heart's content, take showers as long as he wants without using up all the hot water, pop every bag of microwave popcorn in the place. This's going to be a lot easier than taking him to restaurants.*

He did not want to think about the last time he'd taken Chinthliss to a real restaurant. Fortunately, it had been one that catered to the elves at Fairgrove, and the staff was used to some of the customers acting peculiarly.

Like ordering escargot and jalapeno pizza with bleu cheese, and eating it with chopsticks.

While Joe relaxed for the first time since *she* had shown up, sprawling in the living room and watching cable, he left the grocery list on the doorknob and found a phone in one of the bedrooms.

Dottie answered it on the second ring, which was a relief. There was no mistaking her sugar-sweet phone voice. *She* would know that if he *said* he needed to talk to Keighvin, he really *needed* to talk to the boss there and then.

"Fairgrove Industries, Kevin Silver's office," she chirped. "How may I help you?"

"Dottie, it's Tannim," he said. "I need to talk to Keighvin. Something came up out here."

That last was a code signal among Fairgrove employees; it meant something had gone seriously wrong. "I'll page him, I think he's out in the plant," she said immediately, every trace of sugar gone from her voice. "Hold on a minute."

She didn't put him on hold, just put the phone down on the desk, so he heard her when she used the pager. "Keighvin, Line One. Keighvin, Line One. Charlie Tannim."

That would tell Keighvin that he needed to get to the phone *immediately* without telling any visitors to the plant that there was something wrong somewhere. It would also tell him that he needed to get to a secure phone, one without any outsiders anywhere around.

"Okay, I've paged him," Dottie said, picking up the phone again. A moment later a *click* and the background whine of turbines signaled the fact that Keighvin had just picked up a phone somewhere in the complex.

"I have it, Dottie." Keighvin Silverhair's resonant tenor was as unmistakable as Dottie's phone voice.

"Yes, sir," she said, and hung up.

"It's Tannim, Keighvin," the young mage said. "And I've got a problem here."

Briefly he outlined the appearance of the mysterious lady and everything that had happened associated with her. Except for one small detail; he did *not* reveal that she was the one he had been dreaming about for years. Somehow he just couldn't bring himself to; the dreams were so intimate, so much a part of him. And how could they be germaine to the situation, anyway?

Keighvin remained silent all through the narrative, but

Tannim knew him well enough to know that his mind was working at a furious pace, analyzing everything Tannim had told him.

"You've been challenged, lad," he said at last. "It's definitely in the style of the Sidhe, too. But I canna explain those bits of Death Metal; in no way could any Sidhe handle those. She canna be Seleighe nor Unseleighe herself, but she knows our style. Is this the lady ye've been dreamin' of all these years, lad?"

Tannim felt himself flush with anger. "Damn, Keighvin, have you left *anything* in my mind alone?"

"Aye, more'n ye know, lad, but that's na important now. It's her then, is it?"

"Yeah. I think."

"Mmm."

"That's it, just *mmm*, Keighvin?"

"Mmm-hmm. As I said, ye've been challenged with the gloves."

"So what's it mean, really, having gloves delivered?" he asked. "Other than the obvious challenge."

Silence on the other end of the line, as Keighvin Silverhair tried to twist Old World feudal customs into words that a twentieth-century hot-rodder would understand.

"It implies one of two things," he said finally. "I believe that we may eliminate the notion that you hae somehow insulted the lady's honor."

Not unless she somehow found out about my dreams. . . .

Keighvin's accent always thickened when he harkened back to his "other self," Lord Sir Keighvin Silverhair, ruler of Elfhame Fairgrove and all who dwelt therein. "So 'tother implication is that you hae been chosen by th' lass t'prove her ain worth. She didna slap ye with yon glove, did she?"

"Not unless you call pop-riveting the first one to my door a slap, no," Tannim replied. "Unless her slamming into the back of the Mach One counts. Does it?"

"Nay." Keighvin was firm on that. "The *glove* wasna

physically involved. An' you mind, she was very careful to have no impact when she delivered the glove, aye?"

"Oh, absolutely," Tannim said. "No impact at all, or I'd have noticed it for sure. I had no clue she'd done anything until I was out of the car."

"Then she's not issued th' challenge mortal, or at least, she's not been insulted to th' point where she's wishin' your heart an' head on a platter, an' yer privates for remembrance," Keighvin replied, relief clear in his voice. "The meanin' is simply that she sees you as bein' the best t' measure hersel' against. 'Tis a bit like yon drag race; she wishes t' cast ye down, an' rise hersel' in the process. Like the young knights that would challenge their elders, the Lancelots and Gawaines—or challenge us at the cross-roads of a midnight if they were truly bold. Now mind, it can still go t' the challenge mortal, but at th' moment, I'd say she wishes t' gae only to first blood."

"In other words, she's picked me. She can keep it civilized, or she can decide to go for the whole enchilada."

"In essence, aye." Keighvin went silent again as he thought. "I dinna think ye can count on her staying civilized, though."

Tannim heaved a sigh. "Yeah, we have to figure on worst-case scenario. We also can't count on her working alone."

"She could be in th' employ of our darker cousins, aye." Keighvin echoed his sigh. "For that matter, though her intent be innocent now, still, once th' Unseleighe learn of her and her intent, they may yet make it worth her while t' make this more than a contest of wits an' skill."

"Got any ideas?" Tannim asked, hoping against hope that Keighvin, with all of his centuries of experience in situations like this, just might know of a loophole some-where.

"*Don't* reject th' challenge, an' don't run," Keighvin said firmly. "'Twill reduce ye t' th' hunted animal. That's the rules of th' game: run, an' ye become a coward, an' th' coward can be squashed like a bothersome insect. Aye,

and anyone with him. Run, an' Joe an' your parents coul'
be sacrificed, or used as bait t' bring ye in."

Tannim cursed softly, hearing his own thoughts confirmed.

"*But,* for all that she seems t' know a fair bit about ye,
she canna assume she knows all," Keighvin continued,
raising his hopes. "So—my advice is pretend ye dinna
understand."

"You mean play dumb? Like I've never heard of the
challenge game?" The idea had its appeal. "How long can
I drag things out that way?"

"Depends on how much she knows, an' who she knows.
If she's hand-in-glove wi' our cousins, she'll find out soon
enough 'tis an act, and challenge ye outright." Keighvin
put one hand over the mouthpiece and spoke to someone
else for a moment. "Conal reminds me of another aspect t'
all of this. As th' challenged party, 'tis *you* who has the
choice of weapons. Ah, here—"

Some fumbling on the other end of the line, then
Conal's thicker accent and deeper voice sounded over the
speaker. "Eh, lad, has she not yon Mustang too, ye said?"

"Yeah, it's a late-model number. Depending on what
she's done to it, if she's *not* kicking in nitrous injection or
magic, we're probably a match in that department. Hers is
lighter, it's reliable, it handles better. It's easy to boost the
power on it with after-market stuff. Are you saying," he
continued, "that I should accept her challenge and pick
the *cars* as weapons?"

"Make it a race, lad," Conal agreed. "Set the conditions.
Use yer expertise and yer magery on yon pony-car yersel'.
I've not seen a mage here t' match ye i' that department.
An' I know for a fact that t'only driver we hae that is as
good as ye is young Maclyn."

"What if she wants to make it—what did Keighvin call
it? The challenge mortal?" He gritted his teeth, waiting
for Conal's reply.

"There is that." Conal took a deep breath. "Well, an' ye
find yersel' wi' the challenge mortal—where would ye

rather find yersel'? Behind yon blade, i' th' mage-circle, or behind th' wheel?"

He thought long and hard before replying. "Behind the wheel," he said slowly. "I'm better off there than anywhere else."

"I wouldna say *that*—but I would say this. I think ye'd be safer there. I think she canna be th' driver ye are. An' once ye learn whence her magery an' her trainin' come, I think ye can best her. Ah, here's Keighvin back. The luck to ye, lad."

A moment more, and Keighvin came back on the line. "I agree with everything Conal told you, Tannim. Stall her while you learn about her, then when she delivers a challenge you can't refuse, take her to the road. *Don't hesitate to call us.* There's only a limited amount we can do, but what we can, we will. And we'll see to it that yon Joe and your parents stay safe. In fact, we'll begin on that this very moment; 'tis a fair amount we can do even at long distances."

"I'm working on getting someone here who can help me," Tannim told him. Relief spread through him and made him limp as Keighvin *offered* Fairgrove's help. That took a tremendous amount off his mind. With Sidhe mage-warriors watching over the noncombatants, he could deal with this lady with all his attention. He had the feeling she would *require* his entire attention.

"Keep us informed," Keighvin concluded. "Call once a day from now on, perhaps about this time. I'll be havin' some of the rest dealin' with keeping your parents shielded and safe as soon as I hang up."

"Thanks, Keighvin," Tannim said fervently, running his hand through his tangled hair. "I can't even begin to thank you enough for that."

I can even forgive you for funding the horse ranch without telling me.

"'Tis nothing you don't have as your due, lad," Keighvin replied, warmth in his voice. "Now, I'll be off."

"Same here. And thanks again." He waited for the *click*

that signaled Keighvin had rung off before hanging up himself. Protocol, protocol. Never be the one to hang up on an elven lord.

Joe looked at him inquisitively when he descended the staircase using every other step and entered the living room. "Good?" the young man asked.

"Good," Tannim replied. "Keighvin's taking care of some of it, and he and Conal gave me some good advice on the rest." He leveled the most authoritative gaze he had on the young man. "The moment—the *instant* we know that this might mean more than a simple magical drag race, you are out of here. Keighvin's going to see to it. Got that?"

"But—" Joe protested weakly. "But—"

"You're not a two-stroke engine, stop imitating one," Tannim told him, crossing his arms over his chest. "No arguments. If this gets serious, you haven't got the training, the experience, or the power to handle fighting between two mages *or* between two drivers. If this turns into a Mustang shootout, I don't want innocent bystanders making it into Death Race 2000."

Joe flushed and looked chagrined. "All right," he said reluctantly. *Very* reluctantly, for someone who had just yesterday told Tannim that he had not wanted to get involved with magic anymore.

Sheesh, the kid's decided he's responsible for me. Or else he's feeling guilty about leaving me to take this on alone.

"Look, Joe," he said, lowering his voice persuasively, "if this were a regular fight, there isn't anyone I'd rather have working point or tail. I'd rather trust you at my back than anyone else in the state. But it's not a regular fight—it'd be like you going out into a firefight with an ordinary college freshman backing you. See?"

Joe nodded, his flush fading. "Yes, sir, I do see. You're right. I understand."

Oh, the wonders of a paramilitary education. Authority actually means something! Try telling that to one of the

*Fairgrove fosterlings, and you'd find him following you as
closely as if you'd hooked a tow-bar to his forehead.*

"I'll tell you what you can do," he continued. "You can
help me keep my folks from finding anything out about all
this. And if anything happens to me—well, you and
Keighvin take care of them for me, okay?"

Joe straightened at that, and came very close to saluting.
"Yes, sir. I can do that, sir. I *will* do that; your parents
are—wonderful people."

"Yes," he said simply. "They are. And you have taken an
enormous weight off my mind, knowing there will be
someone who'll look after them. And speaking of my parents, we'd better get back; it's almost suppertime, and I
think Mom is planning pasta. I know it seems kind of stupid to go back home after all this, but there are reasons for
it."

Joe rose with alacrity and followed him to the door,
making certain that it locked after them. Tannim found
himself liking the young man more and more with every
hour he spent in Joe's presence.

The odd thing was that having a promise from Joe to
"take care of" his parents *did* take an enormous weight off
his mind. He was an only child, and while he had every intention of staying alive a long, long time—well, the racing
business alone was dangerous, as his own wrecks proved.
Then, once you added in the other complications, well—if
he'd been an insurance agent, *he* wouldn't have written a
policy on himself.

One thing that had always troubled his sleep—besides
the *special* side effects of those dreams about *her*—was
what his untimely demise would do to his mom and dad,
and at times like these it troubled him even more. Now, if
everything went badly, they'd have Joe there to help them
through the mourning and be a second son to them afterward.

*And if everything goes well, they'll still have their first
son, plus a second son. One that can stand horses, to make
up for me.*

This was nothing that Alinor and Keighvin could ever have foreseen when they asked Tannim to pick up the young man. No, this was the kind of magic that had nothing to do with elves, and everything to do with the human heart.

Sometimes, he reflected, things worked out okay. As he popped the locks on the Mustang, he decided that letting the good things happen was the best magic he knew.

SharMarali Halanyn examined herself in the mirror with a critical eye. Her facial fur was perfect; her ears were groomed immaculately, as always. In the reflection of her own green eyes she could see the mirror's glinting circle; she then banished the silvered glass with a thought. All was well. If she looked this cool after being out in the sweltering Oklahoma sunshine, she must have been devastating when Tannim had seen her. She smiled with satisfaction and no little anticipation as she sat back in her overstuffed red-silk chair and gazed at the flower arrangement that had taken the mirror's place.

This looked remarkably like an upscale Manhattan condo, except there were no windows anywhere, and no doors to the exterior, either. There were no windows because there was nothing to look out upon except the emptiness of mist-filled Chaos where she had created her home. And there were no doors, because there was no need for doors. The only possible way in or out of here—other than stumbling on the place by sheerest accident—was by Gate.

Her own Mustang rested in a heavily shielded shelter attached to this apartment, and it had its own Gate large enough to drive through. It had not been easy, bringing so much Cold Iron into this place; the very fabric of Underhill rebelled against the presence of the Death Metal, and the magics of her allies became unreliable and unpredictable around anything ferrous. That was one reason why they did not seek to visit her in her own "den"; and that was the main reason she had insisted on keeping the car here. That, plus the masking properties of silk, kept them just wary enough to suit her needs. Good.

Tannim had looked so wonderfully stunned. That old deer-in-the-headlights look. It was such a marvelous feeling, being able to wipe that self-assured grin off his face and leave him completely off balance. Without a clue! And without even a dime to buy one with!

And it had been so gratifying to know that she could do that to him anytime she wanted. She knew all there was to know about him; he knew nothing of her.

Had he guessed that she was his challenger from last night? There had been some kind of recognition, so perhaps he had. *Or perhaps, just perhaps, he recognizes you from something else entirely,* whispered the little voice from within. *Perhaps he has dreamed of you, even as you have dreamed of him. Remember the candles and satin, and the warmth of his body over you, in you, cupping you and pouring deep. . . .*

She shook the voice into quiescence with a toss of her hair. How could he possibly dream of her? He had no notion that she even existed! Whereas *she* had known of his existence from early adolescence. Hadn't she been trained and groomed to be his opposite number, his ultimate rival, yin to his yang, even as her father was Chinthliss' ultimate rival? She had watched him, studied him for years, and she *knew* he had no inkling that she— or someone like her—was anywhere in any universe.

Even Chinthliss had never told him, although Chinthliss knew very well that she existed, though he did not know where she was. Her father Charcoal had seen to it that Chinthliss was kept abreast of her progress.

The jerkoff. Her father Charcoal, that is, not Chinthliss. Charcoal was no longer a part of her life, and that was the way she wanted it.

No, there was no reason to think that Tannim had recognized her from dreams. Particularly not the kind of dream passages that *she* had about *him.*

Erotic? Oh, a tad. They had certainly been far more

satisfactory than anything shared with her Unseleighe lovers.

She frowned a little at that. There would be no more dalliances with the Unseleighe; she had cut them off from that years ago when she realized how much they were using her. They had no consideration for her pleasure in their spurious loving intimacies; their only thoughts were for their own satiation. She preferred a fantasy-dream with Tannim any night over a real-life assignation with an Unseleighe, however comely the elven twit might be.

Not that the Sidhe were extremely attractive to her. It was just that Tannim was anything but uncomely. When it came down to it, he was far better looking in the bright sun of day than he ever had been in her misty dreams, or in much of the covert spying she had done on him. If he were *kitsune*, she'd be even more in lust with him.

She closed her eyes, and he sprang into her mind with extraordinary vividness.

He looked far younger than his true years; he shared that with her, despite his purely mortal origins. He had a fine face; not handsome in the classical sense, but one that was not likely to be forgotten: high cheekbones, broad brow, firm and determined chin, sensual mouth given to smiles and laughter.

Unlike these dour Unseleighe, who smile only when they kill and laugh only when blood spills across their hands. They all think they are such great kings and warriors. What a bunch of complete weenies.

Despite the fact that Tannim was as slim as a young girl, there was strength to him, in the broad shoulders, the wiry muscles. *Good bones,* her mother would say. And, ah, that wild mane of dark and curling hair; women must go mad to run their hands through it!

But it was the eyes that caught you, when he wasn't staring at you like a rabbit trying to guess the make of the car about to run it over. Huge green eyes that changed hue with the changing of his emotions. Vulnerable eyes; eyes that promised something wonderful to those whom he gave his loyalty and affection. And she had every reason to believe those implied wonders were real, for she had seen how generously he gave of himself once his trust and heart were pledged.

Ah, lucky one, who becomes his true lover. . . .

It was that little internal voice again, and with annoyance she squashed it down. She had *no* business with such thoughts; he was a human and she was most decidedly not, for one thing. And for another—

She was his mirror.

Whether she would be his fate, as the Unseleighe wished, remained to be seen.

She opened her eyes again and interlaced her hands over the red silk covering her knee, thinking in silence. Unlike Tannim, music distracted her. For him it was a focus.

He had, as yet, given her no sign that he recognized the challenges for what they were. Then again, she had given him no chance to respond. She enjoyed this game; she wanted to stretch it out as long as possible, and by teasing him like this, she fulfilled the letter of her agreement with the Unseleighe without actually taking any action against him.

Given how much time he had spent with Keighvin Silverhair, though, he surely must have recognized a Challenge by now. But she could continue to tease him for several days without giving him an opportunity to answer the Challenge. Eventually, of course, the Unseleighe would become impatient with her, and force her to conclude the opening steps of the dance, but for now, she was free to improvise her own patterns on the stage.

A glissando of subtle energies chimed upon her inward ear, and a rustle of stiffer silk than she wore alerted her to the presence of someone who had just crossed the Gate into her private pocket of Underhill. Since that Gate was guarded against everyone but her parents—and since she had long since barred her father from coming anywhere *near* her without her specific permission—there was only one person it could be.

"Mother!" she exclaimed with pleasure, rising to her feet and whirling to meet the Honorable Lady Ako with outstretched arms. The Honorable Lady Ako stepped across the threshold in a flutter of ankle-length, fox-red hair and a rustle of blue-green kimonos, serene as a statue of a saint and graceful as the most exquisitely trained geisha, and she smiled to see her daughter running to greet her.

The Honorable Lady Ako—magician, healer, shapeshifter, bearer of some of the most noble blood in or out of Underhill, and nine-tailed *kitsune*—met her daughter's embrace and accepted it. But something in Ako's eyes told Shar that this visit was not a social call.

Nevertheless, the amenities of civilization must come first.

Shar led her mother to the seat of honor, and with a brush of her hand, changed the silk of the couch to a blue-green that harmonized with her mother's kimonos. *Should there be a tea ceremony?* she wondered, as she settled at her mother's feet. *Perhaps—*

But Ako laid one gentle hand on her daughter's before Shar could summon the implements for a proper tea ceremony. "Tea, but no ceremony, my love," Ako told her firmly. "I must speak with you, and I have little time."

Shar summoned perfectly brewed tea and translucent porcelain cups with a gesture, handing the first cup to her mother before taking up her own. Ako took a sip, then placed the cup back down on her own palm. The amenities had been observed. Now for business.

"I have learned that you have been abroad," Ako said delicately. "That you have been there at the behest of— your father's friends."

Ako would not mention the Unseleighe by name, nor Charcoal. She had long ago fallen out with the blood-father of her daughter—rightly, Shar thought, since Charcoal was insufferable in all ways. She would have no commerce with Charcoal's friends and allies. And when Ako declined to mention someone by name, it meant that she declined to acknowledge their existence, given the option of doing so.

Reluctantly, Shar nodded. She was too well-trained to flush, but the feeling of faint shame was there, as if she had been caught in something dishonorable.

Ako studied her daughter's face, her green eyes grave in the white-porcelain doll-face beneath the crimson waterfall of her hair. It was all that Shar could do to maintain eye contact with her mother. "I know what it is that they wish you to do," Ako said finally. "You know that I do not approve. This young man has done nothing to harm you; he has done nothing, save to be the protégé of Chinthliss. But that is not to the point. Are *you* so certain that you wish to visit destruction upon this young man?"

For a single, bewildered moment, Shar wondered if her mother could somehow have learned of her years of dreams. She shook her head, and bit her lip. "Honorable Mother, I am not to be commanded by such as—my father's friends. I do what I will. At the moment, it amuses me to occupy this young man. It may amuse me to deliver him to them. But it will be of *my* will or not at all."

She raised her chin defiantly, willing her mother to recognize that she would not be tamed by any creature.

Ako looked deep into Shar's eyes, and the young female found herself hot with the blushes she had conquered earlier. "I will say only this to you: look deeply into your thoughts and your heart, your instincts and your memories, before you commit yourself to any action," she said. "Do nothing irrevocable until you have determined that you can live with the result for all of your life. I say this, my dearest child, so that you do not follow in the path of your mother. Do not make mistakes you will regret, and prove unable to correct."

And with that, as Shar sat in stunned silence, Lady Ako rose with the grace of a bending willow, and summoned the Gate to life. She glided toward it, and paused on the threshold.

Then she turned, and caught Shar's eyes, so like her own, one more time. "Remember the past," she said simply.

Then she stepped across the Gate, and was gone.

❋   ❋   ❋

Stuffed full of pasta and garlic bread, Tannim and Joe arrived at the old barn just at sunset. Once again, Joe spotted for Tannim as he drove—carefully—into the long grass and parked the Mach One beside the barn. Joe was the first one out of the car, and Tannim waited for him to give the "all clear" signal before he got out himself.

If the mysterious woman was watching, and she meant no more than a simple challenge, their behavior would seem very consistent for someone who had not understood the meaning of what she had done. And if she meant worse than that, well, she would see that they were alert and would be hard to catch off guard twice.

Once he and Joe were inside the barn, he activated the *entire* set of protections on the place. It was a pity he couldn't get the Mach One in here anymore now that the door was a wreck, but the Mustang had its own defenses.

The protections rose, layer on layer, forming a shifting golden dome inside the barn. It would take something like a magical bomb to penetrate the shields on this place now, plus a physical one to do otherwise.

"Remember, you can't leave till I take this all down," he reminded Joe, who stared in wonder at the glowing dome over them. "Chinthliss did a lot of this; I don't know everything it's set against, I only know that I haven't come across anything that can break in or out."

"Won't somebody see the light and think—I don't know, maybe it's a UFO or something?" Joe worried.

Tannim laughed and hit the young man in the shoulder lightly. "You've been hanging around elves too much," he chided. "Turn your mage-sight *off*."

He watched as Joe frowned in concentration, then grinned with relief. "Nothing," the young man said. "There's nothing there."

"Right, it's only visible to those with the *ability* to see it." He considered the lovely golden dome overhead. "I suppose there might be a few folks around here who would notice it if they looked this way, but they're also the kind who'll stay out of anything they haven't been invited to. Not because they aren't curious—but because they'll have learned 'don't touch' the same way I did. The hard way. Nothing like getting your hand burned to teach you to watch that fire."

He grinned, and Joe shook his head in mock sadness. "Maybe you shoulda had a dose of military school," Joe told him with a spark of impudence.

Tannim blinked at the unexpected display of wicked humor. "That's what my dad kept saying," he admitted. "I guess I ought to be glad he didn't have the money for it."

Joe sized him up as if he were looking at Tannim for the first time. "You'd either have done real good, or real bad," the young man replied at last. "Depending on whether you got to be the brains of an outfit or not."

"Probably real bad," Tannim told him. "When I was younger, I never could learn to keep my mouth shut. Only thing that kept me out of trouble in high school was that the jocks knew *I* knew how to fix cars, and if they beat me up, next time they were stuck out in the parking lot with a fuel-line block or worse, I'd keep right on trucking."

And the fact that people who beat me up tended to get blocked fuel-lines or worse—and always when they were miles away from a gas station and I had cast-iron alibis. Not my fault they never bothered to get their cars serviced regularly. A little regular maintenance, and their mechanics would have found my little presents.

Ah, well. His former tormentors were like snow on the fired-up gas grill of life, and he had a whole *new* set of tormentors to deal with.

So who's after my hide now that Vidal Dhu and his crew are out of the picture? That was a good question, actually, and one he would really like to have an answer to. The Unseleighe were less cohesive than a rolling barrel of bullfrogs; it was hard to get them to agree to anything long enough to get beyond the "nuisance" stage. Vidal Dhu had nursed a feud with Keighvin's folk for centuries before

Tannim ever came on the scene, and he had targeted Tannim for elimination largely because he was Keighvin's most reliable outlet to the human world.

Could it be that they've decided I'm dangerous to the Unseleighe as a whole, even without my connection to Keighvin? That was possible, and it had happened before. When one human came to know too much about Underhill, that knowledge was often seen as a threat by the Unseleighe. Rightly so; they relied on invisibility in their predation on humankind, and when a human knew what they could do and how they operated, he would be able to tell when something was simply misfortune and when it was *caused.* And he could move to stop what was going on. Humans always had three things going for them against all the magic of the Sidhe: cleverness, sheer numbers and Cold Iron. Those things alone could stop the Sidhe dead in their tracks.

And when a human knew how to make Cold Iron into a *weapon* . . .

That made him much more of a danger.

And I'm training Seleighe Sidhe in Cold Iron Magery 101. Yeah, I can see why they might tag me as a problem.

The sun set with a minimum of fanfare; after a cloudless, hot day there was very little color in the west, nothing but a fattened, blood-red ball gliding down below the horizon. *It won't be long now,* Tannim thought. *Chinthliss has a lot of faults, but tardiness isn't one of them.*

Full dark came quickly; within fifteen minutes the first stars were out, and within a half hour the only light was from the half moon directly overhead.

Moonlight poured down through the open roof, and Tannim frowned a moment as he contemplated the slowly twisting patterns of moonlight crossing the barn floor. Then he realized what was affecting the moonlight. *Jeez! The Gate!*

As he ushered Joe out of the way, he felt a little smug for noticing the patterns. Did Chinthliss know that his magic interfered with moonlight just before mage-senses could feel it? For *now* he sensed that odd internal chiming that meant someone had called up a Gate between this human world and another, and a moment later, the Gate itself appeared.

He'd seen it all before, of course, but Joe never had. The young man's eyes widened as the air where the Gate would be twisted in geometries no mathemetician of this world had ever encountered. *Something* darkened, rotated through dimensions human eyes were not built to perceive, and formed into a gossamer arch made up of hundreds of thin threads of pure power, as if an unearthly spider had been coaxed into spinning the structure.

Then it flared, plates formed across the threads, and sheets of light played with each other in oil-on-water colors.

Tannim patted Joe's shoulder. "Don't worry about it," he said easily. "It's just Chinthliss' way of being invisible."

"But—" Joe said, gesturing at the light show. Then he grinned as he realized what Tannim really meant. "Oh. Yeah."

The entire Gate-structure flared again, and the magelight built until it would soon be impossible to look at. Tannim pulled out his Wayfarers and flicked them open. Joe shielded his face and winced away. Tannim simply put on his shades and smirked.

Then a note deeper than that of a huge bronze templegong vibrated across the barn. It thrummed in Tannim's chest, and he had to close his eyes behind the protection of his dark glasses when the final flare ended.

And then came the deafening silence. Magic was like that sometimes.

The crickets resumed their interrupted nuptial chorus, and Tannim reopened his eyes and took off his glasses.

Directly below where the peak of the arch had been, framed by the blackened walls and silvery moonlight, stood a gaunt but obviously powerful man. His thin features were vaguely oriental. He wore an impeccably-tailored Armani suit, and Tannim knew, although the moonlight was too dim to see colors, that it would be bronze silk.

The man straightened his bolo tie, and the eyes of the little dragon curling around the leather winked with bright topaz flashes.

The man raised one long eyebrow at Tannim in a gesture that Tannim knew perfectly well had been copied after long study of Leonard Nimoy.

"Could you manage subtle, do you suppose?" Tannim asked wistfully, thinking of all the Sensitives for miles around who would be suffering with strange dreams and unexplained headaches thanks to Chinthliss' lust for the dramatic.

His mentor simply raised that eyebrow a little higher, though Tannim could not imagine how he'd done it.

"No," he replied.

• CHAPTER FIVE

"Well," Tannim said as they walked into the suite. "It's not home, but it's much."

Chinthliss gazed about with delight and immediately began exploring all of the amenities. Joe was perfectly willing to show him around.

Once they reached the bedrooms, with amazingly spacious closets, Chinthliss produced *luggage* from somewhere. Armani, of course. Tannim had no idea where the luggage had appeared from, since the dragon hadn't brought anything across the Gate and hadn't loaded anything into the Mach One. Still, Chinthliss spent the first half hour unpacking.

And people accuse me of being a clotheshorse! Then again, Chinthliss didn't wear this form very often, and Tannim knew he found the concept of clothing-as-persona fascinating. *Just please, God, don't let him have brought any leisure suits.*

Tannim waited, joked, and curbed his own impatience. There was no point in rushing Chinthliss. He would get around to the problem at hand when he felt settled, and not before. Rush him, and you were apt to end up with more trouble than you had in the first place.

At least he was happy with the suite, which was a relief. When Chinthliss was annoyed, he grew uncooperative, and right now, Tannim needed glasnost more than detente.

His old friend finished with his prowling and settled onto the sofa in the living room as Tannim tuned in the local classical station on the radio/TV console. On the table at his mentor's elbow was a tall cola with a great deal of ice; unlike the elves, Chinthliss had no trouble with caffeine, and unlike most of his relatives, he hated tea with a passion. His jacket had been tossed carelessly over the back of a chair, and he had rolled his silk shirtsleeves up to his elbows. He was ready to work.

"Now, tell me again everything that has happened when this young lady appeared, in as much detail as you can recall," Chinthliss ordered, leaning forward to listen intently. The topaz eyes of the dragon bolo tie at his neck glowed with their own muted power.

Tannim obeyed, closing his eyes to concentrate. When he finished, he fished the gloves out of his jeans pocket and handed them over. "They're custom work, I can tell that much," he said as Chinthliss studied the gloves minutely, then applied the same care to studying the parchment slips. "I didn't realize it until later, but they're both from the right hand, so evidently she doesn't mind wasting whole pairs of custom-made gloves. There's no maker's mark on them, no labels, and the leather isn't stamped. I think they're deerskin, but they're made of very light leather, lighter than any deerskin I've ever seen. They seem to be hand-stitched—"

"They are," Chinthliss interrupted. "With silk thread, which is unusual, to say the least. And the 'string' of the backs is also silk."

Tannim gnawed his lip, and reached into the pocket over his right thigh for a cherry-pop. "Where would anyone get silk yarn like that?" he asked, as he unwrapped the candy and stuck it in his cheek.

Chinthliss shook his head. "It is available in your world, but not in too many places," he replied. "And the supply is very limited. It is silk noil, made from the outer, coarser threads of the cocoon. It is normally used to weave heavier material with a rougher texture than this—" He pointed to his shirt. "Under most circumstances, one would not waste such threads, however coarse, on making string for driving gloves. Unless—"

"Unless?" Tannim prompted.

"Unless the wearer wished to make use of some of the magical properties of silk as an insulator," Chinthliss said, and shook his head. "The leather is unusual also; not deerskin, but *fawnskin*. Very difficult to obtain, and unless I mistake your laws, not legal in this country. The paper, as you probably noticed, has no watermark, and the texture is *too* even; it might not have been manufactured, it might have been produced magically. The quotes were written with a real quill pen, not metal, but a goose-quill; you can see how the nib has worn down on the longer piece by the time she reached the end of the quote. See there, where the lines are just a little thicker. The ink is of an old style that does not dry quickly and must have sand sprinkled over it to take up the excess. Here—"

He held out the second quote, and tilted the small square of paper to catch the light. Sure enough, the light sparkled off a few crystals of sand stuck in the ink.

"All of this points in only one direction, unless your mysterious lady is so *very* eccentric that she drives modern cars yet uses the most archaic of writing implements. And unless she is so very wealthy that she can afford to discard hand-tailored driving gloves made with materials one would have to search the world to find."

"Well, we knew she must be using magic," Joe said thoughtfully. "But you're implying there's more than that."

Chinthliss nodded. "These small things indicate a radically different upbringing than you would find in your America, Tannim. I believe these things indicate that she cannot be from this culture, perhaps not this world. She may well not be human."

Joe looked queasy. Tannim wasn't so sure about his own health at the moment.

"Unless she was using illusion to change her eyes, she

isn't Sidhe," Tannim interjected. "The Sidhe all have cat-eyes, with slit pupils, not round."

"But most, if not all Sidhe, Seleighe and Unseleighe, use illusion to cover their differences when dealing with mortals," Chinthliss countered. "There is no reason to think that she would change that pattern with you."

Tannim sucked thoughtfully on the cherry-pop and nodded. "Why two right-hand gloves?" he asked.

"Because at the moment she does not wish to kill you," Chinthliss replied. "As my brother taught me once, there is a reason why the left hand is called the 'sinister' hand."

Tannim swallowed. "Well, that's handy," he said as dryly as he could. Which was not very. He could not help thinking that she had two perfectly good *left*-hand gloves somewhere, doing nothing, taking up drawer-space. . . .

And where in the hell was Fox? He hadn't shown in over twenty-four hours!

Wait a minute. . . . "FX was *with* me just before she showed up the first time. He took one look out the back window of the Mach One, said 'Oh-oh,' and flat disappeared," he said. "He hasn't been back since, and he *had* been bugging me hourly. Old lizard, I think he *recognized* her. I think he *knew* her. Wouldn't a *kitsune* recognize another *kitsune*, even if a human didn't pick up anything at all? Sort of like a scent on the wind—"

"You are more likely being hunted by a succubus or the like, but that is a very good point, and the answer is probably yes," Chinthliss responded. His brow creased and his eyes narrowed. "Bear in mind though, just as a Sidhe would be sensitive to the 'scents' of those creatures from *his* world, a *kitsune* is going to be more sensitive to the 'scents' of those from his. A *gaki*, for instance, or a nature-spirit. But that does give me something to work from."

"Can't you do something magical with those gloves?" Joe asked. "I mean, can't you use magic to find out something about her from them?" He bit his thumbnail as Chinthliss turned to look at him, obviously ill at ease with the whole concept. "Isn't that why you shouldn't let something that belonged to you fall into a wizard's hands, because they can use it to put a hex on you or something?"

"Cogent," Chinthliss agreed. "And if these were ordinary gloves, from an ordinary person, such things would bear fruit. But they are the gloves of a mage, and she has made use of the properties of the materials to remove as much of the essence of *herself* from them as she can."

"Which means it will take some real work to get anything useful out of them," Tannim translated for Joe. "And probably a lot of time."

Chinthliss put the gloves down and stretched. "I shall be comfortable here, and I will need nothing. It grows late. *You* should sleep, Son of Dragons." He lanced Tannim with a penetrating stare. "You were in need of rest when you came here, as I know only too well. I will consult with my allies and send them sniffing along the path these gloves have traced."

Tannim stood up, and Joe followed his example. "Yes, Mother," he said mockingly. "And I'll take my vitamins and brush my teeth before I go to bed."

Tannim chuckled, and he and Joe let themselves out, leaving Chinthliss sitting on the couch, studying the gloves.

Shar smiled and petted the little air elementals that flocked around her, vying for her attention. Cross a kitten with a dragonfly and you might have something like these creatures. Less like a classical sylph than a puffball with wings, they were some of her chief sources of information when she did not care to go and gather it herself. They were not very bright, but they could be very affectionate. They seemed to like her.

One in particular was very affectionate, and extremely reliable; that was the one she called "Azure," and set him the particular task of keeping a constant eye on Tannim. She sent him off on his duties with a shooing motion and continued with her own preparations. She had a scheduled meeting with Madoc Skean, the chief of her "allies," and she was not looking forward to it.

The Unseleighe Sidhe was a sadistic, chauvinistic, selfish braggart, and a traitor to his own kind to boot. Most Unseleighe were born "on the dark side," so to speak: boggles and banshees, trolls and kobolds. But some, like Madoc, chose that path. Until recently, he had served as a knight in the court of High King Oberon. Oberon was a fairly tolerant fellow when it came to his subjects and their "games" with mortals—outright mischief was well within the bounds of what was considered amusing. Further, if he felt some foolish human deserved punishment or needed to learn a lesson, he saw no reason why a Seleighe shouldn't do whatever was needful so long as he stopped just short of killing the mortal. But some things he would not abide—and he caught Madoc at one of them. What it was, precisely, Shar did not know, though she could guess—but it had been enough to send Oberon into a red rage. He had *physically* cast Madoc out, blasting him through several layers of Underhill realities before he came to rest in a battered, broken heap.

It took Madoc some time to recover; once he did, he used the powerful charisma that had made him a brilliant manipulator in Seleighe Court politics and turned it on the Unseleighe left in disarray after the demise of Vidal Dhu and Aurilia. He not only organized them, but he attracted others to his side, including Unseleighe Sidhe far more powerful than Vidal Dhu had been.

Powerful Unseleighe Sidhe tended to be solitary souls; they did not like to share their power with anyone, and would support a "retinue" composed of vastly inferior creatures that were easy to control. They formed a "court" mostly as a means of amusement; they seldom agreed on anything. Innate distrust made alliances tenuous at best—an "I won't destroy your home if you don't destroy mine" cold war. But somehow, Madoc won them. And won them to his pet project.

Get rid of Keighvin Silverhair's little pet, the mortal called Tannim.

He managed to persuade them that Tannim, knowledgeable as he was in the ways of the Sidhe and Underhill, was far more of a danger to them than their traditional enemies, the Seleighe Court elves. He convinced them that Tannim was unlikely to turn against his friends, but that there was nothing stopping the young man from marching on Underhill and taking over the areas held by Unseleighe with a small army of Cold-Iron-wielding humans.

He even half-convinced Shar. She had been trained as a youngster by the Unseleighe, after all, in the time before she had broken off with her father. Why shouldn't Tannim think that she was just the same as them? She was the daughter of Charcoal, Chinthliss' great enemy—and she had been groomed by Charcoal to be Tannim's rival in magic ever since Chinthliss took Tannim as a protégé. Allying with Madoc Skean became a matter of self-defense.

Until she came to learn more about both Tannim and Madoc, that is. Then it became obvious, at least to her, that this tale Madoc had spun about a human mage mad for power was full of what they threw on the compost heap. Tannim was no more a conquering Patton than she was. He might consider moving into some little unused section of Underhill one day, just as she had, but conquering vast sections of it would simply never occur to him. It was only Unseleighe paranoia that made such a thing seem possible.

But by then she had already committed herself to Madoc. She'd been having second thoughts for some time now.

The very fact that her blood-father was friends with the Unseleighe was enough to make her think they were worthless. What she had learned about them since she had cut off all ties to him only confirmed that. Only her own paranoia had made her listen to Madoc in the first place; only his incredible charisma had persuaded her to give the Unseleighe one more chance.

But Madoc had grown more and more arrogant with her every time she had spoken with him since she first pledged her help. *He* needed her; she was the only creature allied with him that could handle Cold Iron with impunity. He knew that, and yet pretended that it was otherwise.

And the more she saw and learned of Tannim, the less she liked Madoc or wished to put up with him.

So she donned her armor; armor that the Unseleighe would understand. Her hair she braided back in a severe and androgynous style that left the impression of a helmet. She wore tunic and pants of knitted cloth-of-silver that cleverly counterfeited fine chain-mail and minimized her femininity. Her belt *was* a sword-belt, with a supporting baldric, and the empty loops that should support a sheath spoke eloquently for her capabilities.

She looked herself over in the mirror, analyzing every nuance of her outfit and stance for clues that might hint at weakness. She found none.

She banished the glass again and turned toward the Gate, activating it and setting it for an Unseleighe-held portion of Underhill where she could Gate to Madoc Skean's stronghold. Although this was a poor strategic move, coming to him like a petitioner, she would not permit him here. Allow him here but once, and there was no telling the mischief he could cause.

Or what he might leave behind, besides his smell.

Her Gate had only three settings: Unseleighe Underhill, her mother's realm, and her father's. The last, she would not use. To go to the human world, she must use the Gate in the "garage." A bit awkward, sometimes, but neccessary.

She stepped through her Gate, felt the shivering of energies around her as it sprang to life and bridged the gap between where she *was* and where she wanted to be.

As usual, it was dark. She blinked, and waited for her eyes to adjust. Many Unseleighe creatures simply could not exist in bright light, so most Unseleighe realms were as gloomy as a thunderstorm during an eclipse, or dusk on a badly overcast day. She stood at the head of a path that traveled straight through a primeval and wildly overgrown forest. Forests such as this one had not existed on the face of the human world since the Bronze Age, if then. It was the distillation of everything about the ancient Forest that primitive man had feared.

And it contained everything dark and treacherous that primitive man had believed in.

The trees were alive, and they hungered; strange things rustled and moaned in the undergrowth. There were glowing eyes up among the branches, and as Shar stepped out on the path, the noises increased, the trees leaned toward her, and the number of eyes multiplied.

Something screamed in pain in the distance, and something nearer wailed in desolation.

Shar looked about her with absolute scorn, as the sounds and eyes surrounded her, and the trees closed in.

"Will you just *chill out?*" she snapped, putting a small fraction of her Power behind her words. "I've been here before, and you know it. I am *not* impressed."

A moment of stunned silence, a muttering of disappointment, and within a few more seconds, the trees were only trees, and there were no more scuttlings in the underbrush or eyes in the branches overhead.

"Oh, thank you," she said sarcastically, and made her way to the second Gate. So much of the power of the older Unseleighe depended on fear that the moment anyone faced them down, they simply melted away. That might be why there were so few of these unadapted creatures active in the humans' world these days, and Cold Iron had nothing to do with them fleeing to dwell Underhill. The modern world was frightening enough that most people *couldn't* be scared by these ancient creatures. Where was the power of glowing eyes to terrify when rat eyes looked out at children every day from beneath the furniture of their ghetto apartments? How could a man be terrified by reaching tree branches when beneath the tree was a crack-addict with a gun? Moans and cries in the darkness could be the neighbor pummeling his wife and children to a pulp—and he just might' come after anyone else who interfered, too, so moans and cries were best ignored.

The supernatural lost its power to terrify when so much of the natural world could not be controlled. These elder creatures were forced to abide in places like this one, where, if they were lucky, some poor unsuspecting being from another realm might stumble in to die of fright.

But the Unseleighe who had adapted found the modern human world rich in possibility. They fed on human pain and misery, so anywhere there was the potential for such things, you found them in the thick of it. Sometimes they even caused it, either as sustenance for themselves or as a hobby. Some considered inflicting suffering on humans to be an art form.

She had been taught by her father and his friends that humans were no business of hers. They were cattle, beneath her except to use when she chose and discard afterward.

But she had been taught by her mother that humans were not that much different from her. More limited, shorter-lived—but did that mean that a human confined to a wheelchair was the toy of humans with no such limitations?

For a long time she had been confused by the conflicting viewpoints, especially while the handsome Unseleighe Sidhe had been courting her, seeking her favors. They seemed so powerful, so confident. They had everything they wanted, simply by waving a hand. They were in control of their world, and controlled the humans' world far more than the mortals knew. They were beautiful, charismatic, confident, proud. . . .

But after a few bitter and painful episodes, she began to see some patterns. Once an Unseleighe got what he wanted, *he* discarded *her* exactly as they urged her to do with the humans. Her father, whom she tried desperately to please, cynically used her childish devotion to manipulate her.

The lessons were branded deeply; as deeply as the ones she was *supposed* to be learning. Little by little, she changed her own approach. She began learning, fiercely, greedily. She stole knowledge, when it was not given to her.

She spent more time in her mother's company. No one, not even the powerful Unseleighe lords, dared to block the approach of a nine-tailed *kitsune* to her daughter, and Ako made certain they were given no reason to think she was undermining their teaching.

Then, when the time was right, after Shar had established her own tiny Underhill domain, and she had learned everything she could, she began severing her connections to the Unseleighe and to her father.

She had cast Charcoal out of her life first; he had made the mistake of trying to coerce her when she refused to cooperate with some unsavory project of his. She no longer even remembered what it *was;* it had been trivial, but she had not wanted to have any part of it, and for the first time, she had the power to enforce her own will.

After barring him from her domain, she began pursuing her own projects—the first of which was to spend an entire year with her mother and her mother's people.

That year had been the most eye-opening time she had ever passed. She had moved among *kitsune* with poise, not posturing. She had learned manners rooted in respect, not fear of repercussions. She had heard laughter that was not aimed at anyone but instead filled the room with its warmth. At the end of that year, she had withdrawn to her own domain and begun planning what she truly wanted to do with her life, and more importantly, plotting how to rid herself of the Unseleighe influence without a loss of power or status.

She shook herself out of her reverie as she approached the Gate that would take her to Madoc Skean. This one was guarded, by literally faceless warriors, but she had the signs and the passwords, and they ignored her. There were four of them, of the "immortal" type; no weapon would kill them except Cold Iron, and even then it would have to penetrate their mage-crafted armor. The Gate was a real, solid structure, four pillars supporting a dome above a platform, all of black-and-red marble. The faceless ones stood at each corner, staring out into nothingness. They had no wills of their own, never tired, never needed food or drink; they were enchanted flesh and metal, sustained by the mage-energies of their master.

She walked up onto the platform beneath the dome, closed her eyes, and "knocked" with her power. At the third "knock," she opened her eyes on the audience chamber of Madoc Skean, Lord of Underhill, Magus Major and Unseleighe commander.

As if to emphasize how *different* he and his Seleighe rival Keighvin Silverhair were, everything in Madoc's domain was of the most archaic mode. This "audience chamber," for instance. Shar was fairly certain that he had copied it from a movie about a barbarian king and his barbarian rivals—all the Sidhe seemed to love movies. Built of the same black-and-red marble as the Gate, the main body of it was lit only by torches in brackets along the walls, so that the high ceiling was shrouded in gloom. Pillars ranged along each side of the room, their tops lost in the shadows. The floor, of the same marble, held a scattering of fur rugs. A fire burned in the center of the room, held in a huge copper dish supported on bronze lions' feet. At the end of the room, on a platform that raised him above the floor by about three feet so that anyone who approached him would be forced to look up at him, was Madoc. He sat in a Roman-style chair, made of gold and draped with more furs. Torches burned in golden holders on either side of him, and the rear wall was covered with a huge tapestry depicting Madoc doing something disgusting to a defeated foe. Two more of his faceless guards flanked his throne; their black armor was ornamented with gold chasing and rubies the same color as drying blood.

Madoc wore a heavy, primitive crown of gold, inscribed with Celtic knotwork and set with more rubies, on his handsome, blond head. He made no attempt to disguise his cat-pupiled green eyes or pointed ears. His costume was an elaborate and thickly embroidered antique-style tunic and trews made of gold and scarlet silk; on his feet were sandals that laced up over the legs of the trews. The leather was studded with gold, as was the heavy belt at his waist. A crimson mantle of silk velvet was held to his shoulders by matching Celtic circle-brooches. His jewelry, aside from the crown and the brooches, consisted of a pair of heavy gold armbands and a gold torc with monster-head finials.

Shar could not help thinking that he looked like an art supply catalog on two feet.

Shar stepped carefully down from the platform, which held the physical counterpart of the Gate in the Forest, and made her way across the vast and empty floor. She kept her face impassive right up until the moment that she came to Madoc's feet.

Then she allowed her face to assume an expression of amused irony. "I think you owe Frank Frazetta licensing fees," she said.

Madoc frowned, a flash of real anger, as his impassive mask slipped for a moment. Shar smiled. Madoc hated being reminded that the elves copied everything they did from humans, and he hated it even more when she recognized the source.

"Don't mention Frazetta's name to me again. He has caused the Unseleighe enough trouble. You're making no progress in dealing with Tannim," he said abruptly, as she crossed her arms over her breasts and took a hip-shot, careless stance designed to tell him without words that she was not impressed.

She shrugged. "It's coming along. You know as well as anyone that Oberon has been taking an interest in Keighvin and his crew, and that includes Tannim. Challenge him without all the proper protocols and you could wind up answering to the High King. Again. Just because he threw you out of the Court once doesn't mean he can't choose to come after you."

Madoc flushed. "You haven't stayed long enough to get Tannim's response to your challenge!" he accused. "You're toying with him! Enough of your foolishness! We are not engaged with this plan to amuse you. Deal with the man and have done with it!"

She lowered her eyelids to hide her anger at the tone of command he had taken with her. He should know better than to take that attitude with her—

Suddenly, a soft popping sound signaled Azure's arrival into the throne room, speeding towards her with obvious excitement. *Something* must have happened to make her pet seek her out here! She raised her hand to warn Madoc not to disturb the creature—

Too late.

He was already irritated with her, and this intrusion gave him an excuse to vent that anger on something connected with her.

He blasted the hapless creature into the back wall with a flick of his hand. It whimpered once, and died.

Shar felt stunned, as if she had taken the blow herself. She stared at the remains of her pet, then transferred her gaze to Madoc. The Unseleighe yawned, rubbed his chin, and smiled at her lazily.

"Next time," he purred, "curb your dog."

At that moment Shar made up her mind about which side she was on.

She gave no outward sign of her thoughts. Instead, she said, "What do you want me to do? Don't you realize what weapon he's likely to choose for the Challenge? *Cars.* Racing. His Mustang against mine." She gritted her teeth and went on with the deception. "In anything else, I could best him, but not that. He's better than I am or ever will be, and no amount of magery is going to counteract his skill."

Madoc frowned, as if that had never occurred to him. "Well, *kill* him, then!" he snapped.

But again, she shook her head. "Oberon," she said

succinctly. "If you don't want Oberon's attention, play by the rules of the game. We've *issued* the Challenge; we can't kill Tannim out of hand now. Remember, if you violate the rules, no Unseleighe will ever trust you. He has to accept the Challenge, and you're going to have to figure out some way of making him choose magery or some other weapon I am superior with. That's why I've been drawing things out; I've been trying to get him off balance enough that he won't think of racing as the response when I finally let him respond."

There. Bite on that awhile.

She seethed with anger at the wanton, *pointless* destruction of Azure; she would mourn the poor little creature later, when her privacy was assured. But the best way to get revenge on Madoc was to frustrate him, to make *him* angry. If he lost control of himself, he would do something stupid, and he might lose all of his allies. That would put him right back at square one, all of his plans in ruins, all of it to do over again. But this time it would take much longer to undo all the damage. Look how long it had taken Vidal Dhu to regain *his* reputation after losing to Keighvin Silverhair the first time!

Madoc frowned fiercely at being confronted with the truth—but then, unexpectedly, he smiled.

"But he cannot choose *racing* if he has nothing to race *with*, can he?" the Unseleighe lord said with glee. "'Tis simple enough: we steal his precious Mustang with magic, and bring it Underhill! There are pockets we can armor against the harmful effect of so much Cold Iron—and I myself have enough power to bring the vehicle here!"

She blinked, taken aback—then quickly recovered. "What if he comes after it?" she countered. "What if he brings help with him, armed with Cold Iron weapons?"

"Then he but proves my point to Oberon," Madoc retorted with triumph. "And we can lay a trap for him. Oberon cannot object to our squashing him like an impudent insect if he brings Death Metal into Underhill!"

She was too well-trained to panic, but her mind raced as it never had before. "Let me deal with the car and set the trap," she said quickly. "Why waste your energies on dealing with something I can handle with impunity? Then you can confront him yourself, power intact."

Madoc nodded slowly. "You have a point," he admitted. "It would exhaust me to bring the car Underhill; it would serve us little if I cannot be the one to defeat him here." He straightened regally on his throne. "Very well," he said, his arrogance as heavy a mantle as the red velvet shrouding his shoulders. "Deal with it, Shar. Bring the car to the Underhill pocket nearest the Hall of the Mountain King. The Norse are used to the presence of metals; it should cause a minimum of disturbance to their magics. And if it troubles them—" he smiled, a snake's smile as it prepared to sink its fangs into the neck of the prey "—well, I offered an alliance, and they refused me. They can deal with the consequences."

She nodded shortly and turned on her heel, striding to the Gate at the other end of the hall and presenting him with her back instead of retreating, walking backward, as an underling would do. In that much, at least, she could offer open defiance. Her jaw was clenched so hard it ached, and her hands twitched as she forced them to remain at her side without turning into fists.

He had gone too far. He had neither the right nor the cause to callously slay Azure. Now it was time for her to think, plan everything with absolute care, and then act. She must kidnap the Mustang; she must make sure that Tannim *would* follow it. But the result of that would not be what Madoc supposed. She would best Madoc at Madoc's own game.

And, fates willing, feed him his own black heart at the end of it all.

Shar crouched in the gravel of the driveway of Tannim's house. Her fur was almost black under the pale moon, and she laid out the last components of her spell with care.

Her tail lashed as she spun out the energies, linked them all in together, and *flung* them with handlike paws at the Mach One—

She held her breath, waiting, as the spell settled into place, a gossamer web of her power laid carefully over the layers and structures of Tannim's spells on his Mustang. As delicately as this was made, it *still* might set off his alarms—

It didn't, and she let out her breath in a rush. It had been damned difficult to get past all his mage-alarms and shields and this close to his parents' house, even wearing the true-fox shape. She had never been so close to triggering someone else's protections in her life, and she suspected that only her form had kept her from setting off all those alarms. It would have been disaster if she somehow set off the protections on the Mustang.

She had known from the moment Madoc opened his mouth to order the Mach One's capture that Tannim would, if the car was merely *taken,* simply write it off as a loss. He would *know* it was going to be bait in a trap. When he refused to come after it, Madoc would insist that she make good on the Challenge, assuming that Tannim would have to choose some other weapon.

The trouble was, Tannim could *still* choose racing. He could have the damned Victor GT sent down here to him if he wanted. He could buy two identical cars off a showroom floor.

Madoc would know she could not match him on a race course. He could do something stupid to hex the race, but he would do it in the mortal world, where he could not operate as freely as she could. Yes, she could work this into Madoc's downfall, but there would be a sacrifice she no longer wanted to make.

Madoc would murder Tannim, as he had murdered Azure. SharMarali Halanyn vowed, on the spirits of her ancestors, Madoc Skean would have no more victims.

She had to do something to make it look as if the Mach One's disappearance was an accident. If it happened while *he* was doing something to the car, he would not assume it was a trap.

So, she laid in a spell to open a Gate to the appointed place the moment Tannim tried to set another spell of any kind on his car. With her nipping at his heels, it couldn't be long before he did just that. She would be ready to snatch his car away before he knew what was happening.

And since the Mach One would *not* end up anywhere near Unseleighe domains—as per Madoc's orders—he would assume that something had backfired in the spell *he* had set, and come after his wandering Mustang.

Or so she hoped, for his sake. If he did that, she had a chance of saving him *and* engineering Madoc's downfall.

The only other way of saving him would be for the two of them to join forces and take Madoc on. She knew how strong she was—and in a head-on confrontation, Madoc would win over her. He was the better fighter. The strengths of the *kitsune* lay in subterfuge, trickery. The strengths of the dragon—

She had not learned. Not well enough. Her father had not taught her enough to become a rival to his power. If Ako had remained with Chinthliss, perhaps—

Perhaps changes nothing, she scolded herself, and crept carefully down the driveway, still in fox-shape. She was strong enough to hold her independence only because Charcoal would not challenge Ako and her family, and because the Unseleighe did not realize how she had come to despise them. *They* thought they still ruled her, and permitted her what they thought was the illusion of independence. She could not protect Tannim alone. He could not withstand the full power of the Unseleighe alone. His friends from Fairgrove could not reach him before Madoc murdered him, if Madoc struck without warning.

They would have to join forces, and for that, she would have to show herself as his ally.

She looked back over her shoulder at the house once she was safely outside the perimeter of Tannim's shields. A single light burned in the room she knew was *his*.

What was he doing? Trying to extract information from her carefully Cleansed gloves? Thinking? Dreaming?

Of her?

She shook her head violently, her ears flapping, and sneezed. Then she spun around three times, a little red fox chasing her tail, and reached through the thrice-cast circle for her Gate to home.

Tannim pulled the Mustang into Chinthliss' slot just before sunset. His mentor had told him on the phone when Tannim called him this morning not to bother to appear before then; his own researches would not be completed before dark.

So he and Joe cruised around Tulsa in the afternoon. Fox still hadn't put in an appearance.

But the mysterious, dark-haired woman in her black Mustang certainly did. She was tailing them.

She made no attempt to hide, but she also made no further attempt at contact of any kind. In fact, the two times he had tried to turn the tables on her and force a confrontation, she had managed to vanish into the traffic.

She stayed no less than three cars behind him, and no more than five, no matter what route he chose; even when he was certain he'd managed to shake her, she always turned up again. He thought he'd lost her when they pulled into one of the malls, but when he and Joe came out again with more clothing for Joe, she was there, parked three rows away from the Mach One, watching them.

When he stopped to fill up the tank, she was in the parking lot of a fast-food joint across the street. When he turned onto the Broken Arrow expressway, she followed right behind. He got off and thought he'd lost her for sure when he didn't see her following on the little two-lane blacktop road he'd chosen—but as soon as he came to a major intersection, there she was again, as if she had somehow *known* where he was going.

She finally vanished when he pulled into his folks'

driveway, hot and frustrated, and doing his best not to take his frustration out on Joe.

He certainly hoped that Chinthliss would have better news for him than all of this.

She hadn't shown up on the drive to the hotel, so that was a plus. Maybe following them around all day, between the power-shopping and the aimless driving, had been driving her as buggy as being followed had driven him.

She sure as hell hadn't learned anything interesting. Unless it was which stores had his favorite brands of clothing.

They piled out of the car and started up the walkway in the blue dusk. Chinthliss met them at the door, letting them in without any of his usual banter. That was enough to make Tannim take a closer look at his friend. Chinthliss had a very odd, closed expression on his face.

"What's wrong?" Tannim asked bluntly.

Chinthliss shook his head and waved them both to seats on the couch. The two gloves lay on the table, in the exact middle, side by side, both of them palm showing. As Chinthliss took his own seat, Tannim watched him closely. Something was definitely up.

"I believe I have the identity of your challenger," Chinthliss said, abruptly, with no warm-up. "I don't know *why* she has challenged you, for certain, but I can guess. And I hope that I am wrong."

"So who *is* she?" Tannim asked when Chinthliss had remained silent for far too long.

Chinthliss drew himself up and tried to look diginified, but succeeded only in looking haggard. "I would rather not say," he replied. "It involves something very personal."

That was the last straw in a long and frustrating day. Tannim lost his temper. Chinthliss liked to play these little coaxing games, but Tannim was not in the mood for one now.

"*Personal*, my—" Tannim exploded, as Joe jumped in startlement at his vehemence. Then he forced himself to calm down. "Look, lizard," he said, leaning forward and emphasizing his words with a pointed finger. "I've told you a lot of stuff that was *damned* personal over the years, when it had a bearing on something you needed to know. You know that nothing you tell me will leave this room. Time to pay up. I have to *know* this stuff. It's my tail that's on the line, here!"

Chinthliss licked his lips and tried to avoid Tannim's eyes. Tannim wouldn't let him.

Finally Chinthliss sighed and let his head sag down into his hands. "It is very complicated and goes back a long time," he said plaintively, as if he was hoping Tannim would be content with that.

Not a chance. "Ante up, Chinthliss," Tannim said remorselessly. "The more you stall, the worse I'll think it is."

Chinthliss sighed again, and leaned back in his chair, eyes closed. "It all began twenty-eight years ago, in the time of this world," he said, surprising Tannim. *Huh. He wasn't kidding about it being a long time. That's a year longer than I've been alive.*

"This occurred in my realm. There were two young males, constant rivals. One was called Charcoal, and one, Chinthliss," his mentor continued. "They both courted a lovely lady of the *kitsune* clan. She was young and flirtatious, and paid the same attentions to each. Very—ah—personal attentions. Chinthliss was the one who temporarily won her, mostly because Charcoal became insufferable. But it was not Chinthliss who fathered the daughter she bore."

Tannim sat bolt upright. Chinthliss—and a *kitsune*?

"The daughter was charming and talented, and Chinthliss had no qualms with accepting her as a foster-daughter, even though Charcoal had gone beyond being his rival and had become his most vicious enemy. But—he had many things on his mind, and eventually the Lady Ako became disenchanted with the lack of attention he paid her, and left him." There was real pain on Chinthliss' features, the ache of loss never forgotten and always regretted. "When she left him, she took her daughter. He never saw either of them again."

He opened his eyes at last, and Tannim locked his lips on the questions he wanted to ask. "That was when Chinthliss realized that he needed others, and began looking for someone—yes, to take the places of Lady Ako and SharMarali. Stupid, I know, for one person can never *replace* another, but I have never been particularly wise, no matter what my student might say to flatter me. . . . " His voice trailed off for a moment, then he looked Tannim straight in the eyes. "I never found anyone to match Ako, but I did find an eager young mind to teach, a protégé, someone to take the place of little Shar. That was why I gave him the name, 'Son of Dragons'; not only as a joke on the name of his real, blood parents, but because he became a kind of son to me."

Tannim licked lips gone dry, and prompted him gently. "Is this—Shar—the one who's been following me?"

Chinthliss nodded painfully, as if his head was very heavy and hard to move. "I don't think there can be any doubt," he said. "Especially since there is only one *kitsune*-dragon I know of, and in the past, I heard rumors, rumors I had thought I could discount. I *thought* that Lady Ako had Shar safely with her; the rumors were that not long after I began teaching you, Charcoal asserted his parental rights over the girl and took her off to be trained by himself and by his allies. The Unseleighe."

At Tannim's hissing intake of breath, Chinthliss grimaced. "You see, the rumors I heard were that he intended to make her into the opposite of you."

Joe scratched his head thoughtfully. "I can see that," he said. "It all matches, if she's supposed to be the anti-Tannim. Even the car she drives is a Mustang. Late model, old versus new. The same, only different."

"So you see why she would be challenging you," Chinthliss continued unhappily. "And why it's happening here and now, in Oklahoma, where I first found you."

Tannim shook his head and groaned. "Oh, God. I'm in an evil twin episode. If this were a TV show, I'd kick in the screen about now."

Joe snickered; Chinthliss made what sounded like a sympathetic noise deep in his throat.

Tannim looked up at Chinthliss again. "Okay, we can figure it's Shar; we can figure she's sleep—ah—working with the Unseleighe. She's challenging me, and figures she's going to wipe me. Keighvin and Conal said that since I have choice of weapons in a Challenge, I should choose racing."

Chinthliss brightened a little at that. "The laws of challenge are clear on that point; you have the right of any weapon you choose—and I rather suspect that they would never think of racing as a weapon. I cannot imagine how even Shar could best you in a contest of that sort. Unless her allies make it something less than a fair fight."

Tannim leaned back in his chair and ran his fingers through his hair thoughtfully. "Okay. Let's assume they do. What can they do? Booby-trap the course, do something to *her* car to turn it deadly, do something to *mine* to make it fail on me."

"I can prevent them from interfering with the course," Chinthliss replied quickly. "I have more practice working in this world than they."

"No matter what they do to her car, they have to get it close to mine to make any weapons work." Tannim unwrapped a pop, stuck the paper in the ashtray and the cherry-pop in his mouth. "That just takes a little more finesse on my part. *I've* had nasties after me. If she's never done combat-driving before, she's no match for me."

Chinthliss shrugged. "Where would she have learned?" he asked. "Who would have taught her?"

"More to the point, where would she have gotten the practice?" Tannim put in. "SERRA keeps an eye out for reports of driving 'incidents'; things like that sometimes mean there's a mage out there that isn't trained or mentored. I think we'd have a tag on her if she'd been messing around on her own. Hell, she'd have run into one of ours by now, for sure."

"That only leaves—sabotaging the Mach One," Joe said. "But how do you keep someone from messing around with your car when they can do it magically?"

"Easy," Tannim and Chinthliss said in chorus. "More magic."

Joe sighed. "I shoulda known."

Tannim half grinned. "So," he said, looking into Chinthliss' eyes, "feel up to anything tonight? Time might not be on our side. Your wicked stepdaughter was trailing us all over Tulsa today."

"Mmm. I will help, yes," Chinthliss replied. "Most of today's work was not mine. And I have a few ideas that I would like you to try anyway."

"Shall we?" Tannim rose and bowed, gesturing toward the door.

"Let's shall," Chinthlis said with a sigh. "Tannim, this is not how I wanted to find her again."

"I can imagine." Tannim led the way out to the Mustang. It was fully dark now. The stars above dotted the sky even through the light-haze thrown up by Tulsa. Out in the country they would be able to see the Milky Way.

Joe automatically wedged himself into the backseat, leaving the front to Chinthliss. "If this girl's half kit-whats-it," he asked, leaning over the seat as Tannim pulled out of the parking slot, "would that be why Fox just disappeared and hasn't come back?"

"Exactly so," Chinthliss told him. Tannim let his mentor make the explanations; he was too busy watching for that black Mustang. "Shar's mother is a nine-tailed *kitsune*; she can shape-change into a *real* fox if she chooses, or into anything else. She can act and be acted upon as a real human woman. She has powers I could wish I enjoyed. Nine tails is an enormously high rank, and I have never personally heard of or met a *kitsune* with more tails. The number of tails indicates the rank and power in a *kitsune*; I doubt that Shar, in her *kitsune* form, has less than six. FX has only three tails, which is why he can affect nothing in this world; he could not possibly best her, and if he crossed her, she *could* take one of his tails."

"So?" Joe wanted to know.

Chinthliss shrugged. "So, he would definitely lose rank and power—and there are some who say that the number of tails also means the number of *lives* a *kitsune* has. Lose a tail and you lose a life."

"Oh." Joe sat back to digest this.

Tannim knew that the young man must be confused as all hell. *Kitsunes*, dragons, magic-enhanced cars . . . it could have flattened a less stable person. Maybe in some cases old what's-his-name was right: "that which does not kill us, makes us stronger." It sure seemed to work for Joe.

Helluva way to grow up, though.

The barn seemed the right place to go, even though they'd have to do any magic on the Mach One "without a net," outside the protections available inside the barn. But with two mages here, one of them a dragon, what could go wrong that they couldn't fix?

Joe went out ahead with a flashlight, just to make sure that their little playmate hadn't booby-trapped the access with tire-slashers. He walked all the way to the side of the barn, examining the flattened lines in the grass, and waved an "all-clear" when he reached the barn itself.

Tannim pulled up beside the barn and got out. Chinthliss followed.

He stood looking at the Mach One for a long time, fists on his hips, feet apart and braced. Then he took a deep breath, and stepped back.

"All right folks," he said quietly, as the crickets and mockingbirds sang in the distance, and a nighthawk screamed overhead. "It's show time."

Although Tannim had never done anything synchronized this way before, Chinthliss wanted to set up all of their spells in a complex net, so that they all meshed and could all be triggered together.

Tannim had argued against that, but not very forcefully, because he had known Chinthliss was right about one thing. Once Shar got a whiff of magics out here at the barn, she'd *know* that Chinthliss was involved. And once she knew that, she might change her mind about keeping her distance. They'd really better do everything at once, because they might not get a second chance.

The trouble was, he had no idea how well all this stuff was going to "take," given the protections that were already on the Mach One. And he had no idea how it would integrate with what was already there. *Hell*, he thought ruefully, as Chinthliss laid out the last of his webs of power over Tannim's own "crystalline" geometric structures, *I've got no idea how half of what he wants to do is going to work!* It was worse than computer programming.

Chinthliss surveyed his handiwork and stepped back a pace. "Ready?" he asked.

"Ready," his former pupil replied, though not without considerable misgivings.

"Right. On my count." Chinthliss walked to the tail of the car and raised his hands, and Tannim copied his gesture, standing at the nose. "Four. Three. Two. One. *Fire.*"

Tannim triggered his spells.

What *should* have happened was that a structure a great deal like the dome inside the barn would form, then shrink down to become one with the Mach One's skin.

What actually happened was that the dome formed and shrank, all right—

But as soon as it touched the skin of the Mustang, there was a blinding flash of light.

Tannim shouted in pain, and turned away, eyes watering, swearing with every curse he had ever heard in his life. He scrubbed at his eyes frantically—*What did we do to my car?*

There were spots dancing in front of him, but it was perfectly clear what they had done to his car.

Because the Mach One was no longer there; only a flattened place in the grass, and a single chrome trim-ring from one of the wheels, gleaming in the moonlight.

"Ah, *hell!*" he half groaned, half shouted. *"Now* what am I gonna do? How do you explain *this* to State Farm?"

• CHAPTER SIX

Tannim stared at the chrome trim-ring for a moment longer, then waded through the tall grass and picked it up. It felt warm, as if it had been sitting in the sun for a long time. "The Mach One can't have gone far," he said finally. "At least, I don't think it could have. We didn't put *that* much power into those spells, not enough to have teleported a car for miles—"

"If it went Underhill, 'far' is relative," Chinthliss warned. "My guess is that's where it went. It would not take a great deal of power to open a Gate into some truly outré realm."

Tannim felt himself blanch, and the bottom dropped out of his stomach. Underhill. It wasn't just Keighvin and his "good" elves who lived Underhill. So did the Unseleighe, the efrits, and a lot of other nasty characters. Underhill wasn't *one* place, it was many places, all lumped in the same generic basket. Some of those places held people who didn't care for Tannim very much. "If it went Underhill," he said slowly, "and the bad guys get ahold of it, I am in deep kimchee. I've got a lot of personal power invested in that car. They could get *at* me through it. I've got to get it back before they know it's there."

"Do you think that is wise?" Chinthliss asked, looking skeptical and a tad worried. "You could end up in more difficulties than if you simply left it there."

"I don't think I have a choice," he retorted. "It's either that, or cut it off from me entirely, which I'm not sure would work, then try to explain to my folks where my car went. They know I'd never sell it. Shoot, I'd rather deal with Unseleighe."

Not to mention the long walk back. *I could say someone stole it. But then I'd have to go through the whole police show, and meanwhile I still have Shar on my tail and I wouldn't have all the protection I built into the Mustang.* It did occur to him that he could borrow an elvensteed from Keighvin—after all, if Rhellan could look like a '57 Chevy, surely another 'steed could look like the Mach One. But that would mean calling in yet another favor from Keighvin, and that would still leave the problem of the Mach One in possibly unfriendly hands. *It won't take them more than a couple of days to figure out that it's down there; all that Cold Iron unshielded is going to make a helluva distortion in the magic fields Underhill. It'll only get worse the longer I wait. If I just get in and get out again, everything should be fine.*

Besides, he loved that car. There were a lot of important memories tied up in it. It had carried him through a lot of bad situations, and more than a few good ones. He wanted it back.

"It hasn't been down there that long; I can't imagine anyone would have found it this soon. I can use this to scry with," he continued, holding up the trim-ring as he pushed through the waist-high grass to get inside the barn. "It shouldn't take me long to find it. Once I know where it is, I can go get it and bring it back with me. It's easier to open up a Gate from there to here than vice versa. Right?"

"That depends—" Chinthliss began.

But Tannim ignored him. After all, if it hadn't been for Chinthliss insisting that they trigger *all* the spells together, none of this would have happened. Although how that particular batch of spells could have conspired to open up a hole into Underhill, he could not imagine.

Of course, no one knew how programmers got Windows 3.1 to run, either, and it had at least as many ways to go wrong as their cobbled mass of spells.

He put the trim-ring down on the ground once he got inside the protected area of the barn, triggered some of the primary protections, and then laid a mirror-finished disk of energy within the trim-ring. That turned the whole trim-ring into a scrying mirror, very like some of the scrying pools Underhill, but set specifically for the Mach One. Chinthliss came in behind him and conjured up a magelight that provided real-world illumination. In the dim, blue light, Joe wore an expression of worry and puzzlement. Chinthliss was, as usual, inscrutable.

He crouched down on his heels beside the ring as Joe and Chinthliss joined him. Joe stared nervously down over his shoulder, but Chinthliss kept chewing on his lip and casting suspicious glances everywhere except at the ring.

The surface of the mirror glowed with a milky radiance like fog lit up from within. Silently, Tannim commanded it: *Show me the vehicle of which you were once a part. Show me where it is, and the condition it is in.*

He continued to stare down at the ring as the light within it shifted restlessly, showing only vague shapes, and hints of wavering forms within its misty depths.

Finally, faint color tinged the fog, red and gold, purple and deep blue. He willed more power into the mirror, and the image within it strengthened and the colors intensified.

Then the whole image trembled violently, and settled; the huge oblong of deep, deep red in the center cleared and became the Mustang, while the rest of the image focused into the background.

The Mach One sat sedately in the exact middle of what could only be a huge audience chamber, literally fit for a king. She looked terribly odd there: the only modern object in a room that resonated with a feeling of *ancient times*. Her four tires rested on a floor of polished amber; behind her was a wall covered with a geometric tapestry of red, blue, purple, and gold. Benches of gold and amber sat beneath the tapestry, and in between the benches were ever-burning lamps of gold and tortoiseshell, or stands holding antique weaponry.

A thick patina of dust lay over everything except the car.

Tannim chewed his lip, trying to figure out just *where* this was. Underhill, obviously, since of the humans of this world, only a Russian Tzar could ever afford to have a room with a floor of amber, but the question was, *where* Underhill?

Chinthliss finally looked down at the image within the mirror and frowned. "That's the audience chamber of the Katschei, the one he used when he was in a good mood," he said. "It's not that far from the Nordic elven enclaves. Once the Katschei was dead, I'd have thought for certain that something else would have taken over his Underhill holdings, but it looks abandoned. Maybe there's a curse on the place or something."

"Yeah, look at the dust. Well. The Nordic elves are deep Underhill. Keighvin says some of them haven't come out for centuries." That gave him distance and direction; he ought to be able to Gate from here to there with Chinthliss' assistance, using the trim-ring as an anchor, then return the same way. The ring, having been part of the car, should keep the path between them open and clear.

He stood up. "Well, if it's as abandoned as it looks, this should be a piece of cake. I can Gate over and Gate back before three in the morning." He grinned at Joe, crookedly. "Be glad you're with me, otherwise Mom would have you under a curfew."

"I really don't feel comfortable with this," Chinthliss began, then shook his head. "Never mind. I fear it was my work that caused this; I shall have to defer to your judgment."

"I told you why I can't just leave it there," Tannim replied. "If we were home, I'd grab Keighvin and a bunch of the polo players and go riding cross-Underhill to get it.

But I'm not, and we don't have time to call them in. If I go now, before anyone realizes the big anomaly that just plopped down there has a physical focus, we should be fine. Underhill's not that stable, and stuff causes mage-quakes all the time down there."

And people are always watching for mage-quakes, bonehead. Sometimes interesting things surface after one. Yeah, you'd better get your tail moving before somebody finds this particular "interesting thing" and gets the pink slip on it.

Chinthliss shrugged and stepped back a pace. "Have it your way. I can at least establish the Gate for you."

Tannim nodded, and cast a glance back at Joe. The young man looked very worried, but he said nothing, perhaps because he felt so out of his depth with two obviously practiced mages.

Chinthliss stared fixedly at the trim-ring for several minutes, then raised his hands slowly. The trim-ring rose smoothly and rotated sideways until it was facing Tannim and balanced on edge, forming a shining "O" that hovered in midair. Joe's eyes widened. Chinthliss spread his fingers, and the trim-ring shivered and expanded, an inch at a time, thinning as it did so, until it was about a half an inch thick and tall enough for Tannim to pass through. The scene inside the ring remained the same: the Mach One, crouched on the amber floor as if in the heart of a showroom. As the ring widened, the scene expanded so that it was possible to see a bit more: the geometrics on the tapestry proved to be only a very wide border; now the legs and lower torsos of humans and other creatures engaged in combat were visible, all of it woven in the same flat but colorful style, like a lacquer box. Then, as Chinthliss shifted the focus of the spell from *seeing* to *going*, the scene vanished, replaced by a dead-black wall.

"I can't hold it long," Chinthliss warned in a voice that showed strain. "If you're going, go now!"

Tannim did not hesitate. He stepped across the edge of the ring, closing his eyes involuntarily as he felt the internal lurch and tingle that a Gate-crossing always gave him. He experienced a moment of disorientation and blackout, accompanied by a jolt as he dropped about a foot. He flexed his legs automatically and dropped into a crouch, one hand touching the floor.

When his eyes opened again, he found himself not more than a couple of feet from the Mach One, one hand resting in about a half inch of dust. Beneath the dust, the amber floor glowed slightly, adding to the illumination in the room with a warm, buttery light.

The same depth of dust lay everywhere—except around the edge of the room, in a path about three feet wide. *Odd.*

He repressed a sneeze, straightened, and turned around. It was virtually the same behind him. The tapestry on that wall showed twelve lovely maidens dancing around a tree loaded with golden fruit, in the heart of a walled garden. The chamber itself was immense, as big as a high school gymnasium at least. The benches were pushed up against three of the four walls; gold and transparent amber, rather than the opaque butter-amber of the floor and walls. The fourth side held a raised platform with a gold-and-amber throne standing in lonely splendor on it. The hanging on that wall was plain purple with gold fringe as long as his arm on the bottom hem. There was no hanging on the opposite wall; it held a set of huge golden double doors, both gaping open. Beyond them lay darkness; light from the audience chamber was swallowed up by that darkness immediately, as if it was just as big as this room. Above the doors, the wall had been inlaid with mosaics of cabochon gemstones forming a pattern of flowers.

He tensed as sound came from beyond those doors. Instinctively, he sprinted to the side of the Mach One and crouched down beside the headlights, ready to use it for cover.

The noises continued; they sounded like someone shuffling, out there in the darkness. He listened carefully and caught another set of sounds: a steady brushing in a rhythmic pattern, scraping, and something like the sound of squeaking cart wheels.

What the—

Something moved out there in the darkness. He tensed, and crouched a little lower beside the fender, one hand in the dust and one clutching the chrome. He smothered another sneeze. He strained his eyes into the murk; magical ever-burning lamps might have been a neat touch, but they didn't give off a heck of a lot of light, and neither did the glowing floor. The sounds neared.

And finally, the maker of the sounds appeared.

A gnarled and twisted old man, dressed in nondescript rags, shuffled in and stood by the hinge of one of the open doors. He was mostly bald, but with a ring of long, unkempt, yellowish-white hair straggling down the back of his head, and he had an equally unkempt white beard that reached to his knees. He held a push-broom and shoved it in front of him with laborious strokes. There was a cart tethered to him by a rope around his waist, which followed him, wheels squeaking, creeping forward with every shuffling step. He made short, hesitant strokes with the broom, then put the broom down painfully, leaning it against the cart; he then reached into the cart, and picked up a whiskbroom and a dustpan.

He got down onto his knees with little whimpers of pain, felt his way to the edge of the area he had just swept, and brushed the little ridge of dust he had collected into his pan.

He got back up to his feet in the same laborious fashion, turned, and felt around the cart. His hand touched the mouth of an open bag resting in the cart, and he carefully tapped the dust into the bag. Then he picked up the broom and began it all again.

What the heck is this—the janitor of the damned?

The old derelict came fully into the audience chamber—and only then did Tannim see *why* he was doing his work with such slow and stilted motions.

Where his eyes should have been there were two gaping, old, but still unhealed, wounds.

Tannim's hissing intake of breath alerted the old man to his presence. The old fellow turned his sightless eyes in Tannim's direction, holding the broom defensively in front of him.

"Who be ye?" he called in a quavering, rusty voice. "What ye want?" His country-English accent was so thick that Tannim could hardly make out what it was he had actually said. *I haven't heard an accent like that since I watched one of those BBC nature shows. It's almost another language entirely.*

Tannim stood up slowly, but he made no move to approach the man. Appearances could be deceptive Underhill. It was hard to tell what was a trap and what was harmless.

"My name is Tannim," he said slowly and carefully, so the old man could make out the words through his own American accent. "I am here to retrieve something that was lost."

"Lost? Lost?" The old man shook his head in senile bewilderment. "Naught's been lost here, boy, 'cept me." He grimaced with pain, his face a mass of wrinkles. "This be no place fer an honest Christian. There be boggles here." He turned his head blindly from side to side, as if looking for the boggles he could no longer see. "Ye seem a good, honest lad. There's danger here. Best leave whiles ye can."

"I found what it was I was looking for, sir," Tannim said placatingly. "But I've seen no danger."

"What ye cain't see kin getcha," the old man retorted, and cackled crazily. "I come here lookin' fer treasure, an' see what it got me! No doubt ye look at all th' gold, an' there's lust in yer heart fer it. Pay it no heed, boy! 'Tis fairy gold, an' not fer any man of God! Take yerself and yer lost thing away, afore them boggles git ye, an' ye find yerself like me—" the voice shook, and tears trickled from the eyeless sockets "—all alone, i' th' dark, ferever an' ever. Never t' see m' lovely Nancy, nor m' ol' Mam. Never t' see nothin' an nobody again. . . ."

The old man stood there, weeping horribly from the ruins of his eyes, rattling on about how he had come to be here, as he clutched his broom. Tannim pieced out from the rambling discourse that the man had somehow come upon one of the rare doors into Underhill that opened at specific times—one of the solstices, for instance, or at the full moon. He had seen a rich hall beyond the door and had returned with bags to carry away the loot, full of greed.

But those who had owned the hall beyond the door were not Seleighe elves, who would have tricked him, terrified him for the sport of it, but let him go relatively unharmed. They were Unseleighe, who used that hall as a tasty trap for the unwary. They throve on pain and fear, and nothing pleased them more than to have a human captive to inflict both on.

They had tormented him until they grew bored with his antics, then had decided on one last torment. They blinded him and sent him here. Where "here" was, he had no clue. His task was to "keep the place clean"—and his life depended on it, for once a day he was to return to a specific spot somewhere in the depths of this place, and the dust he had collected would be transformed into an equal amount of bean-bread. Ironically, the rope that held him to his cart, the sack in the cart, and the cart itself were all tools he himself had brought to carry away his loot. It was an irony that obviously had not been lost on the Unseleighe.

Blinded, he could not see where he had cleaned, and apparently he was a fairly stupid man, who had not figured that he could tell where he was in a room by the echoes from the walls, as many blind people Tannim knew had learned to navigate. That was why he cleaned no farther into the room than he could reach with his broom, despite the tantilizing fact that he *knew* there was thick dust just beyond that point. He had ventured into the middle of a room once, and had been hopelessly lost until he had managed to crawl into a wall again. After that, he never dared make a second attempt.

He was in constant pain, he was more than half mad, and the two oozing holes where his eyes had been made Tannim sick to his stomach to look at. If he remembered his name, he never told it to Tannim. But he was—or had been—a human being, once. However stupid or greedy he had been, he did not deserve a fate like this one.

Yet when Tannim offered to take him away, the man cowered against the wall, wept, and babbled in sheer terror. Clearly, he had been tricked by Unseleighe pretending to "rescue" him before this. Every time Tannim tried to touch him, he only winced violently away. The only way Tannim would ever get the oldster into the Mustang would be kicking, screaming, and utterly mindless with terror. Which right now, could attract a whole lot of unwanted attention and get them both caught.

Finally, Tannim did the only thing he could think of to help the man. He cut bits of the gold fringe from the bottom of the tapestry at the end of the hall and knotted the pieces together until they formed a very long, heavy rope, which he gave to the old man.

"Tie this to the rope on the cart," he explained patiently. "Tie the other end to your waist. You can go as far into the center of a room as you like, and as long as you *don't* pull the cart after you, you can always follow the rope back to the wall."

He had to explain it several times before the old man finally grasped it, and if the lesson would last past the next meal, Tannim would never be sure. But he had tried. And the old wreck was weepingly, pathetically grateful. But *not* grateful enough to lose his suspicion of Tannim's motives or identity—his paranoia was too deeply ingrained for him to trust anyone to take him away.

There was something else that occurred to Tannim: time passed oddly Underhill, and the Seleighe and Unseleighe had ways of staving off old age from mortals when they chose. But those methods did not work in the human world, where magic was not as strong. Assuming that he *could* persuade the oldster that he was to be trusted, Tannim could rescue the poor old goat and bring him across a Gate, only to see him crumble into dust on the threshold.

Would that be a kinder fate than the one he currently had? Given a choice—

Yes, but it's his choice, not mine.

There was enough cutlery in this audience chamber alone, in the weapon-stands, for the old man to have ended his life long ago if he chose. Evidently he preferred living, however miserable that life might be. Maybe it wasn't all that miserable by his standards. Presumably he still had a home, something in his memories worth living for. Perhaps the unknown of death presented a more terrifying prospect than the quiet horror of his daily existence here.

He doesn't trust me, and I can't promise him anything, anyway.

The old derelict filled his sack to the top and shuffled off into the darkness, muttering happily to himself. The cart-wheels creaked, marking his progress, until at last the sounds were swallowed up in the thick darkness.

Shar shuddered and came awake with a smothered gasp.

The internal lurch as Tannim triggered Shar's trap caught her asleep in her own pocket-domain, and took her completely by surprise. She really hadn't expected him to try anything magical for another twenty-four hours at least! She had been so tired after all her work of last night and the ruse of tailing him today that she had thrown herself down on the couch as soon as she returned "home," and must have fallen asleep. The aftershock of so much Cold Iron linked to her hitting the fields of mage-energy Underhill resonated through her as she sat bolt upright, shaking hair and sleep-fog out of her eyes.

She swore to herself as her head rung with a very physical sensation of impact. There was no way that Madoc would ignore *that!* And since he knew that Shar was bringing the Mustang Underhill, he would know what had caused this particular mage-quake. She massaged her temples and swung her feet down to the floor, and wondered what particular imp of ill luck she had annoyed enough to plague her with all these miscalculations.

Oh, most excellent, she told herself sarcastically. *Madoc knows where I was going to dump the car. He'll be there, either as soon as or before I can get there. He won't wait for me to tell him I've caught Tannim—he'll go to gloat over the car! He might even decide not to trust me further and set up an ambush of his own! Why didn't I think of that in the first place? I swear, I get tired of having to second-guess these Unseleighe pricks!*

Tannim would, probably, follow his car as soon as he knew where it had gone. He might already be there. Oh, damnation, if he'd been *in* the car when it made its little journey, he *would* be there already!

Better count on it. If he's not, I can revise things.

Her mind buzzed with a hundred plans, but all of them hinged on one thing—whether Madoc went to the Katschei's Hall alone, or with his troop of mage-warriors. Alone, she and Tannim could probably best him and be away. But with his troops backing him, there wasn't a chance.

Ah, damnation, I've never seen him leave his hall once without a full escort. He'll have them with him.

Her plans had been based on the notion that she could bring the car Underhill without Madoc knowing when she did. Why hadn't she foreseen that the Mustang would cause such a ruckus?

Because I was basing it on my *car, and I plain forgot how much of Tannim's car is steel and Cold Iron, and all of it filled to the roof with spellwork. I should have done my homework, and now it's too late—*

How soon would Madoc get there? How much lead time would she have? *Better plan on not having a lot. Better plan on none. Better assume that he'll beat me unless my short route is faster than his.*

If Tannim was there, and she had a few minutes, she would probably be able to give him some kind of warning. If she had no time, perhaps she might still be able to do something. *Convince Madoc—no, wait! He must have a dozen Unseleighe lords who all have their own plans for Tannim! If I let them know Madoc has the man, I can get them all tangled up in arguing with each other long enough to get him out of there—maybe . . .*

The more she thought about it, the better it sounded. The beauty of it was that she would not even have to identify herself to let the information loose. All it would take would be a few well-placed anonymous messages. If all they had was the car, and Tannim *didn't* follow it immediately, Madoc's allies would be all the more annoyed that Madoc hadn't told them of his plans to trap the human.

So she delayed her departure just long enough to send Madoc's allies their little messages, magicked into pockets and other handy places by the same means she'd used to tack her first note to the panel of Tannim's Mustang, though this time sans pop-rivet. In a few moments, as they discovered their messages, they would all go looking for their titular leader. If Madoc showed up now, it wouldn't be with his own hand-selected guards, but with a following of "allies," all of whom had their own axes to grind on Tannim's skull.

She faced her Gate and set it for that first Gate in Unseleighe lands, from which platform she could descend through another series of magical portals and wind up in the Katschei's Hall, in the room beside the audience chamber. There were very few places Underhill that led directly into each other. For reasons of defense on the part of the Seleighe and neutral realms, and paranoia on the part of the Unseleighe, one could only Gate into halls, Elfhames, or other residences from carefully guarded external Gates, which in turn could only be reached from Gates in friendly or neutral territories. Her one advantage would be that she knew a way to the Katschei's Hall that involved fewer Gates than Madoc did.

She set the Gate and stepped through, but remained on the platform where she had arrived. With a chanted phrase and a sigil drawn in the air, she reset it to another currently vacant domain.

That's where I did do my research, she comforted herself, stepping through and arriving at the edge of a swamp. *If you know who* used *to be allies, you know where the Gates are set.* Each Gate had a maximum of six destinations; many were not set for more than three or four. No one ever went anywhere in a straight line Underhill, and often a traveler would have to physically walk from one Gate to another in neutral lands in order to reach a Gate that would take him in the direction he wanted to go, and not likely even close to his true destination. It was like trying for connections at Dallas/Ft. Worth airport.

Fortunately, this was not one of those places. Shar would not have enjoyed a stroll across any swamp, but this one, which once had housed Egyptian crocodile-spirits, was particularly unpleasant. *They* had simply vanished over time; the theory was that something had used these swamps as hunting grounds, and picked them off, one by one. Life was dangerous Underhill; the creature that trusted in his own invincibility and immortality often discovered how misplaced that trust was.

But the Egyptians once allied with the efrits, and the efrits with the vampires of the Balkan states. Those in turn had alliances with the Nordic elves—the sort that corresponded to the Unseleighe—and they contracted an alliance with the Katschei. All of those connections were as long distant as the things that once prowled this marsh, but Shar made a point of discovering such alliances and making mental maps of all the Gates that interconnected. Such maps had served her well in the past, and no doubt would again.

Five Gates later, she walked into the audience chamber of the Katschei, a Russian creature, half-monster, half-mage, who had been defeated and killed by a clever human and a benevolent Russian bird-spirit, the Firebird.

A great many of the Russian counterparts to the Seleighe and Unseleighe were bird and animal spirits. The Mare of the Night Wind, for instance, and her sons inhabited the same realm as the Firebird.

According to all that Shar had learned, there were not many creatures who cared to share the Katschei's realm with him. Most of the Katschei's underlings had either been his own creations, or creatures which quickly fled as soon as he was no more. No one had ever taken over this domain afterward, partially because of a superstitious feeling that a place where an "immortal" had been destroyed was very unlucky for other "immortals."

Most of the Katschei's palace now lay in complete darkness, except for the gardens outside and the audience chamber. The garden contained a Gate to the human world, but it came out in the heart of Old Rus, not far from what was now Moscow. Probably not the best place for an American with no passport, no luggage, and nothing but his vehicle to appear, even in the current enlightened times. . . .

Assuming Tannim was already here, and that she had *so* great a lead time over Madoc that she could help him get the Mach One out of the palace, into the garden, and through a Gate that hadn't been used in centuries. Assuming Tannim would cooperate.

The glow from the audience chamber lay ahead and to the right; she moved carefully across the hallway, and paused for a moment on the threshold.

He was there, all right, standing with his hands in his pockets and his legs braced apart, staring at the car. Already it was a disruptive presence Underhill: little crackling tendrils of energy crept across the hood and roof from time to time, and the longer it remained here, the worse the effect would be.

She stepped into the room, making no effort to be quiet. The heels of her boots made muted ticking sounds on the amber floor.

He whirled, hands held out to attack or defend.

She waited for him to say something, but he remained silent. She kept her own hands down at her side, and walked slowly toward him. She did *not* hold her hands out; in a mage, empty hands did not mean "no threat," and such a gesture could be construed as aggressive. He showed no sign of relaxing.

She stopped when she was a few feet away from him. Already she sensed the Gate in the other room gathering energy; it would take longer to transport Madoc and his guards than it had to bring only her, but her time was still short.

But he spoke first. "I know who you are, Shar," he said flatly. "I know who your teachers were, and who you've allied yourself with, and they're not exactly friends of mine."

His use of her name shocked her into unconsidered speech, and she flinched as if she'd been slapped. *How* had he learned her name, much less anything else about her? Unless—

Chinthliss? Could he have contacted Chinthliss?

"They aren't exactly friends of mine, either, monkey-boy," she snapped before she thought. Then she shook her head, and continued, talking so quickly she sounded like a New Yorker so that she could get everything out before Madoc arrived. "Look, you don't have to trust me, you don't have to believe me, but I want to help you. I'm not what I seem, or what you think. But I'm going to have to play along with these jerks to get some room to act, so cut me some slack until the next time you see me, okay? Things are changing faster than you can guess, and I don't much like the idea of being your opposite. I really don't like being forced into it."

He started to answer; she waved him to silence. The Gate had just opened again. She backed up several paces, then said, "Sorry about this," and slapped a spell of paralysis on him just as a clamor of metal signaled that Madoc had come with his guards. Madoc walked through the door into their midst.

"I told you I would bring him, Madoc Skean," she said calmly, without turning around. "I told you, and I have."

Madoc didn't quite run, but he certainly hurried his walk, pushing his escort aside. His eyes gleamed with eager greed as he surveyed Shar briefly, and her prisoner in a more leisurely manner. "You did. Well done," he replied absently. "Now, if you'll just turn him over to me and—"

"Not so fast, Madoc Skean!" said another Unseleighe, who joined Madoc at her side. The sounds of many boots behind her warned that, as she had hoped, the rest of the Unseleighe lords had gotten her message and had taken it seriously. "Not so fast! I have my own claims on this mortal! Did he not slay my own sister's son, Vidal Dhu, with that Death Metal chariot? I swore I would have revenge on him!"

"And what of *my* claim?" cried another. He was joined by the rest, all of them claiming a piece of Tannim. Shar waited; it was *her* spell that held him, and protocol dictated that they could not have him until and unless she let him go.

When the clamor of voices ceased, she spoke into a moment of silence. "My claim supersedes all of yours," she said flatly. "My Challenge to him still holds. And you dare not touch him until it is discharged—you know well the rules of the Challenge. Once issued, it must be answered unless the challenger is willing to be otherwise satisfied. I am not satisfied. And High King Oberon will be less than pleased if you violate so simple a tenet of the laws that bind us all."

There was an uneasy stirring behind her as soon as she mentioned the name "Oberon." Madoc's face was set in a frozen snarl.

She could not look at Tannim's expression; she confined her gaze to a point just below his chin. She was afraid to look in his eyes and see the bleakness of betrayal there.

"But his vehicle is causing harm in the aether of Underhill," she continued. "I will release him to you, Madoc Skean, only if you pledge to hold him unharmed until I can deal with the vehicle and take it somewhere safe. Only I have the ability to handle so much Death Metal—as well you know."

Madoc's snarl increased a trifle.

"You cannot leave this metal beast here," she reminded him. "Look you, how already it causes rifts in the energy-fields, and warps magics about itself. It will not be long until its influence reaches even to your own realm."

He nodded slowly, reluctantly. "I will hold him unharmed," he said finally. "I pledge it upon my True Name."

"Then give me your True Name," she replied immediately. The True Name did not have the power that some granted it—to give absolute control over another mage—but it *did* make it possible to penetrate most of his defenses. That effect was largely psychological, rather than magical.

With a growl, he leaned over and whispered it into her ear. She kept herself from smiling in triumph, and released the spell into Madoc's hands.

"Remember," she warned, "you pledged to hold him unharmed until my return to your court."

"Aye," he said, tightening his "grip" so that Tannim paled. "But mind, we all have our claims as well."

She gave him a look of warning, and he loosened the cocooning paralysis spell enough to let Tannim breathe easier again. "I will not be gone long, Madoc Skean," she told him. "Be aware of that. This man must be in good health and unharmed, ready to take my Challenge, when I return to your court."

Madoc merely smiled. She dared not stipulate more than she had; she knew very well that Madoc had any number of ways of inflicting suffering that caused no permanent damage to body or health. She only hoped that Tannim's tolerance of such things was as good as she had been led to believe.

She did not watch as Madoc had his guards surround his prize and then released the paralysis spell. She turned her back as Tannim was escorted from the room inside a ring of guards, followed by the dozen or so Unseleighe lords who wanted a piece of him, and then by Madoc himself. She feigned indifference and pretended to study the Mach One. The less real interest she showed in the mortal, the safer he would be. Madoc would not hesitate to use him as a weapon against her, if he thought her interest was anything other than the Challenge itself.

When they were all gone, she studied the Mustang in earnest, for there was no doubt in her mind that she had better do something to make it safe, both for the sake of Underhill and for Tannim. She cast a spell of Creation, reweaving it three times before it fell correctly, and summoned a sheet of silk. That, at least, helped ease some of the disturbance its mere presence was creating, and made it less likely that the neighbors, those surly and unpredictable Nordic types, would come storming across the threshold in the next few moments.

I'll have to actually build another Gate-spell of the kind I put on it in the first place, she decided. *I can't just drive it off. For one thing, I don't have the keys and I bet he's put some nasty surprises in there for anyone who tries to hot-wire it. For another, the only Gate big enough for this thing is the one in the garden. I could certainly fake my way as a Russian, but this is not a Trabant—and how in hell would I get it back to the USA, anyway? Slap a FedEx sticker on it?*

So, the question now was, how much power did she have to spare to move the Mach One somewhere else? She didn't want to send it to her "garage"; that was too obvious a place, for one thing. For another, she wasn't certain she could manage to bridge that much physical distance.

Whoa, wait a moment. I told Madoc I'll be moving it, and that's just about as good as actually moving it. The very last place he'll look for it is here, *and if I put enough shrouding spells on it to negate the effect of all that Cold Iron, no one will ever know that it's here. Except for that poor old blind beggar that sweeps this place, and he won't*

*know it isn't supposed to be here, he won't even know that
it's not some peculiar sculpture or piece of furniture.*

The amount of power she would need for those shrouding spells was much less than the amount it would take to open a Gate for even a short distance. Look what bringing the thing here had done to her—she'd slept like a mortal for a dozen hours, then fallen asleep again as soon as she relaxed at the end of the day. There were better uses for that power.

And there was a distinct advantage to not using all that power. Madoc would assume she was drained, as he would be after such an attempt. Or else, he would believe her to be stronger than she actually was. In the latter case, he would not presume to block her, and in the former, he would seriously underestimate her strength.

She nodded to herself as she made her decision and began spinning the gossamer webs of spells that shielded the Mustang from the aether here, and the aether from the Mustang. Each spell settled over the bulk of the car like a delicate veil. Such spells broke the moment whatever they protected moved away from their protection, but that was all right. The only person who would be moving this car was Tannim himself, and if she had him in the driver's seat, it probably wouldn't matter how much disruption they caused.

Finally, the last veil settled into place, and the mists of power flowed through the hall with scarcely a ripple of disturbance.

Shar turned briskly and headed back out the door. She had done all that she could here.

Now she needed to see what she could get away with under the eye of Madoc Skean. Her draconic side knew how deadly a contest of powers this would be—but beneath all the seriousness, her *kitsune* heritage kept reminding her gleefully how much fun this contest would be, especially if she won.

This much was sure; if ever there was to be a test of her full abilities of craft and cleverness, this was surely it.

❋ ❋ ❋

Things were happening a little too fast for Tannim to react to them. But he had least had one thing straight. *No point in fighting six guys armed with sharp, pointy things. Especially since they'd really like it if I would. It would give them the perfect excuse to use those sharp, pointy things on my soft little body.*

So Tannim stayed uncharacteristically meek and polite—and silent—as the six faceless guards marched him out of the amber room and into the darkness. Their very appearance had given him a bit of a shock, when he'd realized that behind the faceplates of their helms was nothing but empty darkness. He'd never seen this particular kind of Unseleighe before, and he wasn't certain if it was some creation, or something that had intelligence and will of its own. It really didn't matter; in either case, the guy who thought he was in charge, the one Shar had called Madoc Skean, would be only too happy for an excuse to have Tannim roughed up. It was in Tannim's best interest to make sure he had no excuses.

He was still trying to recover from the shock of Shar's little speech. He prided himself on his ability to read people, to pick up on the most subtle of body language, and everything he had "read" indicated that she was telling the truth. She sounded—she acted—as if she wanted to be on his side. Could he believe her? Could he trust his ability to read body language when he was dealing with a *kitsune*-dragon hybrid who only looked human?

After all those years of dreaming about her, he wanted to believe her; he wanted to believe it with an ache of longing that he simply could not deny. Yes, it was stupid to believe her. Yes, he might be pinning his hopes on a creature as evil and devious as Aurilia nic Morrigan. Like her, Shar could be a female who would betray him simply because it amused her to do so. But long ago he had made up his mind that his life was always going to be precarious at best. He could expect the worst of everyone, be paranoid and fearful, and spend his life being miserable and driving away people who really *did* want to be friendly. Or he could expect the best out of everyone, treat them that way, and enjoy himself. He might not increase his potential lifespan, but it was even odds that he wouldn't shorten it, either. And he just might gain himself a whole lot of allies against the day—like today—when the real enemies he had made or inherited caught up with him.

Some of the Unseleighe had left mage-lights hanging in the air of the corridor and one room beyond. They weren't much—as a whole, the Unseleighe preferred a gloomy twilight—but they helped keep him from stumbling over his own feet. By the time the guards marched him up onto a stone platform in the middle of a very dimly lit room, he had made up his mind to believe Shar, or at least believe that she intended to help him. If half of her heritage came from Chinthliss' enemy Charcoal, still, half of it came from a *kitsune*-woman who was clearly someone Chinthliss still cared for and admired deeply.

Besides, he reminded himself, *evil isn't a genetic trait.*

He and the guards stepped through the archway over the stone platform. The mental and physical jolt that accompanied a Gate-crossing hit him and disoriented him; one of the guards shoved him when he didn't move quickly enough off the new platform, and he sprawled facedown on the ground beyond it. Fortunately, it was soft turf, but he scrambled to his feet quickly before one of them could follow up the shove with a kick in the ribs.

He had expected that he would be marched immediately off into a prison or some other place where he could be locked up, but to his surprise, he found that they were standing beside a huge, naturally flat stone in the middle of a grassy meadow. To either side of them was a row of long, turf-covered mounds. It was twilight here, the perpetual twilight he'd noted in many places Underhill; the "sky" overhead looked like that of an overcast day. His guards moved forward, and he perforce had to move with them. They marched down the row and turned between two of the mounds; there were openings in the middle of these mounds, dark holes with no doors, the sides supported by stones. His escort waited while the rest of the party caught up with them.

While they waited, he tried to remember where he had seen this Madoc Skean before, or had heard the name, and could come up with nothing. Not altogether surprising; there were a lot of Unseleighe, in a vast number of sizes and types, and he'd collected enemies from among many of them just by being Keighvin's friend. Hell, look at Vidal Dhu, for instance; he'd never done a *thing* to that particular Unseleighe lord, but Vidal had sworn to exterminate Keighvin's entire clan, and Tannim stood in the way of that. No doubt Keighvin or Conal could identify this particular Unseleighe lord, and likely tell off at least part of his family tree, but it took one of the elven folk to do that. It was enough to know that he wanted Tannim disposed of, and if Shar hadn't intervened, he'd likely have done the disposing then and there, back in the amber room.

That made him wonder about something else. Shar had said that *she* had brought Tannim Underhill; could she have been responsible for what happened to the Mach One? If so, when had she decided to turn her coat? Or had she been on his side all along, but forced into helping capture him?

His head swam with possibilities, and in the long run, none of them really mattered. What did matter was that she had forced Madoc into keeping him alive and unharmed for a time, and if she could be trusted, before that time was up she would find a way to get him out of here.

Once the entire party had assembled, the guards marched him forward into the mound. Or that was what he thought—but as he passed under the capstone of the arch, he felt that same disorientation of a Gate-crossing as he had before.

And once again he found himself on a stone platform;

this time a simple slab in the middle of the mist of the Unformed areas. They took him through ten or twelve more Gates before they were through, and from the impatience he thought he felt from his captors, he didn't think all this was for the purpose of confusing him. No, they had no choice but to take this route.

Other than very occasional visits to Elfhame Fairgrove, he'd never been Underhill except to visit a couple of the other Seleighe Elfhames and the one ride through the Unformed lands between the Gate Vidal Dhu had established and Elfhame Fairgrove. He'd had no idea that travel around here was so complicated.

And now a new twist entered the picture. If travel was this difficult, it was going to make escaping a stone bitch. Without someone who knew the way from realm to realm and to the human world, he could wander around in here forever.

Finally, after passing through a Gate into a dark and eerie forest, taking a path right out of a horror movie through that forest, they reached a stone platform guarded by more of the faceless warriors. After this last crossing, he found himself at one end of a huge room of black marble that seemed hauntingly familiar. Finally, after a moment, he realized why. He'd seen it, or one just like it, in the cover paintings of sword-and-sorcery barbarian epics.

He almost earned himself a whack on the head right then by laughing out loud. *Creativity.* The elves just didn't have it, and here was a striking example of exactly how much they lacked it. Given the power and resources of one of these Greater Lords, a human would have come up with something at least a *little* original.

The elves simply couldn't; it wasn't in their natures. Everything they had was a copy of something that humans had already done, from the chrome-and-glass Art Deco splendor of Elfhame Fairgrove to the Tolkienesque groves and tree-dwellings of Elfhame Outremer. Elsewhere, he'd been told, there were realms copied from such diverse sources as Italian science fiction movies and King Ludwig of Bavaria's famous palace. It didn't matter if the source was real or fictional. There had never been a "barbarian kingdom" in the history of humanity that would have produced a throne room looking like this; the mythical, fictional character those books purported to describe never existed, nor did his kingdom and palace. But the elves had copied it as faithfully as if it were real.

In fact, this was a much more slavish copy than anything the Seleighe elves ever produced. They generally elaborated, and often improved, on the originals. Apparantly the Unseleighe lacked even that ability.

He wasn't given long to gawk, however; as soon as the rest of the little party had passed through the Gate, it was time to march off again, this time down to a Hollywood nightmare of a dungeon. While part of him tried very hard to seem nonchalant, and another part of him gibbered and groveled in stark panic, a detached third part wondered if they had any idea how to use half of the stuff in here.

Of course they do. It's their specialty, he chided himself. *The one place you can count on an Unseleighe to show some originality is in the ability to hurt someone.*

Beads of sweat trickled down his forehead and neck, making him shiver. *My only hope is that the guy in charge is going to keep his promise to Shar. Oh, please, please, make him keep his promise to Shar.*

Tannim was not a coward, but at that moment he came as close as he had ever come to flinging himself at Madoc Skean's feet and blubbering. He'd had enough injuries to know only too well how it felt to have bones broken, flesh slashed, skin burned. . . .

There was a peculiar contraption hanging in one corner—literally hanging, in fact. It was a cube about four feet on a side, suspended at one corner by a chain; he couldn't decide if it was made of stone or metal. It lacked the sheen of metal, but seemed too heavy to be stone. That same detached part of him wondered what it was; he'd never seen a device quite like it before.

As two of the guards seized him by the arms and dragged him toward it, he realized that he was about to find out just what it was.

One entire side pivoted up on hinges, revealing an interior composed of panels of blunt-pointed, fat spikes, about six inches in diameter at the bottom and three inches tall, set into the walls of the interior so that their sides touched. As he discovered when the two guards grabbed his elbows and heaved him unceremoniously up off his feet and tossed him inside, they were not sharp enough to pierce, but they were certainly sharp enough to bruise. And there was no way to escape them.

They slammed the wall shut on him, leaving him in almost total darkness. Almost—because a little air came in through the top corner, where the chain was strung through a pair of holes. The box was not big enough to stand in or lie down at full length, and the spikes made it impossible to sit comfortably in any position. Despite the ventilation holes, it was stuffy in there. And to add insult to injury, water dripped in steadily from the chain.

Very clever. The "room of little comfort," new improved version. This would certainly not harm him, but it would exhaust him and keep him in a state of constant discomfort, very nicely obeying the exact letter of the promise.

But the situation only made him think faster. *What else would I do if I was one of them? Ah—I'd put a telepath on watch, to see if I was thinking of escape, and glean information.*

He settled himself in a position that was as close to comfort as he was likely to get and waited, listening, both with his ears and his mind. Though no telepath himself, Keighvin had taught him how to recognize the touch of a telepath on his thoughts some time ago.

Interestingly enough, they hadn't taken anything from him, neither his watch nor the contents of his pockets. Granted, some of it, like the pocketknife, could hurt them, but he had no doubt they could find some way around that. Perhaps they meant to show him how contemptuous they were of his abilities. Perhaps they simply assumed, with typical elven arrogance, that there was nothing a mere mortal could do against their magics once they had him in their grasp. The watch alone was a godsend; with it, he knew exactly how much time was passing. After about thirty minutes, he heard the scrape of a chair on stone outside. And a moment later, he felt an insidious little brush against the outside of his mind.

Keighvin had taught him that it took a moment for a telepath to accustom himself to his target's mind, but that once he was inside it, only determined effort would keep him from learning what he wished.

Unless, of course, the target could provide something else to completely distract himself and his eavesdropper. Something as insidious as advertising jingles, for instance.

For the first time since his capture, he grinned. *So. They want to know what I'm thinking about, hmm? Let's see if I can provide them with something . . . completely unexpected. Oh, Yogi, the ranger isn't gonna like this!*

He cleared his throat, took a deep breath—and began to sing.

"I'm your only friend, I'm not your only friend, but I'm a little glowing friend, but really I'm not actually your friend but I am—"

Beat, beat, beat—

The manic grin spread widely over his face as the chair scraped again.

Ladies and gentlemen of the Unseleighe, you are about to be treated to a nonstop concert of They Might Be Giants. Have a nice day.

The thing about the lyrics of a lot of the songs that particular duo came up with was that they were so completely illogical that it required concentration to remember them. You couldn't just infer the next line from the line previous to it. He caroled at the top of his lungs, concentrating *only* on the incredibly infectious melody and the unbelievably bizarre lyrics. *Get that out of your head, not-friend. I sure as hell can't!*

As he began the second verse, and got to the part about "... countless screaming Argonauts," he thought he heard a faint whimper.

As he began his second tune, "She'd like to see you again, slowly twisting in the wind," the whimper was no longer faint.

Just wait until I start on the Apollo 18 album.

He settled back, protecting the back of his head with his hands, and sang with great gusto at the holes in the metal above him.

• CHAPTER SEVEN

Joe stood back in the murky shadows cast by the ruined walls of the barn, where Chinthliss and Fox wouldn't notice him unless they really looked for him, and kept his mouth shut. Fox hadn't been here long—just long enough for Chinthliss to get both their tempers to the boiling point.

When Tannim didn't return, Chinthliss decided to do something—the first thing that apparently came to his mind was the need to interrogate FX. And despite what Tannim had said about not being able to bring FX here, Chinthliss was evidently not bound by any such constraints. A few mumbled words, a clenched fist slapped into a palm—and there was Fox, the photo-image of James Dean, except for his fox-feet and the three tails that lashed furiously behind him, his whole body tense with anger and apprehension.

This was the first argument Joe had ever seen between two mythological creatures; there was no telling in what direction it might explode, or who might get splattered when it did. He decided to stay out of it for the moment, while he let his subconscious work on the problem of getting Tannim back.

Chinthliss had backed the *kitsune* into what was left of the wall beside the door, and he must have done something that made it impossible for FX to disappear, because so far Fox seemed stuck right where Chinthliss wanted him. Surely Fox had made at least one attempt to get away by now, since he certainly looked as if he wanted to be far, far, away from here. Whatever he'd tried, though, it hadn't worked.

"Look," FX said, his eyes widened pleadingly, as Chinthliss loomed over him. Fox spread his hands to either side in entreaty. "What was I supposed to do? I couldn't cross her, I didn't *dare!* I'm a lousy three-tail, she has *nine!* I get in her way, and I end up being called 'Stumpy' for the rest of my short life!"

"You could have told Tannim what she was," Chinthliss growled, looking less human with every passing moment. "You could have called on *me.*"

"How was I to know you knew her?" Fox retorted, tails rigid for a moment.

"You knew she was challenging Tannim; you knew that Tannim is like a son to me. *Of course* I would be interested in anything or anyone challenging him, whether I actually knew the creature or not!" Chinthliss thundered, standing tall and dark against the glow of magic shields. Joe shivered; when Chinthliss talked like that, he sounded powerful. Very powerful. Scary, too.

"You don't understand *kitsune* politics," Fox retorted, dropping his eyes and staring at his furred and clawed feet sullenly. "Hell, that's what got you into trouble with Lady Ako in the first place."

Chinthliss' expression darkened perceptibly, and he seemed to grow a little. Joe decided this might be a good time to intervene.

"None of this is getting Tannim back," he pointed out. "We don't even know where he is. We don't know if he's in trouble or not—"

But FX shook his head and raised his eyes to meet Joe's. "He's in trouble," Fox replied glumly. "When I ducked out, I ran back home to check on the nine-tail who was following Tannim. There was only one unaccounted for; that was Lady Shar, and everyone knows that Lady Shar's been playing footsie with the Unseleighe. And whether or not you can smell it, old man," he added, regaining a little courage to glance insolently at Chinthliss, "this young nose tracked the scent of her all over his Mustang. She's probably the reason it went AWOL in the first place."

Chinthliss' eyes narrowed, and he tensed. For a moment, Joe was afraid that Chinthliss might actually strike the *kitsune*. Or worse. But Chinthliss regained control of himself with an effort after a sidelong glance at Joe.

"Fine," he said acidly. "And if you are so very clever, why don't you find out where he is now?"

"Because I can't," Fox replied, deflating abruptly. Now he looked depressed, and no longer even remotely insolent. "I tried, and I can't. Whoever has him crossed through too many Gates and I lost the scent."

Chinthliss growled and turned away. Fox hung his head and his shoulders drooped. Joe tried to pat him on the back consolingly, but his hand went right through Fox's body.

Funny: Chinthliss could touch him. . . . Never mind. The important thing was to find Tannim.

"Well, we know where the car is," he reasoned out loud. "If Tannim *has* been caught by somebody, that's the first place he'll go, right? And if he's just gotten lost or something, it's still the first place he'll go! Why don't we just wait there for him to show up?"

But Fox only looked panicked at that idea, and Chinthliss shook his head. "This is not like a trip to the mall, young friend," he said, just a little patronizingly. "Tannim will not simply return to where the car is parked. He may decide to abandon it; he may decide that it is wiser to come back after it with a force. He may—be unable to come."

Chinthliss' voice faltered on that last, and Joe's resentment at his patronizing tone faded into worry. "Well, what can we do?" he asked. "Should we go there and see if we can track him or something?"

Fox shook his head fiercely, his eyes wide. "No! Oh, no, no, no! She's been all over that place, and I bet she comes back! That's a very bad idea!"

"But it would be no bad idea to try tracking him from somewhere Underhill," Chinthliss mused. "Magic is more available there, and more reliable as well. We still have the chrome circle to keep track of the Mustang, and we have other things of his to use to find Tannim. Hmm. I believe we could do this."

"If you're going to start messing around with *her*, I'm—" Fox began, as he sidled away from Chinthliss. The latter shot out a hand and caught his jacket collar before he could sneak out of reach.

"You will remain with us to help," Chinthliss rumbled dangerously. "A nine-tailed *kitsune* is not the only creature that can change your name to 'Stumpy.' *I* can change your name to 'Mulch.' It is at least in part your fault that he is missing; you *will* help us to find him. And if you try to slip away, the first item I conjure will be *hedge clippers*. Understand?"

Fox shrank in Chinthliss' grasp, but said nothing and did not struggle.

"Now, the question is, where are we to go?" Chinthliss continued, with FX still dangling from one outstretched arm. "Not a Seleighe Elfhame; the very nature of the place would make it impossible to find him from within one. Besides, we need somewhere less—law-abiding."

"Jamaica?" Fox suggested hopefully. Chinthliss shook him a little, and his teeth rattled.

"Are there neutral places there?" Joe asked. "Like Switzerland?"

Chinthliss nodded. "The trouble is they are most often densely inhabited. There are more creatures that are neither good nor evil than there are creatures of either persuasion."

Joe thought for a moment. "Is that bad?" he asked. "I mean, would it be bad for people to know that Tannim's missing and might be in trouble? Maybe some of them would help us if we came up with the right price. And—well, if the bad guys have got him, how can it hurt to have other bad guys know? Either they're going to know

already, or else they just might be pissed off that somebody else got Tannim first and try and get him for
themselves."

Fox brightened considerably as Chinthliss tightened his
lips and drew his brows together in thought. "We might be
able to spring him while they're fighting over him," Fox
pointed out. "Maybe some of the neutrals would help us
because they owe Tannim a favor. You know how the neutrals are: if the scales ain't balanced, they're not happy. I
know of a real good place to go looking for critters that
might owe him, too. Furhold. News travels faster there
than anywhere else Underhill."

Now Chinthliss smiled, a thin sliver of a smile full of
sardonic irony. "Oh, yes. Indeed it does. Not surprising.
The Furholders have a privileged life, and a rich economy.
They have little else to do but find new ways to entertain
themselves, and invent exotic drinks. Chocolate khumiss,
indeed."

Joe looked from one to the other and back again, and a
strange idea occurred to him. "Is this place—the one you
want to go to—anything like a Mexican border bar?"

Chinthliss' lips twitched with reluctant amusement. "It is
a comparison that has occurred to me, yes," he admitted.

Joe nodded, feeling a little more on secure ground. Not
that he had ever been in a Mexican border bar, but plenty
of the men in the Chosen Ones had, before they were
"saved," and a lot of loose talk went on in the barracks.
The *shapes* might be different, but there would be drunks
and bar girls, pushers and pimps, out-of-town tourists, students looking for a thrill, out-of-work self-styled
mercenaries—and he should be able to recognize each
type for what it was, no matter what shape it wore.

"Let's go," he urged. "I'm not too bad in a fight."

Now Chinthliss let go of FX, turned, and looked at him
sternly. "I did not mean for you to go," he protested. "Tannim would be most displeased."

"No, he wouldn't," Joe lied fluently. "Besides, I bet I'm
a better shot than either of you."

"He can't take a gun across the Gate, can he?" Fox asked, looking interested and eager. His tails twitched with nervous energy.

Chinthliss shrugged. "If a Mustang can cross over into Underhill, I fail to see why a gun should not. The only question is, where can he get a weapon at such short notice?" He tilted his head in Joe's direction and waited for an answer.

Joe grinned. He was in! They were already talking as if his presence was an accepted thing. "I've got one in my baggage, back at Tannim's house," he told them both gleefully. "A .45 M1911A1, GI-issue. And ammo, too. I didn't tell Tannim, but Frank didn't want me unarmed, in case some of the old Chosen Ones might have gotten away the night of the raid. It's not that far a run; I can be there and back in no time. Besides, I'd better leave a note for Mr. and Mrs. Drake, otherwise if we aren't there in the morning, they'll be really worried."

That was something else he'd considered—what if they couldn't bring Tannim home by dawn? His parents would think something bad had happened to him. Well, something bad *had* happened to him, but Joe didn't want the Drakes to know that, and he was certain Tannim didn't, either.

"You don't want me there alone, if we can't get him back soon," Joe continued with warning. "They'll start asking questions I can't answer. But if I leave a note saying that an emergency came up and Mr. Silver from Fairgrove needed us to run up to Kansas City, they'll probably figure we're fine."

Chinthliss sighed and shrugged. "You are an adult by the laws of your land," he admitted. "You are fully capable of making your own decisions. We will wait here for your return."

"And I'll be back before you know it," Joe promised, and turned and vaulted the doorframe into the tall grass. Excitement chilled his skin and gave his feet extra spring as he ran out into the night.

✳ ✳ ✳

Shar did not go straight to Madoc's domain; she was fairly certain that he would keep the exact letter of his pledge. Tannim would be alive, sane, and in relatively good health when she returned. Bruises, hunger, thirst— all were easily cured, all were trivial.

She needed advice, and there was only one completely trustworthy source for that advice.

She returned to her own place and composed a carefully worded message, writing it properly in elegant calligraphy on rice paper, folding it into the shape of a flower, before finally encapsulating it and sending it away with a brief exercise of power.

Then she waited, with folded hands, for her little Gate to activate. If Lady Ako did not appear within an hour, she would take her own chances, unadvised, with Madoc Skean.

She forced herself not to look at her watch. The minutes crept past with agonizing slowness. She kept thinking of all the things that could be going wrong. And what if Tannim had contacted Chinthliss before he came Underhill? What if Chinthliss was looking for him? That was another complication that she had not counted on.

The hour ticked slowly to the end, and she rose, preparing to activate the Gate herself to take her to that relatively neutral point in the Unseleighe lands. She had actually touched it with her power, although she had not yet done anything, when the Gate came alive under her hand.

She disengaged her own magics and backed up a pace. Her mother stepped through the dark haze within the doorway as soon as she had cleared the way.

But this time Lady Ako was *not* the image of the proper *kitsune* lady.

She looked scarcely older than Shar; her long hair had been braided into a single tail in the back, and she wore a spotless white t-shirt and form-fitting black jeans. She raised a perfectly manicured eyebrow at her daughter, and set her hands on her hips.

"I have been making some inquiries among the lesser *kitsune*," she said without preamble. "There is a young fox that you have rattled badly, and I fear that your actions will have effects reaching up to the highest tables."

Shar flushed, although she could not imagine what her mother was talking about. Unless—

"Saski Berith, who calls himself Foxtrot X-ray, is now among the missing," Lady Ako continued. "I believe that he is in the humans' world even now. He is known to have been a friend of Tannim, and he told some of the others that a lady of nine tails was interested in 'one of his friends' in a way that was likely to jeopardize that friend's health. I can only conclude that he sensed you and ran. And, unfortunately, talked. I am probably not the only *kitsune* who has put all the pieces together by this point in time."

Shar flushed more deeply. "I didn't know there was another of our kind about," she confessed. "Actually—to tell the truth, Mother, I didn't think to look."

Lady Ako shook her head. "Draconic carelessness," she chided, none too gently. "It may cost you. There are questions being asked. *Kitsune* of nine tails are not to involve themselves seriously in the lives of mortals unless that mortal is a relative, or unless the *kitsune* is under divine direction, you know that. And when it comes out that the young man was being challenged by you because of your involvement with the Unseleighe—"

Shar hung her head; she couldn't look into her mother's eyes. "I did not think that it would matter."

"Say rather only the first four words of that statement, and you will be closer to the truth, my daughter," Lady Ako said sternly. "And have you brought the mortal to harm by your meddling, or is the situation yet salvageable?"

Shar raised her head slowly. "He is in the hands of Madoc Skean, but will not be harmed until my Challenge is satisfied or revoked," she replied. "That is what I wished to ask your advice upon, Mother." She put pleading into her gaze, but her mother's youthful face did not lose its expression of disapproving judgment.

"You knew what you were doing," Lady Ako replied implacably. "I warned you, and you did not heed the warning. Now there is a mortal Underhill in the hands of his enemies, it is your fault, and it has come to the attention of the clan. This is not a good thing. You will be asked to balance the scales. It would be better for you if you even them yourself, before you are ordered to do so and find you cannot, because the one you should aid is dead."

Shar clenched her jaw in anger. "How?" she demanded. "If I help him, it is only the two of us against all the Unseleighe that Madoc Skean has under his sway!"

Lady Ako shrugged, as if it mattered little to her. "The way of the *kitsune*," her mother said. "Trickery. Guile. Craft. Divide them; make them quarrel amongst themselves. Plant rumors; engineer incidents that make the rumors appear to be the truth. Fling the pebble among the bandits, and see them argue over which of them tossed it. I need not tell you these things; you should know them already."

Shar remained silent, waiting for her mother to answer her real question, the one that had been in her letter.

Lady Ako pulled her braid over her shoulder, and toyed with the end of it for a moment. "As for the rest—it is sufficient that you have placed yourself in a position of obligation to this mortal. Discharge that obligation; get him free. Only then can you proceed in any other directions."

"And if I don't?" Shar asked, with a touch of rebellion.

Her mother did not respond to the tone of her voice, only to the words. "If you *choose* not to, you will be liable to answer to the clan; what will happen then, I cannot say. It will depend on how cleverly you argue your case. You could lose a tail; you could get off with little more than a reprimand. If you try, but cannot aid him, what happens to you will depend on whether the Unseleighe detect your meddling." She shrugged. "If you escape the Unseleighe alive at all, I suspect the clan will judge your attempt enough to balance the scales. You will be lectured, and shamed, but no more than that."

Trust Lady Ako to answer her literally! What she wanted was advice of the heart—which, having given it earlier, Lady Ako would not give a second time.

But she had to admit, her mother was right. Before she could decide what to do *about* Tannim, she must even the scales between them—yes, and confess what her part had been in all of this. If he could not deal with that, well, then there was no point in pursuing a mouse down a hole. All that would happen would be sore paws from trying to dig through granite.

And meanwhile—well, she had an answer of another sort. Her status among the *kitsune* was in danger because of her own actions. If the clan had never come to hear of this, or if that lesser *kitsune* had not been frightened, she might have come through this with an unsullied reputation. Now the least of it would be a blot in her record. How big a blot would depend on how well she managed to set things right. If she managed to not only set things aright, but did so in archetypically *kitsune* manner, spectacularly, she would even gain status from it. *Kitsune* respected style in any form.

She bowed formally to her mother. Lady Ako nodded her head in return. While Shar remained bent over her knees, the lady turned and left, without a farewell.

A bad sign, both for the state of her mother's temper and the temper of the other high-ranking *kitsune*. For a moment, Shar indulged in a fit of resentment.

Didn't she used to be a rebel? Can't she remember what that was like? To have two suitors, to ally with one but bear the child of the other? Isn't that as scandalous as anything I have done?

But her conscience came up with the answer.

It had not involved mortals. It had not changed the lives of humans. Like it or not, human mortals were considered to be beings deserving of pity for their limitations. Ako's had only changed her life—and Ako had no scales to even. That was the difference.

Scandal was one thing. Upsetting the balances was far more serious.

What could she do? She could deal with it. She could follow her mother's advice.

Or she could ignore it all, stay here, and face the consequences.

But her feet were already on a different path than indifference to what she had done to Tannim; they had taken the first steps the moment she asked him to trust her. She was under an even heavier obligation than Lady Ako knew.

So I deal with it. She nodded to herself, faced her Gate, and activated it. *Now—just what kind of pebble can I throw among the feasting bandits, I wonder?*

And despite her mother's real anger and the gravity of the entire situation, she felt herself smiling a true vixen's-grin.

This had the potential to be so much *fun!*

The dripping water turned out to be less of a nuisance than Tannim had thought; it gave him something to drink to ease his throat. At least he wasn't too hoarse yet. His singing voice wasn't too bad even after a couple hours of abuse, though he didn't think there were any recording contracts in his future.

"This is where the party ends, I can't sit here listening to you and your racist friends," he sang, wondering what his enemies were making of all this. Most of the Unseleighe he'd seen with Madoc looked as if they hadn't been out of Underhill since the sixteenth century—the very meaning of many of the words he sang had changed since that time, and some words hadn't existed. They were probably analyzing every little syllable, trying to find some meaning in it. He *knew* he'd heard someone cry out in tones of despair, "The White Eagle I know, but what in the name of the Morrigan is the *Blue Canary?*" The White Eagle was an alchemical term; were they trying to find alchemical formulas in the lyrics? No wonder they were going crazy out there!

He had held the thought firmly in mind since he had begun that he was working on some kind of spell to set him free. Halfway through the lyrics of the *Flood* album, it had occurred to him to concentrate also on the accordion as a vessel of incredibly potent magical power just to confuse the issue even further. So now they were trying to make sense of senseless lyrics and wondering what the heck made an accordion so magical. Would there be a rash of mysterious accordion thefts from pawnshops and music stores all across the USA after this? Had he just inflicted the madness of the accordion upon the Unseleighe?

The horror . . . the horror . . .

In fact, if he hadn't been so damned uncomfortable, this would have been a lot of fun. He was pretty certain he was on his third telepath by now; one had collapsed, and the second had begun moaning and been taken away a few minutes ago.

Mom used to claim my music drove her crazy. I didn't think it would ever be the literal truth.

Since about the third song, they'd stopped giving the cube occasional shoves to set it swinging. He was rather glad of that; one major disadvantage of being so thin was that he didn't have a lot of padding between him and those spikes. He was going to be black and blue by the time they let him out of here.

There was a scrape of chair legs. "No more," a voice said firmly, and the light touch on his mind went away. "I will bear no more of this. And I do not think you will find another to take my place, Madoc Skean. There is no treasure and no revenge worth this madness!"

Tannim grinned wider in the darkness of his prison, and sang lustily, at the top of his lungs: "When you're following an angel doesn't mean you have to throw your body off a building. . . ."

More footsteps retreating, and the muttering of voices. Were they actually giving up?

No point in taking any chances. Better start repeating the most infectious song he knew.

"Throw the crib door wide, let the people crawl inside. Someone in this town wants to burn the playhouse down. They want to stop the ones who want a rock to wind a string around. . . . "

Take that, Madoc Skean!

Shar stepped through the Gate to find Madoc Skean's throne quite empty. The Unseleighe prince was in the center of a huddle of his allies and underlings. Two of them were simply monsters: an ogre, and something Shar suspected was a Greek lamia. There were about a half dozen of the Unseleighe elves, dressed in their ornate brocades and silks, enchanted armor, and elaborate jewels, the evidences of the power of their magic. The rest were retainers, each in the livery of his master's colors. "No more," one was saying, firmly, his face creased with strain. "He tortures us with his conundrums more than we torture him."

At that moment, one of the little hobgoblins that served as lower servants trotted by, singing to itself. The melody was incredibly catchy, but the words—

"They want to stop the ones who want prosthetic foreheads on their heads," the little hunched-over creature crooned happily. "But everybody wants prosthetic foreheads for their real he—"

A tremendous *smack* interrupted the song, as Madoc Skean whirled and slapped the small creature into the wall. "Enough!" he roared into the sudden silence. "Is it not bad enough that the fool mortal carols us with his arrant nonsense? Must I hear it from the basest servants as well?"

The hobgoblin whimpered, picked himself up off the ground, and scampered away.

Madoc turned and saw Shar. He was appallingly easy to

read; she wondered if he had any idea how easy it was. Even if she had not heard him arguing with his putative allies, she would have known from his thundercloud expression that things were not going well for him. These Unseleighe made no effort to control themselves or their emotions.

Throw a pebble among the bandits? Ah—when better than right now?

"I have investigated the vehicle, Lord Madoc," she said smoothly, offering him the title of honor although she seldom accorded it to him. "I have come to some disturbing conclusions. I am not entirely certain that the creature we have now is truly the human Tannim."

Madoc's blank look of shock came very close to making her smile; she repressed it and continued, with the gravest of expressions, pitching her voice so that all the assembled Unseleighe heard it. "There are a great many traces of magery on the vehicle. They are not magics as a human would practice them; they are not Seleighe. I cannot identify them."

That much was the strictest truth; the very best kind of misdirection.

"If I were to hazard a guess, I would say it was not impossible that these traces were from a neutral creature, or even—" she hesitated a moment, then continued "—even an Unseleighe. I do not think it would be going too far to warn you that this thing we have taken prisoner might be a shape-shifter, or a changeling. It might even have been sent as a kind of expendable assassin by one of your enemies. For that matter, Lord Madoc, *you* might not even be its target; it might have been intended for one of the other lords and ladies here."

She nodded at the gathered Unseleighe, who were eavesdropping without shame, their sharp features betraying their alarm at this unwelcome news. "It could be that one of your allies is the real target, and whoever sent this creature intended the blame for the death to fall upon you, Lord Madoc."

The ploy was working! Already the other Unseleighe edged slightly away from each other, casting glances of suspicion at one another and at Madoc. Lovely! Now if she could just make Tannim vanish from his place of captivity. . . .

Wait a moment—

"Perhaps we had best see if your prisoner is still there, Lord Madoc," she continued earnestly, wondering if he had noticed by now that she had called him "lord" no less than three times now. That was more honorifics than she normally accorded him in the course of a week! "If this creature is a shape-shifter, he may already have escaped. If he is more powerful than we realized, he could have vanished without you ever knowing."

One of the others laughed scornfully. "Escaped? How? When we have heard him a-singing like a foolish jongleur this past hour and more?"

She leveled a glance at the speaker, an ogre, in a way that made him snap his mouth shut on his laughter. "And how better to make you think that you had him still than to leave a voice singing there? It need not even require magic! Did this creature not *come* from the human world? Have none of you heard of the mechanical wonders the humans build? Did any of you think to search it for one of those human devices by which words and music may be captured and replayed? Why, such things are made that are no larger than this!" She measured out the size of the palm of her hand. "It could easily have concealed such a thing in its clothing! And there are spells enough to accomplish the same thing. Am I to understand that you are no longer keeping a mind-reader a-watching of his thoughts?"

At Madoc's reluctant nod, she shook her head, as if she was impatient with all of them. "The moment this creature knew that its thoughts were no longer subject to scrutiny, he could have made his escape. Any shapechanger could become a snake, and slip through holes. A vampire could become a mist or a fog and do the same. A changeling—

who knows what it could become at the will of the one
who sent it?"

"This is all speculation," snapped one poisonously lovely
woman, a pale blond in an Elizabethan gown of deep
green brocade with a huge ruff of silver lace about her
long neck. "Let us go and see whether he is the mortal we
wanted or no! If not, and if it has escaped somehow, we
must recapture it and discover what it wants. And if so,
well, this *lady* wishes to discharge her Challenge, and the
sooner this is done, the sooner we may deal with the
mortal."

Whatever Madoc wanted was moot at this point; the
rest of his allies clamored for an immediate visit to his
dungeons. Shar simply looked grave, and let them carry
her along with them.

And while they were arguing about it all, she exercised
just the tiniest bit of her powers in a spell of illusion.

The entire group pushed and shoved through the doors,
still arguing. Shar brought up the rear, confident of what
would happen and wanting to be out of the way when it
did.

"Sir!" one of Madoc's guards called out over the noise.
"The mortal seems to be repeating his songs now. I
thought that it might be a ruse to make us open his prison;
I restrained Lord Liam's liegeman from breaking the
seal."

"Yes, my Lord Liam, *he* kept me from the performance
of my duty!" another guard called out resentfully. Shar
raised an eyebrow in surprise at the number of guards
crowding the room. It looked as if every one of Madoc's
allies had insisted on having his own guard here.

Good. That meant they trusted each other even less
than she had thought. She reached into a pocket while
they were looking at each other and palmed the first thing
she touched that would serve for her next ruse; a cheap
pocket-calculator she had broken and shoved into a
pocket, then all but forgotten.

"Open it now!" Madoc ordered, waving peremptorily at

the guard. This was not one of the faceless creatures Madoc generally favored, although Shar would have preferred one of those to this monster. It wasn't so much the single eye that bothered her as the very pink skin that glistened around it. The creature bowed and propped his pike up against the wall, then turned to the suspended cube and broke the seal on it. Then he swung the side up—to reveal an empty interior.

The singing stopped in mid-phrase.

The heavy side slipped from his fingers as he gawked in startlement and slammed it back into place. Another guard quickly pulled the side back up, though everyone here had already seen that the cube was completely empty, just as Shar had predicted. She reached out herself and "plucked" the calculator from the interior with a neat bit of sleight-of-hand palming.

"Look!" she said, waving it aloft. "What did I tell you? Here is the device the mortal used to trick you into thinking he was singing in there! Now he has fled, and who knows where he might be?"

She flung the calculator down at Madoc's feet. No one here would recognize it for what it was; they'd have to take her word for it. Since it was already broken, they could play with it forever and not get it to "work." And just as she expected, pandemonium erupted as one of Madoc's servants hastily scooped the device up.

Accusations flew for a moment, most of them leveled at Madoc, who had gathered his bodyguard around him and was backing up toward the door. Shar prudently got out of his way; it was never a good idea to be between an Unseleighe and his exit. But after a moment, the accusations and counter-accusations became general. Each of the Unseleighe gathered his underlings to him (or her), and followed Madoc Skean's example, backing toward the exit while screaming imprecations at everyone else. Shar's suggestion that Tannim might be an assassin had fallen on fertile ground; none of them were willing to risk the chance of being the target of that assassin.

There were some tense moments as the several parties collided at the door; those who had more retainers with them intimidated those who had fewer. Madoc, with the most, was the first out and heading toward some place where he might barricade himself into relative safety. The ogre was next, followed by the beautiful Unseleighe elven lady. The rest sorted themselves out, glaring at each other in mingled fear and accusation, until they all got out into the freedom of the hall. Then they headed elsewhere. Where, Shar did not particularly care, so long as they left her in sole guardianship of this room for a few moments.

When she was certain that the last of the Unseleighe were gone, she swung up the unlocked side of the cube and banished the illusion of the empty interior. Tannim sat there for a moment, arms wrapped around his legs, chin resting on his knees, regarding her with a wry expression and the hint of a tired smile.

"I'd love to know how you managed that," he said finally. "I figured I was about to become Spam when I heard all the voices out there. And when they all stared at me instead of grabbing me, I couldn't figure out what was wrong. That *was* your doing, wasn't it?"

"Yes," she replied. "But unless you've grown fond of that thing, I suggest we might find someplace else to have a discussion about what just happened. They could be back any moment."

Tannim took the hint and scrambled out of the cube in a way that suggested to Shar that he had probably acquired a few bruises in there. He brushed himself off as he straightened up, and gave her a look that clearly said, "Now what?" But wisely, he kept silent; she had to give him a lot of points for that.

She simply gestured to him to follow. The less talking they did, the better; there were spells that could reach back in time to see what had happened in a particular area, and if there was no dialogue to *tell* the spellcaster what they planned to do, following them out of this room would be a matter of hit-or-miss.

Tannim seemed ready enough to trust her; or at least, he was going to trust her until he had a chance to strike out on his own, or *she* explained herself sufficiently to him.

Well, as long as they were in this palace, he would be very stupid to try and strike out on his own, and she hoped he had the good sense to realize just that.

There was noise enough in the direction of the audience chamber; she had a fair notion that at least two or three of Madoc's former allies were fighting their way to the Gate there. Madoc's men, in absence of any other orders, had probably assumed that the "allies" had become "enemies" and were trying to keep them from the Gate. The Faceless Ones assumed nothing, and there was no telling what they were doing. Madoc might have told them to oppose anyone who tried to leave, he might have told them nothing at all. In the latter case, the Faceless Ones would let anyone who was already on the approved list to go through the Gate as they wished.

She hoped that was the case; their own escape depended on it. The Gate in the audience chamber was always guarded, but the Gate she intended to use would very likely be as well.

There was no point in putting a dungeon underground when you were already Underhill; the reason for having a prison beneath the earth was to prevent easy escape. Well, there was no such thing as an "easy" escape for someone in Unseleighe lands and Unseleighe hands. Even if you made an escape, you were forced between one of two choices. You could take your chances on whatever Gate you might find unguarded, or you could take your chances in the Unformed. You might run into a solid wall out there; you might not. One's sense of direction went all to pieces, and people had wandered in small circles until they dropped without ever reaching a barrier or the place they had left. You might discover that the "land" you had escaped and the Unformed surrounding it comprised an area of less than one hundred acres. You might discover it was the size of a small continent—or, as in Shar's case, the size of a generous townhouse with attached garage.

Just to make matters even more entertaining, you might or might not find a physical opening into another realm or domain. Shar knew where a few of those were, but no one knew them all. Few cared to trust their safety to the Unformed to explore the possibilities. The mist was strange stuff; very sensitive to magic and to even the thoughts of those within it. Your fears, if you dwelled upon them for too long, could become reality. . . .

Well, just at the moment, Shar had no intentions of dashing off into the dangerous mist outside the walls of Madoc Skean's realm. She had a better plan.

As soon as they penetrated beyond the prison section, she made a sharp right, away from the black-marble corridors lit with torches in gold-chased sconces, and into a hallway built of some dull gray stuff that could not even be identified. Two lefts and a right later, and they were deep into the maze of passageways that only the servants used.

There weren't too many of those about; the noise of fighting, shouts, and the occasional clash of metal-on-metal penetrated even here and warned all but the very dullest that it was not wise to be abroad just now. Only the occasional hobgoblin skipped by, humming to itself, oblivious to everything except the last task it had been given.

The corridors remained the same: gray walls, floor, and ceiling made of something that might even have been taken for plastic elsewhere. Maybe it was, anyway. Out of sight of anyone to impress, Madoc might well have eschewed tradition for sheer practicality. Plastic was one of the easier substances to *ken* and reproduce, after all.

There was no mistaking the light source, however. Dim witchlights bobbed at intervals near the ceiling. Madoc was not one to waste energy on creating comfort or convenience for the sake of mere servants; there was *just* enough light to keep from falling on your nose, and no more.

No matter. Shar already knew where she was going and

could have felt her way in the dark, if need be. Madoc might not know it, but she had prowled the halls of his domain in several shapes until she knew it better than he did. She had been a hobgoblin, an Unseleighe elven lady, even one of his very own Faceless Ones. And wouldn't he have been surprised to know what she had seen in *that* form!

It was not the brightest of moves, to invite a shape-changer to be your guest. . . .

Two rights, a left, and a smell that just bordered between savory and unsavory wafted down the hall, telling her that she was nearing her goal. Tannim followed—flowed, actually; for a mortal, he was surprisingly graceful. A little knife in his hand told her that he was not as guileless as he looked; she wondered where he'd hidden it. A leg sheath, perhaps?

She motioned him to wait as they neared the door to the kitchen. She straightened and concentrated for a moment, shutting her eyes as she shifted her form.

When she opened them, she was quite a bit shorter, and her neck strained from the odd angle she was forced to hold her head at. Never mind; she wouldn't have this form for long. She glanced back at Tannim and grinned a little at the dumbfounded expression on his face.

Well, it probably wasn't every day he watched a "human" woman shift into a hunchbacked female troll.

Now, if luck is on my side this little while more, every servant in the Hall will have fled to places of safety while their betters are squabbling.

She shuffled into the kitchen door as if she had every right to be there—which in this servant-form, she theoretically did. The strange mix of smells nauseated her for a moment until she dimmed that particular sense down to something bearable. Some of Madoc's allies and servants ate perfectly palatable foods. But then there were creatures like that ogre—

Best not think about what might be floating in the soup kettle on the hearth. Not all the bodies from midnight gang fights on the streets of big cities ended up in the hands of the coroner. Not all the old winos who vanished in the night were ever accounted for.

Enough; her guess was correct: the kitchen was empty. The work tables were clean, since the evening meal was long since over, but the soapy water and pottery shards on the floor and the heaps of soiled dishes showed that cleanup had not been completed when the servants learned of their masters' quarrels. They might be routed out and sent back to work, but not within the next hour.

She shifted back to her preferred form and waved Tannim in, then headed to the doorway on the opposite side of the room. If it had been gloomy in the hallway, it was positively dark in the kitchen, and hot as Hades. All the light came from the fires in the two fireplaces, and both put out enough heat to melt lead on the hearthstones.

She wrestled with the bar across the door for a moment, then it came free; she lifted it and pulled the latch, slipping out into the eternal dusk outside. Tannim followed, and stood looking cautiously around as she closed the door behind them.

They were in what would have been the kitchen garden in the manor-house that this hall had been copied from. Here Underhill, in Unseleighe lands, where there was no reason to grow things for a purpose, this was simply a rank and weed-filled annex to the main garden. Black vines covered with decaying leaves clung to the walls, their branches infesting the brickwork. Where plots of herbs and vegetables would have been, spiky, gray weeds and limp, dispirited grasses attempted to choke the life out of each other. Trees reached clawlike branches against the deep gray sky beyond the weedy plots, marking the edge of the "pleasure gardens."

But Shar's interest lay here, not out there. Food for Madoc, his guests, and the horde of servants had to come from somewhere, and it was not from anywhere within his realm. Instead, there was a Gate out here, a Gate set to a neutral area where Madoc's servants could obtain the needed foodstuffs. It would probably be a fairly unpleasant place to visit, but Shar didn't intend to be there for long.

She signaled Tannim to follow her, and across the garden to the wooden platform and arched roof that marked this Gate position. Somewhat to her surprise, it was *not* guarded; a dropped spear proved that the goblin that usually guarded this Gate had deserted his post. Beside the platform were burlap bags full of garbage, and it occurred to her then that the Gate could be as useful for disposing of kitchen refuse as it was bringing the raw material in. For a moment she toyed with trying that setting—

No, I think not. I don't believe I want to visit an Unseleighe garbage dump.

Not so much because it was a garbage dump as because such a place would be a fine place for scavengers. Unseleighe scavengers were generally not things you wanted to meet under any circumstances.

Unless, of course, you happened to be toting an AK-47.

In her guise as a kitchen servant, she had been once to the "market," and she had noted then how the Unseleighe seneschal had set the Gate. She triggered the spell herself this time, and the crude wooden arch filled with a dark haze. She motioned to Tannim to enter; he bowed mockingly and shook his head.

"After you, lady," he said quietly. So, he didn't trust her? Well, she couldn't exactly blame him.

She walked right through the Gate, ignoring the brief internal jarring as she crossed the boundary between *here* and *there*. A moment later, Tannim joined her, and she banished the Gate quickly, before anyone in Madoc's hall could stumble into the garden and notice that it had been activated.

After the relative silence of the garden, the noise here left her a little numb. The stench of the place could only be compared to a cross between a feedlot and a garbage dump. Fortunately, the merchants here were too busy trying to sell their wares to pay any attention to a couple of human types standing beside the Gate platform looking stunned.

"Come on," Shar said, nodding her head at the Gate. "We aren't going to be here long. I can reset this thing to a place that's a little friendlier." She saw that he was staring at the rows of meat merchants and added, "You really don't want to know what they're selling. Trust me."

He was already about as pale as a human could get; he swallowed hard and nodded. "Ah—by the way, I don't suppose we could get to my car from here, could we?"

She considered the question for a moment; his suggestion had a lot of merit. She already knew the Mach One had some very complex spells worked into its fabric, and there was every reason to think that he might be using it as a kind of magical storage battery as well. It might prove very useful.

"Not directly," she said after a moment. "Why?"

"Because it has a lot of protections on it," he replied with open honesty. "Other things, too. It's Cold Iron; lots of things down here can't cope with it. We're already in trouble; couldn't we really use a safe haven, a rolling base of operations?"

She nodded, and not at all reluctantly. "It's going to take us about a dozen Gates to get there, but yes, I can get us there from here eventually."

Tannim looked over his shoulder at the marketplace and shuddered. "How about if we start now—before someone out there needs to replace his inventory?"

One of the meat merchants, a boggle, had noticed them, and his eyes narrowed with speculation. Granted, a lot of the Unseleighe had human servants, or rather, slaves—but such slaves usually didn't loiter anywhere. They didn't dare.

"Good idea," she said shortly, and turned to reset the Gate to one of its other destinations.

Anyplace with fresh air. . . .

• CHAPTER EIGHT

Tannim slid into the driver's seat of his beloved Mustang, shut the door, and simply leaned back in the familiar surroundings. He had never been quite as happy to see any material object as he'd been to see his Mustang still waiting there in the middle of the amber room. The journey to reach it had been a harrowing one in terms of all the strange and menacing slices of Underhill they'd had to traverse. He was still astonished at Shar's ability to pick her way across all of those Gates. She must have an incredible memory. . . .

But they made it, and without any opposition to speak of. For the first time since he'd come Underhill, he felt relatively safe. There was Cold Iron between him and any enemies now, and lots of it. There were spells of protection and defense built into the very sheet metal. He had reserves of magical energy stored here as well; energies that he badly needed.

And his magic-imbued crowbar, his weapon of choice in any confrontation with the Unseleighe, was right under the seat where he could grab it.

The other door opened and closed as Shar slipped into the passenger's side and shut the door as soon as she was seated. He noted that she *locked* it, too, and did the same on his side. She fumbled for a moment with the controls on her seat before getting the hang of it and sliding it back as far as it would go.

Shar. Now, there was a mystery wrapped in an enigma: half-*kitsune*, half-dragon, all perplexing—

And one I'd better figure out before she turns around and stabs me in the back.

Chinthliss himself hadn't known where she stood but had assumed she was not on the side of truth, justice, and apple pie. Tannim had been so happy to see her, though, back in that Rubik's Prison, that he hadn't given a thought to what Chinthliss had said about her. Or, frankly, a fat damn about her motives in cracking him out of there. Her motives didn't matter, as long as she was getting him free. If she was leading him into another and different trap, well, maybe it would be easier to escape or talk his way out of than the last. The important thing was that he was buying a little more time, and in an uncertain universe, every moment counted. It gave him a little more opportunity to think things through. Something unexpected might happen.

So far, so good.

"All right, we made it. Now what? Aren't Madoc and his Merry Men going to come straight here as soon as they get over fighting with each other?" he asked, opening his eyes and blinking them wearily. How long had he gone without rest? Long enough; his eyes felt puffy and swollen, very heavy.

He looked over at Shar's lovely profile; she smiled a little and shook her head. "No," she said with a ghost of a chuckle. "No, I put a lot of masking spells on your car to deaden the effect of so much Cold Iron here—then I told them that I'd moved it to a safer place. Madoc won't go anywhere in person if he has the choice. The spells work like that silk sheet we put in the trunk; your Mach One is insulated from the energies Underhill now—which means that they are not going to be able to detect it by its effect on the world around it. They have absolutely no reason to think I left it here. I don't believe any of the Unseleighe Madoc's got know these masking spells are even possible, so they're going to take me at my word if they don't see

Death-Metal effects here. And scrying is so costly in terms of time and energy that I don't think they'll make the attempt. They'd have to have something of yours, mine, or the vehicle's for scrying to find it anyway. We can actually afford to get a little rest, then be on our way."

"How?" he asked skeptically. "Drive out of here?"

To his surprise, she nodded. "This place was meant for creatures larger than this vehicle; the doors and hallways will all accomodate it, and this room is on the ground floor. We can drive it out into the garden; there is a Gate there as well as the one in here. We will have to take our chances on *where* it goes, though; the only setting that I know of would land us in a fairly unpleasant and unfriendly place. I can see how many other settings there are, and you can pick one, and we'll hope it takes us somewhere familiar."

He nodded. She turned to him then, pulling her hair away from her face and looking at him rather wistfully. "I don't suppose you have anything in the way of food in here, do you? I'm awfully hungry. I *could* get something from the garden, but I'd rather not leave the car, frankly. This is about the first time I've felt safe outside of my— my own place."

He lifted an eyebrow at her, quite well aware of gnawing hunger in his own innards. "You mean our gracious host didn't offer you dinner?"

She made a little face. "You saw the kitchen; you saw what was in it. Would you eat anything prepared there?"

He had to grin, just a little, and reached behind the seat. "Here—" he said, handing her one of the high-energy sports-bars he kept back there. "I fool my body into thinking this is food all the time. It's not exactly cordon bleu, but it'll keep you going." He looked back around the side of the seat. "I've got crackers and Spraycheeze back there too, if you'd rather."

"This will be fine," she responded, unwrapping the bar and nibbling on it.

There were dented drink-boxes of Gatorade back

behind the seat as well; he fished out a pair and handed her one. She nibbled at the bar daintily, but not as if she disliked the taste. He wondered what a *kitsune* normally ate; not sushi, surely. Somehow she didn't seem to be the sushi type.

He made short work of his own share and reclined the seat to its fullest. After sitting in that cube for hours, the car seat felt as luxurious as a featherbed. He was going to have to get some sleep; this seemed to be the safest place for it.

But worries swarmed through his mind, preventing any relaxation. How long, real-time, had he been Underhill? Time often moved very differently here; by the chronology of his own world, he could have been down here a few minutes, or a few months. His folks would be frantic—

I hope somebody thought of a story to tell them.

Chinthliss had obviously lost the link to the Mustang; *he* might be able to reach back to the human world with a Gate, but only at the price of expending everything he had and leaving himself open to any attacker.

That might be just what Shar was waiting for, in fact. Just because she'd been chummy with him so far today, that didn't mean she was on his side. She could be waiting to catch him in a moment of vulnerability.

Yeah, like asleep in this car.

But he didn't want to think about that. He didn't even want to consider it. He wanted to hear that she had somehow seen what her former allies really were like and had rejected them.

I want to find out that she's turned into a good guy, darn it. I want—hell, might as well admit it. I want her to be the girl in my dreams.

Well, there was another objection to opening up a Gate on his own. He was no Chinthliss; he would need quite a bit of time to establish that Gate, and such a huge expenditure of power would signal his presence as effectively as a Las Vegas–style neon sign.

Yeah. "Good Eats Here." Bad. Very bad.

So how was he going to get home again? Drive cross-Underhill? What was *that* going to do to the Mustang? He could create small planes of force, like magical ramps, all day long. They weren't too tough to make. He could even create those from inside the car, while it was in motion, so that should take care of stairs, lumps, and small ravines.

And where in heck are the gas stations down here, anyway?

Where did Shar figure into all this? What *was* she all about? Was she friend, foe, or neither?

"So," he said carefully, staring through the windshield at the throne at the other end of the room. "Why don't you start with some explanations? Like, how come you're suddenly my friend?"

She stiffened a little, then wrapped both hands around her drink-box, propping it on her knee. "You know who I am," she stated. "Who my father is." Her voice was completely neutral, and he nodded just as neutrally.

"Your name is Shar, your father is a dragon named Charcoal. He is an enemy of my mentor, Chinthliss, and an ally of the Unseleighe." He waited for her response; it was a curt nod. "I'm assuming you are, or were, an ally of the Unseleighe yourself. Your mother is a *kitsune*; Charcoal and Chinthliss both courted her, and Chinthliss won her, temporarily at least. That's basically all I know."

"My blood-father is a manipulative control freak," Shar replied bitterly. "I was raised supposedly as *your* opposite number. I was supposed to be everything you are not. Fortunately, Mother made certain that Charcoal wasn't the only creature with a hand in my upbringing. I parted company with him some time ago; our parting was less than friendly and he has forgiven neither Mother nor myself."

She glanced at him to see how he was taking this; he kept his expression neutral, but nodded.

"Unfortunately I was taught by Unseleighe and spent a lot of time in several of their domains. I began severing as many ties with his old allies as I deemed feasible, but—

much as it galls me to admit this—there were some I didn't dare cut off completely. If I had, they would have been mortally offended." She bit her lip, and looked at her hands.

"And offending an Unseleighe prince can have very permanent results," Tannim commented. He could understand that; heck, he lived it. "They hate everybody, and it's only when they want something out of you that you can trust them within limited bounds. It's just a good thing that there are rules even they don't dare break."

"Exactly." She blinked rapidly, and rubbed her eyes. "I was still *supposed* to be your opposite; I went on studying you, partly because it didn't do any harm, and partly because if Father wanted me to be your opposite, I wanted to see what I was supposed to be the opposite of. You posed something of a challenge, actually, trying to come up with things I could do to match your skills. I've been watching you, on and off, for years. Since you were in high school, in fact."

She'd been studying him? For *years?* He couldn't conceal his shock and surprise—and it was that shock that made him blurt out what he would not otherwise have revealed. "Did you dream about me the way I—"

She brought her head up like a startled deer and stared directly into his eyes, her pupils wide with shock and surprise. "You dreamed about *me?* When?"

Good one, Tannim. You really stepped on your dick that time. Well, it was too late now; might as well fess up. "At least once a month, sometimes as often as every other night, for years. Since Chinthliss first came across to my side of the Hill, anyway." He couldn't help himself; he felt his ears turning hot as he flushed. Would she guess just what some of those dreams had been about?

But she averted her eyes, and pink crept over her cheeks. "I—dreamed too, about you. I thought it was just because I was studying you."

Quick, get the subject back on track before you really stick your foot in your mouth. Don't ask what she dreamed about! "Right," he said more harshly than he intended. "So—*now* what? How do you figure into this mess? Besides challenging me, I mean; I suppose that was on this Madoc Skean's orders. Why'd you get me out of that prison?"

"I caused it," she said in a very small voice. Her blush deepened to a painful crimson, and she stared fixedly at her clenched hands crushing her empty drink-box. "It's my fault you're Underhill in the first place. I was the one who brought your car here."

So that's why—! Damn it—

"I didn't expect you to follow it so fast!" she continued, an edge of desperation in her voice, as she finally turned to meet his accusing gaze. "I was—oh, I was under pressure from Madoc Skean. I didn't know what to do, I mean, I really got a rush out of challenging you, but he kept pushing for me to—"

"To get rid of me," he supplied, flatly. "So?"

"So I was trying to buy time for both of us! I couldn't risk a direct confrontation with Madoc Skean, I didn't want to actually consummate the challenge, and I was trying to buy us both time!" Her hands tightened on the drink-box. "I thought—I thought you'd follow the car in a few days at best, and by then, I'd have some idea of how to put Madoc off further, or I'd have managed to create a rift among his other allies, or you'd have gotten in touch with your Seleighe friends. And I had no idea this car was going to make such a huge disturbance when it came across!" The muscles of her throat looked tight, and there was a line of strain between her brows. "Madoc had a lot of ideas; he thought that without the Mach One you might choose something other than 'racing' as your weapon. And in case you decided to go chasing after it, he expected to use the car as bait in a trap, and I was the only one that could bring it Underhill for him. My plan was to keep the fact that I actually had it hidden from Madoc until I could talk to you. . . . "

Her voice faltered and died, and she licked her lips

unhappily. But she did not avert her gaze, and she seemed sincere. He looked into her eyes and saw no falsehood there.

Could he believe her?

Ah, hell, why not?

"Okay," he said into the thick, leaden silence. "Okay, I'll accept that. Now, why are you helping me?"

She dropped her eyes for a moment, then looked up again, with a spark of defiance in her expression. "Because I got you into this," she said. "The scales have to be balanced before we decide on anything else; that's *kitsune* law and custom. I got you into this, but now I've gotten you out of this. You have to release me from that debt."

But he shook his head slightly. She was not going to get off the hook that easily. *He* was still Underhill, and so was the Mach One; springing him from Madoc Skean's little reception didn't even things out. "Sorry," he told her. "I can't do that. I'm not *out of this* yet, I'm only out of Madoc's clutches, and that may just be temporarily. I can't release you from your debt until I'm back in my world, and my car, too."

She flinched, but she nodded; she obviously saw the justice of his demand. Her cheeks were so pale that he longed to touch her and reassure her.

He wanted to do more than just touch her, if it came down to that. Unbidden dream-memories told him of any number of ways this could go—

But this wasn't a dream. He couldn't make that kind of assumption.

He tore his gaze away from hers and stared out the windshield again, trying to calm the chaos of his mind and heart.

He just wasn't certain how to act—did he behave as if she was a stranger, or as if she really *was* the person he had dreamed about? This was as confusing as all hell; it felt as if he *knew* her, as if he had known her intimately for years! It was all those damned dreams, where she'd figured as his lover. They'd had a solid feeling, a reality to them, that made the current situation positively schizoid. He didn't *know* her in any sense; they'd never met before she'd nailed that glove to his Mustang. Yet at the same time, all the little things she did, the tiny quirks of behavior, the ways she reacted, the bits of body language, were all exactly the way he "remembered."

"I hate to ask you what your dreams were about, if they were anything like mine," she whispered across his confusion.

"If you knew," he replied, trying desperately to make a joke about it, "you'd slap me into next week."

"Oh, I don't know about that," she said, which was exactly what he would have expected her to say if this was a dream, and not at all what he had rationally expected to hear. He looked over at her in startlement to find her smiling wanly at him. "After all, I am half-*kitsune*. We have a certain reputation; one that's been known to attract even dragons."

His body reacted in a predictable manner before his mind took over and gathered up all the reins firmly. *This isn't the time or the place,* he told his galloping libido firmly. *We're surrounded by potential enemies, we're exhausted—and on top of that, the front seat of a '69 Mustang is absolutely impossible. These are bucket seats. The backseat is practically nonexistent. You'd have to be a contortionist.*

"Trust me," he said firmly. "You'd smack me so hard I'd lose teeth."

He closed his eyes for a moment—just for a few seconds—

It was long enough; she struck as swiftly as a cobra. Before he could open them again, she'd writhed around in her seat, leaning over the center console, and planted her mouth firmly on his. One hand snuck around behind the back of his head, holding him so he couldn't jerk away.

Not that he wanted to!

Without the use of anything as confusing as words, she was letting him know that her dreams had probably been along the same lines as his own. And in no uncertain terms, she was telling him that she had enjoyed those dreams.

When she'd succeeded in setting every nerve afire and causing a complete meltdown of his brain, she let him go, returning to her seat with a teasing smile on her lips. "I don't think I would smack you, if those dreams were like mine—unless you asked nicely," was all she said.

"I—guess not." He blinked and tried to make his frontal lobes function again, after having the blood supply to his brain rush off elsewhere. Should he follow up on this?

If I do, I could get into more trouble than I can handle right now. If I don't, it could still be trouble, but not as complicated.

"This isn't a—a good time to get into anything—ah—distracting," he ventured. "We aren't really *safe* here, just safer for the moment than a lot of other places." He hoped she understood; the lover who had shared more than just his bed would have.

"You don't like it dangerous?" she purred.

"No, and you wouldn't, either."

She nodded; reluctantly, he thought, but in agreement. "Damn. You're right. I'm not happy about it, though." She smiled weakly. "I shouldn't have done that, but I couldn't resist. Let's just call that a—a promissory note, a raincheck, until a better time."

Jeez, some raincheck! Makes me want to call Fighting Eagle for a thunder-dance! He yawned, exaggerating it a little. "Look, Shar, I'm not capable of thinking or much of anything at the moment. I am beat, and I need some rest badly. Can you stay awake long enough for me to catch a couple of hours of sleep? Once I can think straight, we can make some plans, but right now, I wouldn't want to make any kind of decisions. I'm two burritos short of a combination plate when I'm this tired."

She nodded, and to his relief, she did not seem put out by the fact that he didn't follow through on her tacit invitation. *But the Shar I know—knew—think I know would understand.* "Get some rest, then," she said with surprising gentleness. "I'll keep watch."

Could he trust her?

Did it matter?

Not really. If he couldn't trust her, he was already doomed, and he might as well get some sleep. And if he *could* trust her—

—he might as well get some sleep.

"Thanks, Shar," he said, and smiled. He reached out and squeezed her hand. "Thanks a lot. It's nice to have somebody watching at my back in this."

Her reaction—blinking as if such a thing had never occurred to her—made him wonder about her past. Living with the Unseleighe would only teach you that there could be no such thing as a partner. But someone or something had to teach her that it was possible.

Has she ever had someone she could depend on? Her mother, maybe.

"I can see that it would be," she replied wistfully. Then she shook her head and became her usual, confident self. "You get that sleep; I probably need a lot less than you do, anyway. When you wake again, we'll make some plans."

"Right." He smiled again, and closed his eyes firmly. Having her so close was such a temptation—

Go to sleep, Tannim. And—jeez, if you can help it, don't dream about Shar.

Joe padded up to the old barn a little more than two hours after he'd left it, sweating, but not even close to being winded. It had felt good to run full-out like that, with the cool night air all around him and the drone of cicadas coming from all directions. When he was doing something like running, he didn't have to think so much about things. Like how all of this was more than a little crazy.

He'd let himself into the Drake's house and had left a note propped on the kitchen table, explaining pretty much what he'd suggested to Chinthliss. Kansas City was far enough away that the Drakes would not expect to hear anything for at least a couple of days, especially since this was supposed to be an emergency. And if they weren't back with Tannim in a couple of days, then things really would have gone seriously wrong.

To lend credence to the note, Joe had rummaged through Tannim's room and his own, making it look as if some things, but not all, had been taken. Then he had gotten what he'd come for from its hiding place up inside the boxsprings of his bed. A .45 automatic, basically the same handgun as the military surplus he'd trained with. Pity that it wasn't an M-16 or some other fully automatic assault rifle, but—well, it wasn't supposed to have been a bullet-hose for all-out attacks but something to defend himself from one or more of the Chosen Ones until the real law showed up. He had to keep reminding himself that he was *supposed* to be a civilian now. Most civvies didn't even have *this* much firepower, when it came right down to it. They saw guys like Dirty Harry in the movies, and that was about the extent of their gun knowledge.

Which was why, of course, whenever one of them *did* get scared over something and get himself a weapon, the people who usually got hurt or killed by it were people in his own family. Frank had once remarked that for a bunch of paranoid nut cases, the Chosen Ones had the best gun-safety classes he'd ever heard of. Joe had not only taken those classes, he'd taught them to the Junior Guard.

He had strapped on the shoulder holster, and slung extra pouches of ammo on their web-belts around his waist. They were heavy, but you never knew. . . . Better take all he had; there probably weren't any gun shops where he was going.

He was used to running with full pack and kit; this had been nothing, really, no kind of weight at all. He had let himself out of the house, moving so quietly he didn't even make the floor creak, and took off back the way he had come.

i

He was halfway afraid that Chinthliss had used his aquiescence as a ruse, or had changed his mind, and that when he got back to the barn he would find the other two gone. Then what would he do?

Call Keighvin at Fairgrove, he supposed, and let him know what had happened. And hope that he didn't let anything slip to Mr. and Mrs. Drake when they asked him where their son was.

But the glow of heavy shields over the barn told him that Chinthliss and Fox were still there, and as he ran back up the track through the tall grass, intermittent flashes of bright white light beneath the golden glow indicated that they were up to something. None of this was visible if he did that little mental trick and turned what Tannim had called his "mage-sight" off. This other kind of sight—it was so strange, seeing colored glows around people, and the occasional figure that he knew wasn't "really" there for the rest of the world. It had started when he'd seen Sarah for the first time, and thanks to the training Bob and Al had given him, it was getting stronger all the time. Every time he used it, he saw more. Was this how everyone at Fairgrove saw the world, bathed in extra colors and populated by more creatures than anyone else knew existed? Or was this something only a few people could do?

Well, he'd find all that out later, if he made it through this.

If.

He had to think of it in those terms. He had no illusions that this was going to be some romp through Wonderland; Fox was terrified, and even though Chinthliss tried to seem glib about the situation, Tannim's mentor was worried. There was danger here, much more real than the "danger" his father had prophesied.

He was about to get into something he hadn't really wanted to deal with, and something he wasn't really prepared for. Magic. What the hell did he know about magic, really? Not much when push came to shove. Not enough to use it as a weapon, probably not enough to put up an adequate defense of his own.

But Tannim, in the short time that Joe had known him, had become a "big brother," just as Jamie was his "little brother." Not a blood relationship, but one that went far deeper than blood and bone and genes. Tannim was family. You stood by your family. When they were in trouble, you helped them.

Fox stood beside the gap in the wall that had once been the doorway, his tails swishing nervously. Joe trotted up. The tall grass resisted him a little and caught on his jeans. Chinthliss stood in the center of the barn, as Tannim had stood not that long ago. He didn't *seem* to be doing anything, but Joe knew better than to assume that nothing was going on.

"What's up?" he whispered to Fox, wiping the sweat off his forehead with the back of his arm.

"He's building a Gate," Fox whispered back. "The whole thing; all the Gates where we want to go are booked up and unless we build our own, we can't get there from here. I gave him all the *oomph* I had to spare, so now he's channeling in everything he can get from outside. It's not that easy, building a Gate in your world; magic runs thinner here. We're just lucky that it hasn't been tapped around here much."

Just as he finished that last sentence, Chinthliss exclaimed in satisfaction, and a tiny glowing dot appeared in the air in front of him, at just about eye-level. Chinthliss cupped his hands before him, catching the spark for a moment so that his hands glowed and the bones showed through the translucent flesh. Then Chinthliss slowly spread his hands wide; the dot became a glowing ring, which grew as he spread his hands, until it was a circle of light taller than he and broader than his outstretched arms. A dark haze filled it, a haze you couldn't see through, and which made Joe shiver for reasons he didn't quite understand.

"You've come exactly in time, Joe," Chinthliss said

without turning around. "We are ready, now. You and I, that is," he amended. "Fox can journey there without the need of a Gate; one of the advantages of being a spirit-form."

"Right. See you at the bandstand?" Fox replied, and vanished without waiting for an answer.

"Will he really be there?" Joe said a bit dubiously, for all that Fox was his old "friend" from childhood. Even his memories painted Fox as something less than reliable and inclined to tricks.

"He'll be there," Chinthliss replied grimly. "If he's not, well, he knows that *I* will be looking for him when all this is over. Being called 'Stumpy' will be the least of his problems."

Joe stepped across the threshold of the barn to join Chinthliss in front of the circle of light. "So what do we do?" he asked bravely, putting the best face he could on all this. "I—I'm afraid I don't know a lot about this kind of thing."

Chinthliss looked down at him, and the dark eyes changed from hard and purposeful to warm and kindly, all in a single moment. "We simply step across," he told Joe. "There will be a moment of disorientation, then you will find yourself in the place we wish to go to. And you are doing very well, young man. You are bearing up under some very strange experiences, and doing so with more composure than many with more years than you."

Joe looked up into those odd, oriental eyes, saw or sensed *far* more years than he had dreamed, and swallowed. "I don't supppose you have any advice before we do this, do you?"

Chinthliss shook his head. "Nothing that would help. Are you ready?"

Joe took a very deep breath, allowed himself to be *conscious* for a moment of the weight in his shoulder holster, and remembered with a flush of pride how good a marksman he was. Heck, he wasn't too bad at hand-to-hand, either. Chinthliss had obviously included him in this party because of that expertise. If he simply kept his eyes, ears, and mind open, obeyed his orders, and behaved in a professional manner, everything should be all right, no matter how strange the external circumstances became.

"I'm ready, sir," he said, proud of the fact that his voice did not break or quaver, and that he stood tall, straight, and confidently. "You first, or me?"

In answer, Chinthliss gestured at the circle of light. Joe repressed a shiver when he remembered how Tannim had stepped into an identical circle and vanished. . . .

He took a convulsive grip on his belt and stepped through; his skin tingled all over, as if he'd grasped a live wire, his eyes blurred, the world swirled and spun around him, and he gasped as his stomach lurched, exactly as if he'd gone into free-fall for a moment. He flexed his knees involuntarily.

Then with a shock, he went from night into full day, and his feet landed on soft turf. Since his knees were already flexed to take the strain, he only staggered a little to catch his balance. As he straightened, he saw that he stood in the center of what looked like a city park, with a white bandstand or gazebo in the middle. By the bright light, it had to be just about noon, and where they'd come from, it was around two in the morning.

Overhead, he heard someone whistling.

He looked up in startlement to see a cartoon sun in the middle of a flat, blue sky, staring down at him jovially. You could look right *at* it without even blinking; lemon-yellow, it had round, fat cheeks, blue eyes, a wide mouth, and a fringe of pointed petal-like rays. It smiled at him as soon as it saw he was looking at it, winked broadly, and waved at him with one of the petals.

Stunned, he waved back automatically. It grinned, and went back to whistling and bobbing a little in time to the song—a *real* song—that was also being whistled by a vivid blue and red bird perched on the top of the gazebo. Puffy, flat-looking marshmallow clouds sat in the sky with the sun, a sky that was an unshaded, turquoise blue, without any variation from horizon to horizon. The emerald grass under his feet was more like carpet than grass, and did not crush down under his weight. There was no breeze, yet the air smelled fresh and clean. In fact, it smelled exactly like freshly washed sheets.

They also weren't alone. The other creatures were not very near, and they didn't seem to care that a Gate had been opened in the park, although many noticed. There were otters and foxes, though none of the foxes looked like FX. There was a massive cobalt-blue unicorn, and a centaur with a black, d'Artagnan beard. They were having a picnic with what could only be called a foxtaur, and a small golden-colored dragon, and an oddly hunched, very large bird. A white unicorn mare chased playfully after a humanoid, black-horned unicorn wearing black leather and spikes, howling taunts. And overhead, a red-and-umber gryphon with broad coppery wings glided in to join the rest.

He turned as a crackling, sizzling sound beside him startled him again. There was nothing there for a second—then a familiar arm clad in Armani-tailored silk phased into existence, as if the owner was pushing his way through an invisible barrier, exactly like an expensive special effect. The rest of Chinthliss followed shortly as Joe watched in utter fascination. He seemed to arrive suspended a few inches above the plush green lawn and dropped as soon as all of him was "there."

Chinthliss landed with flexed knees, just as Joe had. He straightened, looked around, and nodded with satisfaction.

"Good," he said. "At least we made *our* transition safely. Now, where is Fox?"

"Right here." Fox strolled up from behind them, although Joe could have sworn that there hadn't been anyone there a moment earlier. He was in the fox-footed, three-tailed James Dean form, the one with the red leather jacket. "Now where?"

"One moment." Chinthliss glanced at Joe. "Young man, would you please grasp our friend?"

Joe didn't understand what Chinthliss was trying to prove—he couldn't touch Fox, he already knew that—but he shrugged, reached out, and made a grab for Fox's arm.

And with a shock, realized that he was holding a very solid, completely real, red-leather clad arm.

"What—" he said, startled. "How—but—"

Fox looked at Chinthliss in irritation.

"So what were you trying to prove?" he growled. "You *know* I'm real here!"

"That's what I was trying to prove," Chinthliss said with ironic satisfaction. "That you were not playing any of your *kitsune* tricks with me and projecting a spirit-form here as well, rather than risking your real self. Thank you, Joe."

"You're welcome," Joe responded automatically, dropping his hold on Fox's arm and backing up a step. He hadn't expected that. If Fox was real here—was that cartoon sun up above real as well?

He didn't want to think about it.

But then he suddenly realized that he really didn't *have* to think about it. His part in this mission was very simple. He didn't have to try and figure out what was real and what wasn't; all he really had to do was keep a lookout for trouble and hit it or shoot it if it got too close. And if it turned out that all this was just one big hallucination, well, no problem. He'd wake up from this dream, or in the looney bin, and pick up his life where he'd left off. Right?

Yeah. Sure.

"I think our first logical destination would be the Drunk Tank," Chinthliss continued, unperturbed. "All news comes there, sooner or later—and if any of Tannim's friends are here, that is where they will go."

Fox sighed with resignation, but shrugged. "Suit yourself," he replied. "You know this place as well as I do, and you know Tannim's friends better than I do."

"Are you going to build a Gate again?" Joe asked nervously. He hadn't liked the sensations of crossing into this place, and he wasn't certain that he wanted a repetition of the experience quite so soon.

"Build a Gate?" Chinthliss said. "Here? Good heavens, no."

"Then how are we going to get to this place?" Joe asked, more than a little confused now, since there didn't seem to *be* anything here except lush grass, a few fairly normal-looking trees, some benches, the gazebo, and the cartoon sky. Literally; the sky appeared to intersect with the ground no more than a few hundred yards away on all sides.

"How?" Chinthliss said, and whistled loudly, waving an arm.

And a fat taxi, bright yellow with black checks, shaped rather like an overgrown VW Bug, pulled up beside them. Joe blinked; he *knew* that thing hadn't been anywhere near them a moment ago, yet there it was!

A creature like a mannish badger leaned out the window. "Hiya folks!" the thing growled. "Where to?"

"The Drunk Tank," FX told it blandly.

"This is how," Chinthliss said to Joe, opening up the door and gesturing for him and Fox to enter. "We take a taxi, of course. It's too far to walk."

"Of course," Joe echoed in a daze, climbing into the rear seat. "A taxi. Of course."

"Well what else would we use?" Chinthliss retorted, as he wedged himself inside as well, with Fox squeezed between them making Warner Brothers cartoon faces. "A dragon?"

The taxi accelerated toward the flat blue sky, which looked more and more like a wall as they drew nearer. Joe closed his eyes and gripped the seat—they were going to hit! He waited for the impact, his teeth clenched tightly.

But a second later, the taxi screeched to a halt. "Here we are, folks!" came the cheerful voice from the front. "Thanks for riding with me! See you soon!"

The door popped open on its own, and Joe stepped cautiously out onto the pavement.

Real pavement. Real, cracked cement.

The sky above them was dark here, with a haze of light-pollution above the buildings. This looked like any street in any bar-district in any big city he'd ever been in. The street was asphalt, the sidewalk and curb were chipped and eroded concrete with cracks in it, but there were no cigarette butts and other trash scattered around. Dirty brick buildings on both sides of the street stood four or five stories tall, with darkened storefronts on the ground floor, and lighted or darkened windows that might lead into offices or apartments in the stories above. The taxi had pulled up in front of another brick building with a neon sign in a small window, set into a wood panel where a much larger window had once been. The sign flashed *The Drunk Tank* twice in red, then flashed a green neon caricature of a tipsy tank with a dripping turret the third time. To the right of the building was a parking lot; to the left, a vacant lot with a fence around it. The lot was about half full of the kind of "beater" cars most people of modest means drove in a big city. They were just about in the middle of the block, which seemed to be pretty much deserted. A couple of cars and a panel-truck were parked on the other side of the street, in front of a black-and-silver sign which read *Dusty's Furley-Davidson*. Below it was what could only be an authentic Springer Softail. With a warning sticker.

The cartoonish taxi did not belong here, but the driver didn't seem to care. It waited until Chinthliss got out, then buzzed off down the street.

Fox still had his fox-feet, but he'd lost the tails somewhere. Chinthliss still looked entirely human.

"Do bullets work here?" Joe whispered to FX as Chinthliss led the way to the red-painted door.

"Oh, yeah," Fox replied, a little grimly. "Yeah, bullets work just fine. You're not in some kind of cartoon, no matter what it looks like. The last bunch of city planners were animation buffs and made the sky and all look like this, but this is real. This may look weird to you right now, but bullets work, knives work, crossbows and darts work, getting hit hurts a *lot*, and dead is very, very dead. No second chance, no resurrection, no magic spell to bring you back. Keep that in mind if trouble starts."

Joe gulped. "Right."

Fox followed on Chinthliss' heels into the bar; Joe followed on Fox's.

Inside, the bar looked a lot bigger than it had from the outside. A lot nicer, too—kind of like one of those fancy nightclubs in movies about the Roaring Twenties and the Depression. They stood in a waiting room at the top of a series of descending tiers that held two- or four-person tables. Each table was spread with a spotless white tablecloth, centered with flowers and a candle-lamp. Wall-sconces made of geometric shapes of black metal and mirrors fastened invisibly to the white walls held brilliant white lights. To Joe's left was a check-room with a hat-check girl and the hostess' stand; beyond those was a curving balcony looking out over the tables, with a few doors leading off of it. To his right was the bar, which curved along the wall behind the top tier of tables as one immaculate, unbelievably precise arc of mahogany. Everything else was done in shiny black, chrome, and glass. At the bottom of the tiers was a dance floor with a geometric pattern in black and white marble laid out on it—and somehow lit from below—and behind that a glossy black stage large enough for a complete big-band orchestra. From the stands pushed to one side and the classic grand piano, it often held such a band, but right now there was a combo composed of a keyboard-player, a drummer with a full electronic rig, a guy with an impressive synth-set, and a female vocalist. They were covering "Silk Pajamas" by Thomas Dolby, and those in the crowd who were actually listening seemed to be enjoying it. And singing along.

But Joe had to do another reality check when he looked the crowd over.

Around about half the folks here were human; plenty of them were wearing outfits that would have had them barred at the door in the real world. Said "clothing" ranged everywhere from full military kit to as close to nothing as personal modesty would allow. In the case of some people, that pretty much meant clothing-as-jewelry—or, as Frank had once put it, "gownless evening straps." Joe tried not to stare at the blonde girl in the G-string, fishnets, diamond-choker, and heels; she was centerfold-perfect—and her brawny, saturnine escort could have picked him up with one hand and broken him over his knee without breaking a sweat. *He* was done up in what looked like medieval chainmail, the real thing. The sword slung along his back was certainly real looking.

Fortunately, both of them were too busy watching the stage and the dancers on the dance floor to notice his stares or his blushes.

The rest of the patrons—including most of those on the dance floor—were definitely *not* any more human than the creatures he'd seen in the park. The couple drawing the most attention at the moment was a pair of bipedal cat-creatures, one Siamese, the other a vivid red lynx, who were showing off their dance steps. But sharing the floor with them was a female with green hair and wearing what appeared to be a dress made of leaves who was dancing alone, a couple of elves, two fox couples, a pine marten dancing with a large monitor lizard, and a pair of beautiful young sloe-eyed men, dark and graceful, with the hindquarters and horn-buds of young goats, who were dancing together in a sensuous way that made Joe blush as badly as the blonde girl had.

He averted his eyes and fixed them firmly on Chinthliss' back. The dragon was speaking to the hostess—who seemed to have a wonderful personality, if you didn't mind the fact that otherwise she was a dog. She nodded, and wagged the tail that barely showed below her Erté dress. Chinthliss made his own way towards the bar. Joe and Fox followed him.

Chinthliss ordered "yuppie water"; Fox, with a defiant glance at Chinthliss, ordered a rum-and-Coke. Joe waved the bartender away. First of all, he had no idea how he was going to pay for a drink, or in what currency—and secondly, it was a bad idea to have your hands busy with something else if a situation came up.

Chinthliss scanned the crowd, then turned back to the bartender as the man (Arabic-looking, but with pointed ears) brought him his drink and Fox's. "So, Mahmut, have you heard or seen anything of Tannim?" the dragon asked casually, as he pushed what appeared to be a coin made of gold across to the bartender. The being slid it expertly out of sight, as he pretended to polish the bar with a soft cloth. "Not recently, Chinthliss," Mahmut replied, rubbing industriously at a very shiny spot. "Why? Are you looking for him? He *never* comes here anymore; in fact, as far as I know, he never goes out of the Seleighe Elfhames these days, if he leaves America at all."

Chinthliss sighed, and sipped the bubbling water. The band finished its number to the applause of the dancers and some of the people at the tables. The lights came down, and a pair of women, one very, very pale and in a long, white, high-collared dress, and one with long blond hair right down to the floor, wearing what appeared to be a dress made of glittering green fish scales, took the stage. The one in white sat down at the piano; the blonde took the microphone. A spotlight centered on the blonde, who lowered her eyelids for a moment and smiled sweetly.

The bartender tapped Joe on the shoulder; he jumped. When he turned to see what the man wanted, the fellow was holding out a pair of earplugs.

"You single?" the man asked. Joe flushed, and nodded. "You wouldn't be a virgin, by any chance, would you?" the bartender persisted, this time in a whisper.

This time Joe flushed so badly that he felt as if he was on fire.

"Thought so." The bartender nodded. "You'd better wear these if you don't want to end up following Lorelie around like a lost puppy for the rest of your short life." He held out the earplugs. Joe looked at Fox and Chinthliss, who both nodded.

"We're protected. I wouldn't worry so much about Lorelie, but her friend has appetites you wouldn't want to satisfy," Fox said solemnly. "Lamias are like that."

"Th—them?" Joe stammered.

"Yeah, them," Fox said. "Think of them as the Cocteau Twins gone horribly wrong. The L&L Music Factory, embalming optional."

Lamias? Lorelie? Something about both those names rang a dim and distant bell in his mind, but he couldn't put a finger on what they meant. Still, if not only this bartender but Chinthliss and Fox thought he ought to put in those earplugs—well, maybe he'd better.

He took them gingerly and inserted them. And he discovered, rather to his surprise, that even with them in his ears he could hear perfectly well, if a little distantly.

There were waitresses circulating among the tables, he saw now, and they were handing out more earplugs. But oddly enough, only to the men—or rather, male creatures. The two young men with the goats' legs laughed and waved them away, as did one or two others, including the pine marten and the lizard, but most of the men took them and fitted them into their ears.

Interesting.

The pale girl at the piano began singing as soon as the last of the earplug-girls retired; Joe recognized the song as "Stormy Weather," and after a few bars, Lorelie began to sing.

She had a low, throaty voice, rather than the bell-like and pure tones Joe had half expected; there was no doubt, though, that in *his* world she'd have a lot of people offering her record contracts. Especially with that face and figure behind the voice. But he couldn't help but wonder what all the fuss was about—and why the earplugs?

Oh, well. When in Rome . . .

He turned his attention back to Chinthliss and the bartender.

" . . . and we think he might have bitten off more than he can chew," Chinthliss was saying, as Mahmut listened attentively. "Look, I know you're on the Seleighe side of the fence, so to speak, at least most of the time. You know some of the kid's friends. If any of them show up here, can you pass that information on for me?"

Mahmut nodded gravely. "For a dog of an infidel, that one is a good boy," he replied. "For me, he arranged a lager distributor from America. He has done several of my friends a service or two in the past. For a chance to even the scales, I think that they would do much."

"What kind *is* his kind?" Joe whispered to Fox. FX shrugged and muttered something that sounded like "gin," although that couldn't possibly be right. It was probably the earplugs. Joe made a move to take them out; Fox grabbed his hand to prevent him—

Just as someone entered the bar, stared at the singer below, and stopped dead in his tracks, as if transfixed.

It was a young man; one with branching antlers rising from his head, but otherwise quite normal-looking. As Joe paused with his hand on the plug in his ear, the newcomer shook his head violently, turned a deathly white, and made a kind of odd moaning noise.

His eyes glazed over, and he stumbled down the stairs between the tiers of tables, ignoring everything and everyone in his path. He staggered across the dance floor towards Lorelie, who ignored his presence completely, and dropped down at her feet in a crouch, gazing up at her with the adoration of a saint at the feet of the Almighty.

If Joe hadn't chanced to look in her direction, he might never have seen the piano player's reaction. If Lorelie was indifferent to her worshipper, the pale girl was *not*.

She stared at the young man with such pure, naked hunger that the word "hunger" simply did not describe the expression she wore. He might have been a thick, juicy steak, and she suffering starvation. Then she licked her lips and smiled.

Her teeth were all pointed, like a shark's.

"Poor kid," the bartender said distantly. "She got

another one." And somehow Joe knew what he meant. Lorelie might have snared the man, but her accompanist was going to devour him somehow. Not just figuratively, either.

Joe rounded on the bartender, suddenly suffused with anger. "So why aren't you doing anything about it?" he hissed, one hand on the Colt. "Why do you let her sing here?"

Mahmut's eyes narrowed dangerously, but his voice remained calm and even. "Look, kid, we have placards in the lobby announcing that Lorelie's singing in here. The hat-check girl would have offered him earplugs. The hostess would have offered him earplugs. How much more do you want us to do? Shove the plugs in his ears? This is a neutral realm; Lorelie's free to sing, we're free to hire her, and he's free to ignore the warnings. Who knows? Maybe he was suicidal. You may not like it, son, but you're not in Kansas anymore, either."

This is a neutral realm. Maybe he was suicidal. They know he's going to die, and no one is going to help him.

Joe felt cold all over. He looked at Mahmut's flat black eyes; looked back down at the bandstand, at Lorelie, at her admirer, at the piano player. He shivered, and briefly considered the ramifications of running down there and trying to save that poor guy—

Then he caught Fox's eyes. The *kitsune* shook his head slowly. He remembered all of Fox's warnings, shuddered, and turned away.

Mahmut spoke to him again. "Sometimes we get people doing that because there are a lot of ways to drain a man. Those two know most of them. I have been told that many are pleasurable and leave the man more alive than before. Some think the risk is worth it for the experience. The young buck there isn't likely to die—and he might enjoy it."

He *still* might have tried to think of some way of getting Lorelie's victim free, but he never got the chance.

At that moment, one of the waitresses (a delicate

creature like a winged lizard with veil-like wings sprouting from her shoulder blades) came over and tapped Chinthliss on the arm. "Sir," she said, "the lady over there would like you and your friends to join her in the Blue Room."

Chinthliss shook his head impatiently, as the young creature pointed. "I do not have time—" he began, looking in the direction she indicated.

Then he stopped speaking, frozen with shock that even Joe could read. And beside him, Fox went as white as the girl at the piano.

Joe turned to see what they were looking at.

On the other side of the room, behind the last tier of tables where the bar was on this side, there were several doors that presumably led to private dining rooms. There was someone standing in front of one of those doors.

She wore the kimono and elaborate hairstyle of a traditional Japanese woman—Joe could only think "geisha," since he had no idea who else wore the kimonos with the long, trailing sleeves, or the hair pierced through with so many jeweled pins that her head looked like a pincushion. But although the body beneath the gown was that of a human woman, the face was that of a fox.

And behind her, fanned out like the glory of the peacock, was an array of fox tails that clearly belonged to her.

"Oh, shit," FX said weakly. "It's—it's—"

Chinthliss cleared his throat with difficulty.

"Tell the Lady Ako," he managed, after several tries, "that we would be honored to join her."

• CHAPTER NINE

Shar watched Tannim out of the corner of her eye, hoping it wasn't obvious that she was watching him. If he felt her gaze resting on him, he probably wouldn't be able to sleep; he'd assume she was waiting for him to fall asleep so that she could do something unpleasant to him.

Well, she wouldn't *mind* doing something to him, but it wouldn't be unpleasant. If she had gotten his hormones dancing with that kiss, she'd sent her own into orbit. There hadn't been anyone who'd had that effect on her for a long, long time.

At least she knew one thing, now. She knew he'd had the same kind of erotic dreams of her that she'd had of him. The way he'd responded to her impulsive kiss had left no doubt in her mind of that. Enthusiasm under the surprise—and a great deal of heat under the control. He would feel *so good*. . . .

But Shar knew he was also not going to presume on those dreams. He didn't trust her yet and she couldn't blame him. But there was another thing: he didn't assume that her personality was anything like the person he'd dreamed about. He didn't know anything at all about her, and he acknowledged that. *I knew he was a cautious and clever man,* she mused as his breathing deepened, and he began to relax minutely. *This is just one more example of that. I have the advantage here; I know that the lover in my dreams is virtually identical in personality to the real*

man—or at least, as much of the real man as I have been
able to observe over the years.

And yet, even though he didn't trust *her* yet, it seemed
to her that he was willing to give her the benefit of the
doubt; he was apparently willing to give her the time to
prove to him by her actions that she could be trusted.

She sighed quietly. If that kiss was anything to go by,
he was just as talented and considerate as the dream-
lover had been. A far cry from the Unseleighe, or the
relatively shallow and skittish *kitsune* males. Those were
the only creatures of male gender she'd spent any time
with; she'd avoided human males simply out of disinter-
est. And if Charcoal and Chinthliss were examples of
dragonkind—

*They're either manipulative, selfish bastards who'll run
over the top of anything and anyone to get what they
want, or they're fast-talking, charming rogues who'd
rather lose everything they have than make a commitment.*

Bitter? Oh, a tad.

Tannim sighed and nestled down a little further into his
seat. Was he truly asleep? She shifted slightly, touched the
door handle and made it rattle just a little. He didn't stir;
his eyelids didn't even flicker. There were dark shadows
under his eyes, shadows that spoke eloquently of just how
exhausted he'd been. In sleep, he looked frighteningly
frail, and now she realized just how much of his appearance of strength depended on his personality.

Well, now what? They couldn't stay here forever; they
probably shouldn't stay here longer than it took Tannim to
catch up on some rest and recover a bit. So, how to get
out of here?

There was the Gate in the garden; that was probably
their best bet. As she had pointed out, there would be no
difficulty in simply driving the Mustang out into the hall
and out the door into the garden. The Katschei had used
that particular Gate to get into the mortal world to steal
his collection of princesses, but there were five more

settings on it. They'd have to take their chances, but at least she *would* recognize a potentially dangerous setting for a destination she had encountered before. That would keep them out of Unseleighe domains, even if it did dump them off into unknown territory. If they kept traversing Gates, sooner or later she'd find her way back into a place she knew.

A pity that the Katschei hadn't left at least one setting empty; she could have used that to Gate somewhere friendly. Or at least, to somewhere neutral.

I would be very happy with neutral, she decided. *Particularly neutral and familiar. Most neutrals can be bought, and usually remain bought. In neutral territory I might be able to buy some help, or a way out of Underhill.*

Tannim slept very quietly; barely breathing, it seemed, head turned slightly into the seat that cradled him, one hand curled up beside his face. She touched his hair hesitantly. *So soft,* she thought with wonder, as she pulled her hand back before it betrayed her by turning the touch into a caress.

There was nothing impulsive about the strength of her reaction to him; in a way, it was inevitable, given how long she had studied him. If he had not interested her, she would have given up on her studies a long time ago, and none of this would be happening now. If he had not attracted her as well as interested her—

I probably would have done exactly what Madoc Skean wanted me to. I'd have gotten rid of him a long time ago.

And if she had not met him in her dreams? Difficult to say. She'd enjoyed her little glimpses into his life. She found him in some ways completely alien to her. Perhaps that was part of the root of her attraction; she couldn't predict him, and her *kitsune* heritage would always be intrigued by anything she didn't understand and couldn't predict. Just as she would always be repelled by something that bored her.

Tannim was anything but boring. . . .

On the other hand, Madoc Skean was *quite* predictable,

and she ought to be trying to predict what *his* next move would be, not hovering over Tannim like some lovesick nymph.

She sat back in her own seat, reclining it to match Tannim's, but turned her gaze outward, staring at the wall. Madoc had fled the dungeon with his own guards, and probably went straight to the isolated wing of the keep that contained his own quarters. Paranoid as any Unseleighe, he would not live in a place where he could not defend against all comers.

But as his allies fought their way to his Gate and left, and nothing whatsoever happened, he would collect his courage and his few functioning brain cells. What conclusions would he come to?

The most obvious would be that Tannim—or Tannim's impersonator—was somewhere in his stronghold still. But he had means to discover if that was true, and he would put those means in motion as soon as he knew his people had cleared the entire holding of potential troublemakers.

Sooner or later, he would learn that there his fears were completely groundless. He would learn that Tannim was not in his dungeon, nor anywhere else in his own domain. Then what?

Well, his allies had all deserted him. Even if he decided to first go after them, it would take a great deal of coaxing to bring most of his allies back. It would be possible to chase after Tannim without them, but Madoc Skean was a cautious sort, and he always preferred to operate from a position of strength. He really had two options at this point: try to mend the mess that had been made of his alliances and then pursue Tannim, or go after Tannim without any help.

She could hope that he would pursue his allies; she must plan that he would pursue Tannim. She would *have* to assume that Madoc would figure out that she was with Tannim, given that she had been there when they all discovered he'd "vanished."

Madoc would waste some time trying to figure out where she had gone in order to escape his stronghold. Sooner or later, he would narrow the possibilities to the Gate in the courtyard. Then he had six possible destinations; eventually he would find the Gate that led here, but unless he had a way to trace her movements, every succeeding Gate they took would lead to no less than three and as many as six more possibilities. So it was safe to assume that they had time enough for Tannim to get some sleep.

But after that—they should assume that Madoc could be no less than a single Gate behind them. Tannim and Shar could even have the misfortune to Gate into the same place at the same time as *they* tried to find them.

So who or what is Madoc going to have with him? Probably all of the Faceless Ones; they were the most faithful of his fighters. Madoc's own ego tolerated no better mage than himself among his followers, and she was better than they were. Madoc himself would be the one to watch out for, magically. Unseleighe got to the top of the "food chain" by cutthroat competition. Literally cutthroat, sometimes. She didn't know exactly how powerful he was, and she didn't want to find out by going head-to-head with him.

The trouble was, it was going to take a lot of work to find a way out of Unseleighe domains. Gates generally connected like with like; out of every three Gates, the odds were that only one of them would have a connection to neutral lands, and then only a single connection out of the six possible. Their best hope was that the places those Gates *did* go to would be empty and unused, deserted like this one, or only a transfer point.

The best thing will be to keep moving, she decided. *The more we can muddle the trail, even by simply moving at random, the better off we will be.*

So—given that they had no choice but to use the Gate in the Katschei's garden, where was it *likely* that the settings on that one went?

No love lost between him and Baba Yaga; I doubt he had one set there. In fact, he didn't have any alliances with any of the other Russian myth-figures, not even the neutrals. He did have an arrangement with some of the Chinese demons though. . . . No, that would not be a good idea. The yush *eat human souls and use the bodies. I'd be safe enough, but if they all ganged up on Tannim, they might be able to take him before we got out. He had a private hunting preserve that would probably not be a healthy place to go, either.*

She rubbed one finger behind her ear as she tried to recall the rest of his historical alliances. *Something from India . . . oh, no, I remember now! He had something going with the* rakshasha! *That would be a very, very bad place to end up!*

The only remotely safe places she could think of were with other national equivalents to the Unseleighe and certain minor Unseleighe folk: ogres, trolls, and the like. Most of those folk were a great deal like the major lords Madoc Skean had courted; they had shut themselves off from the human world a long time ago, and the sight of the Iron Chariot that was Tannim's Mustang, moving through their realms and causing no end of damage in the process, could be enough to frighten them into panic. Certainly they would be confused and wary enough to leave the two of them alone while they studied the situation. She and Tannim should have time to find another Gate or another setting on the one they had just used and get out before anyone mustered up enough courage to oppose them. The only awkward part was that she would have to physically get out of the vehicle in order to read the Gate and reset it; that created a time of great vulnerability. Ah well, it couldn't be helped.

Once they found such Gates, they could only hope that the creatures there did not decide to find Madoc Skean and tell him where they had gone.

Damn. We'll be moving; it won't be possible to keep those special shields on the Mustang for long. We'll show up just by the disruption we cause. The more magic there is in a domain, the more disruption will take place.

No help for it; while she could not tell from in here just how much magic Tannim had infused into this vehicle, there was no doubt that it represented a major undertaking. Protections were layered on protection; and was that an energy reserve? It could be. They would be much safer in the Mach One than without it.

So it'll be a lot like taking a cross-country trip in a tank. Maybe we'll leave a swath behind us, but most of what people shoot at us should bounce off.

She massaged the back of her neck with the ends of her fingers. *I got myself into this,* she reminded herself. *I have to get myself out of it. There were a hundred things I could have done to prevent all this, including simply taking shelter with Mother when Madoc Skean demanded I help him. I was so sure that I could stall Madoc and have a good time doing it—and I just didn't want to hide behind my* kitsune *kin.*

No point in pretending that if she hadn't done what she'd done, Tannim would still be in trouble from some other ally of Madoc's. Whether or not that was true, it was irrelevant. *She* had made her decisions, *she* had put her steps on *this* path, obliterating all other possibilities. Now she was the one who must deal with it all.

And she had never felt quite so alone and uncertain before. Or quite so vulnerable.

Joe followed in Chinthliss' wake, walking just behind FX, as the dragon moved slowly toward the fox-lady on the other side of the balcony. Fox had sprouted all of his tails again, but they trailed dispiritedly on the ground behind him, telegraphing major submission. And as they neared the door which presumably led to the private room that Lady Ako had reserved, past a very attractive and very large female bat, Fox's clothing was mutating as well.

By the time they actually reached the door, the red leather jacket had become a short, wrapped red jacket along the lines of a karate *gi,* and the jeans had become some other kind of loose blue pants. Both looked like silk to Joe; both were very rich and shiny. Chinthliss' silk suit was impressive enough without turning it into anything else. Joe wished *he* had Fox's talent; he felt terribly under-dressed in his fatigue pants and white t-shirt.

Well, maybe if he pretended as if he was Chinthliss' bodyguard, he wouldn't look as conspicuous as he felt. No one ever expected a bodyguard to be dressed in any kind of fancy outfits, after all. They only wore tuxes in the mov-ies, right? The rest of the time a bodyguard surely dressed comfortably. They weren't there to provide scenery but protection, right?

Whatever.

He kept his eyes on Chinthliss' silk-clad back as they reached the doorway, resisting the urge to stare at Lady Ako. Her head wasn't precisely like a fox; the lips were more mobile, he thought; the muzzle blunter. Her eyes were lovely, large, and exactly the same color as melted chocolate. Her hands were entirely human, but like Fox, she had fox-feet. Then there were all those tails. . . .

He tried to tell himself that she wasn't any different than those cat-creatures down on the dance floor. She certainly was not at all cartoonlike. Her wide brown eyes rested briefly on him as he passed; she blinked, and he got the oddest feeling that it was with surprise at his presence.

Now why should someone like her be surprised at him?

Then again . . . he hadn't seen too many *humans* down here, only people that looked human from a distance. If he'd gotten closer, who knows what he would have seen? Scales, fangs, more tails? His kind might be pretty rare, actually. He might look just as outrageous to her as she did to him.

What an odd thought that was! It made him feel acutely uncomfortable. He'd been trying not to stare at the other creatures around him, but what if they'd been gawking at him all this time?

Lady Ako closed the door behind him. Chinthliss stood off to the far side of the room, and as he took his own place, standing in a kind of parade rest behind Chinthliss, he saw that the Blue Room contained only four flat cushions, a very low table with four brown-glazed cups and a teapot on it, plus a couple of things he didn't recognize. He wasn't sure what he should do next, but Lady Ako solved the question for him.

"Please," she said, in a gentle voice that nevertheless brooked no argument. "Sit. We will have Tea."

The way she said the last word, with a subtle emphasis on it, made him think that this was not going to be a silly affair with cookies and cream and sugar. She made it sound rather like some kind of holy ritual.

"Ako!" Chinthliss exclaimed, his voice pained. "Please, we don't have time—"

"We will have Tea," she repeated firmly. "You have accepted my invitation. You will find the time."

"Don't argue with her, lizard," Fox hissed, and then bowed deeply over his knees and took his place on one of the cushions. With a grimace, Chinthliss did the same; after a moment, Joe did likewise. Fortunately, a great deal of his martial-arts instruction had been very traditional, so he was used to sitting Oriental-style on the floor.

"What's going on here?" he whispered to Fox behind Chinthliss' back, as Lady Ako clapped her hands and another brown kimono-clad fox-woman entered, carrying a few more implements on a tray. This one didn't have the elaborate hairstyle of Lady Ako, and her kimono-sleeves were much shorter.

"The Tea Ceremony," Fox breathed back. "I'll explain it all to you later; just be quiet and don't fidget. It's very important and very meaningful, and you're supposed to be contemplating the cosmos through all of this."

Well, that confirmed his feeling that this was supposed to be some kind of ritual or other. But "contemplating the cosmos"? How did that have anything to do with drinking tea? It must be a fox thing.

The only tea he'd ever had much to do with was in the form of the gallons of iced tea he usually put away in the summer, and there wasn't much *there* to inspire a ceremony.

Oh, well. Hopefully, Lady Ako would ignore him. Hopefully, he wouldn't get involved with this at all.

"Who is this young human, Chinthliss?" she asked in a quiet voice with no discernable accent. "I do not know him."

"He is the pupil of my pupil, Ako," Chinthliss replied with a sigh of resignation, as she took up what looked like a small bowl and a shaving brush. "My pupil is missing; this young one wishes to help me find him. When last seen, Tannim was Underhill, but we do not know where. We fear that he is in some danger. He has enemies Underhill."

Is he going to say something about Shar challenging Tannim? Joe wondered. *Is he going to say anything about Shar at all?*

Chinthliss said nothing more, however, and after a glance at Joe, Lady Ako's eyes twinkled for a moment with some secret amusement. "Then, since this young man you bring is new to both Underhill and the ways of the *kitsune,* this will be a new experience for him," was all she said.

Oh, great. "A learning experience." The traditional three-word preamble to a burial. Terrific.

It was certainly that. Joe had never seen anyone make so much fuss over a cup of tea in his life. Lady Ako went through so many ritualistic passes you'd have thought she was concocting the Elixir of Life. It made as much sense as gold-plating popcorn kernels by hand. She was very graceful at it, however; she made the whole thing seem like a dance. Maybe that was the point. Who knew? He hadn't understood Fox all the time when he'd been a kid, and this Lady Ako made a fine art out of creating mystery and obscurity.

Anyway, when he finally got his cup of tea, he was

rather disappointed, much as he had been the first time someone gave him a glass of what was supposed to be a fine vintage wine. The tea was odd, rather bitter, very strong. On the whole, he would have preferred a cola. He would have liked to add sugar at least to make it more palatable, but there didn't seem to be any, so he hid his grimaces and sipped at it while Chinthliss and Lady Ako discussed poetry and music. Joe tried not to fidget while they exchanged what were probably terribly Meaningful and Insightful remarks.

It all took *hours*.

Finally, *finally*, she clapped her hands and the other fox-woman came and took the tea things away. They all sat in complete silence while the other female carefully placed each object on her tray, bowed, and took it all away.

But when the serving-fox was gone, and Chinthliss started to rise, Lady Ako tilted her head to one side and gave Chinthliss a warning look that made him sit right back down again.

"You are seeking Tannim," she stated. "I suspect that you are also seeking my daughter."

Chinthliss wore no discernible expression at all. "There was some indication that she has challenged him or intended to challenge him in the near future," Chinthliss replied levelly. "I don't see any demonstrable connection between that and his disappearance. I am not making any accusations, nor can I imagine why Shar would want to—"

"Please," Ako interrupted. "Don't take me for a fool. You know why Charcoal asserted his rights over her. You know what he intended to do with her. Must I put it in simple terms for you? *He wanted to make her the enemy of your human, this Tannim.* He sees all that you are, and ever moves to make himself the image in the darkened mirror. Charcoal would steal from you whatever he can. *I* do not know why." She glared at him, and the mighty Chinthliss, much to Joe's surprise, seemed to shrink into himself a little. "I *never* knew why. I never understood this rivalry of yours."

She drew herself up in profound dignity, and Joe suspected that she had said a great deal more with those words than he had perceived. Chinthliss closed his eyes for a moment, as if in acknowledgement of that.

"Well," Ako said after a moment. "He did not succeed in his endeavor; I had far more influence over her than he ever guessed, and she broke off all connections with him four years ago. She refuses to see him, speak with him, or communicate with him in any way whatsoever."

"She did?" Chinthliss showed his surprise, briefly. "But—in that case, why challenge Tannim? What's the point?"

Ako sighed, and carefully arranged the fold of a sleeve before continuing. "She maintained some alliances with some of Charcoal's Unseleighe connections; I do not know why. She told me that these alliances amused her. I think there was more to it than that, and I can hazard a guess or two. I believe that these alliances were too powerful to flaunt, and she was too stubborn to seek shelter with the *kitsune* from their anger. One of those connections, an Unseleighe elven lord named Madoc Skean, wanted your pupil, Tannim. I warned her that pursuing this human would have grave consequences; she disregarded that warning, and due to her meddling, this young man was trapped by Madoc."

"*What?*" Chintliss roared, starting to leap up off his cushion.

"Calm yourself!" Lady Ako snapped, before he could get to his feet. "Do you think that I would have brought you here and led you through Tea if I thought he was in any danger? We of the tails have obligations to this world and the other and to the Balance between them!"

Chinthliss sat down again, slowly, but Joe sensed that he was smouldering with anger and impatience.

Ako's nose twitched with distaste. "I advised Shar that she would have to remedy the balance herself. She agreed, and took herself back to Madoc's stronghold. Madoc had Tannim but briefly, and he has the young human no longer. Further, his allies have scattered, and his own domain is in confusion. I don't know where your young human pupil is right now—and I *also* do not know where Shar is. I believe that we can assume that they are together, and that she at least took my advice and freed him from the captivity that she sent him into." Lady Ako directed a chilling look at Chinthliss; the dragon gave her back a heated one. "I told her that by leading this human into captivity, she had seriously unbalanced the scales not only between them, but between our world and his; that she and she alone would have to bring them back into balance. Her actions attracted the attention of the Elders, and she will be called to account for what she has done before a Council. I informed her of this, and that how she fares will depend entirely on what she does now to rectify the situation."

"Did she tell you what she planned to do?" Chinthliss asked, after a long moment of silence. Joe glanced at FX; the *kitsune* gazed at Lady Ako with rapt astonishment, all of his tails twitching. Evidently, all of this was news to him as well as to Joe and Chinthliss.

"No," Ako responded. "She came to me for advice and I could give her none, other than what I just told you. I assume by the confusion in Madoc Skean's holding that she rescued him successfully, but she has not attempted to contact me nor to put herself at the disposal of the Elders, as she would do if she had also returned him to his side of the Hill."

Chinthliss nodded, slowly. "So they are still Underhill, somewhere. Where? Her own domain? I assume she has one—" He smiled, ironically. "I cannot imagine her sharing a domain with anyone."

"Oh—" Lady Ako said very casually. "*I* can. Eventually. Still, that does not matter at the moment. If she had reached her own domain, she would have been able to bring Tannim out of Underhill, for she has a direct outlet to the human side there, in America. So, she has not. I suspect that she is wandering Unseleighe Underhill,

searching for a Gate that will bring her into neutral holdings, or even out of Underhill. I think that we must begin
looking for her ourselves. Where she is, your pupil will
most certainly be."

"We?" Chinthliss did jump to his feet this time. "*We?*"

Joe blinked. They had been looking for an ally. He
hadn't expected one like this.

Wonder how good she is in a fight, he thought. Then he
sized her up with a practiced eye, ignoring her sex, the
fancy outfit, the hair, and the fox-face, concentrating only
on the strength of the muscles, the lithe body. *Huh. Pretty
good, I bet!*

"Of course, we," Ako said with complete composure.
"You didn't think I would allow you to go chasing off after
my daughter without my presence, did you?"

Shar had slept in less comfortable places than the front
seat of a 1969 Mustang. The front seat of *her* Mustang, for
instance. She had chosen her own car with the view to
personifying the "modern" version of Tannim—but after
seeing all the electronic gear in here, and experiencing the
greater comfort-factor at first hand, she was having second
and third thoughts.

Tannim woke, rested and cheerful, after a few hours of
very deep sleep—so deep that he had hardly moved, and
Shar had needed to check him now and again to make certain he was still breathing.

It was her turn to be yawning. She was happy enough at
that point to let him stand watch while *she* caught a quick
nap; by then, even she felt the strains of the past several
hours and needed to recharge.

She thought, just as she finally dropped off, that he was
watching her just as surreptitiously as she had studied
him, but she was just too tired to be sure. . . .

She woke with a start at a noise from outside the Mustang, a shuffling sound, the scraping of a pair of feet. She
sat bolt upright in alarm, but there was nothing in the
amber room with them, the noise was coming from the

hallway outside. Tannim wasn't alarmed, either. He just shook his head at her.

"Don't worry about that sound," he told her, watching the hall door, a shadow of melancholy in his eyes. "I know who it is; I ran into him the last time I was here. It's just a poor old man that the Unseleighe left here. He might be more than half mad by now. I think he was English, and I'm afraid he was taken more than a hundred years ago. I can understand him—barely—so he can't have come from much longer ago than that."

The cursed human. But why would he be here? Why would the Unseleighe put one of their captives here? It's horribly hard to get to this place! Unless—they got tired of him, but they wanted to keep him alive, just in case they ran out of amusements.

That would certainly be like them. And it wasn't as if they managed to get *too* many humans to play with these days. Not like in the old times, when they could kidnap people at will, practically. No, by the late 1800s, they probably *had* figured out they couldn't snatch people off the face of the earth without it being noticed, and when they got a toy, they kept it, even if they were tired of it.

She forgot all her questions, though, as the old man shuffled into the room, pushing his broom and dragging his cart. She felt an unexpected surge of pity for the old creature—and then she caught sight of his eyeless face.

She stifled a gasp with the back of her hand. Not that she hadn't seen the cruelties that the Unseleighe worked on their captives before—but there was something about this man. He struck something unexpected inside her, clothed in his rags, with his wrecked face—held captive here, in this magnificent room, a prison whose beauty he would never see—

The contrast was so great, it shocked her. Tannim watched the poor old wreck with an expression she could not read. Then, before she could say or do anything, he popped the door and was out of the car, walking quickly, heading for the old man.

She opened her own door and hurried to catch up with him, wondering what he thought he was going to do. Tannim was already talking to him, when she caught up with them.

" . . . aye, sir, an' thankee," the old man was saying, with something like a smile, if such a heap of misery could produce a smile. "I hae' bread enow for many a day, thanks to ye."

Shar couldn't help but try to analyze the accent; English, obviously, and probably from the Shires. It was an accent that hadn't changed much until the advent of a radio in every home. "Would you like more than bread?" Tannim asked, leaning forward with nervous intensity. "Would you like to be free of this place forever?"

"Free? Free?" The old man shook his head, alarmed, and shuffled back a pace or two. "There's nought free for Tom Cadge!" He held up his hands before his face in abject fear. "Are ye one o' them blackhearts, that ye taunt me wi' bein' free, an—"

But Tannim seized one of Cadge's hands and put it over his ear before the old man could pull away. "Feel that, Thomas Cadge!" he ordered fiercely. "Is there a single one of the People of the Hills that has *round ears?*"

The old man stopped trying to escape and stood as still as a statue except for the hand that hovered over Tannim's ear. The trembling fingers explored the top of the ear as the face assumed an expression of confusion. "Well, sir," the old man said very slowly and in great perplexity, "I dunno. I don' think so—"

"And here, follow me!" Tannim yanked the improvised rope free, took Tom's wrist, and led him in a rapid shuffle across the floor of the amber room, to end up beside the Mustang. He put the old man's hand flat against the Mach One's hood. "Feel *that!*" he ordered. "That's steel, Thomas Cadge; Cold Iron, from nose to tail! It's a carriage, a Cold Iron carriage, and *that* is how we plan to escape from here. In it! Could *any* of the Fair Folk, kindly or unkindly, bear so much as the presence of a carriage like this? Could any of their magics ever touch someone inside it?"

Thomas Cadge began to tremble, though Shar could not tell if it was from excitement, apprehension, hope, or all three. "N-n-no, sir," he whispered. "That they could not, and there's an end to it. They could no more bear the touch of yon carriage than I can fly."

"Then come with us, Thomas Cadge," Tannim urged. "I won't pretend that there won't be danger—we're in a strange and dangerous place, and we don't know our way out of it yet. I have to admit to you that we're just a bit lost at the moment—and that the same Fair Folk that put you here are probably after us."

Thomas Cadge shook his head dumbly. "I canna think what worse they could be doin' to me, sir," he replied, in a kind of daze. "They could only kill me, eh?"

Tannim sighed. "I don't think we can get you *home*. I don't think you want to go back to your home, anyway—"

Tears dripped horribly from the dark sockets where the old man's eyes had been. "Nay, sir, 'tis one'o the things they mocked me with, that the world I knew is a hunnerd years agone an' more. An' I knew it, aye, I knew that in that they spake true enough. Ye think on all th' auld ballads, an' how a day Underhill is a year in the world above, an' I knew they spake truly. Nay, sir, I canna go back—"

"But I have friends Underhill, if we can find them," Tannim interrupted. "*Good* people—people who will help get rid of your pain and take care of you. I'd like to leave you with them. Will you come with us, Thomas Cadge?"

"Us?" The old man was quick; he swung his blind face around, as if searching for the other person. "Us?"

"He's talking about me," Shar said hastily. "Please, come with us—I don't want to leave you here. If the Unseleighe decide they want entertainment again, and come back for you—" She left the rest unsaid. "I don't want that on my conscience," she added simply.

And although she had been aghast when Tannim first urged the old man to join them, she was surprised to find that she meant the offer as the words left her mouth. Tannim cast a surprised smile at her, one with hints of approval in it, and she was even more surprised to find that the idea of rescuing the old man felt—rather good.

Ah, well, why not? Perhaps the Elders will think of this as a sign that I am striving to rebalance my earlier actions.

"I—ye hae a sweet voice, milady," old Tom quavered shyly. "If ye will ha' me, aye, I'll come wi' ye."

It took some work to wedge Thomas Cadge into the backseat of the Mustang, but once there, he exclaimed over the softness of the seat, the smoothness of the "leather" on the cushions. And when Tannim put an unwrapped sports-bar into one hand, and a bottle of spring-water into the other, the old man nearly wept with joy. It made Shar feel very uncomfortable, and very much ashamed. To this poor old wreck, the cramped back seat of the Mustang, the sweet treat, and the bottle of pure water were unbelievable luxury. And a few hours ago she had felt slightly sorry for herself for "having" to sleep in the front seat and "make do" with a sports-bar and a Gatorade.

Admittedly, it helped that although Thomas Cadge was shabby, he was clean. She had to admit to herself that she would not have felt so sorry for him, nor so willing to take him along, if he had been filthy and odorous.

Thomas Cadge devoured his meal in a few bites and gulps, and promptly curled up in the blanket Tannim got out of the trunk. Tannim came back with an armload of things besides the blanket; Shar welcomed the extra crowbar with fervent glee, and with another body in the car, the extra rations were going to come in handy.

So were the heavy flashlights, the highway flares, the first-aid kit, and the bayonet-knives he piled into the passenger's-side footwell. Other domains would not neccessarily be lighted, and there were plenty of creatures who would fear the flame of a highway flare.

She swiped one of the breakfast bars and went over to the other side of the room to open up both doors into the hallway. When she returned, Tannim had strapped himself in—and Thomas Cadge was asleep in the back seat with an improvised bandage of white gauze from the first-aid kit thankfully covering the ruins of his eyes. Now the old man was truly a sight to inspire anyone's pity, rather than horror or revulsion. He looked like a wounded, weary old soldier from some time in the long past; still trying to keep up his pride, though the infirmities of his own body had betrayed him.

Taking her cue from Tannim, she strapped the seatbelt across her shoulders once she had shut the door. "Go out those doors, take a sharp right, and the door to the gardens will be at the end of the hall," she directed. "You'll have to use your lights; I'll get out and open the doors into the garden once we reach them. Then it's down a set of four very shallow stairs, and follow the garden path. The Gate will be at the end of it, and it will be night out there."

He nodded, and started the car. The sound of the engine seemed terribly loud in all the silence, but Thomas Cadge did not even seem to wake up. It occurred to her that this must be the first time he had slept with any feeling of safety or security in decades.

Poor, abused old man. No home but yourself.

"Now what?" Tannim asked from the front seat.

Artificial stars gleamed down from a flat-black sky; the Katschei's round, silver moon sailed serenely in its track above them. Although no one had tended the garden for centuries, most of the plants here were much as they had been when their creator died; that was part of their magical nature, to thrive without being tended. Flowers bloomed on all sides, all out of their proper season. Trees had flowers, green, and ripening fruit, all at the same time. Perfumes floated on the faint breeze, and bowers beckoned, promising soft places for dalliance. All a cheat, of course—there had never been any dalliance here. The Katschei's captives had been quite, quite virginal; this was merely the appropriate setting for a dozen of the most beautiful maidens in Rus. The Katschei had surrounded them with fresh beauty and all the stage-dressing of romance. The setting was still here, and it was more romantic in its overgrown state than it had been when neatly tamed and pruned.

And even if we weren't in a hurry, we have a chaperone, damn it all.

The Gate here was a rose trellis; the rose vines had overgrown it somewhat, but it was still quite useful. Roses of three colors cascaded down over it, saturating the air with their mingled fragrances of honey, damask, and musk. Only the Katschei would have had night-blooming roses. Only the Katschei would have covered a Gate with them.

And only the Katschei would ever have placed the Gate back to their homelands in the heart of the garden his captives had been imprisoned in.

None of them could use it, of course. He would never have carried off a princess with even a touch of magical power. But he surely enjoyed the irony: his prisoners danced in and around the very means of their escape, if they could only have learned how to make it work. Doubtless, he told them that very thing. He had been an artist, in his way, juxtaposing cruelty with beauty, wonder with tragedy. If *he* had been the one who had captured Thomas Cadge, he would not have blinded the old man. No, he would have done something artistic with him; perhaps gelded him, shaped his face and body into that of a young god, and left him to guard his flock of lovely virgins.

Shar studied the Gate with her eyes closed, testing each of the six settings. One, she already knew, came up in Tannim's world, but only a few miles from present-day Moscow. However improved current conditions were, he would have a *damned* hard time explaining his presence there—and such a destination was likely to be as hazardous in the end as anything Underhill.

One definitely ended in the domain of the *rakshasha;* man-eating shape-changing creatures of India, and another was set for the realm of the *yush*. Bad destinations, both of them; neither she nor Tannim could ever hold their own against a group of either monsters.

That left three other settings, none of which she recognized. They all felt very old, older even than the setting to the other side of the Hill. They might represent alliances the Katschei made before he began his collection of human maidens.

What the heck.

She returned to the car and reported her findings. "And I can't even tell where those last three go," she warned. "The third one is the nearest, and that's all I can tell you about it."

Tannim only shrugged. "Door number three sounds all right with me," he opined, as she got into the car and strapped herself back into her seat. "If you don't recognize it, chances are whoever lives there won't recognize us, right?"

"That's the theory, anyway." She lowered the window and leaned out from inside the safety of the steel framework. Feeling very grateful that *she* knew the effect of Cold Iron on her magics, and knew it intimately, she reached out with a finger of power and invoked that setting.

The rose vines quivered for a moment, and then lit up from within with a warm, golden light. The magic ran through every vein, illuminating the flowers from within, as Shar stared, transfixed. How had the Katschei *done* that? She'd never seen anyone incorporate living things into a Gate before, at least not in a purely ornamental fashion.

Trust the Katschei to do it if anyone would.

"Now there," Tannim said with detached admiration, "was a guy who had style."

The center of the arbor filled with dark haze. Whatever lay on the other side, they were now committed to it.

"Ready?" she asked, pulling her head and arm back into the steel cocoon of the Mach One, and rolling her window back up again. Not that the glass would provide any protection at all, but at least it gave her the illusion of shelter.

Tannim managed a wan smile, and a thumb's-up. "Here we come, ready or not," he said lightly, and put the Mach One into gear, driving slowly up to and into the arbor.

Shar repressed a shudder as the dark mist seemed to swallow up the light, then the headlights, the hood, and crept toward the windshield. It was just as well that Thomas Cadge was not only asleep but blind. He'd have run screaming from the car if he'd seen this.

She closed her own eyes involuntarily. Her skin tingled as the magic field passed over her; her stomach objected to the moment of apparent weightlessness.

Then, with a jolt, it was over.

The Mach One bounced slightly as it dropped about an inch, and she opened her eyes.

And her jaw dropped as Tannim quickly hit the brakes, stopping them dead. Just in time, since they had a reception committee, and a few more feet would have put the Mach One within range of their weapons.

The weapons were the first things that *she* noticed; the headlights gleamed from the shining surfaces of huge battle-axes, smaller throwing-axes, spear points, and knives and swords.

Evidently someone here had sensed the Gate coming to life and had gathered a crowd to greet whatever came through it. From the looks of the group, they had not expected the visitors to be friendly. ·

"A little strong for the Welcome Wagon, don't you think?" Tannim said, as the twenty or so armed warriors stared into their headlights.

Whoever these fellows had been expecting, Tannim figured it wasn't Ford's Finest. They obviously didn't recognize him, Shar, or the vehicle; the way they glared at the headlights suggested that they didn't even notice the passengers, only the car, and they didn't know what it was.

He didn't recognize them, either. Sidhe of some kind, that was all he could tell; pointed ears thrust through wild tangles of very blond, straight hair, and the slit-pupiled green eyes were unmistakable in the bright lights from the headlights.

Elves. Why did it have to be elves?

But the clothing they sported was not anything he recognized. In fact, by elven standards, it was downright primitive. That was the amazing part.

The elves he knew, even the Unseleighe, reveled in the use of ornament and lush, flowing fabrics, of intricate goldwork and carved gems, of bizarre design and exotic cut. The elves he'd associated with wore armor so engraved and chased, inlaid and enameled, that it ceased being "armor" and became a work of art. They carried weapons of terrible beauty: slim, razor-sharp swords as ornamented as their armor, knives that matched the swords to within a hair, bows of perfect curve and silent grace, so elegant that their bowstrings sang, not *twanged*.

These warriors carried small, round shields of plain wood with copper bosses in the middle; they had no helmets at all, and only corselets, vambraces, and leg armor of the same hammered copper. The blades of their swords and heavy axes also appeared to be of copper or brass. None of the metal-work was chased or engraved; there was a tiny amount of inlay work, but not much. Under the scant armor, they had donned short-sleeved woolen tunics of bright colors, with bands of embroidery at all the hems. They wore sandals and shoes, not the tooled leather boots favored by the elves Tannim had seen. Their hair looked as if it had never seen a pair of scissors; a few of them had it bound up in braids, but the majority sported lengthy manes that would have been the envy of any human female.

They seemed frozen in place, staring at the Mach One in horrified fascination.

"You don't recognize these jokers, do you?" he asked Shar quietly. She shook her head. While the reception commitee stayed where it was, he took a moment to get a

look at *where* they had landed. Maybe the setting would
tell him something.

Except that the roof took him rather by surprise.

A cave? He blinked, very much amazed. Even when an
Underhill domain had originally looked like a cave, those
who inhabited it usually took pains to make it look like
something else—someplace outdoors, usually. This was
the very first time he had ever seen a domain that looked
like what it was.

It was an awfully big cave, though. Bigger than Mam-
moth Cave, or Meramac, or the largest room in Carlsbad
Caverns. The ceiling had to be at least a hundred feet up,
a rough dome of white, unworked, natural rock. The rest
of the place was on a scale with the ceiling; from here to
the other side of the room was probably fully half a mile.
The floor between here and there was not of stone,
though, but of wood, smoothed only by time and wear,
and not put together with any level of sophistication. In
fact, it looked something rather like a deck built by
drunken beavers or very, very bad industrial-arts students.
At regular intervals a round platform of stone rose above
the level of the wood for about a foot, and these platforms
were topped with huge bonfires. Oddly enough, though,
the fires didn't seem to be giving off any smoke. That was
the first evidence of magic he'd seen here.

Spitted over these fires were the carcasses of animals;
deer, pig, and cow. Beside the fires were barrels that he
presumed contained beer or ale—but these barrels had
not been tapped, as the kegs he knew were. Instead, the
end was open, and people came along and dipped their
cups into the liquid to fill them.

There were fur-covered benches around each fire;
some of them even held prone figures, possibly sleeping
off that beer.

Most of the people in this place, however, were staring
at the Mach One with the same postures of surprise as the
warriors directly in front of it.

There were women out there—or, at least, Tannim

assumed they were women, since they wore dresses. Hard to tell with elves, sometimes. Simple T-tunic dresses, of the same bright colors as the tunics the men wore. Over the dresses, most of the women wore a kind of apron. The straps were heavily embroidered and were attached to the embroidered panels of the front and back by large, round brooches of copper, silver, and gold. Their blond hair was bound around their foreheads with ribbon-headbands and covered with small veils; some of them wore their hair unbound except by the headbands, but the rest wore it in two braids. Their ears were as pointed as those of the men, and the nearest had the same cat-slitted, elven eyes.

One of the nearest men, one who had a gold headband, finally got over his shock. He gestured with his copper sword and shouted something to the rest. It was a fairly long speech and involved a lot of sword-waving and pointing at the car.

It wasn't in any language Tannim recognized. He'd heard his own elves spouting off long strings of Gaelic curses often enough when they dropped something heavy on a toe, or a wrench slipped and skinned knuckles. Whatever this was, it wasn't Gaelic, and neither were these lads. Funny, it *almost* sounded like the Swedish Chef from the old Muppet show—

Shar narrowed her eyes as the leader continued his speech to the headlights, pointing and threatening with his blade. At that point, Tannim realized something. *Huh. He's shouting at the* car! *Does he think it's alive?*

To test that theory, Tannim tapped lightly on the horn.

With a yell, *all* of the fighters leapt back a pace and stared at the front of the car as if they thought it might suddenly shoot out flames.

"Oh hell—" Shar said into the silence. "I know where we are. These Sidhe haven't seen a human for fifteen hundred years! They sealed themselves off so long ago that not even Madoc could get them to come out. They're Nordic—we're in the Hall of the Mountain King!"

Tannim bit off an exclamation as all the clues fell into place. *Right—copper and bronze weapons, copper armor—these were some of the first elves to be driven Underhill and seal themselves off from Cold Iron and the world above.* "I don't suppose you speak their lingo, do you?" he asked hopefully. Those axes might only be bronze, but they could do plenty of damage if the fighters decided to attack the Iron Dragon. They'd go through glass just fine, for instance. "It would be really nice if you could apologize for breaking up their party, tell them that we're just passing through."

"No," Shar said shortly. "Sorry. I don't think there's any-one alive who does understand them without a telepath. They not only sealed themselves off from your world, they sealed themselves off from the rest of Underhill. *Maybe* there's a scholar in your world who speaks Old Norse, or Old Swedish, or Old Finnish—but I wouldn't count on it, and I doubt he's going to suddenly teleport into the back seat."

Tom Cadge? Tannim thought—

"I can't help ye, sir," came an apologetic voice from behind them. "Whatever yon spouted, 'tis pure babble to me."

Tannim studied the situation: the leader finished his speech, and he and his followers went back to staring into the headlights, as transfixed by the light as a bunch of moths.

"Shar, can you reset the Gate behind us to somewhere friendlier?" he asked quietly, and glanced out of the corner of his eye at her. She bit her lip, then cranked the window down.

Slowly.

Just as slowly, she edged one hand and a bit of her head outside, turned to face the rear of the car, and stared back at the Gate behind them.

"There's a very shallow stone platform the Gate rests on right behind us, just past the rear wheels," she said quietly. The elves didn't seem to have noticed her head and hand sticking out; maybe the headlights were obscuring whatever he and Shar did. "That was why we bumped down when we arrived. The Gate is one of those stone arches like at Stonehenge, and it looks big enough for an elephant. I think the Mach One will fit in there with no problem."

So far, so good.

"One of the settings is the Katschei's palace, obviously," she continued. "I just don't recognize the others—but if these people have been cut off for as long as I think, I wouldn't. There are plenty of places Underhill where I've never been, and plenty more that sealed themselves off from the parts that continued to progress. I don't know a darned thing about this lot, who their allies were, or anything else."

"Okay," Tannim replied after a moment of thought. "Pick one, I don't care what. I'm going to drive slowly toward these guys, and see if I can't get them to clear off enough to give me room to turn around."

This *was* a "dragon" made of the Death Metal, something these elves had gone Underhill to avoid completely. With luck, they were too terrified of it to touch it. With equal luck, if he was very, very careful, they would realize in a moment that he didn't want to hurt them.

Then again, maybe they were too busy thinking about hurting him to notice.

He put the car into motion, creeping forward an inch at a time.

The elven warriors backed up, an inch at a time, staring at the headlights. From the way they glared at the Mach One, they evidently read this as an aggressive move. The moment of truth was going to come when he spun the car and turned his back to them. Would they rush him?

They might. If they realized he was going to escape, they might very well.

Look, Sven, we killed the Iron Dragon and it had eaten three humans!

"Can you gear that Gate up so as soon as I get these

guys cleared, I can pull a doughnut and get the heck out of here?" he asked anxiously. "I don't want to have our back to these guys for more than a minute, max."

"No argument here." Shar poked her head a little further out of the window, as he continued to creep the Mustang forward. The elves cleared back a bit more, their eyes narrowing, their knuckles going white as they clutched their weaponry tighter.

"Got it," she said, after far too long. The elves in front of him were beginning to look as if they resented being backed up, and he didn't think he'd be able to force them back much further. He took a quick glance in his rearview mirror, and another over his shoulder.

There was enough room for the maneuver he wanted to pull. Barely.

Barely is still enough!

"Hold on!" he said through gritted teeth; then he leaned on the horn.

The elves screeched and jumped back; he'd succeeded in frightening them back another precious foot or so. He floored the accelerator, smoked the wheels, and slung the steering wheel over.

The tires screamed; the rear slung sideways, then around in a complete half-circle, while the elven warriors shrieked in answer and threw themselves wildly out of the way. Tannim stabilized the spin, until the nose pointed straight at the dark haze under the trio of huge, rough-cut stones looming up in front of them. He let up on the gas for a moment, then floored it as the elves leapt at the rear of the car with hideous war cries.

The Mach One roared through the Gate as Tannim saw the blade of a throwing-axe sail past the rear end, and in the rearview mirror, the leader buried the blade of his huge battle-axe into the wooden floor, scant inches from the rear bumper.

Then there was a moment of darkness, and of dizziness, and then they were through.

He slammed on the brakes quickly, and looked up at a

full moon and a sky full of stars under a snow-filled and seemingly endless plain.

"Maybe you'd better turn on the heater," Shar suggested mildly, and rolled up the window.

• CHAPTER TEN

Tannim reached over and automatically turned on the dash-heater, and a moment later was grateful that Shar had prodded him to do so.

It must be thirty below out there!

Cold penetrated the window glass, and the side-window on his side frosted over between one breath and the next.

"Where the heck are we?" he asked, peering up through the windshield at the sky. Only the fact that the stars did not twinkle proved that this was another Underhill domain and not some place on the other side of the Hill: Siberia or Manitoba. Otherwise the sky was a much more accurate copy of the real thing than the one over the garden they'd left.

Except that there didn't seem to be any constellations he recognized.

"I have no clue." Shar craned her own neck around to look up through the glass at the stars above them. "No clue at all. I don't recognize the stars up there; for all I know, they might not even represent the constellations, they were just thrown up there randomly. This could be an analog of anywhere: Alaska, the Arctic, the Gobi Desert in winter—heck, even the Great Plains. Your guess is as good as mine."

Maybe if he got out and took a look, he might get a clue. "Hang on a minute. Keep the heater running." He was going to have to get into the trunk again, anyway; it was just a good thing the trunk on a Mach One was so big and he never took his survival supplies out, no matter what. They were going to need some of his winter emergency stash.

He opened the door and got out in a hurry; his nose was cold and his fingers were frozen by the time he reached the trunk and extracted two Mylar blankets and three of green wool. Army surplus, of course.

There wasn't a lot of snow; it wasn't much past calf-deep at the worst. It formed an icy crust over long grass, beaten flat, and held down by the weight of the ice. He crunched his way back to the front of the Mustang, hands and feet numbed, grateful for the warming effect of his armor. The driver's-side window was completely frosted over, and the air was so cold it hurt to breathe. Hopefully they wouldn't be here much longer; the Mustang's heater was not going to keep up with cold like this. He could make do with one of the wool blankets, but old Tom and Shar had probably better have the Mylar as well as the wool. . . .

He pulled open the door and slid in quickly, then turned to Shar and stared.

"Hi," Shar said, turning a pointed muzzle and a pair of twinkling eyes at him. "You didn't seem to have a fur coat around, so I grew my own."

He dropped his jaw and the blankets; fumbled the latter up off the floor. The warm air curled around him as he stared at the lovely fox-woman with Shar's eyes sitting on the passenger's side of the Mustang.

An arctic fox, no less, with thick, white fur, and a blunter nose and smaller ears than the red fox FX usually morphed into. He stared like a booby, and she winked at him.

I'm taking this all very well, aren't I?

"Eh, excuse me, young sir, but if ye've brought a bit more blankets—" Tom said humbly from the rear seat as Tannim sat and gawked. "—'tis gettin' a bit chill here."

He didn't move. It really was Shar. And it really was a human-sized fox. It was one thing to know intellectually that Shar was half-*kitsune*, but to actually *see* the proof of it—

"Oh, yeah, of course." Tannim shook himself out of his daze, passed back the Mylar and one of the wool blankets, and kept one of the wool ones for himself. He turned back to Shar and offered her the remaining blankets. "Do you—"

"Just give me a wool one," Shar replied. "I may have fur, but I want to spend some time studying the Gate this time before we jump, and I'll have to do it from outside the Mach One."

Wordlessly, he handed her the scratchy old wool blanket and left the little silver packet of Mylar for later.

He couldn't keep from staring at her; *this* had never happened in any of his dreams! Jeez, if anything came of this between him and Shar, he was going to have one heck of a fascinating love life . . . or did something like this come under the category of bestiality?

Boy, I hope not. Otherwise I'm a lot kinkier than I thought.

And to think that he'd had trouble explaining some of his other girlfriends to his mother!

"Hi, Mom, this is my girl. By the way, have you got a spare flea collar around? And she's due for her shots." She gets one look at Shar like this, and she'll be praying for me to go back to Teresa and her red Mohawk!

Shar didn't seem to be in the least offended by all of his staring. "I—ah—" he began.

"You're taking this very well. Oh, I don't do this very often around humans, not nearly as often as Mother," she offered casually. "Being brought up around the Unseleighe, I tended to keep to the elven look. It was bad enough that I wasn't Sidhe; they tend to regard any of the anthropomorphic forms as very much inferior. Has Saski Berith—FX—ever gone completely fox on you?"

"Not for long," Tannim admitted. The thick, white fur looked so incredibly soft—and the eyes were still human, still Shar's. And never mind that the voice came from a muzzle full of pointed teeth, it was still Shar's voice. Shar's clothes, for that matter; she'd left them on when she changed. Fascinating.

"It has its points." She regarded her hands—very much fur-covered human hands, except for the long claws. "I can inflict a lot more damage this way if there aren't any weapons available. And raw meat and fish taste much better in this form than in the human. Still, does it disturb you?"

He shook his head. "I don't think so." Belatedly, he remembered what he'd been looking for when he'd gotten out of the car. "Oh—I think we might be in a Native American analog to the Great Plains, or to the steppes of Russia. The grasses look right, anyway. Tall grass, I think, or whatever equivalent grows on the steppes. If that's true, there's going to be a lot more Spirit Animals around here—the steppes-herdsmen have a lot of the same shamanic equivalents to the Native Americans. That's one massive generalization, of course, but what the hell."

"Really?" she said with acute interest. "I wonder why the Gate went *here*, then?"

"Eh, who knows?" Tom put in. "The Fair Folk, they ne'er did make allies an' enemies th' way us mortal folk do. It don't matter t' them whether a land were across the sea Above the Hill; 'tis all Underhill here."

"True enough," Tannim agreed. "The other possibility is that this place was abandoned a long time ago. Who wants to live in eternal winter? Even Spirit Animals prefer summer to winter, on the whole. It might be that this is only used when someone is doing a Vision Quest in winter, or needs to make part of the Quest through a winter setting."

"I don' know naught about quests, sir," Tom replied, "but there's a mort 'o places down here that go beggin'. Some 'un gets t' playin' with it, an' it goes wrong, they give it up an starts over, like. Could be some 'un was tryin' for a nice place for winter huntin', long gallops an' no places for your horse t' bust his leg, an' this is what they got."

"Well, if so, it better not be fox hunting that they were planning," Shar replied, baring her teeth and snapping playfully. "This fox might just chase them!"

Tannim grinned. It really felt *good* to be working with Shar, even though they really knew so little about each other! He'd have to be mindful of those teeth, later, when they—

The old man had a point, though; it wouldn't do to linger here. Just because the place looked abandoned, that didn't mean it was. And if it was someone's private hunting preserve, it would be a good idea to get out of here before the hunter returned. Not that they needed any more reasons for urgency!

"Whenever you're ready, Shar," Tannim said quietly. "Take all the time you need. I've got a near-full tank, and at idle, the Mach One won't be drinking too much gas." He thought a moment. "Actually, I have an idea."

We're both in trouble together. She's made the effort to get me out. And just in case I don't make it—I can add to her chances to survive this. Even if everything goes to hell.

"Hold on a minute before you go out there." He closed his eyes, sank his own awareness into the fabric of the Mustang, and began to chant quietly.

He didn't leave his body this time, but with his mage-sight tapped into all the myriad possibilities Underhill, he had to blink a few times to get *here and now* clear.

Beside him, Shar was particularly disconcerting. Lovely woman, flirtatious fox, and—something else. Not *quite* like Chinthliss' draconic form; Shar was more delicate, graceful, *entirely* feminine. But the resemblance was there. The three forms washed in and out of focus, but the strongest was not the draconic but the human, followed by the fox.

Jeez, and I swore I wasn't going to date outside my own species. Even at Fairgrove. She's so sexy!

He reached out with his real hand; Shar put hers into his without any prompting on his part. Physical touch gave him physical linkage; he pitched his chanting a tad higher and plugged her into the Mach One's energy reserves.

"Oh!" she exclaimed. And then thoughtfully, "Oh . . . my."

He sealed the connections to her and dropped back into the real world. She was sitting in absolute, Zen stillness, head cocked to one side, eyes unfocused, her attention concentrated on what he had just given her.

He watched her face; interestingly, it was as easy to read the vulpine expressions as the human ones. Finally, her eyes focused again, and she came back to reality, turning a face still full of surprise to him. "Tannim—" she said very slowly, her expression full of wonder and gratitude. "You didn't need to do that."

He shrugged, covering his mingled feelings. He was filled with pleasure at her thanks, and nervousness at having given her the key to so much of himself. "Gives us both an edge," he replied. "Gives us both a source of power to draw on when we don't want to let the locals know that we're mages. Now, you go out there and study that Gate. Here, take the other Mylar blanket, too. Put it over the wool. Sit on the hood. The engine'll keep your— ah—tail warm, and you'll have a pure and reliable power source to draw on."

Tom took all this in, head tilted to the side, a slight smile on his face. "I'll be havin' another bit of a nap, if ye won't be a-needin' me, eh?" he said, when Tannim had finished.

Tannim chuckled weakly. "Sounds good to me, Tom," he said, and the old man curled up, tucking his head under an improvised blanket-hood so that his face could not be seen.

Shar laid her hand on the back of his. "Thank you," she said quietly. "Thank you very much. It is a noble gift, and a generous one. I'll never forget it."

Then, before he could reply, she popped the door open and slipped out with a crackle of plastic. She stood wrapped in Mylar in a reversal of "woman in a silver dress, wrapped in a fox-fur cape." He turned the car around carefully, so that the nose faced the Gate. Like the one in the Mountain King's Hall, this was a simple arch of three rough stones and appeared to be the only structure here for as far as the eye could see.

She slid up onto the hood of the car and sat just in front of the air-intake, breath steaming up into the air, pointed ears perked forward. Tannim took it upon himself to sit guard for her, watching with *every* sense, in every direction except the one she faced, for any sign of living things.

He sensed her slipping into deep meditation; she must have felt him putting out warning-feelers, and trusted to him to guard her back.

It was the second such evidence of trust she'd granted him, the first being when she had slept for an hour or so, back in the amber room.

And despite their precarious situation, he felt his mouth stretching in a silly grin.

Or maybe not so silly. *Because maybe, just maybe, this is all going to work out . . . .*

"You will come with me, please." Lady Ako rose gracefully to her feet; Joe discovered that he was not as practiced at sitting on the floor as he had thought, when he tried to follow her example.

Chinthliss and FX didn't seem to have much more luck than he had, fortunately, or he'd have felt really stupid.

The *kitsune*-lady led the way not to the door into the nightclub but to the door through which their *kitsune*-server had come.

"We will use the private entrance," she said, turning her head to speak over her shoulder.

"I didn't know there was a private entrance," Chinthliss observed with mild surprise.

Lady Ako smiled slightly. On a fox-head, that translated to showing the barest tips of her teeth. Definitely an unsettling sight. "You were also not aware that the majority partners in this establisment are five-tail *kitsune*, I assume."

FX started with surprise. "I'd wondered about the Tea Ceremony," Chinthliss replied with equanimity. "There aren't too many nightclubs equipped to perform it at a moment's notice."

Lady Ako said nothing; she only opened the door for them all and bowed without a hint of servility. They all filed through, Joe taking the rearmost position.

The door led into a perfectly ordinary, utilitarian hallway, white-painted, terrazzo-floored, with ordinary light fixtures overhead. Odd creatures squeezed by them as they passed, emerging from other doors along the hall. Some were in the uniforms of the cocktail waitresses and waiters, some in full tuxedos, a few in very little other than strategically placed spangles.

Joe blushed; he couldn't help it. Bad enough when these females were at a distance, but they brushed past him without a trace of embarassment, full breasts practically in his face. His cheeks and neck felt as if he had the worst sunburn in his life, and he was certain he looked like a boiled lobster.

"Two sequins and a cork," Fox muttered in his ear as they threaded their way past another group of girls with butterfly-wings in matching—outfits. "Placement optional."

Joe blushed so hard he could have blacked out from the rush of blood to his skin. And elsewhere.

Finally Lady Ako brought them to a door at the end of the corridor and opened it for them. Joe had only a moment to notice that the doorframe seemed filled with a hazy darkness—

Then, before he could stop, his momentum took him through.

His stomach lurched for a moment. *A Gate?* he thought in confusion; then his leading foot came down solidly on the "other side."

His eyes cleared; he shook his head to clear it as well, taking a firm grip on his weaponry.

"No need," Lady Ako said mildly from behind him.

He blinked, finding himself in bright sunlight on an immaculately groomed gravel path. Sculptured mounds crowned with carefully placed, twisted trees, stone statues, and iron lanterns rose on either side. Ahead of him was a bridge that arched over a tiny stream, with a curve as gentle as a caress. Beyond the bridge, on a perfectly shaped miniature hill, stood a pavilion with a peaked roof and white paper walls.

"You are at our embassy here; you have not left your original section of Underhill," Lady Ako stated calmly. "We will be able to search for Shar and Tannim from here—and we will be able to alert our allies and agents in unfriendly domains to watch for them."

It was not until she came around in front of them that Joe saw she had changed significantly. She was no longer a fox-woman, but was, to all appearances, perfectly human. She still wore her kimono, but she had discarded the elaborate black hairdo somewhere. Now she wore only what Joe assumed was her real hair: a long, unbound fall of fox-red, with a streak of white, ornamented by a single clasp in the shape of a carved fox of white jade. That hair color looked distinctly odd on someone with otherwise Oriental features.

She moved to the front of the group, but did not lead them to the pavilion as Joe had expected. Instead, she brought them, after a short walk, to another building altogether.

Joe got the oddest feeling that Lady Ako was giving them the runaround. But why would she want to do that? Wasn't it her daughter that was in trouble here?

He put his feelings aside; surely he was mistaken. It was just because this was all so weird that the only way his mind could cope with it was to be suspicious.

This was something like a bigger version of the pavilion; it had a wide, wooden porch around it, with more little flat tables and cushions arranged neatly and precisely. Lady Ako brought them up onto the porch and took her place on one of the cushions; they did the same, arranging themselves around her.

"Now," she said, when they were all settled, "we shall have Tea."

"We will *not* have Tea!" Chinthliss exploded, shattering the serene silence and frightening some little birds out of a sculptured bush near the porch.

Ako fixed him with a look of stern rebuke. "We will have Tea," she repeated stubbornly.

But Chinthliss had evidently had enough. "We will not have any damned Tea!" he shouted, leaping to his feet. "Tannim is missing, you don't know where Shar is, an Unseleighe enemy of Tannim's *and* mine wants Tannim in small pieces, and *you* want to serve us another bowl of your damned green glop?"

"She's stalling!" Joe blurted.

All eyes turned to him—including Lady Ako's, and she was not happy with him or his observation. But Joe couldn't help it; now that his subconscious had come up with what was really going on, he had to report it to Chinthliss, his "superior officer."

"She's stalling, sir," Joe said to Chinthliss, deliberately avoiding Lady Ako's gaze. "I don't know why, but she's been taking as much time as she possibly could to do everything. It isn't just that tea-stuff, it's everything; if she really wanted to get something done, couldn't she have met us at the park? Or if she had someone watching to see if we came to the Drunk Tank, couldn't she have brought us straight here?"

The sheer numbers of people crowding that hallway, too, had been way out of line. "She even had everybody working in the club out there in the hall, just to keep us from moving through it too quickly." Now he cast a quick glance at Lady Ako; she looked distinctly chagrined. "Sir, she's been throwing every single delay at us that she could. She probably even had some kind of 'emergency' planned, so that she could shut us up someplace for a while."

Chinthliss stood, towering over her as she remained seated on her little cushion. "Well?" he asked icily.

She averted her eyes. "I haven't the least idea what the boy is talking about," she protested, though it sounded to

Joe just a bit feeble. "Why would I do anything like that?"

"The reasons are as many as your tails, Ako, and only you know which of them are true." Chinthliss was clearly out of patience. "The only thing useful to have come out of this is that you have told me that Shar and Tannim are likely together, and that Tannim is pursued but no longer captured. Thanks to all this taradiddle of yours, that may no longer be the case."

He jerked his head a little, and Joe took his place behind him. FX vacillated for a moment, then joined them.

"You may do what you like, Ako," Chinthliss said, his voice coldly emotionless. "I am going to find a taxi. I suggest that you do nothing to stop us."

Tannim's nose and feet were awfully cold, but the rest of him was warm enough, wrapped up with his armor beneath it all. Tom Cadge slept blissfully on in the backseat, and Shar contemplated the Gate from the hood of the car, a fox of white jade wrapped in shiny silver gift wrap.

She could have been an incense burner, with the fog of her breath for smoke. *Or a baked potato in a microwave? No, she's not at all potato-shaped. And potatoes explode. Hope she doesn't do that.*

Finally, though, she stirred and climbed carefully down off the hood of the Mach One. Still wrapped in her silver cloak, she padded quickly to the door of the car, opened it, and slipped inside. The Mylar crackled annoyingly as she slid into her seat.

"This was good. With leisure to study the Gate, I was able to trace all of its destinations as to *type* if not actual location. Six settings, so I can't add one of my own," she said. "One is back to the place we just came from. One goes directly to the domain belonging to the yeti. We *could* take that one—they have another Gate that goes to the other side of the Hill—but we'd wind up in the Himalayas near Everest, and the Mach One is neither a yak nor equipped with oxygen and climbing gear."

"And I'm not a mountain climber," Tannim added. "We'd have to be damned lucky to survive the Himalayas long enough for Tibetans, monks, or some expedition or other to find us and rescue us. And if we arrived in the middle of one of their killer snowstorms, we're ice cubes. Next?"

"One leads to a swamp. I don't know who owns the swamp, but I suspect something like the Will-o'-the-Wisps." She waited for his reaction, keeping quite still, so that the Mylar wouldn't crackle.

Tannim shuddered; he'd encountered one, the real thing, not swamp gas. Will-O'-the-Wisps were not little dancing fairy lights; they were horrible creatures who lived only to lure living beings into sucking morasses in the swamps they called home. Like the other Unseleighe, they thrived on fear and pain; when their victim was well and truly trapped, and sinking to his death, they would perch nearby and drink in the panic and despair as he struggled and died. The Will-o'-the-Wisp Tannim had encountered had not been content with trying to lure him away to his death; when he had not cooperated, it had tried to frighten him into a morass. Then it decided to take the matter into its own hands.

The experience had not been a pleasant one, to say the least. "I don't think that's a good idea," he said. "Next?"

"Nazis," Shar supplied succinctly.

"Pardon?" he replied, sure that he could not have heard her correctly.

"Nazis," she repeated. "And I must admit, this does solve a little puzzle for me. The Nazis had a secret program of research into magic and the occult. I always wondered where all the Nazi sorcerors went when the Third Reich collapsed; they were too powerful to have been caught, the way the Nazi leaders were, but there was no sign of them after the end of the war. Apparently, they discovered or built a Gate, found a vacant realm and took it over for their very own. They must be some of the very few mortals to succeed in living Underhill without elven aid."

"Nazis." He shook his head. "I hate those guys."

"I doubt that even the Unseleighe would care for them," Shar replied. "They were approaching magic as a science, and their attitude would have turned even Madoc Skean off. So, that's four of the six destinations. The other two end in the Unformed."

Tannim gave that some thought. The Unformed was the generic term for pockets of odd, thick mist in completely unclaimed and untouched areas. There were a few realms that were so large that they were still surrounded by a dense and impenetrable cloud of the Unformed. Elfhame Outremer had been like that—and it was out of the Unformed that their destruction had come, for the mist was psychotropic, and anyone with strong enough psychic powers could influence it, create things out of it.

In the case of Outremer, disaster had come at the hands of a seriously unbalanced child with powerful psychic and magic powers: a deadly combination, when put together with the Unformed.

Anyone who was both psychic *and* a mage could find himself facing down his worst nightmares out in the Unformed. In the old days, that had often been a test of a new mage, the test that proved how good his control was not only of his magic but of himself. There were a lot of mages who hadn't survived this particular ordeal.

There were a number of unclaimed pocket domains that were the results of these trials-by-fire, as well. The one that they were in might well be one of those, come to think of it.

"Any idea how big the pockets are?" he asked finally.

Shar shook her head. "Not even a guess. Can't help you. The only thing I can tell is that one of them might have more than one Gate in it. The other might have a physical connection to another realm. You have to remember that it is very likely that every setting on the Gates there is taken up by a destination we wouldn't like. The Unseleighe and their ilk still prove out young mages in trial-by-Unformed."

"Go for the one with the physical connection?" he hazarded. "That would be my choice. The drawback I can see to the Unformed with two Gates in it is that there's twice the probability that there's something really nasty still roaming around in the mist out there, left over from a trial—and twice the chance that some new Unseleighe mage is going to pop in on us while we're there, and maybe even break the Unformed down around us while he goes through *his* trial."

Shar nodded thoughtfully. "I hadn't thought of that, but you're right. It's going to be hard enough to keep our own thoughts pleasant; I'd hate to meet some Unseleighe nightmares. Actually, a Nightmare may be exactly one 'of the things we'd meet out there."

"A Nightmare?" Tannim had only heard of those, and he had no real wish to meet one in person. Sometimes a skull-headed white horse with her retinue of nine black, man-eating foals, sometimes a grim woman in a robe of storm clouds, with the head of a fanged horse in place of her own, she was, as Dottie succinctly put it, "mondo bad news." If you were lucky, she would only force you to mount and ride her through your greatest fears.

If you weren't lucky . . .

"Anytime I can avoid a Nightmare, I'd prefer to," Shar replied, echoing his own thoughts. "They're classic Unseleighe, so they wouldn't like the Mustang's Death Metal, but why take chances?"

"Heh. Mustang versus Nightmare—now that's something I'd like the video rights to!" He cracked a smile, and Shar pretended to swat him. "So, you want to aim for what, then? The destination with the possible physical outlet?"

She shrugged. "They're all bad; that seems the one with the least risk. With luck, that physical connection will be to something neutral."

"Right." He was under no illusions here; they were in enemy territory, working without a map, and their best hope was to end up *somewhere* Shar recognized. Only then would they be able to make their way to safe ground.

And home . . . .

Unexpectedly his throat closed for a moment, as longing for home hit him like a physical blow, and he bit his lip. God, he was so tired of running. . . . Home had never felt so far away, so unattainable; at least in the past, he'd known where he was, what to expect, what the limits were. Here, it was all up in the air. And he would give almost anything to see a familiar face. Would he *ever* see anyone he knew again?

"What's the matter?" Shar asked, quickly putting one soft hand over his cold one, as his face reflected some of his feelings despite his effort to hide them.

He shook his head, intending to say nothing, but it came out anyway. "I want—to go home," he whispered hoarsely. "All this--it's all so strange. I've never been this far Underhill before. I've never been anywhere but Elfhame Fairgrove, Furhold, and—I just want to go home."

He couldn't continue. *Fairgrove was a short step, and I was back on my side of the Hill. I wasn't lost. And even if someone was trying to kill me, it didn't matter, because I was standing by my friends.* He had to face the reality of the situation: he could die here, and no one would ever know what had become of him. He was pretty sure by now that Shar was on his side, but they could be separated—they would be separated if they were caught—and he would die alone here.

"I've never had a home, as such," Shar said wistfully. "I have my own domain, but it's really just a place to live. I've never felt comfortable enough with the *kitsune* to live in their realm. I certainly don't want anything to do with my father, or his allies. I have a few friends, but not many. Maybe that's why I spent as much time on your side of the Hill as I did." Her tongue flicked out thoughtfully. "Things are simpler there. At least on your side of the Hill I know the rules, and they don't change."

"Simpler—" He nodded. "That's not a bad thing." Then

he shook off his mood of melancholy with a heroic effort. They didn't have time for this. Maybe Hamlet could take time in the middle of a firefight to soliloquize, but real people had to keep on running and shooting.

"I'll go set the Gate," she said, as if reading his mind. "Be back in a few seconds."

She slipped out of the blanket and the car at the same time; a rush of cold air numbed his ears as she opened and shut the door. She stood beside the Mustang for a full minute, staring at the stone arch, one paw-hand raised to it, palm outward.

The stones began to hum.

He didn't realize what it was at first; he thought that the cold might have introduced a new note into the rumbling of the Mach One's engine. But then, as the sound built, he realized that it came from the stones in front of him, a deep note just barely in the audible spectrum, that vibrated in his chest and made his hands and feet tingle.

Shar slipped back into the car, bringing with her another rush of cold air and a sparkle of frost. "Whenever you're ready."

He put the car in motion, creeping slowly forward, as the dark mist filled the space defined by the three stones. This scene was beginning to take on the uncanny feeling of familiarity; as the Gate swallowed up the lights, the hood, crept toward the windshield, he simply braced himself slightly, the same way that he braced himself against the lurch of an airplane take-off.

This time, though, the moment of disorientation was much shorter. The blackout lasted barely long enough to blink twice, then the Mach One moved smoothly into a thick, gray fog, illuminated from everywhere and nowhere.

He hit the brakes as soon as the tail cleared the Gate; red light washed up behind them as the brake-lights reflected through the mist. He killed the headlights and turned off the engine. There was no point in advertising their presence here with the glare of headlights, even though the fog swallowed up most of the light. Behind them, the Gate was a smooth arch carved of white stone, easily lost in the mist of the Unformed now that the haze of activation was gone.

That was probably the point. If a mage blundered too far away from the Gate, he'd better be able to use his powers to find it again, or he was going to be in trouble.

The Unseleighe were great believers in Darwinism, it seemed.

"Tannim—" Shar said suddenly. "Look at what the mist is doing!"

At first he wasn't sure what she meant; a moment later, though, as he followed her gaze to the hood of the Mustang, he realized what it was she saw.

The mist of the Unformed curled away from the Mach One, leaving a shell of clear space between the metal and the mist. Was the car repelling the mist? Was the mist reacting to the metal, trying to avoid it? The mist *was* charged with raw magical energy, after all. Or was the mist reacting to the spells of protection on the Mustang?

Whatever the cause, here was a visible sign that the Mach One affected the world Underhill, one that he didn't need to invoke mage-sight to read. He watched in fascination as the mist pulled back into itself, for all the world as if it reacted in pain.

Shar's features blurred briefly, and returned to the human ones he knew best. She had shifted as suddenly as a sigh, and as noiselessly as the mist. He was not entirely certain she had done so consciously.

"Probably we ought to both recon this situation," Shar said into the silence. But she made no move to leave the Mustang.

He didn't blame her; there was something about this mist, uncanny, sinister. Sad, too; his depression returned in full force, and it was all he could do to keep from giving up and curling up into a fetal ball right then and there.

Right. And if you do that, there's no way you're going to get out of here, bonehead!

Shar stared out the window, her own expression pensive, her eyes full of secrets.

"Your parents," she said out of nowhere. "I watched you with them, and I envied you for having *two* such people to care for and who cared for you. I could not understand why you left your home so eagerly."

It was not a question, but the questions were there, nonetheless. "It's hard to explain," he told her, knowing that it sounded feeble. "I think the world of my folks, and I know that they are prouder of me than they ever let on, but—" He snorted, as a little more of his depression lifted. "This is really going to sound trite, but they honestly don't understand me."

"Well, you *are* a mage, and they are—good, normal folk," Shar replied sensibly.

But Tannim shook his head. "That's only part of it. They would never understand me, even if I wasn't a mage, but that makes it astronomically worse. They don't know why I do what I do for a living, test-driving, all that. Half the time they think I'm going through some kind of a phase, and after a while I'll get tired of all this and become an accountant, or a car salesman." He ran his hands through his hair in distraction. "They worry about me, that I'll wake up some day as an old has-been driver with nothing to fall back on. And that's just the *surface* problem."

"And the deeper problem?" Shar prompted.

"There's the magic, the Sidhe—which I *can't* tell them about." He clutched his hair. "I've tried; they literally don't hear it. Won't hear it. I'm afraid to try anymore; they might think I was on drugs or something. Mom half hinted at that the last time. Usually they just act like they think I'm talking about a book I read or some movie."

"But they love you—" Shar said blankly.

"Love doesn't mean understanding," he replied, letting go of his hair and staring at his hands. "They don't share the same values I have anymore. How can I pay *any* attention to the package a person comes in, when so many people I'm proud to call my friends aren't even human? Then I get home, and Dad starts bitching about the 'foreigners taking over' and signs a petition to forbid every other language in America but English. And that's only the start of it. Dad's a great man—but he's coming down with hardening of the attitude; looking for some group to blame for problems, and not bothering to do something about the problems. Instead of trying to fix things, he's bitching about it."

Shar's mouth formed into a silent "oh." Tannim's lips twitched. "That's one reason why I try to keep my visits brief, because I know that I let things slip that they worry about. Mom isn't happy about my lifestyle; Dad isn't happy that I've turned my back on three generations of Drakes farming in Oklahoma. I'm not happy knowing that, deep down, they wish I was someone more like Joe." He rubbed the side of his head unhappily. "Sometimes I think I'm a changeling. I couldn't be more of a misfit in my family if I'd been left on the doorstep in a basket."

Shar was very quiet for a long time. "But I thought— you said—"

"I said I loved my parents. I do. And they love me. They just don't understand me." He laughed weakly. "Oh, Shar, it's awfully difficult to explain. Sometimes you can care a great deal about someone, and simply not understand him at all. Especially if you're related to him."

She blinked at him. "Forgive me for saying earlier that life in your world is simpler."

"Life is ne'er simple, lass." Tom Cadge spoke softly from the rear seat. "'Twasn't when I was a lad, and likely has got no better. There's more grief 'twixt relations than strangers."

"Don't misunderstand me. I love my folks, Thomas," Tannim protested. "I just don't fit in their lives anymore. Their home—just isn't home for me now. I don't belong there anymore. I can't go back without feeling like an alien."

"Well, now, that's as it should be, eh?" Tom cocked his

head to the side and turned his bandaged face toward Tannim. "The chick don't go back in the shell, do he? Nor the wee bird go back to his mam's nest come spring again? Ye can't go *back* to a home, lad, not once ye be a man grown. Ye have to *make* your home, your *own* home, or it ain't really *your* home, if ye take my meanin'."

"What about those who've never had a home, Thomas Cadge?" Shar asked softly, with a note of bitterness in her voice.

Tom turned his head toward her, creating the odd impression that despite his blindness, he still saw right through the layers of bandage over the grisly ruins of his eyes. "Those who've never got a home has all the more reason to make one, milady," the old man said with odd gentleness. "Even an old man, half mad an' all blind has a reason t' make a home. An' them as never got a home, well, mebbe they ought t' look to them as knows what a good home is, to show 'em how t' build one. 'Specially summat who's a friend. Bain't that what friends be for?"

Tannim stared at the swirling mist as the silence lengthened. "Well," he said, finally, "Before we get out of the Mustang, we'd better get ourselves in a better mood. That mist out there is going to react to what we're thinking, and even more to what we're feeling. The car's got shielding enough to keep us from creating any nightmares, but once we get out to study the situation—"

Shar straightened visibly, and her face took on an expression of determination. "Absolutely right. I think we're letting this miserable place get to us. And absolutely the *last* thing I want to do is conjure up my wretched father out of the Unformed." She made a grimace of distaste. "One of him is bad enough; two would be unbearable."

"Oh, I don't know," Tannim replied, managing a chuckle. "From what you've said, if you created a second Charcoal, they'd be so in love with each other we'd never have to worry again."

Shar actually smiled. "You have a point," she agreed.

"Still, let's not take any chances." She pulled her hair back from her face, and closed her eyes for a moment. "Right. I assume you don't know anything about the Gates, since you haven't volunteered to examine them with me."

Tannim spread his hands helplessly. "Not a hint. Haven't the vaguest notion how to look into the things. I make my own Gates when I need 'em, but only back in America. However, I *do* know a bit about the Unformed, since Fairgrove got involved in the cleaning up after the disaster at Outremer. If the Gate doesn't pan out, I can probably find that physical connection to the next realm."

"You can?" Shar brightened visibly. "Oh good—I can tell there's one out there, but I can't locate it."

"Then I think we have our two tasks laid out for us; nothing like a proper division of labor. And I believe I'm ready for the mist, if you are." Tannim put his hand on the door and gave Shar an inquiring glance.

"As ready as I'm likely to be." She sighed, and opened her own door with an expression of resolution on her face.

The Unformed was not precisely "mist" as any human knew it. It was neither cold nor damp. It had no odor, no taste, nothing to feel—in fact, if Tannim had closed his eyes, he would not have known it obscured everything in every direction. Anything more than a three feet away might just as well be invisible. As he understood it, the theory went that the mist was a physical manifestation of the available energy in these pockets of Underhill. Raw energy at that; the theory was that once that energy was given a form, it ceased to be random and started to obey normal laws of physics. Until then—you had this mist, potential in its purest form.

It tried to trick you into giving it a form, too. There were phantom shapes out there, shapes that teased the mind and made it strive to put definition on the vague shadows. The more the unwary person peered, the more his mind tried to match the half-seen shape, the more the half-seen shape fitted itself to the image in a watcher's mind.

In the case of one particular child, in a sea of Unformed mist outside Elfhame Outremer, those images had been very terrible . . . .

Forget that. Don't look out there. Don't let it trap you. Just hunt for the pathway into the next domain. Shar might be the expert on Gates here, but that was something he *could* do, though it was a tricky bit of work, and akin to echolocation.

There was a peculiarity to the rock walls of Underhill pockets; they reflected magic. Real rock didn't do that, so Tannim could only assume that the caves of Underhill were not exactly made of rock.

I wonder if they only look like caves because that's what the creatures who first came to this place expected. The mist was psychotropic, after all. . . . If you had enough mist, could you form rock walls out of it?

But that wasn't getting anything done. The point was that the rock walls reflected magic, but a place where the rock wasn't obviously didn't. So he had to become the human equivalent of a bat.

He walked around to the front of the car, settled himself on the hood of the Mustang, absentmindedly pulled a cherry-pop out of his pocket, and unwrapped it. He tucked the cellophane neatly back in his pocket and the candy in his cheek, crossed his legs, and went to work.

Shar faced the Gate, the Mach One a solid and reassuring presence behind her, and closed her eyes, sinking her awareness into the fabric of the pale stone arch. One of the settings she already knew; the frozen plain they had left behind. Her first action would be to count the number of settings this Gate had; after that, she would worry about where they went.

She tended to think of them as directions in three dimensions; forward and back, left and right, up and down. "Filled" settings pulsed with power; the "empty" places where settings would be—when there were any such empty slots, which wasn't often in a public Gate—

held power, but not as much, and always felt to her as if she touched the surface of a glass, warmed by sunlight, holding a gentle glow of magic.

"Up" is the plain that we just left. Damn, the rest are active, too. No chance to add a setting of my own. Ah well, it had been a *faint* hope, after all. In pure reflex, she checked "down" first, and got a nasty shock when she recognized it for what it was.

One of Charcoal's domains? As a destination for us? I don't think so! Of course, as a powerful mage as well as a dragon, her father had more than one little pocket kingdom. He might not be using this one; as she recalled, it was smallish, as small as the ersatz apartment she had built for herself. Charcoal preferred grander dwellings; he mostly used this one as a place to leave people he wasn't sure were guests or prisoners. It was one of the places he had graciously allowed her to use when she was a child.

It's tempting, though. There's at least one setting on every Gate he builds that goes someplace neutral. Charcoal might be insufferable, but he wasn't stupid, and he always kept his options open.

Long familiarity with the Unseleighe let her quickly identify the other four destinations. They all were Unseleighe Sidhe holdings, and all of them places she had visited, thanks to her father's habit of playing both ends against the middle: the Shadow Tower of Bredna, the Hall of Tulan the Black Bard, the private hunting preserve of Chulhain Lorn, and Red Magda's stud farm.

Best not ask what she raises. She might feed you to them.

All of them grim destinations, and all too small to escape from readily. Smaller, even, than Madoc Skean's holding.

The one saving grace was that none of the four were on good terms with Madoc. In fact, Red Magda and Tulan had little private feuds with him that virtually guaranteed they would turn him away with a curse if he came to them on the trail of Tannim.

Of course, this did *not* mean that they would help Tannim. Since the young human was an ally of Keighvin Silverhair, they would probably be perfectly happy to hunt him down on their own. Magda hunted any humans she could find or kidnap just on general principles; she preferred the Great Hunt over any other kind. And as for Shar—well, they'd probably treat her the same as a human.

I have no notion how I'd stack up against them. Rather not find out by meeting them head-to-head, either.

It was rather interesting, though, to discover that she recognized all the destinations of this Gate. Were they finally getting back into familiar territory? That could be good or bad news. Good, if it meant finding a neutral destination at last—bad, if all that happened was that they worked themselves deeper and deeper into the holdings of the darker creatures. Shar had heard rumors of those who'd worked themselves into places where even the Unseleighe Sidhe were afraid to go. And once, when she was a child, her father had returned silent and stiff from one of his own journeys of exploration—and he would not talk about where he had been, only sealed off the setting on the Gate that had led there. Now that was an unsettling recollection.

It almost made a foray into one of Charcoal's holdings into a tempting idea.

She disengaged her awareness from the Gate carefully, making sure to leave behind no traces that she had been there. No magical "footprints" or "fingerprints"; nothing to betray her presence.

Moving that circumspectly took time. She only hoped that Tannim had been able to find the physical opening out there in the mist, since this Gate was pretty much a washout. Of course, they could always go back to the plain and try the other pocket of the Unformed that Gate went to. They might have better luck there.

Behind her, she heard Tannim stirring, the *shh-ing* of denim on the hood of the Mustang. Good! He must have found the opening into the next domain. They could compare notes, make some further plans.

The sound of fabric sliding over the metal ended with the faint *thud* of sneakers hitting the soft, white sand of the ground of this place. She was turning to greet him when a hint of movement out of the corner of her eye caught her attention.

Is there something out there? She peered into the mist, trying not to think of anything in particular, but whatever had been there was no longer there.

She still wasn't certain if the momentary curdling of mist had been the result of the mist "wanting" her to see something, or if it had been something very real slinking through the fog, when Tannim screamed.

• CHAPTER ELEVEN

Tannim slid off the hood of the Mach One feeling rather pleased at how quickly he had found the entrance he'd been searching for. He was straightening up, his defenses momentarily down, when the mist-thing streaked out of nowhere and sank its teeth into his arm.

He never got more than a glimpse of it; his brief impression was of a long, lean creature about the size of a Great Dane, as white as the mist, and impossibly fast.

It was possessed of an obscene number of sharp, white teeth, thin as razor blades, most of which seemed to be scraping his arm bones.

Maybe it was a giant white shrew, or a wild dog or an albino weasel. More likely it was someone's worst nightmare. That was certainly the way Tannim felt when the thing's teeth met in his arm as it knocked him to the ground.

He screamed, unable to stop it, no macho posturing or stoicism—he screamed.

He didn't resist the fall, he continued it, rolling over on his back and kicking at the beast as hard as he could with both legs, feet planted firmly in the creature's belly.

The thing let go of his arm as the breath was knocked out of it in a fetid puff, and the force of his kick sent it sailing over his head.

Into the side of the Mach One.

The monster screeched like a chainsaw ripping through

an oil barrel. For a moment, it hung over the front fender, body convulsing as it encountered some of the protective spells. It screamed again, and a crackle of energy arced across its body, a tiny display of fireworks that obscured whatever the beast had looked like. Not that he was in any shape to notice details.

In fact, he wasn't in much shape to notice much of anything, since he was lying on his side, eyes unfocused, trying not to scream loudly enough to attract another one of the creatures.

The thing hung on the fender for a few more moments, then it slid to the ground and burst into flame.

Within seconds, as Shar ran toward him out of the mist, hands ablaze with magical energies, it was gone, leaving nothing behind to show it had ever existed. Except, of course, for the ragged remains of his shirtsleeve, which hardly amounted to more than a few ribbons of cloth over the armor.

And the bleeding puncture wounds, where the beast's teeth had gone *through* the armor.

He clamped his teeth shut on his own pain and stared at the sluggish blood dripping down his arm in shock as the pain turned to numbness, though he knew *that* state was only temporary. The shock was not only because he had been wounded, but because he had been wounded *through the armor.*

Shar dropped to her knees beside him but did not touch him. "Is that arm broken?" she asked, her voice tight.

He shook his head, unable to speak, for *now* the pain began all over again, worse than before, and his arm felt as if he had—he had—

Ah, God this hurts!

With that assurance, Shar carefully picked his arm up by the wrist, and with one crooked finger, deftly made a slit along the joining of the top row of scales. The armor peeled back from his wounded arm, revealing a half-circle of wide, oozing punctures, all of them turning an ugly shade of purple around the edges.

"Is that poison?" he asked in pain-filled and masochistic fascination.

"No," Shar replied absently, "just fast bruising. Mother taught me some Healing; I'm not in her league, but let me see what I can do."

Shar's reaction was automatic and immediate: *I've got to help him!* Without a second thought, she dashed in the direction of the scream, war-magics ready and burning to be thrown, only to see Tannim go over on his back and flip his assailant against the fender of the Mach One.

That was the end of that; Shar didn't need to watch the beast convulse and burst into flames to know that it was finished.

She dropped down beside him and went to work, ignoring the blazing mist-creature, although she thought it was a species that she recognized. The beast, before it had vanished, seemed to be one of the guard creatures Charcoal had created, or else something cooked up along the same plan. Charcoal did that sort of thing on a regular basis, rather than recruiting other creatures to his service. In fact, when she was young, he had made a habit of going to pockets of the Unformed specifically to create such monsters and chimera, bringing them back to his own domains to serve as watchdogs. Madoc Skean had gone Charcoal one better, creating the Faceless Ones the same way. Both of them preferred the expenditure of personal energy in order to obtain servants that were utterly loyal. The only trouble with these little expeditions was that it was quite difficult to keep the new creations rounded up. They always lost one or two every couple of trips, leaving the creatures roaming the mist, waiting for unwary prey.

That explains why Father had a Gate set here, she thought, as she engaged the little set-spell that parted Tannim's armored scales and slit it along the top of his wounded arm. *This pocket of the Unformed must be particularly sensitive*. The mists were not uniformly psychotropic, and those who used them to create living creatures kept the locations of the best mist pockets as a valuable resource.

She couldn't help but notice Tannim's start of surprise at her ability to open his armor. But at the moment her greatest concern was with his damaged arm; if that creature really was one of Charcoal's "shrogs" (her father's "clever" name for a thing based on shrews and dogs— what an idiot), the wounds could and would go septic in a heartbeat, and there wasn't exactly an emergency room with antibiotics handy.

She sank quickly into a Healing trance, held her hands around the wounds, and forced Healing energies into his cells. She worked from inside out; that way she wouldn't Heal the wound only to leave the infection still active inside. There was no telling if there were any more of the creatures nearby, nor when they would appear if there were more, but Tannim's injury *had* to be dealt with *now*.

As she penetrated his defenses, she realized something else.

There was something very erotic about this; it was the first time that she had Healed anyone other than herself of a serious injury. Shar had closed up other peoples' cuts and soothed abrasions, but this was deeper, much deeper. She was aware of him in a way that she had never experienced with anyone else; the touch of her hand on his arm sent pulses of sensuous electricity through *her* arms; she felt what he felt directly, from the tiny ache where he'd hit the back of his head, to the caress of the silk-smooth armor over the rest of his body, including the places where it was so closely fitted that it held swelling down.

Hmm. They didn't allow for it to expand much, did they?

She had never been so *aware* of a male in her life, or on so many different levels. Not the level of telepathy; neither of them were telepaths. No, this was on a visceral level, where the instincts lived. Was this how an empath felt? Small wonder most of them got into Healing of one sort or another and pursued all Arts of the body.

She wasn't good enough to mend the bites completely; she cleaned out the sites of possible infection, dulled down the pain, and stopped the bleeding. Then she accelerated the cell growth as much as she had the skill and the power to do. In another day, he would have a half-circle of mostly healed punctures, and in two, a half-circle of tiny scars.

She got into the car for a bottle of water and washed the blood off him with it, then got a pad of gauze from the first-aid kit. Figuring that nothing preventive was going to hurt, she dabbed each wound with a spot of antibiotic salve, then wrapped the arm in a thin layer of gauze and resealed the armor over the whole.

It was only when she looked up from the final motions of sealing up the scales that she looked up to see his expression of complete disbelief.

"How are you doing that?" he asked, voice a little harsh from the screams, but harsher still with suspicion. She would have been a little hurt by that suspicion if she hadn't been well aware that *she* would feel the same if a secret of hers had been uncovered. "How did you know how to unseal my armor?"

"Very rapid deductive reasoning," she replied as she let go of his arm, and he flexed it to test it, wincing at residual pain. "You're Chinthliss' pupil, there are only a limited number of ways you can seal armor like this, and I know all of the ones Chinthliss uses. The easiest would be the most logical, since you're obviously going to have to get in and out of it at least once a day, and you might have to get into it when you're hurt. Like now. So I tried the first spell, and it worked."

She tilted her head to the side and waited for his reply. It wasn't long in coming.

"Oh—" he said, "but—Chinthliss told me that no one had ever had armor like this."

"He was right," she told him. "No one has. Most people simply work spells into standard armor. A few more have enchanted Kevlar, or something else high-tech. No one has ever combined anachronism, high-tech, and magic to make something like this. But there are still only a limited number of ways armor like this can be opened."

Tannim sighed explosively. "Well, *damn.* And damn it again; he told me the armor wouldn't stop everything, but I'd gotten kind of used to it doing just that."

Shar nodded, with sympathy this time. She recalled the time that she had first discovered that *she* was not invulnerable in her draconic form. It had been a painful revelation. Literally.

"It's not going to stop everything—maybe in your world, but not here. Any time you have a situation where there's a seam, there's a weakness," she told him. "I still have scars on my ankle to prove the truth of that."

"I'm sorry," he said, as if he meant it. "You shouldn't have scars anywhere."

She held her breath, and looked up, to meet his intensely green gaze. "Oh," she said, unable to think of anything else.

What are you doing, Shar? You're a kitsune, *you're supposed to be unpredictable, wild, willful. What are you getting yourself into?*

Just because you've always found this man fascinating, intriguing—just because he's the only male you've ever imagined trusting at your back—and at your front—that's no reason to sit here like a love-struck ninny, gazing into his eyes.

That's no reason to want to kiss him. Or to pull him right down next to you on this relatively soft ground and finish stripping off that armor.

Like hell it isn't!

"Bloody hell!" said a voice just above her head. "What was that 'orrible screeching?"

Tom Cadge had his nose stuck out of the open window; apparently he'd managed to figure out the mechanism to lower it. Both she and Tannim jerked upright; he with a curse as it jarred his arm, and she with a curse for a different reason entirely.

"Nasty piece of Unseleighe work," Shar said, as she got up off the ground and offered Tannim her hand. He was not too macho to accept it, or to accept her help in getting to his feet. "It bit Tannim," she continued, trying to sound matter-of-fact.

"I'll be all right," Tannim added hastily. Then, in an undertone, "I will be all right, won't I?" he asked Shar. A stray lock of hair fell over his worried eyes, and his complexion was pale. "I don't feel all right."

"Don't play any tennis with that arm for a little, and go have a Gatorade. You're just in shock," she assured him. "In fact, it might not be a bad notion to move the car just to that opening you found, and then sit there for awhile. The intersections of domains tend to be rather chaotic and stressed, and I think perhaps that the Mach One won't make as much of a disturbance there." She gave him a sharp look, as she noticed that he was leaning very heavily against the side of the Mustang. "I can drive, if you can direct me."

"I think maybe you'd better," Tannim replied honestly. "I really don't feel very good at the moment."

He went around to the passenger's side and opened the door with a little difficulty. She slid into the driver's side and found the keys waiting in the ignition. As soon as she settled herself, she cast another long look at him, and did not like what she saw. Pale and sweating, he was obviously still in a lot of pain, and very shocky. "Here," she said, fishing behind the seat for another Gatorade. "Just tell me where to go, and I'll get us there. You rest—and when we get there, you should take a longer rest."

"I'm not going to argue," Tannim told her, as he leaned back in his seat and closed his eyes. "Not at all. Forward, about two o'clock."

She followed his directions, murmured between gulps of Gatorade, through the absolutely directionless white mist. Finally, the rock wall of the boundary loomed up in front of them, gray and smooth, rather than craggy as a natural rock face would be. "Right," Tannim said. "I

mean, go right, along the wall. You'll find it in a
moment."

She did; in fact, she spotted the place where the opening was by the turbulent swirling of the mist ahead of
them. The mist itself was no longer white or drifting;
stained with pale colors and random shifts of light, it
eddied and flowed restlessly. It still avoided the Mustang,
however, which was comforting; anything that lived in it
would probably be as vulnerable to Cold Iron as the creatures spawned in the quieter areas.

She parked the car and turned off the engine. "Rest,"
she told him. "The problem might just be a bit of shock;
give your body and mind a chance to catch up with what I
did."

He started to protest, then evidently decided better of
it. "How bad are ye hurt, lad?" Tom Cadge asked with evident concern.

"Not too bad," Tannim replied, as Shar rummaged for a
Gatorade of her own. "Been hurt worse."

"But we are not going any further until you are completely ready for anything," she told him in a voice that
would permit no argument. "I never got a chance to tell
you back there, but we've got more than one choice. We
can try this unknown pocket of Unformed ahead of us, or
we could try something that has—well, risk. The Gate
goes to one of Charcoal's smaller domains. He might be
there, he might not—but it's a place I know, and I can get
to neutral territory from there."

He sipped his Gatorade, a lock of his hair falling over
his eyes, as he sat in thoughtful silence. "So, the choice is
the total unknown, versus a place where we know there's
an enemy, one who may or may not be home right now."

She grimaced, but nodded. "If it were me—I'd go for
the mist. I haven't been in that particular place for a long
time, and Charcoal may have laid some nasty traps for the
unwary in there. And anyway, even if he isn't there, his
serving-creatures will be, and I don't think I could pass
them anymore. But I thought you ought to know that the

option is there; you have as much say in this as I do. If you think we should risk the known danger for the sake of a known way out—"

But Tannim shook his head decisively. "I'd rather take the unknown. You probably know Charcoal better than anyone else, and I'm strongly in favor of trusting an expert." He raised an eyebrow at her. "I take it that the rest of the destinations were equally unattractive?"

She smiled thinly and recited the other four destinations. His eyes widened for a moment at the mention of Red Magda and the Black Bard, confirming her guess that he just might know something about them.

And they just might know something about him, too. I rather doubt that they want to make certain he gets invitations to all their weddings and bar mitzvahs.

"The last possibility is to go back where we came from," she finished. "We could try the other settings on that Gate. The drawback is that if someone is following us, we might meet them."

"The other side of this rock wall sounds better all the time," Tannim said after a significant pause.

"A little rest, first," Shar said firmly. "You need it."

And I am not going to drive his car into another domain. If there's any trouble—I know who the good driver is in this car, and it isn't me or Thomas Cadge.

Chinthliss stalked off down the garden path, with Joe right behind him, and Fox making a reluctant third. "You really shouldn't do this, you know," FX said plaintively. "Lady Ako has some powerful friends. She could cause us a lot of trouble."

Chinthliss did not reply. His stiff back said it all. As their feet crunched along the gravel path, Joe glanced from side to side, nervously. He could not believe that Lady Ako would let them go so easily after detaining them for so long.

He was right. Two massive guards in fancy lacquered armor stepped, literally out of nowhere, to bar their path.

It was really *weird*; they unfolded out of the air on either side of the gravel walkway, then stepped onto it with curved swords bared. Chinthliss stopped abruptly; Joe loosened his weapon in its holster.

"I told you she could cause us trouble! We're doomed," Fox said from the rear of the group.

With a growl, Chinthliss turned abruptly; Joe stepped out of the way, leaving Chinthliss face-to-face with FX. The *kitsune* backed up a couple of steps after one look at Chinthliss' expression of rage. The guards didn't move, and Joe opted to disregard them for the moment, in favor of keeping Chinthliss from disemboweling Fox right then and there.

Fox held up his hands placatingly. "Hey, it was just a comment, you know? A little information? A bit of a reminder?"

Chinthliss took another step towards him.

Fox's hands transformed into a pair of fur-covered paws.

"Wee paws for station identification?" FX continued, with a nervous, feeble grin. "Ah—please accept my apology for the social fox-paws?"

The corner of Chinthliss' mouth twitched, although Joe could not see anything that would have been funny in that last sentence. But evidently the dragon did, and Joe breathed a little easier. Maybe Chinthliss wouldn't kill the *kitsune* quite yet.

"I did not bring you along as my court fool," Chinthliss replied coolly. "Whatever capacity Tannim has you in. I brought you because you are a *kitsune* and Shar is half *kitsune*, and I assumed your knowledge of her would be useful."

"What about the information Shar's mother could give you?" The sweetly feminine voice coming from behind Joe had a distinct edge to it. Joe turned again, and the two armor-clad bulwarks parted to let Lady Ako pass between them.

"Your information would be damned useful, my lady, if you could just bring yourself to part with it instead of offering endless Tea Ceremonies," Chinthliss replied, his own voice honed to an icy sharpness. "Failing that, we will simply seek help elsewhere."

"I have not been *your lady* for a very long time. You will not need to look elsewhere." Lady Ako made this a statement without a hint of apology to it. "There are circumstances surrounding this sad state of affairs that required you be detained." Her tone said, as clearly as words, that she did not intend to apologize for anything, nor did she intend to give any further explanation than this. She matched Chinthliss stare for stare.

Finally Chinthliss broke the silence. "Fine," he said abruptly. "I suppose I'm going to have to assume this has something to do with internal *kitsune* politics, the secrets of which mere mortals are not free to plumb. As long as your little game is over with, I'll put off looking for that cab."

He crossed his arms over his chest and waited, wrapped in dignity, for her to reply.

She bristled. "Do not presume to dictate my actions to me, Chinthliss!"

"I wouldn't dream of it," the dragon replied dryly. "Nor will I be drawn into an argument so as to permit you to delay us even further."

Fox looked from one to the other of them, and finally held up both paws. "He's called your bluff, Lady Ako," the *kitsune* said bluntly. "You might as well admit it, and give us some real help."

Lady Ako stared for a moment longer, then sighed. "He has indeed called my bluff. And the best I have is a pair of twos," she admitted. "All right; I can't seem to delay you any further, so we might as well get down to the business of actually finding them." She started back toward the building they had all stalked away from, and with a glance to the rear at the impassive guards, Chinthliss, Joe, and FX followed her.

"I've had someone watching the boy's car since it came Underhill," she said, as they mounted the steps to the graceful porch, and a few *kitsune* sitting on the flat cushions watched them with covert curiosity. "Not actually watching it, you understand, but keeping track of it by means of the disturbance it causes in the magic-fields. Shar managed to cloak it somewhat, but that much Cold Iron was bound to wreak a certain amount of disturbance no matter how skillfully she shielded it—a disturbance of a distinctive flavor, as you know."

"That makes sense." Chinthliss mounted the wooden steps of the building, keeping pace beside her. The steps creaked slightly under him, as if he weighed far more than his appearance would suggest. "But why track the vehicle instead of the people?"

"Because Shar is better than I at cloaking spells, and I do not know Tannim." Lady Ako held the scarlet-painted door open for them, and they all filed through—except for Chinthliss, who took the brass handle from her and bowed her inside. It seemed to Joe that she smiled faintly at the gallantry. "I knew that Shar would bring Tannim to his vehicle if she found a way to free him, because it represents a powerful weapon of defense," she continued. "And I know that Madoc Skean has no allies other than Shar who could do anything with so great a concentration of Death Metal. Further, I suspected that only Tannim would have whatever other devices were needed to make it work, such as a key. So it followed that no one but Shar or Tannim would be able to move it. Not long ago, my intuition bore fruit; the car moved, and as soon as it moved, Shar's cloaking-spells destabilized, making it easier to track. Since we saw no motive-spells working, it must have moved under its own power."

Chinthliss stopped right in the middle of the white-paneled room. "It did? Where? And where is it now?"

Lady Ako beckoned them to follow, past a room full of flat cushions on the floor, through a sliding paper screen instead of a door, and into the kind of room Joe had not expected to find here.

It was a room full of computer equipment, mostly deep

blue and bright red, with huge screens. There were at least a dozen SPARC stations and Silicon Graphics computers that they could see, with about half of them being used by creatures that were more or less foxlike. Some only had fox tails, some fox tails and feet, and some were humanized foxes as Lady Ako had been when they had first seen her.

They were all dressed in varying costumes, from futuristic jumpsuits to the full kimono-kit that Lady Ako wore. The lady bent over the shoulder of one of the silver foxes in a pearl-gray jumpsuit; this one had long, flowing white hair crowning her fox-mask and cascading down her back.

"It isn't that easy, Chinthliss," Ako said at last. "We know that the vehicle is moving, and we know in general where it is, but we can't tell specifically." She shrugged helplessly. "You simply cannot *map* Underhill; I have tried, with no success. You can go north, then east, then south, and find yourself facing north again. You can go up several levels only to find yourself four levels *below* the place you had started. The Gates do not connect domains in any kind of logical fashion. This room holds the closest thing anyone has to a map of Underhill."

"They're somewhere in the predominantly Unseleighe region, my lady," said the silver fox, tapping the screen with one furry forefinger. "If they can just get into one of the larger domains, one where we can pinpoint them by what Gates they are near, I can give you coordinates. But now— well, the sensors and programs we are using only show that they've used Gates to make domain-jumps, but since we don't have those specific Gates in our lists, it can't locate them precisely." The silver fox looked at everyone assembled. "We have magical sonar, and there's a lot of noise. We don't get a ping on them until they *do* something."

"You see?" Ako held up her hands helplessly. "We can track the perturbation and know that they are moving. Once they reach and use a Gate that we have in the computer, we know where they truly are. But until then, we'd be jumping blind."

Joe nudged Chinthliss. "Sir," he said hesitantly, "what about the trim-ring? Tannim used it to find the Mustang. Couldn't we do the same thing?"

"I wouldn't do that if I were you, sir," the silver fox replied respectfully, before Lady Ako could say anything. She turned around to look Chinthliss right in the eyes. "That much iron and steel is warping the magic fields down there in ways I can't predict, and neither can the computers. We just can't model chaos that well. If you tried to use that artifact to create a Gate, you might end up tearing a hole in the fabric of Underhill. Or you might just end up Gating somewhere you wouldn't like. The odds of actually going where you wanted to go are pretty low. We could run a simulation—but if we had enough data to make an accurate simulation, we'd have enough to find the vehicle, too."

"Laini is my best tech," Ako said, placing a hand on the silver fox's shoulder. "If she says it's dangerous, I'd believe her. And if she doesn't like the odds, I wouldn't take the risk."

Chinthliss eyed both of the *kitsune* dubiously. "So what *would* you do if you were in our position?" he asked.

Laini thought for a moment. "You might use the trim-ring as a magic-mirror, just to *show* you where they are. We use an optical link through a magic-mirror to connect to Internet from here. The Internet is great for hiding things and communicating with obscure locations on Earth—Underhill enclaves with outerworld fronts, allies, informants—just bounce encrypted files from one anonymous site to another. Anyway, we use a tuned laser beamed through two stationary mirrors—one here in Furhold, and one on the other side. If you use a magic-mirror, you get a super clear image most of the time. You might recognize something we could use, or get a photograph sharp enough that we could cross-reference it through our Silicon Graphics image systems here." She pointed one delicately-clawed paw—hand—at the crimson boxes whirring away. "We have thousands of subrealms identified and imaged, and some of them are mapped down to ten-meter grid squares with local magical data. We just don't know all the Gates that lead to them, because that takes a lot more than remote viewing. But we do have some."

Laini looking thoughtful again and tapped at her silvery-black snout. She flicked an ear. "If you can determine a *place*, or give us enough data that we can find it, we might be able to plot a route that could get you there, using the Gates that we know of."

Joe grinned. *Now that's a little more like it!* he thought. Evidently Chinthliss felt the same.

"I didn't realize that you had an artifact," Lady Ako said, "or I would have offered all this a little sooner."

"Is there somewhere secure that we can use to set up a scrying-spell?" Chinthliss asked. "You know what I mean by 'secure,' I trust."

"Of course." Ako smiled sweetly. "This *is* the embassy, after all. We have some very secure places. If you'll follow me?"

Once again, Lady Ako led them all down a maze of corridors, this time with walls of white paper and bamboo rather than white-painted wood. How such a place could be considered "secure" was beyond Joe, but if Lady Ako said it was, he might as well take her word for it. At least no one would be able to eavesdrop on you here—you'd see his shadow through the walls first.

Maybe that was what made it secure?

At length she pushed aside a sliding door and led them into a room containing what was either a very small building or a very large box, lacquered in black, with graceful images of cranes and carp—and, of course, foxes—on the sides, formed in strokes of gold paint. "You will be secure enough in there," she said. "It will be a little crowded, but it is very well shielded."

She opened a door into the box; it looked rather like a sauna inside, with benches against two of the walls and a low table in the middle. Somehow all four of them managed to squeeze inside; Lady Ako and Chinthliss on one bench, FX and Joe on the other.

Ako shut the door; after a moment of darkness, a gentle, sourceless light came up all around them. Chinthliss placed the chrome trim-ring down in the middle of the black-lacquered table.

Here we go again . . . .

As all three of the others bent over the shining circle of chrome, Chinthliss chanted under his breath. A drift of sparks came from his outstretched hand and settled on the ring, exactly as if he had sprinkled glitter down on it. But these sparks spread and grew, until a skin of light coated the whole trim-ring.

Mist gathered inside the ring, and all four of them leaned a little closer. "Damn," Chinthliss muttered irritably, "that tech of yours is right. The Mach One really is warping things all out of shape down there."

Ako laid one hand over the top of his, and a second shower of sparks fell on the ring. The light strengthened, and for just a moment, a picture formed in the middle.

It *was* the Mach One, all right; Tannim was in the passenger's seat, though, and in the driver's seat was the woman who'd shown up at the barn. There was someone else in the rear seat, too, and the whole car was surrounded by a white mist that eddied around the car as if it didn't quite want to touch it.

Then the picture faded, leaving only the shiny black lacquered surface of the table.

"Well, at least we *do* know that they're together," Lady Ako said into the silence.

"But who was that in the rear?" Joe asked. "And where were they?"

"The Unformed," Chinthliss growled. "There are only several hundred places they could be, with that Unformed mist around them. Damn."

But surprisingly, it was FX who shook his head. "That's the bad part; don't forget, the Unseleighe and the Seleighe both have Gates into those pockets. So do the neutrals, for that matter. It's not a big deal; we just need a little more time. We just wait for them to Gate out of there, and see if we can identify where they came out."

"Which means we sit here until the car moves again." Joe sighed.

Chinthliss nodded abruptly, scowling.

Lady Ako looked from one gloomy face to another, and finally ventured to speak. "I don't suppose," she said doubtfully, "that any of you would care for some tea?"

Shar stared at the swirling, pastel-colored mist and wondered if it was half as unsettled out there as she felt. Most disturbing was the feeling that things had gotten completely out of her control.

Her reaction to Tannim being attacked was entirely out of character. If Tannim hadn't already slain that mist-creature, she would have reverted to Huntress-mode and leapt upon it to rend it with her own, sharp teeth right then and there. She *never* leapt to anyone's defense; she always assumed that they could take care of themselves. After all, no one was going to leap to *her* defense . . . .

The strength of her own feelings had shocked her; more shocking had been the way she had automatically reacted on seeing that he had been hurt. She had *never* expended Healing on anyone else before. Not once. She was not a "natural" Healer as Lady Ako was; it cost her a great deal to invoke a Healing spell. There had never been anyone worth the effort before.

And before my mind could weigh all the consequences, I found myself Healing him without even pausing to think about what I was doing. Very strange. Very unlike her.

Tannim did not sleep this time, but he rested as Shar had ordered, slowly regaining color as he sipped at a Gatorade and nibbled at packaged crackers. After a glance at her, which she met with a smile, he fished under the seat and came up with a car magazine. His inquiring glance asked "may I?" and her answering shrug replied "be my guest." He immersed himself in its pages as she stared out at the mist, still sorting her thoughts.

It was logic, she told herself firmly. *Pure logic. This is his car, we need each other at top form to guard the other's back. I Healed him because of that. It has nothing to do with how I feel about him.*

And pigs were certainly flying in tight formation over LaGuardia at this very moment.

"Ready to switch places?" he said into the silence. When she gave him a measuring look, he grinned at her with a good measure of his old cockiness.

"I would certainly not care to take the blame for anything that happened to your beloved car if I ran it into something out there," Shar replied dryly. "Please, Captain, take the helm by all means."

But before popping any doors, they *both* checked the mist for the telltale swirls that signaled something hiding in it. And Shar noted with some amusement that both of them scooted around the car and into their new places so quickly that it would have taken a photo to tell which of them hit the seat first.

She snapped her seatbelts in place. He quirked his eyebrows at her. "Paranoid?" he asked.

"Of course," she retorted. "They *are* out to get us."

"Point taken." He started the car and drove into the mist, heading for the place where the colors and eddying were the strongest.

The gap in the rock walls must have been larger than she had thought; when the rock disappeared on the left, there was no answering darkness up ahead to show where it might resume. Tannim turned the Mach One into the gap, still keeping the wall on the left. The mist was at its most turbulent here; the predominant color was a blue-green, but there were swirls of red, yellow, even purple.

"This place makes me think of an explosion in a tie-dye plant," Tannim muttered under his breath.

Shar peered ahead into the psychedelic fog, every

muscle and nerve alive with tension, and started when Tom Cadge tapped her shoulder.

"Please, lass," he said quietly, "can ye tell me where this magical chariot is goin'? All I know is we been someplace cold, an' now we're someplace else."

"Did you ever—ah—see any of the places that the Unseleighe Sidhe call 'Unformed'?" she asked. She hated to ask it that way, but Cadge didn't seem to mind.

"Before they put out me eyes, ye mean?" He shook his head. "I heard tell of 'em, but I ne'er saw one. I didna see much but Lady Magda's Hall, an' not much o' that."

"Well, that's where we are. It's a place full of mist, and not much else, and someone with a strong enough will and magic can make it into anything he wants," she told him. "Somebody left something nasty behind the last time he was here, and it attacked Tannim."

"Mist?" Tom shook his head. "What can anyone be doin' with mist?"

"It's a special kind of mist," Shar replied absently. "Think of it like clay. That's how most of the domains were made in the first place, right out of the mist. Either one incredibly powerful mage, like Lord Oberon or Lady Titania, or a group of mages with a single plan in mind, would move into one of these places and turn it into what they wanted."

"So?" Thomas replied. "Is that where we are, then? One o' them mist places?"

"Exactly. There are often Gates in there, and that's what we're looking for." Shar continued to stare ahead as she talked to Tom; was it imagination, or was the color slowly leaching out of the swirling mist? "People can make small things out of the mist, too, so they'll come here when they need something and create it."

"So—if ye can make anything ye like, why don't ye make a Gate now?" Tom asked with perfect logic.

Shar sighed. "Partly because I'm not certain either of us is up to creating a Gate at the moment. Partly because this iron carriage that protects us also warps magic around it,

and I'm not certain what the effect of making a Gate
around it would be. Partly because a Gate is one thing you
can't make out of the mist with any certainty at all—it
would be like you trying to juggle a dozen sharp knives at
once. And lastly, making a Gate makes a fearful disturbance; there are people watching for us, and they'll know
where we are and what we're doing."

"Ah." Tom nodded wisely. "So I see. This workin' of
magic, it just purely isn't like—like magic, is it?" He
grinned, amused at his own wit.

"Precisely." She forced a tired chuckle since he wouldn't
be able to see her smile. "Well, we're going to see if we
can't find another Gate in here to take us somewhere
nearer to our friends."

By now the mist had definitely gone to pastel. In a few
more moments, all the color would be gone, and it would
be time to stop the Mustang and see if she couldn't locate
another Gate on this side of the wall.

But as the color leeched out of the mist, the mist itself
thinned. Shadow-shapes appeared in the thinning mist,
not the moving shapes the mist itself produced, but stationary shadows, with solidity to them.

The mist thinned further as the Mustang rolled forward, and the shapes took on substance, color, and
texture. "Are you seeing what I'm seeing?" Tannim asked
quietly.

"I think so," Shar replied, while she cobbled together
the most apt comparison *she* could come up with. "This is
really weird. It looks like somebody's rock collection."

If it was, the collector had to be a giant. Ahead, behind,
and on either side loomed huge slabs and boulders of polished, formed or crystallized stone, each piece as big as
the Mach One or bigger. These slabs balanced upright
somehow, defying gravity, even though their bases might
be no bigger than a foot or so across. The impression of
being in the midst of a rock collection was inescapable
now that Tannim had pointed it out; no two of these huge
"specimens" were alike, and they all appeared—at least to

Shar's uneducated eyes—to be purely of a particular "kind" of rock. Here was a cluster of quartz crystal points, the smallest of them as long as her arm and the largest taller than Tannim—there a polished boulder of amethyst big enough to crush the Mach One—ahead a single giant violet diamond-shaped fluorite crystal balanced precisely on one point.

"This is bizarre," Tannim said softly, staring at the next rock, a milky yellow multifaceted crystal which balanced on a single point like the fluorite crystal now behind them. The one next to it looked for all the world like an irregular slab cut from a geode and polished on both sides. "Have you ever heard of anything like this?"

"Never," she said firmly. "But I'm not sure I like what it implies. *Someone* had to create all this out of the Unformed; that's the only way you'd get things like this, right? So that person had to not only be some kind of rock-nut, but he had to be a complete monomaniac."

"Rock is my life, man," Tannim said automatically, but the joke fell rather flat.

Mist writhed away from the Mach One as they passed the balanced slab and a round boulder of pink quartz appeared to the right. "To the exclusion of everything else?" Tannim hazarded. "Boy, I hope we aren't disturbing his collection, wandering around in here!" He ran a hand through his tangled curls worriedly.

"Why don't you stop for a moment, and let me see if I can find a Gate," Shar suggested, feeling as worried as Tannim looked. "If someone got in here to create all this, there has to be a way out. I think I'd like to find it before he finds us."

Tannim nodded, and stopped the Mustang between a colorful metallic cubic aggregate of selenium and a polished granite egg the size of a Kenworth. Shar got out, checking all around them with such caution that it felt as if every nerve was an antenna, tuned for danger.

Only when she was certain there was nothing within the reach of her senses or her magics did she take a seat on the hood of the Mustang and send her spirit out questing for the peculiar magical signature of a Gate.

"Want to try again?" Joe suggested, as the rather stilted conversation in the crowded room died into silence again for the fourth time.

Chinthliss looked at Lady Ako, who alone of them had not lost her outward serenity. She shrugged. "I told my underlings to come inform us if the Mustang made a sizable change of location. That would indicate a Gate-passage, of course. There's no telling, though, if they were able to locate a domain *within* the Unformed where we saw them. Elf-hame Outremer is such a place; I'm certain the Unseleighe also have domains within the mist. I know that the Grand Bazaar is in the mist, and that it is not the only neutral hold to be in the center of the Unformed."

"Is that a 'yes' or a 'no'?" Chinthliss asked in open exasperation. "Oh, never mind. *I* want to see if your precious daughter is up to anything." He bent over the chrome trim-ring, and once again chanted until a shower of sparks drifted down from his hand and settled on the chrome ring. This time the lacquer tabletop enclosed by the ring fogged over with no help from Lady Ako.

The haze cleared, and Joe leaned over the table for a closer look.

Shar sat on the hood of the Mach One, her eyes closed and a frown of concentration on her face. Tannim stood beside the car in a protective stance, his bespelled red crowbar in his hands, watching warily to all sides. The Mustang itself was parked in front of a huge gray boulder, a rock as big as two cars put together and polished to a glossy sheen. The mist of the earlier vision was thinner here, but there was still nothing really identifiable about the place.

Joe looked up at Lady Ako to see her reaction. She was smiling: a satisfied little smile compounded of equal parts of approval and relief.

"It seems they truly are working together," the lady said with a faint air of satisfaction.

Chinthliss only grunted. "I should give a great deal to know how my foster-son's sleeve came to be so shredded," he replied.

Joe glanced back down at the little scene imprisoned in the chrome circle, and saw with a start that Tannim's right sleeve *was* hanging in rags. But beneath the shirt-sleeve was something altogether unexpected; armor of some kind, he guessed. Iridescent green, of tiny hexagonal scales invisibly joined together, it covered his arm as smoothly as Spandex from wrist to shoulder.

"Pretty," Lady Ako remarked, indicating the armor with a fingertip that did not quite touch the image. "I assume that this is your doing, this armor?"

"As much Tannim's as mine," the dragon admitted with a touch of pride in his voice. "I happen to think that it is very good work. Something must have attacked them, though."

"If so, it learned that he bites back," Ako observed. "Honestly, I do not recognize this place, although I will inform my techs with a description, and we will see if the computer has a match. What of you?"

"Not a clue," Chinthliss admitted, as Ako slipped what looked to Joe like a palmtop computer out of her sleeve and laid it on her lap, quickly scratching something on its screen with a fingernail before returning it to her voluminous sleeve. *I always wondered what they used those huge kimono sleeves for. Heck, you could smuggle Mexicans in there!*

"You seem to be having an easier time holding the vision this time, old lizard," Fox observed. "Got any idea why?"

Chinthliss shook his head. "Probably has something to do with the area they're in. Less instability, maybe. There's a lot less of the Unformed mist, anyway." He turned to Ako. "What's *she* doing?"

"I would guess that she is searching the area for a Gate," Ako told him. "Shar is particularly sensitive to the energies of Gates. Even if she does not recognize a setting, she can sometimes tell general things about the destination."

"No—" Chinthliss took his eyes from the vision in the chrome trim-ring for a moment to stare at Ako in astonishment. "Where did she pick up that trick? From—"

"Yes," Ako confirmed. "I myself do not know how she does this. It is not a *kitsune* gift."

"It isn't a dragon-talent either." He shook his head. "Evidently she is not simply a meld of *kitsune* and dragon; she is something more."

"As I have always maintained." Ako was too composed to beam with pride, but there was a great deal of pride in her voice.

Inside the chrome circle, Tannim walked a wary patrol around the car as Shar remained perched on the hood. There was nothing in Tannim's behavior that suggested to Joe that he was at all worried about Shar or what she might do. If anything, his prowling suggested that he was determined to protect her from anything that might come at her out of the mist.

That certainly suggested they had come to some sort of arrangement, an agreement of cooperation, perhaps.

The vision still wasn't clear enough to make out who was in the back seat of the Mustang. The figure was blurred, as if the focus was a bit out in that one spot, although the rest of the scene was clear enough.

"I can't see what is in the backseat," Chinthliss said with a frown, echoing Joe's own thought. "That's odd. Look, you can see the front seat itself clearly enough, so it isn't the Mach One's shields that are interfering." He glanced sharply at Ako, who only shrugged.

"I could not tell you who that might be," she replied. "Shar has no allies that she would trust in a situation like this. Perhaps it was someone they met along the way?"

"Maybe another prisoner of Madoc Skean," Chinthliss muttered. "Tannim wouldn't be able to leave someone like that behind. Especially not if it was a Seleighe Sidhe."

"Can you blame him?" Fox made a face. "I wouldn't leave a dead cat in the hands of that lunatic."

"Maybe if I—" Chinthliss held his hand over the trim-ring again, his eyes narrowing as he focused his magic. "I would feel a lot better if I could just see who or what that is—"

But his efforts were not only in vain, they undid everything else he had accomplished. As Joe watched in dismay, the vision flared, then faded, leaving only the hint of haze on the black lacquer.

Then even the haze faded, and only the shiny surface remained.

Chinthliss cursed, but Lady Ako remained philosophical. "You can only hold such a vision for so long," she reminded him. "And what good would it do you to sit here and stare at it? You cannot help them until you know where they are."

Chinthliss growled under his breath, but had to admit that she was right. "But I don't have to like it," he added. Joe agreed silently. At least, if they could watch, they had the illusion that they could do something.

"I can—" Chinthliss began, then pulled his hand back before he even began the spell again. "No. No point in wasting magic that we might need later."

"A messenger *will* come if the Mustang makes a large enough movement for a fix," Ako promised. "I gave you my word."

At that, Chinthliss actually smiled. "I do not recall that you actually gave your word before, my lady, but now that you have—I am inclined to trust you."

Ako looked at him in some surprise, and Joe thought, she also looked a little hurt. "Have we grown so far apart, Chinthliss, that you no longer trust me without my given word?" she asked softly.

Chinthliss blinked, and turned to meet her gaze completely. The two of them stared deeply into one another's eyes, unable to look away.

Joe cleared his throat, and they both jumped and looked at him as if they had forgotten that he and FX existed.

Maybe they did forget we existed.

"Can we—ah—take a break, lady?" he asked carefully. "All that tea—"

"I don't—" Fox began, and Joe jabbed him fiercely in the side with an elbow. FX emitted a strangled grunt and fell silent.

"Certainly," Lady Ako replied, ignoring FX. "Saski can show you where everything is. Can't you, Saski?" Now she smiled at FX, to his obvious discomfort.

"Yes, Lady Ako," FX managed. Joe slid the door to the little room open, and he and Fox climbed out. The door slid shut again as soon as they were outside.

"What did you do that for?" FX hissed angrily.

"They *wanted* to be alone, dummy," Joe replied scornfully. "Jeez, man, couldn't you see that? Don't you remember what Chinthliss told us about him and the lady and all?"

"Of course I remember! That's why I wanted to stay there and watch!" Fox told him. "And—*ow!*" he exclaimed, as Joe elbowed him again. "What did you do *that* for?"

"Because you're rude, crude, and not even housebroken," Joe told him, shaking his head in dismay. "Man, I can't take you anywhere, can I? Why don't you show me what passes for a bathroom around here. I really did drink too much of that tea."

Fox sighed and cast a longing look back at the closed doors of the little room. "Oh well," he said philosophically. "We'll figure out whatever they've been up to when we get back anyway."

"You're impossible," Joe retorted.

Fox only snickered.

• CHAPTER TWELVE

Tannim prowled around the car restlessly, the comforting weight of his crowbar filling both hands. He studied the mist as it eddied around the giant mineral specimens, watching it with wary suspicion. Mist alternately concealed and revealed the farthest of the rocks, moving in no pattern he could discern. Unless he was greatly mistaken, the farthest of those rocks was a slice of watermelon tourmaline, a huge irregular wedge of transparent pink and green. He wouldn't even have known that watermelon tourmaline existed, much less what it was called and what it looked like, if Dotty hadn't been so infatuated with the stuff.

She'd be going ape right now, trying to figure out how to cart a five-ton rock out of here. Boy, this place is surreal. I feel like I'm in the middle of a Lexus commercial.

He kept thinking that he saw things moving, just out of the corner of his eye. But any time he turned to see what it was, there was nothing there but a swirl of mist.

Too bad I'm not some kind of superhero. I could sure use an edge right now. Heros in books had magical senses to warn *them* of approaching danger; all he had were his eyes and ears and mage-sight. *My crowbar-sense is tingling!* The mage-sight wasn't doing him a heck of a lot of good; the mist itself was full of magical potential and obscured everything else.

It's doing me about the same amount of good as a guy with a heat-scope in the desert at high noon.

That left eyes and ears. Plain old human senses, backed by red-painted iron and a bit of experience. Maybe a little good sense. It would have to do.

His feet made no noise at all in the sand. None. He might just as well have been walking on a foot of packed feathers. The ground here was as strange as the rest of the place. You could dig down just as far as you wanted, and all you'd find was sparkling white, utterly dry sand. Yet neither the tires nor feet sank in more than an inch, and there was firm, excellent traction, as good as the sands of Daytona Beach. Better. As good as the Bonneville salt flats. *If I could just export this stuff, I'd make a fortune selling it to dirt-tracks.*

He glanced over at his companion every time he passed her, just to see if anything had changed. Shar's face was utterly still, without expression of any kind. Once again, she looked like a statue sitting there; if he hadn't seen her chest rising and falling in slow, even rhythm, he'd have thought she was dead, spellbound, or otherwise incapacitated.

And that chest, rising and falling, up and down, slowly—

It looked as good as the rest of her. He prowled a series of full circuits around the Mustang, still without seeing anything. This bit of magic was taking her a lot longer than the last time she'd done something. Of course, the last time, she'd had the Gate right in front of her, and this time they didn't even know if there *was* a Gate over here.

What would they do if there wasn't a Gate here? *A good question. Turn around and go back, I guess. Take our chances with one of the unfriendly settings, or with the place before that. It was cold and not very hospitable, but we wouldn't have to be there all that long. I hate to backtrack, though. We might meet something on our tail. That would be bad.*

It shouldn't take them all that long to get on our tail, either. All they have to do is figure out that Shar didn't move the Mach One like she said she did.

By now, Madoc Skean must have figured out they'd slipped through his fingers. He and his cronies were surely on their trail in some form or other. How long would it take him to sort through all of the possibilities? He wasn't stupid; he wouldn't have amassed as many allies as he'd had if he was. He had to be on his way already.

There—something flickered at the edge of his vision again. This time he patrolled a few more soundless steps, then made an abrupt about-face, hoping to catch whatever it was in the act of eluding him.

Nothing. Not even an eddy of mist.

Maybe this place is getting to me, making me see things. Haven't been this jumpy in a long time.

He decided that he might as well prowl in the opposite direction, since he was facing that way anyway.

Madoc's not stupid, and he's got a lot of ears in other domains. So, given how good a spy-network Madoc has, by now he's surely heard about our little visit to the Hall of the Mountain King. From there, there're only five destinations besides the one we came from. Given enough people to check them out . . . yeah, he could be on to us right now.

"Eh, lad?" Tom Cadge called from inside the car, sounding anxious. "How long ye reckon afore the black-guards follow us?"

Even the old man was following his thoughts.

"I don't know, Tom," he answered truthfully, leaning against the car to talk through the window. "Could be they're after us right now. The one thing we've got going for us is that they've got to tread the same maze that we do. With any luck, they'll get as lost as we are."

Tom nodded, his mouth solemn below his bandaged eyes. "Mayhap they'll blunder into a nest 'o their own foes, eh? Like knockin' over a beehive. That'd be a choice jest."

"Oh, that'd be the best thing that could happen," Tannim told him, with a mental image of the Black Bard's surprise on finding his home invaded by his old rival Madoc. That would be a lovely sight to see! If Madoc got out of there with half his followers, he'd be lucky. The Black Bard was without mercy when it came to his few friends—and when given a chance at a foe . . .

Tom cocked his head to one side for a moment, then grimaced. "This place is mortal strange, lad. I keep thinkin' I'm hearin' summat off i' the distance, an' then when nothin' comes of it, thinkin' it's nobbut m' addled wits."

"Well you're not alone. I keep seeing things, but when I turn to look at them, there's nothing there." He pushed away from the car as Shar stirred. "Well, it looks like the lady may have found us something. Keep your ears open, all right? They're probably keener than mine."

"Aye, I will," Tom promised solemnly.

Tannim reached the front of the Mustang just as Shar opened her eyes. "There *is* a Gate here, but it's a long way off," she said, stretching her arms and blinking to clear her sight. "I wouldn't have believed this pocket was so big— that Gate must be six or eight miles from here. I can't think of too many places Underhill that are this size, and all of them have huge populations."

Tannim raised an eyebrow at that. "I wouldn't have thought it could be that big either; I would have thought that a pocket this large would have been claimed by now."

"Maybe it has," she replied ominously. "I caught distinct traces of Unseleighe magics out there. Only traces, so this isn't truly a domain of theirs, but they use this place for something."

"Grand." He sighed, and hefted the crowbar just for the reminder of its comforting weight. "Well, let's get on the road, shall we? If we're moving, we're a harder target to hit."

She slid off the hood without a comment, and landed lightly on the sand. He turned around and and headed for the driver's side. He reached his seat a fraction of a second before she took hers, but this time they both fastened their safety belts.

She pointed directly ahead when he looked to her for

directions. "Straight on, the way we were already going," she said.

He nodded, with a quick glance at the gas gauge. He'd started this trek with darn near a full tank of gas, and he'd tried to be careful—

And we're still a hair above the three-quarter margin, he noted with a bit of relief. *Hard to find a gas station out here, and neither of us are Sidhe, to be able to* ken *and* replicate *whatever we want.*

He started the Mustang and drove on, slowly, in the direction she indicated. Visibility still wasn't good enough to warrant going faster than fifteen or twenty. Another towering rock-sample emerged out of the mist right in front of them, this one a huge nugget of pure copper, constructed like a branching coral formation.

Weird. Just too weird. He shook his head, and drove on.

A half an hour later by his watch, the mist had thinned to no more than a veil, upping visibility to about half a mile. The landscape had been changing for about the past fifteen minutes. The rock formations grew smaller, replaced by groves of dead and leafless trees, stretching blackened limbs against the white haze in the distance. Overhead was exactly the same as the nonexistent horizon: white haze. Lighting was a constant semidusk, nondirectional. All the place needed was a vulture or two for atmosphere.

The terrain itself had changed in that time; getting rougher, with increasingly steep hills and deep valleys, and nothing like a road in sight. The Mustang wasn't built for territory like this; heck, the Mustang wasn't built for anything but a real road. The only way to handle this kind of situation was to work his way up and down the hills in a zig-zag pattern, or travel along the ridge until a better crossing place showed up. The ground was still made of that strange sand; why it didn't slide and behave like dune-sand he had no idea. The top layer would slide down a little as the Mustang's wheels touched it, making the going a bit treacherous and tricky to drive, but beneath the top layer, the ground was firm.

That didn't help much, not when his jaw ached from clenching it and his knuckles were white from clutching the steering wheel.

Finally, they topped a rise only to find themselves looking down into a valley with a fifty-degree slope. Tannim stopped the car altogether.

"We can't take this in the Mach One," Shar said abruptly, before he could say a word. "Nothing short of a Land Rover could negotiate a slope like that. Tannim, I'm amazed you got this far—I'd have given up a mile ago. I almost asked you to quit when we passed that hematite boulder."

Tannim stared down the smooth slope, unbroken except for an occasional boulder of some highly polished stone or by a trio or quartet of spindly black trees, and nodded. Finally, after a long silence, he coughed.

"I'm pretty much stuck here without you," he admitted. "I don't know how to work those Gate things without already knowing the setting I want. I guess it's going to be up to you. Do we ditch the Mach One and try for this new Gate on foot?"

He was hoping she would think that was a bad idea. *I'll argue with her if I have to, but we're partners in this. I'm not going to make an arbitrary decision for both of us.*

Shar shook her head immediately. "No," she replied decisively. "Not a chance. This is one we're going to have to do without. It'd take us hours to get there on foot, Tom couldn't do it, and we'd be without our protection, our ability to move quickly, and our power source. That wouldn't be stupid, it would be suicide."

He ground his teeth to relieve his frustration, then gave voice to the only other solution, the one he'd already contemplated. "We go back. And try the other Gate."

She nodded, her own face displaying her distaste for the obvious. "And unless we're willing to take the chance on running into the people following us by going back to the frozen plain—the only other setting we stand a chance with is Charcoal's holding."

"We'll decide that when we get there," he replied. "One problem at a time."

At least he had a good idea how to *get* back. The soft sand didn't hold tracks forever, but he could still make out a clear trail behind them. While the tire-tracks in the sand were still visible, he could follow them. And after that— he'd kept track of the various rock-samples they'd passed. Unless the unknown collector (if there was one) had a habit of swapping them around on a regular basis—or they moved on their own—he'd get back to the point where the mist got so thick he could use *his* talent to find the gap in the walls again.

It didn't feel right, though, turning back like this. Besides being frustrating, it felt as if he had missed a point somewhere. Granted, this wasn't a video game, where you always got the next level if you did things in the right order, but still—turning back felt like a mistake. There *ought* to have been a way, but if there was, he hadn't seen it, and neither had Shar.

One thing was oddly comforting, though, and that was Shar's behavior. Not only had she refused to give up the Mustang—she'd refused to dump Tom Cadge.

That was automatic, too. She didn't lean over and whisper to me that we ought to abandon him with the car. She didn't suggest we leave him and come back for him with help. It wasn't, "we could leave the passenger behind, but that wouldn't be right." Instead, it was, "it would take us hours on foot, and Tom couldn't do it." As if there was no question of keeping him with us—it's a given.

He could trust her. He *could*. That single sentence had told him that much. She had nothing to gain and everything to lose by continuing to help the old man, and she hadn't even given it a second thought. It had been a completely natural response; that she accepted him as a responsibility along with her "debt" to Tannim.

His mood now much lighter, he surprised her by

smiling at her once they got the Mach One turned around
and headed back the way they had come. The furrows cut
by the tires pointed the way, and he followed, retracing
their path exactly. And hoping that he was doing the right
thing.

*Now as long as there isn't someone laying false tire-
tracks for us to follow, we'll be all right.*

"I suppose it could be worse," she said after a moment.
"There might not *be* anyone following us yet. We do have
options still, and there's—"

Her head and Tom's came up at the same moment in
identical startled movements, like a pair of deer alerted by
a danger signal. "Oh, no—" she whispered.

"Tell me I didna hear a huntin' horn, milady," Tom
begged, his wrinkled face white beneath the bandage.
"Please tell me it was just th' wind, or summat like that.
There's only one kind o' pack a-huntin' Underhill—"

He was interrupted by the sounding, faint but clear
over the Mustang's rumble, of a hunting horn. At least,
Tannim assumed it was a hunting horn, since they both
shivered when they heard it.

"The Wild Hunt," Shar whispered, her eyes wide. "Oh
no—we don't need that kind of trouble!"

"Whoa, whoa, what Wild Hunt?" Tannim asked,
responding to the fear on both their faces by speeding up
just a little. "What hunt? What's it mean to us? Who're the
hunters?"

"The lost gods," Shar said fearfully, looking back over
her shoulder as if she expected to see them at any
moment, topping the hill behind them. "The spirits that
once were gods of death and darkness in your world, who
lost their worshippers and were banished Underhill. They
hunt the living, led by their pack and their terrible Master.
Even the Unseleighe fear them and hide when they hear
that horn. It's said that there's no escape from them. Once
they have the scent of you, they *never* give up!"

"Won't all this Cold Iron stop them?" he asked, as the
horn sounded again, and sent a chill running up his spine.

"I mean, we're talking pre-Christian, Bronze-Age guys here, aren't we? Shouldn't the rules that hold for the Sidhe hold for them?"

"The Master of the Hunt bears a spear tipped with the Death Metal from a fallen star," Shar replied, dashing his hopes. "That is why the Unseleighe fear him. They are no more bothered by iron and steel than a *kitsune*. They can cross running water with impunity, and holy things do not bar their way. Only sunlight stops them, and I doubt we're going to get any of that piped in to us on request!"

Tom Cadge had hunched down into his blankets, shivering, his head completely covered, like a child trying to hide from the monsters in the dark. It didn't look as though he had anything coherent to add.

"Great," Tannim muttered. "So what *do* we have going for us? Anything at all we can use against them?"

"We're not predictable." She stared through the back window; the horn-call sounded again, and it was definitely nearer. "They are more powerful than you, I, and all the Seleighe in Fairgrove put together—they used to be *gods*, for heaven's sake! Their horses never tire, nor do their hounds. But they will never have seen anything like this car, and they won't know what it, and we, can do. For that matter, they may not realize that the Mach One isn't alive—remember how the elves in the Mountain King's Hall reacted? If we can get out of this, it'll be by our wits."

"If I can get us into the heavy mist, can we lose them?" he asked. "Do you think that the turbulent area where the two pockets join is going to be confusing enough that they might lose the scent?"

"I don't know—but that just might work." She bit her lip and closed her eyes for a moment, thinking furiously. "Come to think of it, I know more than a few tricks along those lines. If you can get us some lead, *I* can kill the trail so cold they'll never find it, once we get into that mist!" Shar said at last, with determination replacing the fear in her eyes. "There wasn't a clever fox worthy of his tail yet that couldn't baffle any pack, on this side of the Hill or on the other, and haven't I nine tails?"

"That's the spirit, milady," Tom quavered from beneath his blankets. Tannim was surprised that he could respond at all, as obviously terrified as he was.

"All right then," Tannim said firmly. "Just let me get down where I can do some real driving, and I'll buy you that time."

In answer to that, the horn sounded a new set of notes entirely, and faintly beneath it came the deep and baleful baying of hounds.

Not the excited belling of foxhounds, however. These howls had a strange and doleful sound to them, as if the dogs themselves were in pain and wanted nothing more than to inflict that same pain on their quarry. This was a howl of bloodthirsty despair, a cry of doom approaching on four sore paws, whipped on by something even more terrible behind it. The deep cries called on the fear in the soul, the terror of the *thing behind,* the monster in the darkest shadows of childhood.

"They don't have hawks or anything, do they?" Tannim asked, suddenly struck by a horrible thought. If he had to contend with attacks from above as well as the hunters on the ground—granted, a hawk wouldn't be able to do a lot against the Mustang, but if this Master had complete control of them, there were things he could do *with* them. Having them drop rocks on the windshield—or hurl themselves against the windshield in kamikaze attacks.

"Not that I ever heard," Shar assured him. "Hawks can't be forced to course the way that hounds can. Turn a bird loose, however you have coerced it, and it can and will fly away."

One less thing to worry about. "Good."

As the ground gradually leveled, it became easier to drive. The sounds of the Hunt behind them grew ever nearer, as if the Hunters realized that *they* had the advantage here, and were determined to catch up while they still had that advantage. "What kind of rules are they limited by?" he asked, negotiating the downslope of a hill studded with gemlike boulders. "Can they go faster than a normal horse would?"

"I don't think so," Shar replied after another moment of thought. "The whole point is that the Hunt is their sport, and it wouldn't be sporting if they could just run anything down, would it? The quarry has to have some chance."

"Well, how would they react if the quarry fought back?" he asked. "If we took some of them out before they caught up with us?"

"I don't know. I'm willing to find out, though." He glanced quickly at her, to see that she looked determined and stubborn. "I'll throw everything at them I can think of."

"Take everything you can from the Mach One," he told her. "Try not to erode the shields too much, if you can help it, but drain whatever you need."

But she shook her head. "We need the shields too much, if what I've heard is true. No, I'll be throwing everything I can back there, and most of it *won't* be offensive." Another glance at her showed she was smiling thinly. "My training is primarily from mother's side; the *kitsune* way is trickery and illusion. That's what I'll try first."

The horn-call behind them sounded as if the Hunters were close, very close; perhaps no more than three or four hills away. He made out the calls of individual dogs within the general belling of the pack.

Not good.

"I see them," Shar said, as they topped another hill. Her voice was strained and tight. He glanced into the rearview mirror and caught a glimpse of a darkness, a swiftly moving shadow in the distance, a mob of *something* that poured over the top of the hill like a dark flood. Something about that shadow sent a chill across his heart, and a touch of frost into his soul.

But beside them were the last of the dead trees, and ahead of them the first of the really large rock formations.

This hill was the last bad one; after this, he could take them straight on, and since he knew what they were going into, he could accelerate down the hills to get momentum for the climb.

Shar was twisted around in her seat in a position that couldn't possibly have been comfortable, but she didn't release her safety-belts. *Probably a good idea,* he decided. *I don't know what kind of evasive driving I'm going to have to do.*

Tannim dropped the accelerator another half-inch and the Mustang's velocity increased. The white sand went up in a rooster-tail behind them as they put some serious distance between them and their pursuers. The sparkling shapes of the stones blurred past, while the speedometer needle swept toward three digits.

"Tannim, driving like crazy will buy us some time, but it won't stop them. Ten-second quarter-miles won't stop the Wild Hunt."

Tannim grinned. "Here. Hold the wheel. I'll slow 'em down." He rolled down the window on his side, and Shar leaned as far sideways as she could manage with her seat-harness still buckled to grasp the wheel. Tannim let off the throttle, and the Hunt closed on them.

The wind whipped his curly hair around his face as he hung his left arm, still somewhat tattered, out the window. He chewed on his upper lip a moment and sighted along the rearview mirror before turning his head to face the bad-dreams-on-hooves behind them. The Hounds, canine sacks of sharp bone, were solid black with glittering eyes, loping along as fast as greyhounds on a track. The Hunters were all in black—barbarian types in fur and flying capes, crude tunics, but all of it in dead black. They all wore helms that hid their faces completely, which was fine by Tannim. The horses they rode were also black, but they had fangs instead of horse's teeth. What disturbed Tannim the *most* right now was that they were close enough he could *see* such details through the white sand the Mustang was clouding up behind itself!

It was that rooster-tail of sand that had given him this idea, though, so maybe it wasn't all bad. Tannim conjured up one of his planes of force, the same kind he had been using as ramps for the Mach One. He laid it down behind the speeding Mustang, a few feet behind the rear chrome, and dragged it along. The plume of sand grew even taller while Tannim adjusted the angle of it to make it a scoop. He then called another plane into existence. This time it was vertical, and caught the majority of the sand the other one was kicking up.

Then he snapped his fingers and the vertical one dropped back behind them, braced between a monolith of beryllium and a bus-sized lump of coal. He snapped his head around to face forward, grinning like a fool. *What are you doing, you idiot? Are you actually showing off? You are! You are! You're showing off for Shar!*

"That's one!" he said as he dropped the accelerator pedal again and the engine's rumble went up in pitch. "Now for the clincher—take the wheel again—"

Tannim changed the angle of the trailing plane of force, simultaneously making it both wider and taller. In a few moments more, they had a perfect square of white sand following them as they shot between rows of semiprecious stones the size of student apartments. Tannim laminated a second thin wall of force over the sand, let off the throttle again, and to Shar's obvious amazement, stopped the car.

"What are you *doing?*" Shar demanded.

"Hang on. You'll see," Tannim said tersely. He unbuckled and stepped out of the car. With a few hand gestures, he slid the upright square of compacted sand to one side, and then split it in half horizontally. He shuffled that half down to ground level and pushed it off to the other side, then placed one slab of white sand on either side of the tire-tracks.

"What are you doing?" Shar asked again, a note of frantic worry in her voice this time.

The sand they had left in the air behind had settled enough that he could see, with disconcerting clarity, that their pursuers had split around the wall he had put up a minute ago. Some had simply punched through it with impunity. It had, after all, just been compacted sand, held together by the vestiges of a walling spell.

The hellish horses were lathered. They had no eyes, only dark holes where the eyes should be. The Master of the Hunt was the only Hunter whose face was visible; he wore an open-faced helm crowned with stag's antlers, and his horse was practically a skeleton. The Master *looked* like the ultimate predator; there was obviously only one thing for him, and that was the hunt and the kill.

And they were all gaining.

Tannim kept his hand gestures to a minimum, so he wouldn't telegraph to the closing horde what he was up to—by now they must be thinking their prey was exhausted, stopped to make a hopeless last stand.

Well—if that's what they're thinking, I sure hope they're wrong.

Tannim called up three more planes of force, dropped them into place, and dropped back into the driver's seat as fast as he could. His foot was on the accelerator before his door was even closed, and an eyeblink later, the Mustang was moving again. The thickness of the ever-present mist was increasing. Behind them, the Hunters' horn sounded again, audible over the growling engine—

—and was abruptly cut short. Tannim looked in the rearview mirror.

Behind them, the Wild Hunt's dogs and horses were being cut down by the planes of force he had left at knee-height on either side of the upright, double layered, and very rigid walls of force. Horrors of ages past, spectres of ancient armies and spirits of death were being clotheslined at the kneecaps and vaulted, deathless faces first, into the white sand. By a kid from Oklahoma in a fast car.

And beside him, a half-dragon, half-*kitsune* lady was feverishly concentrating on—something—glowing in her hands.

"This is it!" Shar shouted over the howl of the engine. "This is my trump card! If this one doesn't work—"

She didn't finish the statement. She didn't have to. They both knew what the outcome would be if the Hunt caught up with them.

The mist was so thick now that Tannim's effectiveness as a driver was cut in half. The rocks weren't spaced apart at predictable intervals in this section, and there was always the chance he might run into one if he wasn't careful. That would bring a swift end to the Hunt, but not the one they wanted.

So now it was up to Shar to shake their followers off the trail.

There were no fireworks this time; Shar simply held something small in her hand, visibly pouring every erg of energy left to her into it. She finally tapped into the resources of the Mach One as well; Tannim sensed more power draining from it into whatever it was she held, as if she had suddenly opened a spigot at full force.

Then she dropped it—whatever it was—out the window. And collapsed into the seat, her face drained and white, her eyes closed.

A flash in his rearview mirror startled him into glancing up, taking his attention off her for a moment. To his amazement, there was another Mustang behind them, with two occupants in the front seats, speeding away at right angles from their own path!

She's built a decoy! But how—

"A hair from me, a hair from you, and a loose screw from the dashboard," she said faintly. "Wrapped up in a swatch of silk. It won't create tire-tracks, but it's made to leave a strong scent, magical and physical. I hope it'll hold them until we pass the wall into the other pocket. The decoy will incinerate in about twelve minutes . . . but by then, our trail should be cold enough that they'll give up."

However she'd done it, it had taken everything she had in her, and then some. It was obvious that she had held nothing in reserve. She lay back in the seat, pale and drained, so tired that only the seatbelt was holding her erect.

So now it was up to him again; he'd bought her the time to create the decoy, now her creation was buying them the time to escape.

Time to find the gap in the wall, and get the heck out of there.

Tannim waited until the last of the color and turbulence was gone from the mist around them before bringing the Mach One to a halt and turning the engine off. Shar had not moved in all that time; she was as spent as a channel-swimmer or a marathon-runner at the end of the race. She hadn't even noticed that they'd left the realm of the Hunters.

"Are you all right?" he asked, wanting to touch her, but not certain that he dared. As a sort of awkward compromise, he took both of her cold, limp hands in his to warm them.

"Are we there yet?" she replied, without moving or opening her eyes. "Are we on the other side?"

"Yes—and I can't hear the Hunt anymore." That had been a relief; the moment he'd crossed the barrier of turbulence, he'd lost the last sounds of horns and hounds, and they hadn't returned. It looked as if Shar was right; the Hunt couldn't track anything past all that magical confusion. They might not even be able to find their way in it.

"Nor can I, lad," Tom put in from the rear seat. "An' I think I got sharper ears nor ye."

Shar heaved an enormous sigh of relief, and finally opened eyes that mirrored her own complete exhaustion. "I think we've lost them. I didn't dare believe it, but I think we managed to lose them."

"You mean *you* managed to lose them, clever fox," he said, squeezing her hands. She smiled faintly and squeezed back. "If you hadn't created that decoy, we'd never have gotten away from them."

"There ain't many as escaped the Wild Hunt," Tom

Cadge said, with awe and delight. "I didn' think e'en the two o' ye coulda done it!"

"I couldn't have done it," Tannim said flatly. "Not alone. All the fancy driving in the world wasn't going to shake that bunch." He shook his head at her shrug. "No, I know what I'm talking about and—look, Shar, I want you to know something. I know we aren't out of this yet, but—you're free of your debt to me. You've put in more than enough to get us both out of this mess."

At that, a little life and color crept back into her face. "But I haven't gotten you back yet—" she protested. "You were right. I got you into this, and the only way to balance the scales is to get you home again."

"I know," he replied, "but you've done more than you had to. It's not your fault we couldn't go back the same way I came in. So, no matter what else happens, the scales are balanced so far as I'm concerned, all right?"

"If that's the way you want it," she said slowly, "all right. But I'm still going to get you home, and I'm going to get Tom somewhere that will be safe for him."

"I know," he said, letting her hands go, with a smile. "I know. Now, help me find that Gate again, all right?"

Finding the Gate was a great deal easier than he'd thought it would be; Shar didn't even need to stir herself to help. On this side of the wall, with no wind to disturb the sand and no hills for it to slide down, the tire-tracks were still as plain and as clear as if they'd just driven by a few seconds ago. He simply followed his own trail back to where it ended at the alabaster arch in the midst of the shifting mists.

Now there was only one decision left to make.

"Back to the tundra?" he asked out loud, staring at the translucent rock of the Gate. "Or somewhere else?"

"The only 'else' we have available is that little domain of my father's," Shar replied, sitting up and running her hands through her hair in an obvious effort to revive. "It has to be the tundra. We'll just have to go there and hope that we don't meet up with Madoc."

"And if we do?" he countered. "Shar, if we have a plan in place, we'll be one up on him. If we can move while he's still staring, we have a chance to get away."

She nodded slowly. "You're right. The worst that can happen is that we don't use that plan. Do *you* have any ideas?"

"Actually, I do." He stretched and popped a couple of vertebrae in his neck. "I think we ought to keep the Gate live behind us. And if we run into Madoc on the tundra, we duck back through to here before he can react. He won't know where we went, so we'll have a little lead time. *Then,* from here—we go straight to Charcoal's pocket holding."

She stared at him, eyes wide. "You have got to be kidding. That's crazy! Why don't we just stand off in the mist and let them search around, wait until they give up on this destination and then go back to the tundra?"

But he shook his head. "Because Madoc's going to leave someone to guard that Gate on the frozen plain. If we stand off and wait, they can still follow the tire-tracks and find us. But if we go to Charcoal's domain, when they come through here, they just might see the tire-tracks on this side and follow them out across to the other side of the wall. If they do that—they'll run right into the Hunt."

He waited while she absorbed all that and gave it some serious thought—particularly the part about leading Madoc to the Hunters.

"At the worst," he continued, "they'll figure out which setting we used and follow us there. By then, if we haven't gotten into trouble, we'll be following Gates that *you* know, and we won't be flying blind anymore."

"Those are all good points," she admitted. "And I can't think of a better plan." She ran a hand across her eyes and rubbed her temple wearily. "I hope we don't have to make too many fancy maneuvers, though. I don't have too much left in me."

He knew then exactly how much had been taken out of

her by that last heroic effort. She would never have admitted her weakness if she hadn't known there was no energy, no strength in her to call on anymore.

And now he was in the uncomfortable position of trying to decide what was the most risky proposition. Should they stay where they were until Shar recovered a little, taking the chance that the Wild Hunt might find them, or some other, equally nasty inhabitant of *this* pocket jumped them—or Madoc found them?

Time is running out, either way. We're getting hemmed in.

Or should they go on, and take the chance of running into Madoc with Shar in a dangerously weakened state?

"I wish I knew where Madoc was right now," he muttered, running his finger nervously across his chin.

"If I had my old air elementals, I could tell you," she replied, her eyes growing suspiciously bright and wet. "They used to scout things for me, until Madoc murdered one of them, and the rest of them ran off in terror." She rubbed her hand across her eyes. "My favorite . . ."

He sat down beside her and offered his shoulder. He half expected her to refuse it.

But she didn't. She put her head down on his shoulder and wept silently, tears soaking into his shirt, her whole body shaking with quiet sobs. He held her, sensing that the tears were long overdue.

For the moment, decisions would have to wait.

Joe tapped quietly on the door of the black-lacquered room, after intercepting FX just before he yanked the doors open with no warning to the occupants.

The door slid aside after a moment's pause. Lady Ako was the one who opened it, but Joe thought that Chinthliss looked a little less out-of-sorts. He still looked *worried*, but not as annoyed as before.

There was no change in Lady Ako's expression, at least not that Joe could read, but then she surely had a doctorate in inscrutability. He hoped that the two of them had

gotten *some* of their differences ironed out while he and
FX had left them alone.

He'd never have admitted it out loud, but he was kind
of a romantic, and he had heard the pain in Chinthliss'
voice when the dragon had told the story of how he had
lost Ako. Maybe if Ako knew that, it might make some difference to her. Maybe if Chinthliss got over some of his
attitude problems, she'd be willing to give him another
chance.

But Lady Ako's first words had nothing to do with the
relationship between herself and Chinthliss. "The computer has a tentative match with some of the things
Chinthliss and I have seen while you were gone," she said.
"If the match is a true one, it is most imperative that they
make some move to get out of there before very long. It is
a most dangerous pocket of the Unformed."

"Aren't they all?" Fox asked, as he took his place behind
the table.

"Not all pockets are accessible to the Wild Hunt," Lady
Ako said shortly.

"What?" Fox yelped, every hair standing on end. Joe
blinked in surprise at Fox's reaction. He'd never actually
seen anyone or anything but a cat bristle with fear before.
It was a very interesting effect; Fox became twice his normal size for a moment, before Lady Ako's soothing hand
motions calmed him.

"Tell me we *aren't* going there," FX begged. "Please,
Lady, tell me we aren't going there after them! I'm only a
three-tail, I can't take on the Wild Hunt!"

"Not unless we have more than just a 'tentative match'
from a collection of silicon chips to go on," Chinthliss
replied. "The lady has graciously put one of her best sorcerors at our disposal; when we *know* where they are, he
will give us a Gate that will take us directly to them. But
we are not going to waste that advantage until we have no
doubts."

"Indeed," Ako added with a decisive nod. "I wish that
we could work your Tannim's trick with the chrome circle

a second time, but while we are all Underhill, the mere presence of even this much steel—" she tapped the ring with one claw "—changes the effect of our magic. We have not practiced in the presence of Cold Iron as Tannim and Shar have; we do not know how to use the effect."

Joe stared at her as something hit him. Oh, surely the lady had thought of this already! It was so *obvious*—

Oh, what the heck. "Then why not go up?" he blurted, face and ears reddening as he thought about how stupid he must look. "Why not go to our side of the Hill, where your magic won't be affected as much?"

"Oh, it will still be affected," Ako said with a sigh. "The problem is the magic itself, and not entirely the place where it is cast. Your Tannim *knows* those effects, we do not. He could compensate for them, but we have never had the need to learn to do so."

"A mistake, and one that I have pointed out to others," Chinthliss rumbled. "No point in rehashing old debates. I—" He broke off, suddenly, and his expression changed. "Ako, the boy is right! I had forgotten that Tannim used the ring to *build* his Gate! We cannot use the trim-ring to do more than scry here, for a number of reasons—but we *can* make a Gate out of it on the other side of the Hill *because we will make the Gate from it exactly as Tannim did!* You've been assuming we would create a new Gate, not that we would use the chrome circle! And it won't *matter* if the Mustang warps magics where it is, because the trim ring is *part* of the Mach One! It *would* matter if we were trying for Tannim himself, say, or Shar, but *not* if we're linking into the Mustang directly! Magical resonance should . . ."

He went on at some length about "Laws of Magic" and spouting some kind of mathematical equations—Ako replied in the same vein, with great enthusiasm and growing excitement. Within seconds, Joe was hopelessly lost. Fox's gaze went back and forth between the two of them, like a spectator at a tennis match, but Joe couldn't tell if he was actually following the increasingly esoteric conversation or not.

Well, it hardly mattered. Chinthliss thought his idea was going to work, that was the point, and it looked as if he was convincing Lady Ako. Finally she nodded.

"I believe you are right," she said. "And what is more, I believe your logic is absolutely sound, magically and mathematically. There is no need for us to sit here in idleness any longer."

She slid the door to the tiny room open, and the three of them followed her out into the larger room. "Come," she said with an imperious gesture, showing no sign of stiffness after all that sitting in cramped quarters.

Chinthliss winked broadly at Joe and FX behind Lady Ako's back, but followed her with no other comment.

She paused only to shed her fancy outer kimono and collect a belt hung all over with a variety of implements. Beneath the elaborate robe she wore a much more utilitarian outfit, something like the jackets and loose pants that karate students wore, only in a scarlet silk as red as blazing maple leaves in autumn, bound at the waist with a scarlet scarf. She slung the belt over the jacket and pulled it snug.

"So where is this sorceror you promised us?" Chinthliss asked mildly, as she gestured again that they should follow and headed down a corridor that ended in a door. She waited while Chinthliss got the door, nodded gracefully, and preceded Joe and FX through it. It let out onto a perfectly ordinary sidewalk bordering a paved street in the middle of a well-manicured park of the kind that would surround an English manor-house. Grass as perfect as a carpet of Astroturf undulated beneath huge oak trees and immaculately groomed bushes, and made plush paths between beds of flowers in full and riotous bloom. Behind them, the building, which Joe *knew* was huge, was nothing more than a single-storied one-room cottage surrounded by more beds of flowers, picturesque as anything in a fairy tale.

Lady Ako advanced to the street without a single backward glance. "Taxi!" she called, waving her paw-hand in the air, although Joe hadn't seen a single sign of anything like a cab. But within a few seconds, one appeared—this time it wasn't a cartoonish taxi like the last one, but a perfectly normal London cab.

"Where to, mum?" the driver asked in what was definitely an English accent.

"Grand Central Station," she replied, getting into the front, next to the driver, leaving the rest of them to pile into the rear. It was a bit of a squeeze, with Joe stuck in the middle, but they all made it. The cab smelled pleasantly of leather and metal polish; it made a U-turn and proceeded down the tree-lined avenue at a modest pace. There wasn't any other traffic, and no one on foot, either.

Fortunately, the ride wasn't long. "That's it, up there," Chinthliss said, waving at a building rising above the trees ahead of them. Joe had no clue what the real Grand Central Station looked like, but it probably wasn't anything like this . . . .

Carved of white marble, the place rose several stories tall, covered in arches and staircases—and it made Joe dizzy just to look at it, because it was all so completely *wrong*. Staircases were at right angles to one another, even running upside-down, arches gave out onto platforms that were at the tops of staircases that nevertheless went up from the platform, even though the platform was already higher than the staircase. . . .

Worse yet, there were people walking all over this thing, upside-down, sideways—though always at the correct angle to the surface they were walking on.

"Don't think about it," FX advised him in a kindly voice. "It's all right, it just isn't operating by the rules you're used to."

If that wasn't the understatement of the century! At least the *bottom* story looked normal enough as the taxi pulled up to the single entrance. Joe decided that the best thing he could do would be to fix his gaze firmly on the ground in front of him and not look anyplace else.

Lady Ako paid and tipped the driver, and they all piled

out of the cab onto the white marble sidewalk. Joe refused to look any higher than the first floor, but that was impressive enough. The whole thing was white marble, and every inch of it was carved with patterns of flying birds that became fish that became birds again, or lizards, or rather bewildered-looking gryphons.

"The sorceror?" Chinthliss prompted. Lady Ako just smiled.

"I've always said that if you want something done right, you should do it yourself," she replied. "Why should I delegate something this important to someone else?"

"Ah." Chinthliss only nodded. "Hence Grand Central Station."

She shrugged. "It will save me some effort," she replied, as if that answered everything. "The price of four tickets is far, far less than the cost of the safety of my daughter."

Chinthliss only bowed, and gestured to her to lead them on again. She did so, taking them under an archway upheld by two pillars carved with sinuous, intertwined lizards.

Once inside, Joe forgot his resolution to only look down at his feet. He stared upward, gawking. They were inside a single enormous room of white marble that reached into the misty distance. Around the edge of the room was a ramp spiraling upward until it dwindled far above them into a mere thread. Giving out onto the archway were doors with names carved over them and inlaid with black marble. Joe simply couldn't read most of those names; they weren't lettered with anything he recognized. The words were as foreign as Arabic or Chinese.

People were coming and going from those doors; not many, and not at any regular intervals, but there did appear to be a certain amount of steady traffic.

"Don't worry about those," FX told him, nudging him to get him moving again. "What we want is over there—"

The *kitsune* pointed to another arch, this one quite plain, but with a ticket booth at one side. Lady Ako was already there, buying tickets, while Chinthliss waited beside her. There was a single word carved above this archway as well: *Home*.

Home?

"Come on," Fox urged, as the lady turned away from the booth with tickets in her hand.

"What the heck does that mean, 'Home'?" Joe asked. "What's going on here?"

"All those doors you see up there are Gates," Fox explained as the two of them hurried to catch up. "You can get here from just about any domain Underhill—this is the other side of the park from the gazebo where we came in. If you don't want to use up your own magic in building a Gate to somewhere, you can always come here and use the public Gates. Underhill couldn't exist without this place, actually, it's sort of the center for everything. This is *the* most neutral spot in the universe. You could meet your deadliest blood-enemy here, and no matter how much you hated each other, you'd both better smile, nod, and ignore each other. The guardians of this place don't interfere with much, but break the peace, and they'll squash you flat."

FX giggled. "We call 'em Sysops."

"What's that got to do with 'Home'?" Joe persisted, as they came up to where Chinthliss and Lady Ako were standing just beneath the archway.

"This is a unique Gate in all of the domains," Ako supplied, handing him a ticket. "It requires an enormous amount of magic to operate—and it will take you home. Wherever your home is. It responds to *your* desire, to the place you feel is truly home to you—anywhere Underhill, or anywhere on your side of the Hill, from Warsaw, Poland, to Warsaw, Indiana; from Athens, Greece, to Athens, Georgia. For that reason, although the other public Gates here in Grand Central Station are free or of nominal cost to use, use of *this* Gate is very expensive—but I do not grudge the expense. I will need all my powers once we reach your side of the Hill to build the Gate to reach Shar and Tannim; this will help me save them for that."

"So Joe, it's up to you," Chinthliss said quietly. "We

need to get back to the barn, or somewhere near it, so we can use the trim-ring as a Gate." He handed Joe a different ticket from the other three: metallic gold, it felt very much like a very thin sheet of metal, embossed with odd characters. "You're the one with the Master Ticket for this trip; the Home Gate will take its setting from you. Take us home."

Home? For a moment, his mind was a complete blank. He'd never *had* a home, not really, so how could he take the others there? Not the succession of low-rent apartments that he and his parents had lived in while his father was working out his Grand Plan. Certainly not the old mansion outside Atlanta. *Definitely* not the bunkers of the Chosen Ones in Oklahoma. Not even the military school, which was the only place until now where he'd ever felt comfortable . . . .

Until now. Suddenly his thoughts settled. What was wrong with him? Of course he had a home now! Tannim's parents had made that clear, that he was welcome and wanted there. Needed, too, when it came to it; he could pull his own weight there and know he was useful, and be sure of getting thanks afterwards.

No, there was no question of where home was. Not anymore.

"Ready?" Chinthliss asked, looking searchingly into his eyes.

He nodded, confident now, and led the way under the vast, white arch of stone, knowing what he would find at the other end of it.

Home, he thought with a longing, and yet a deep contentment, as he felt that now-familiar disorientation take hold of him.

● CHAPTER THIRTEEN

There was the usual moment when he was blind, deaf, and directionless; this time Joe flexed his knees automatically and stepped forward confidently, walking out of blindness into—

Darkness. It took his eyes a moment to adjust to the dark after the dazzling whiteness of Grand Central Station.

Don't panic; we left at night, it should still be night, shouldn't it? How much time *had* passed while he was Underhill? Several hours, certainly. Should it be dark, then? Shouldn't it be dawn by now? Were they even where they were supposed to be? What if they were in Atlanta, or even the military academy?

Then, to his immense satisfaction, the bulk to his right resolved itself into the Drake house at the end of the driveway, and the flat to the left became the road.

"Good job," came a whisper to his right; Chinthliss, he thought. "Right on target."

"When are we?" FX whispered urgently.

Joe swiveled and reached out involuntarily, only to find that his hand passed right through FX. So they were definitely home, the world he knew, where Fox was nothing but a spirit. *When? What does he mean by that?*

Chinthliss raised a shadowy arm and a bit of blue light flashed up from his wrist. "Good," he said with satisfaction. "Very good! Only four in the morning, same night that we left."

Another shadow-shape touched his arm, this one slim and graceful. *Lady Ako.* "The time between Underhill and your world runs at different paces," she offered in low-voiced explanation. "Your sense of *place* is very strong, and includes a solid feeling for the exact time you came Underhill. Because Underhill has not been precisely real to you, your sense of *place* was not influenced by the apparent time you spent there."

If that's supposed to be a simple explanation, I don't want to hear a complicated one! he thought, bewildered. Nevertheless, he bowed his thanks to the Lady without revealing that her explanation left him as baffled as before.

"I'd like to get back to the barn," Chinthliss said, scanning the house and the road quickly. "The shields on it are good ones, and I don't want to leave a live Gate open behind us without shields. The only way we're going to get them out will be if we leave the Gate open at our backs."

"A good point," Ako murmured. "This is your place of expertise, Chinthliss, and I will follow your istructions. I have only visited here on this side of the Hill, and none of those visits was very recent."

"Which way is the barn from here?" Chinthliss asked Joe in an undertone. "I don't remember."

"Not a problem." Joe took the lead with confidence, even in the thick darkness of the last hour before dawn. The others followed, accepting him as the temporary leader.

The Junior Guard had followed him and his orders once—but it had been out of habit to obedience, and not because they were particularly confident in his ability.

But this was different. At this moment, despite anxiety for Tannim and worry about what lay ahead, he was as content as he had ever been. He was trusted for himself, now, and not because he was Brother Joseph's son, or the duly authorized leader of the Junior Guard, or even an officer in the ranks of the Chosen Ones.

It felt good.

He owed this, all of it, to Bob, Al, Tannim, and the other Fairgrove people he hadn't even met yet—a family of his own choosing, if it came right down to it. They'd given him a place where he belonged, where he could find out what *he* was all about. He owed them for something beyond price, something not too many people ever got, really.

Well, he thought, lengthening his strides when he sensed that the others would be able to keep up with him, *in that case, it's time for some payback*.

"I'm sorry," Shar said, wiping her nose on the tissue Tannim offered. Her eyes were sore; her throat and lungs ached. She felt vaguely as if she should have been embarassed; she'd never broken down like that before in front of anybody, not even her mother. Charcoal, Lady Ako, some of the Unseleighe had seen her anger, her rage, but never her tears. Grief until now had been a private thing.

But she wasn't embarassed. It had felt so *good* to lean on someone else, even for just a little—so good to let loose all that grief, all the frustration. So good to be held by someone who wasn't going to expect the very next moment to be a passionless roll in the sack.

"Hey," Tannim said, patting her hand awkwardly, "you were just tired, that's all. You still are. Just wait until we're somewhere safer, and you get a chance to rest; you'll be all right then."

She sniffed and blew her nose, then looked up at him to meet his peculiar, weary, lopsided smile.

He handed her another tissue. "I wish all I did was cry when I get tired. When *I'm* beat, you can't trust my aim with anything. That's one reason why I don't carry a gun around."

"Really?" she said, seizing the chance to change the subject gratefully. "I can't imagine you being unskilled at *anything*."

He nodded solemnly. "Honest truth. Scorched one of

my own friends with a mage-bolt once during a firefight
with the Unseleighe; gave him a reverse Mohawk."

"No!" She giggled as he nodded with a touch of chagrin
as well as amusement.

"'Fraid so." He sighed and looked around at the eddying mist outside of the Mustang. "Look, I hate to try and
push you, but we really need to make some decisions
here. What are you going to set the Gate for? The frozen
plain first? Or do we jump right into the fire and try Charcoal—"

Without warning, the Gate flared into life.

Tannim's reactions were faster than she would have
believed possible for a mere human. He had the Mustang
in reverse and skidding away from the Gate in a flash.

It just was not quite soon enough.

The sand came to life with a roar and rose up in a barrier
behind them. It acted as if it was alive, or something was
alive and burrowing beneath it, heaving upward in a towering mound with sides too steep for the Mustang to climb.
He slammed on the brakes, and spun the wheel to the side,
throwing the Mach One into first and accelerating into the
mist at right angles away from the brand-new mound, only
to find the way barred by something entirely unexpected.

A wall of shadow and dulled silver. A living wall.

A wall with ten talons, each as long as an arm.

He slammed on the brakes, just short of it. Shar stared
through the windshield at the two enormous foreclaws,
each half as large as the Mustang.

A *dragon . . . .*

There was only one dragon in all of Underhill that
peculiar metallic gray, like polished ash, or matte-finished
hematite.

Charcoal.

Father.

She bit back a gasp of fear, and felt a wave of chill wash
over her.

Her hands were on the door handle. She tried to take
them off and couldn't. They would not obey her.

She found herself opening the door of the passenger's side, *entirely* against her will; found herself getting out, standing beside the Mustang, mist eddying around her ankles. Her hands shut the passenger's door as she strove to regain control of them, to no avail. She should have been angry, but all she could feel was rising panic.

Charcoal shares my blood; he must have—the ability to control my body—

More shapes moved in on them, out of the mist: bipedal shapes in black armor, with surcoats and cloaks of midnight black, a dozen or more altogether. They paused in a group for a moment, in complete silence. One of them strode out of the midst of them with his sword drawn and his faceplate up.

Madoc Skean. He looked rather pleased with himself. *Bastard. He got Father to track us down!*

"Ah, Charcoal," Madoc said with false good humor. "I see you've found them. Now, just hand them over to me, and—"

The dragon coughed, and warm air laden with the scent of aged stone washed over her. He bent his neck down to stare at Madoc, his sulfur-colored eyes wide with amusement. "Hand them over to you? Aren't you getting above yourself, Madoc Skean? It was *you* who came to *me* for help, as I recall, and not the opposite." Charcoal's voice boomed overhead, kettledrums and distant thunder, a vibration in the breastbone. "If it had not been for me, you would never have found them, would you? If it had not been for me, you would not have known the Gate into this domain, nor would you have been able to hold it."

Shar found herself free to move again, as Charcoal's attention was momentarily on Madoc, and she backed up, one slow step at a time. *So he doesn't control me unless he's concentrating on it!* Maybe if she could get a little out of reach, where the mist was thicker, she could make a run for it. And if she broke and ran, that would give Tannim an opening to try something. Her magic was exhausted, but there was still his, and he was no amateur. Tension corded every muscle in her body as she edged past the rear of the Mustang. A little more. A little more . . . .

Madoc's expression changed from genial and self-satisfied to petulant and angry. "I thought we had a bargain, Charcoal," Madoc replied harshly. "You would find them, I would—"

"You would what?" Charcoal laughed so loudly that Shar winced involuntarily. She knew that laugh. Charcoal was sure he held the situation completely under his own control. "Dispose of the human? Punish *my* daughter? You would *presume?* I claimed this human as my prey a *long* time ago, elven fool—and such as *you* are not fit to polish the talons of one of *my* kind! However she has offended you, she has previously offended *me,* and she is *mine* to deal with, not yours!"

Charcoal's tail lashed, scattering Madoc and his followers, and the barrier of sand collapsed as Madoc took his attention from it. But the overall effect, when Madoc's Faceless Ones gathered around him again, was to put Shar and the Mustang directly between Madoc and Charcoal, with the Faceless Ones between her and freedom. This was not an improvement.

"I will challenge you for them if I must, impertinent lizard!" Madoc shouted, gesturing with his sword. "The human has slain my kin, wrought havoc among my kind! She broke faith with me! She violated the terms of our agreement! I have first claim on her and on him as well!"

"*My* claim takes precedence over yours, oh cream-faced loon," the dragon retorted, raising his head again. "She broke faith with me long before she broke it with you. In fact, I would say that *you* owe *me* for making a separate peace and an alliance with her when you knew that she and I were at odds."

The Faceless Ones were creeping up on Charcoal from behind, working their way across the sand silently, using the mist as cover. Shar wondered if he noticed—

Then his tail lashed again with sudden, deadly purpose. Most of them evaded it, but one did not; the creature was caught across the midsection by twenty feet of scale-covered muscle as big around as the trunk of a tree and sent hurtling, broken-bodied, out into the mist. It did not return. Not surprising; most created creatures disintegrated when damaged beyond repair.

And what will happen to me when I am damaged beyond repair?

"And as for the other, the human, my prey," Charcoal continued, as if nothing had happened, "I will deal with him as I see fit. His very existence is offensive to me, and has been since my rival chose to make a protégé of him."

Tannim opened the driver's-side door and slowly emerged from the Mustang to stand beside it. But Shar got the distinct impression that *he* had not been forced, as she had been, that he was getting out under his own control.

Tannim, no—don't do anything, don't say anything—

The young mage ran a hand through his tangled mop of hair and looked up at Charcoal with no sign of fear. "Don't you think it's a little early to start calling me 'prey'? I mean, we just met," Tannim said mildly.

Shar stiffened at his casual tone, now more afraid for him than she was for herself. *Oh no—no, Tannim, don't provoke him!*

Charcoal bent his gaze on the human below him, his eyes glowing with pent-up hatred. "Oh really? Perhaps you need to be reminded of how tiny you are."

Tannim folded his arms across his chest, and casually leaned against the car. "If you're trying to intimidate me, it's not working. I know all the tricks. And size doesn't impress me in the least."

What was he trying to do? Did *he* have some clever plan to get them both out of this? Shar clenched her fists until her nails cut into the palms of her hands, desperately trying to muster up even the tiniest amount of energy. The sparks of her magic sputtered and died as she tried to fan them into life. Surely he couldn't be counting on her to back him up—he *knew* she was exhausted!

This was a hazardous gambit Tannim was playing, if

what he was doing was trying for time by bluffing—and she didn't think it had a snowball's chance of working.

Charcoal's eyes narrowed. "You are an arrogant fool," he rumbled, his talons flexing in the soft sand as if he longed to sink them into Tannim's body. "As big a fool as that Unseleighe idiot who was hunting you."

But Tannim simply shrugged and leaned a little more against the car, dropping his left hand down behind the open door, paying no attention whatsoever to Shar. "Really? You think so? Then you haven't been paying attention."

His left hand flickered once, quickly, out of Charcoal's line of sight; the keys to the Mustang fell at Shar's feet, the sound of their impact muffled in the soft sand. Charcoal was so busy concentrating on Tannim that he didn't notice.

The dragon's eyes narrowed to mere slits. "You tire me," he hissed. "I believe it is time to squash you, and—"

A whiplash of mage-energy crackled across the distance between Madoc and Charcoal. Shar ducked involuntarily as it arced over her head, and Charcoal's head snapped back from the impact on his muzzle, precisely as if Madoc had slapped him.

"First there are *my* claims, worm!" Madoc cried, his voice high and tight with anger, his hands glowing with the residual energy of the mage-bolt. "This mortal is *mine!*"

"Don't you think both your claims are a little premature?"

Shar turned, for the voice had clearly come from behind her. Another figure loomed out of the mist.

Tannim oohed. "The gang's all here."

Loomed was precisely the word; the shape moving through the mist towards them was just a little shorter than Charcoal—although in this mist it was difficult to judge. In the next moment, a blast of wind from a pair of huge, fanning wings blew all the mist away from the immediate area.

It all began to drift back immediately, of course, but not before Chinthliss made an impressive entrance in the wake of the wind.

Shar had never seen Chinthliss in his full draconic

splendor before, and she felt her eyes widening with surprise. He stalked onto the sand, bronze scales shimmering subtly as the muscles beneath them moved, head held high on his long, flexible neck, wings half-spread behind him like a golden-bronze cloak. Beside him, the rest of his party looked like dolls—

Dolls? Perhaps that was not the best comparison. Perhaps they were no match for him in size, but that did not mean they were not formidable in their own right.

On Chinthliss' left, and nearest Shar, was the young blond human Tannim had been partnering before Shar kidnapped the Mustang; he had a drawn weapon in his hands, and Shar might have been the only creature present other than Tannim who knew just how deadly that tiny piece of metal really was. Beside him, in full battle arousal, was a three-tailed kitsune, his fox-mask convulsed in a snarl of rage, every hair on end, his paws crackling with mage-energy.

And on Chinthliss' right—

Mother!

Lady Ako was as serene and outwardly unmoved as a statue of a Buddhist nun; only someone who really knew her well would see the anger in her eyes and sense how close she was to the boiling point. And Shar knew that scarlet outfit she wore so regally, that belt with all of its many surprises. Lady Ako had come prepared in her own way for battle.

Tannim hadn't moved a muscle, although both Charcoal and Madoc Skean had backed up and shifted a few involuntary feet. Shar allowed herself to hope, just a little. Charcoal stared at the newcomers with the first signs of surprise Shar had ever seen him display. Shar took advantage of the distractions to bend down and snatch up the keys to the Mustang, knowing what that had cost Tannim—and what it meant to her.

He had sent her a message, as clearly as if he had spoken it to her. *If I buy it—it's yours, the car and all the power in it. Everything.*

Her heart ached. It wasn't the Mustang that she wanted . . . .

Shar, Tannim, and the Mustang were now the exact middle of a triangle, the points of which were Madoc and his Faceless Ones, Chinthliss and his allies, and Charcoal. Shar was already several feet behind the tail of the Mustang. With the change of position, Madoc was nearest Tannim, Shar nearest Chinthliss, the Mustang between Tannim and Charcoal.

"*Chinthlisssss.*" Charcoal's hiss of recognition was so full of hatred that Shar could taste it. "I might have known *you* would show up."

The bronze dragon shrugged; an oddly human gesture. "I am not as careless of my protégés as you, it seems. Nor am I inclined to abandon my allies as my whim suits me."

Charcoal ignored the sally and dropped his gaze to Chinthliss' feet. "Ako," he said in a tone that Shar could have *sworn* was one of reproach—if she hadn't already known that Charcoal was a master of manipulation. He assumed an expression of noble hurt. "Ako, I am surprised to find you with—this brat. I thought you had more dignity and pride than to be taken in by a manipulating charlatan."

Lady Ako looked Charcoal up and down, her face so full of open scorn that even Tom Cadge must sense it. "I do," she replied shortly. "That is why I left *you.*"

Charcoal reared up as if he had been struck. The three-tailed *kitsune* openly snickered. Chinthliss' mouth widened slightly in a draconic smile.

"I believe," he said genially, "that we have a stalemate, Chinthliss."

"Foolish worms!" Madoc Skean shouted furiously, startling them all. "You are forgetting me!"

He rushed Tannim, sword held high over his head, the blue-black blade alive with crawling actinic-white tendrils of mage-power. But Tannim was not as unready as he had looked—nor as relaxed.

Tannim reached down into the Mustang's front window,

and turned with one smooth motion to face Madoc's charge. As Madoc's blade slashed downward toward his head, Tannim brought up both hands with something between them. Madoc's sword met Tannim's red crowbar instead of Tannim's head.

However tempered the elven blade was, it was no match for a solid bar of Cold Iron, doubly-tempered with spells. With a scream that sounded almost human, the blade snapped in half, leaving a charred stump in the hilt in Madoc Skean's hands.

The Unseleighe lord stared at the remains of his weapon for a single stunned second. That was long enough for Tannim to make his countermove.

Showing all the expertise of any battle-honed elven warrior Shar had ever seen, Tannim swung the crowbar in a two-handed slash toward Madoc's head. The elven lord ducked aside at the last moment, and the crowbar only caught his upraised arm.

Sparks flew from Madoc's spell-strengthened armor, and Madoc staggered back a few steps.

But now the fight was no longer one-on-one. The Faceless Ones closed in to come to the aid of their master. Tannim whirled to parry their blades, but there were many of them and only one of him.

Tannim! He could never fend them all off—not without help!

Shar managed to summon up the power for a magebolt. Her hands blazed with magical energy; she screamed at the top of her lungs with the pain it cost her, but she blasted the nearest of the Faceless Ones full in the unprotected back, just as Tannim connected with a second, a raking blow straight across the chest with the pointed end of the crowbar.

Both disintegrated in a shower of sparks, empty armor dropping to the sand with a clatter.

Tannim dove through the opening presented by the loss of a faceless warrior, turning the dive into a somersault that brought him up onto his feet much nearer Shar, and outside the circle of Faceless Ones. Out of the corner of her eye, Shar saw that the young human with Chinthliss was trying desperately to find a target, but was clearly afraid of hitting Tannim. Tannim swung on another Faceless One, catching it in the back. Another shower of sparks and tumble of empty armor marked the loss of another of Madoc's creations.

Now it was Madoc's turn again; he charged Tannim with a wild war cry, his hands full of a much cruder weapon than his prized mage-sword. This was an ancient Celtic war-club, a massive piece of lead-weighted wood, previously strapped across his back. Tannim's crowbar was no match for it—and Madoc was a warrior trained since his birth hundreds of years ago in the art of wielding such weapons.

The club came down; Tannim deflected it rather than blocking it, but Madoc recovered swiftly and used the momentum of the deflected swing to come in from the side. Tannim deflected it again, but only partially; he got a glancing blow in the ribs that made him gasp and go double for a moment.

Madoc brought the club around again—

No, you bastard!

Shar's mage-bolt to the side of Madoc's head was weak, but enough to distract him for a moment. She crumpled to her knees, gasping with pain that brought tears to her eyes, but Tannim took advantage of Madoc's distraction to recover, and landed another blow against Madoc, this one a solid hit to the knee with the full weight of the crowbar behind it.

Madoc's leg crumpled and he went down on the other knee, as Tannim shuffled backward, getting out of range of the vicious club.

That gave the young human enough room to begin shooting.

Yes! Shar exulted.

Faceless ones dropped like puppets with cut strings as the human's bullets connected. Joe emptied one clip, and slapped in a second without pausing. He wasn't just a good shot; he was an expert. For every *crack* of gunfire, another Faceless One fell, until the only set of black armor still moving was the one containing the Unseleighe Lord.

Madoc was in full battle-rage, oblivious to the decimation of his followers. In this state, only his own chosen target had any place in his maddened mind. In a condition of berserker mindlessness, he felt no pain, and would not notice injuries or even broken bones. He regained his feet and charged again, limping slightly, heading straight for Tannim.

But the young human beside Chinthliss wasn't finished either.

In a flurry of rapid fire, the young man emptied three well-placed torso-shots into Madoc Skean's breastplate.

Madoc's body jerked backward with each of the three shots. Three fist-sized metallic dimples appeared in the carapace of Madoc's armor, where the spent bullets hit metal after passing through breastplate and flesh.

Silence. Shar's ears rang from the noise of the shots.

Madoc dropped down to one knee with a clatter of armor, leaning on the war-club.

Blood poured from every seam, every hole in Madoc's armor, yet the Unseleighe lord somehow remained erect.

The young human ejected the second clip and slapped in a third, leveling the sights on Madoc, although he did not resume firing.

Madoc's helm came up, the eye-slit pointing at Tannim. There was a gurgling sound as Madoc tried to speak, but nothing coherent emerged. Then, like a tree falling in slow motion, he dropped over sideways to land sprawled in an ungainly heap, blood still oozing from his armor.

The young man swiveled instantly to train his sights on Charcoal, but the dragon's attention was not on him, nor on Chinthliss, nor even on Tannim.

Shar met her father's eyes and could not look away from the burning yellow gaze. His eyes grew until they filled her entire field of vision, until she was lost in them, drowning in them, helpless to look elsewhere.

Once again, fear overwhelmed her, chilling her very soul.

She felt her body moving forward, one slow step at a time.

"This is no stalemate," Charcoal thundered, his voice vibrating her bones and shivering along the surface of her skin. "If you try to stop me, you will all suffer. Chinthliss, you are no match for me, and never were. Ako, your powers lie in cunning and in Healing; the lowly three-tail beside you cannot even muster the latter, much less courage. *No* human born could ever harm me. Even if you should conquer me against all odds, some of you *will* die, and all of you will suffer. You cannot risk that."

Shar fought Charcoal with every atom of her will, to no avail. Her feet continued to move, dragging reluctantly through the sand, taking her ever nearer to him. She sensed the Mustang within reach; it might as well have been on the other side of the Hill for all the good it did her. She could not even feel her hands clutching the keys: they were completely numb.

"Nevertheless," Charcoal continued maliciously, "I shall grant you this much. You may go; even the human called Tannim. I will permit you to escape this time. But I will have my daughter."

"No!" Ako cried, and Shar bled inside to hear the pain in her voice.

"Yes." Charcoal's icy tone sent a frost of fear down Shar's spine. "She is of *my* blood; see for yourself how I control her body. As I created her, she is mine, and I will have her."

"You couldn't hold her the last time, Charcoal," Tannim said defiantly. "She isn't *yours*, she isn't property. She'll slip your leash and run."

But Charcoal laughed, and the sound froze the blood in Shar's veins.

"Not when I am through with her, she will not." The

dragon chuckled maliciously. "I shall see to it that there is nothing left in her mind that I have not placed there, no image that I have not approved. *This* time my dear Shar will be everything a doting and dutiful daughter should be—body, mind, and soul. And the body, mind, and soul will be *mine*."

She knew he could do it. He had the power to erase everything that she was, and replace it with whatever he wanted.

To unmake her,

No! she cried out in horror, but only in her mind. *No!*

And her feet stopped moving.

Fear gave her strength she didn't even know she had. Encouraged, she continued to fight: she stared into Charcoal's eyes and forced them *away* from her, fought against the control of her body until she shook as if she were fevered. Feeling came back to her hands, her arms—

Charcoal's eyes narrowed in anger; his breath escaped in a hiss, and he snapped his jaws together with impatience.

"Do not fight me, girl," he snarled. "Do not fight me, or I shall make your friends suffer."

She ignored his threats, knowing that while she fought his control, he would not be free to turn his attention elsewhere. With a snarl like cloth tearing, he changed his tactics.

She screamed as pain struck her with a thousand fire-tipped lashes, convulsed and dropped to the sand, holding her head in her fisted hands as agony lanced her in both temples.

"Stop it!" cried Ako, in shared agony. Shar saw through eyes blurred with tears of pain that her mother stood as rigid as a stone, her face a mask of anguish. In answer, Charcoal only sent another assault of pain through his daughter.

"I can continue this as long as her mind resists," he said with a laugh that filled her ears and mind, and echoed in her heart. "And you can do nothing to prevent it."

"I'm—not your property!" Shar managed through teeth gritted against the pain. "I—will—not—surrender!"

"Then you will suffer," Charcoal replied, and suited his actions to his words. "And when I am finished with you, if the rest of these fools have not taken advantage of the opportunity to escape, I shall turn my attention to one of them."

A different kind of pain grated on her nerves, racing up her arm from her left palm. She realized that she still held the keys to the Mustang.

And she still held the key to the power *in* the Mustang.

In the brief interval between waves of excruciating pain, she reached for that power. Held it.

Used it.

She threw up a shield between herself and her father; a crude thing, but strong, and she panted with relief as the next wave of pain broke on it and failed to reach her.

She used the moment of respite to refine it and reinforce it, before he realized what she had done, and that his punishment no longer reached her. Slowly, she got her balance back; slowly she raised her head, defiant once again. She got to her knees, then to her feet, and stood staring at him, daring him to try something new.

Charcoal was clearly taken aback by this development and stared back at her with open astonishment.

"I am not your property, Charcoal," she said in a voice hoarse from screaming. "I am not anyone's property. Anything I owed you before, you lost all right to when you tried to control me."

Charcoal's eyes widened in speculation, and she sensed that he was thinking furiously. "Shar—" he said then, his voice sweetly persuasive and hypnotic, "I don't know what this human has been telling you to turn you against me, but humans are by nature deceitful creatures. Whatever he has promised you, there is no way that he intends to make good on his promise. It is easy for humans to promise more than they can deliver—they never live long enough to be forced to account for those promises! You have not seen as much of the worlds as I have; I have only been trying to protect you from all the lies and trickery that—"

"That you are the master of," Shar snapped, holding her head high. "That always has been your way, hasn't it? When you can't force someone, you hurt them, and when you can't hurt them, you try to manipulate them. It isn't going to work with me."

Charcoal reared up to his full height, and only then was it apparent that he was *much* larger than Chinthliss. But his voice remained smooth and calm, even though malice underlay it.

"In that case, daughter," he said silkily, "I shall simply have to destroy you, as I destroy any flawed creation."

The fear returned, fourfold, holding her helplessly hostage. Shar sensed him gathering his power, and winced back behind shields she *knew* were inadequate, waiting helplessly for the blow that would be the last thing she ever felt. She closed her eyes, trying not to show that she was paralyzed with terror.

Any moment.

Her skin crawled as she threw the last of her power into her poor shields.

Now . . . now . . . .

"Stop it!"

The blow did not fall. Shar opened her eyes.

"Stop it, Charcoal," Tannim said wearily, stepping away from the car. "That's enough. Leave them all alone. Leave *her* alone."

Charcoal turned his burning gaze on the battered young human.

"And why, pray, should I?" he asked.

What is he doing? Shar stared, trying to fathom what new trick he was going to pull. Did he have anything left? Surely he must—

"Because you don't want her. If you want revenge on Chinthliss, you want *me*. So take me." He held his arms wide, and her breathing stopped as she realized what he was saying.

"Take me instead. I surrender."

• CHAPTER FOURTEEN

"Take me. I surrender," Tannim repeated, dropping the crowbar to the sand with a dull *thud* as if to emphasize his words. A dispassionate part of his mind noted the shock in Charcoal's eyes with grim amusement. This was the last thing the old lizard had expected.

"An interesting offer," Charcoal replied slowly. "I fail to see what prompts you to assume that I will take it."

"Oh, please, I'm not that dense." He allowed a weary sarcasm to color his words. "Don't you think Shar's already told me *why* you spent all that time training her? You wanted her to be my opposite, right? The counter-weapon to Chinthliss' little 'Son of Dragons.' That's all you ever wanted her for. Well, here I am; all yours. You won't need her anymore, you make Chinthliss unhappy, you get rid of me, you've got the whole enchilada."

He had known the moment Charcoal started in on Shar that the gray dragon was right; they *couldn't* fight him. If they did, they'd all get hurt. Probably at least three of them would be killed—Shar definitely, Joe the most likely after her, Fox and himself as a tie for third victim. Joe would die because he had no idea what he was up against, and a fight with Charcoal was no time to learn. Like the new recruits in the trenches, he wouldn't have time to gain the experience he needed to survive.

They couldn't abandon Shar, leave her to be murdered or mind-wiped by her father. *He* couldn't abandon her.

And even if they *did* abandon Shar to her father like a bunch of cowards, the moment Charcoal finished with her, he'd start on the rest of them anyway.

No matter what happened, *Shar* would die, physically or mentally, and she didn't deserve any kind of death, much less the kind that Charcoal would give her.

Unless *he* gave Charcoal what he really wanted.

And if I'm going to die, I'd like it to be keeping my friends safe. Keeping Shar safe.

Right, Tannim. Very brave. Very noble. Very stupid.

What the hell. When we played soldiers, I was always the one who fell on the grenade and got the terrific funeral. Too bad I won't be around to see this one. Damn. Life's been good.

He took a slow step forward, feeling every bruise, and savoring the pain as the last thing he was likely to feel. He was acutely aware of the soft, shifting sand under his shoes, the oddly clean taste to the air, the faint ache where that mist-thing had bitten him. "Here I am," he repeated. "I won't fight you. It won't cost you a thing. Take me."

Shar could not believe her eyes and ears, as her throat closed, choking back her cry of horror. What was he doing?

He was sacrificing himself, that was what he was doing.

She tried to grab him, to stop him, to counter his offer with one of her own, but she was held frozen, paralyzed. And what *could* she offer? She had just defied her father—should she make Tannim's offer worthless by surrendering herself now? Charcoal would never take her surrender and let Tannim go. Tannim was right. Charcoal didn't want *her* and never had; he wanted the human. She had never been more than the means to get Tannim.

Tannim stepped forward again, arms still wide. "Think about it, Charcoal," he said, as calmly as if he was not writing out his own death warrant with every word he spoke. "Think about how much you gain. You make Chinthliss *miserable*. Since you let Shar loose, you *don't* make Ako unhappy; in fact, you might even stand a chance of getting her back. Ako doesn't give a damn about me, she only wants her daughter safe, and she knows you won't want her once I'm gone. You get rid of *me*. As an added bonus to that, there's a bunch of Unseleighe who'll be so happy with you for getting rid of me for them, you'll be able to write your own ticket with them. Madoc Skean wasn't the only Unseleighe lord who wants me dead."

Everyone's attention was on Tannim, so only Shar saw that Thomas Cadge had crept out of the rear seat and was stealing out of the Mustang on all fours. He had taken the bandage off his head, and although she could not see his face from where she stood, he did not appear to be acting in the *least* blind.

He waited for a moment, crouched behind the shelter of the driver's-side door, then twirled his fingers in a peculiar gesture.

A thick eddy of mist twined up to the door, and he slipped off out of sight under its protective cover.

Shar nearly choked on bitterness, and fury shook her along with her grief. *He must have been Charcoal's confederate—he was the one leading Charcoal to us, and here we thought we were trying to save him! I should have thrown him to the Wild Hunt.*

If she ever saw his cowardly face again, she *would* throw him to the Wild Hunt.

"Well, Charcoal?" Tannim waited, now just within Charcoal's reach, the droop of his head and his slumping shoulders reflecting weary resignation. "How about it? Is the offer good enough?"

No— Shar wailed silently. *No, Tannim, please—*

—don't leave me alone—

Charcoal looked down with smoldering eyes for a long moment at the small human at his feet. Silent tears cut their way down Shar's cheeks, and her heart spasmed with agony.

"Yes," he said at last. "I believe that I shall take advantage of this situation."

He stared down at Tannim for a moment longer; then, before anyone could move or speak, he struck.

He lashed out at Tannim with a foreclaw, all talons extended, striking sideways, like a cat.

Shar reached out—uselessly, with agonizing slowness. Every second became an eternity, enabling her to see the tiniest of details. Charcoal's talons hit Tannim in the chest and bent against his armor, tearing at the remains of his shirt. Only one of the five three-foot-long talons caught and penetrated the armor, but it was enough. It pierced his chest completely, going through the armor, the entire torso, and emerging from the back, a needle-shaft of blood glistening in the light.

Charcoal flexed his talons open, then closed his fist around the body for a moment, as it convulsed in his foreclaw, and he screamed in triumph. Then he flung it contemptuously at Chinthliss' feet.

"Tannim!"

Shar screamed.

Her heart caught fire in mingled pain and anguish, despair and rage, and something broke within her, unleashing a fury she had never known was inside.

She reached for power, found it in her rage and hate.

Charcoal was going to pay in blood. No matter what it cost her.

Right up until the last moment, Joe was sure that Tannim was going to pull some rabbit out of the hat. Even as the gray dragon lashed out, he was positive Tannim was going to do *something* clever.

It wasn't until Tannim's broken and bleeding body flew through the air to land at Chinthliss' feet that he understood the truth of the situation.

There had been no way out. Tannim's offer had been genuine. And Charcoal had taken it.

He didn't realize that he was screaming until he ran out of breath; didn't realize he was shooting until the hammer clicked on an empty chamber. He ejected the clip and slapped in another, emptied it, and slapped in the last, tears running down his face and into his open mouth.

Then he paused for a moment, for now Fox was a streak of red lightning, launched into the air, then slashing at Charcoal's muzzle and eyes until Charcoal roared and slapped *him* down into the sand, where he lay stunned and unmoving.

Lady Ako was on her knees beside Tannim's body; Joe didn't bother to wonder why. Once Fox was out of the line of fire again, he emptied the last round into Charcoal, trying for the eyes.

Just as he dropped the last bullet into the dragon, *Shar* opened up on him.

She stood in the center of a pillar of white-hot flame, her two hands aimed for the gray dragon, and from those hands she poured the fires of the inferno itself down onto Charcoal. She looked like a living flame-thrower.

That, Charcoal felt.

He screamed and tried to fend the fire off with his foreclaws; the webs of his wings withered in the yellow-green flames and started to crisp around the edges—

Then the fires died, and Shar stood wavering for a moment, then collapsed bonelessly onto the sand.

Charcoal was still standing.

All the damage seemed to be superficial. Joe stared at him, frozen in place, unable to breathe or move, tears still scorching his face.

What does it take to kill this bastard?

Charcoal turned toward Chinthliss, and shook himself once. Flakes of ash fell away from him as he glared at the bronze dragon.

"Now," he snarled. *"You die with the human."*

Chinthliss gathered himself, preparing to spring at Charcoal's throat. Joe looked frantically for a weapon and saw nothing even remotely useful.

We're all going to die—

A huge shadow uncoiled itself out of the mist behind Charcoal. A dark bronze, fisted foreclaw lashed out of the shadow and slammed into Charcoal's head in a fearsome backhand *smack*.

The gray dragon rocked back on his heels, as a second bronze dragon, darker and larger than Chinthliss, and faintly striped with deep gold, strode past him across the sand to stand beside them all, facing Charcoal.

"I don't think so," said the newcomer.

"Thomas?" Chinthliss gasped, his fanged mouth gaping open in blank astonishment.

The new dragon grinned toothily. "You haven't been home in ages, Chinthliss. Just keeping up the tradition of bailing you out of trouble, little brother." Thomas turned his attention back to Charcoal. *"You,"* he said, contempt dripping from his voice. "You may take your miserable carcass out of here and slink back to whatever hole you call home. You may do so *only* because we have other concerns at the moment, more important than dealing with you."

"And if I don't?" Charcoal hissed.

Chinthliss drew himself up to his full height. "We, my brother and I, will kill you. This I pledge."

Charcoal looked from one to the other and back again, and evidently believed them, for he snarled and limped off into the mist.

Now Joe unfroze; his knees turned to jelly and he sank down on the ground, closing his eyes in despair. *Oh, Lord God, what do I tell Tannim's mom and dad? He must have had some kind of premonition this was going to happen— he asked me to take care of them if anything ever happened to him. Now he's gone—oh, God, what do I do now?* His shoulders shook with sobs, his throat was tight, and his chest ached as he hugged himself in his grief.

"Boy—" Someone was shaking his shoulder. He looked up, to find an old man—well, older than Chinthliss, anyway—shaking him. "Boy, go help your *kitsune* friend. Lady Ako needs me to aid her."

He nodded dully, responding to an authority automatically, and stumbled to his feet. He shuffled across the sand to Fox, who was stirring and moaning faintly. Just as he reached the *kitsune*, Fox opened his eyes and looked up at him, clearly still in a daze. He'd reverted to the semi-human form, the one with James Dean's face.

"Dial nine-one-one, would you?" FX asked weakly.

"Yeah, sure," Joe replied. "Is anything broken? Can you sit up?"

"No. Yes." With Joe's help, Fox managed to get into a sitting position, holding his head with one hand. "Ah, hell. Being physical is *not* all it's cracked up to be. For every kiss I get when I do this, seems like I catch ten punches."

"Right." Joe had no idea what he meant, and right now, he didn't much give a damn. He hurt too much inside to care about much of anything. All he could think of was the last time he'd seen Tannim, standing beside the Mustang, trading jokes with Chinthliss . . . .

Never again. Never again.

Chinthliss was a few feet away, back in his human form, helping Shar to her feet. The old man and the other dragon were nowhere in sight.

Or was the old man the other dragon?

The young woman leaned heavily on Chinthliss' shoulder, and Joe thought she might be crying, for she hid her face behind the curtain of her hair and her shoulders shook. He was saying something to her that Joe couldn't hear.

Chinthliss led her over to Lady Ako; lacking any other orders, Joe got Fox up and helped him stagger in that direction as well. He averted his eyes as they neared; he just couldn't bear to look at—

"I believe I have him stabilized, with Thomas' help," he heard Ako say in a voice so faint with weariness that it was hardly more than a whisper. "If we can get him to further help quickly, I believe we can pull him through, but he shouldn't be moved without more Healing than we can give him. We are at the end of our strength."

For a moment, the words made no sense to him. Stabilized? Healing? *What?*

Could she mean Tannim?

He let go of Fox's arm, and stumbled the remaining few steps to where Thomas and Lady Ako knelt on either side of Tannim's body. A body which *was* breathing, shallowly. There was an awful lot of blood soaking into the sand around him. Although the green, hexagonal-scale armor he must have worn under his shirt gaped open over the chest, there was no huge wound, only a raw red line, the kind you saw on a wound that had just been sutured.

"The talon missed the heart," the old man was saying. "Just. It would seem your protégé's luck is holding."

"How long can you hold him?" Chinthliss asked, as Shar picked up one of Tannim's hands and held it as if she was willing her remaining strength into his body.

"With Thomas' help, an hour, perhaps more." Ako smoothed the hair over Tannim's pale forehead. "I am not sure that anyone will ever be able to heal the damage completely. I fear he will always bear the marks of this encounter. And he may well still be lost to us."

Chinthliss looked straight at Joe. "The Gate to the barn is still open," he said. "If I send you through it with the Mustang, can you get to a phone, call Keighvin Silverhair, and get him to us within an hour?"

Joe had no hesitation. "Yes, sir!" he replied.

"I'll stand watch for trouble," Fox offered. "I've got enough left in me for that."

"I'll hold the temporary Gate for you and Keighvin. It'll be faster if he Gates to the barn, then takes my Gate here. He'll waste time trying to find us otherwise," Chinthliss said. Then he looked at Thomas. "I'm going to want to know everything later," he said firmly. "But now—let's move. Tannim is still near death, and slipping away."

Joe did not need any urging. Shar pressed the keys into his hand, though how *she* came to have them, he had no idea. He ran for the Mach One, and with Chinthliss leading through the mist, took it to the Gate they'd made of the chrome circle.

This time he drove out of the barn under a dawn sky—

and headed straight for the nearest Quik Trip. There was a quarter burning a hole in his pocket.

There were some tense days ahead.

Reality seemed to float like a feather.

Even now.

Concentration returned to him easier now, despite the fact that his mother was on the phone.

"No, it's all right, Mom, really. Mr. Silver has taken care of everything. Don't worry. Really." Tannim hung up, sighing—carefully, since any movement of his lungs hurt like hell—and Shar took it from him, putting it out of the way in the headboard of The Bed. She handed him a Gatorade and made a little face of apology.

Fox—insubstantial, Tannim assumed, since he was in the real world—perched on the top of Tannim's TV set on the bureau at the foot of The Bed. He shrugged sympathetically, and twitched *four* tails.

"How are they taking it?" Shar asked. "I hated to make you talk to them, but they've been calling here three times a day, and this was the first time you've been awake enough to deal with them. I've been passing myself off as a private-duty nurse, telling them you've been taking pain-pills and you're sleeping."

He coughed, and a sharp stick stabbed him under the ribs again. "About as well as you'd expect. They hate it when I get hurt."

Shar nodded, her face full of sympathy, and sat crosslegged on the foot of his side of The Bed. He slowly tucked up his feet to make room for her.

At least his legs weren't broken this time.

"Hey," Fox said, "look at it this way. If they'd actually *seen* you, they'd have been having fits, followed by lots of really expensive therapy."

"He's right. It could be worse," Shar told him. "Joe was very quick to think of a plausible accident, to account for—" She nodded at his chest. "*I* certainly would never have thought of a runaway glass-truck."

"At least you can tell your mother the truth," he said, just a little bitterly. Then he shook his head and grimaced. "I'm sorry. It's just post-injury depression. I'm a rotten patient." He managed to drag up a little smile for her. "Usually, once Keighvin's Healers get done with me, there isn't anyone here who has to put up with me. That's why I bought this monster bed. As long as I'm not full of IVs, I can pretty much take care of myself if I have to until I'm mobile again."

"Wait. You bought a *huge* bed to be all alone?" she replied, one eyebrow arching. Fox smirked.

"Let's say it works out that way." He shrugged—carefully. "It's got room for my electronics, anyway."

"I found the fridge and the microwave in the headboard, and all the controls to everything else," she said with a fellow gadget-lover's admiration, "but I was afraid to try any of them; I didn't know what they did and I didn't want to turn you into a sandwich."

"Jeez, or worse," FX put in. "I can just see trying to explain to Lady Ako how come Tannim's laminated!"

Glad for the change of subject, Tannim demonstrated his prize for her. The Bed was the only piece of furniture he'd ever really hung onto through all of his many moves, after he found it in a Goodwill. The years of ordeal-after-injury-after-trauma had all been survived with this one item intact. Though he'd modified it for the electronics, someone somewhere had spent a lot of money designing a bed for a market that didn't exist. Or a market of one, depending upon how you looked at it.

He had awakened more than once in The Bed after one of his close encounters with severe pain—but never after quite such a close encounter with death. His last memory—looking down at his chest, his vision filled with seeing Charcoal's talon sticking into it, deep into it, as everything went red and black—played back. He wasn't certain he really wanted to think about that very hard; but he couldn't help it. If he did think about it, he was going to start shaking, and he was afraid he'd never stop, never have the courage to leave this room again. Still, the sequence of events played through his mind, and he felt his control slipping again. Then his mind cleared and the memory mercifully faded away.

His next clear moment had come a couple of hours ago: waking up in The Bed, and finding Fox on the TV and Shar sitting on the edge, pretending to read, but watching him. *That* had been enough to drive all other thoughts from his mind, at least temporarily. Then his parents had called, frantic with worry, and some story about a wreck— that he'd gotten hit by an out-of-control glass-truck and had gotten a huge shard of glass in the lung. Joe was with his folks, keeping them calm.

Just like I asked him to. Am I getting prescient?

In a few more days Joe would "fly" here, once the Drakes were sufficently calmed. Actually, Keighvin was going to send Alinor after him. Joe had said, with a laugh, that Al had orders from Keighvin to "outfit him."

God. Al has great taste, but he's gonna turn the kid into a bigger gadget-hog than me. At least Joe no longer had any problem with accepting Fairgrove's generosity.

He *thought* he'd come to a few times in between that moment Underhill and now; he had vague memories of Chinthliss and Keighvin hovering over him, of a woman with long red hair and oriental features, of Lidam, one of Keighvin's Healers, of Fox and Shar, and of Thomas Cadge. He did think he remembered waking up in terrible pain several times only to be soothed back into sleep by a gentle hand on his forehead, a hand he associated, for some reason, with Shar. He thought he'd dreamed of voices, of Shar and Fox talking together about him.

And he had a particularly vivid memory of awakening in the middle of the night to see Shar asleep in an exhausted tangle of hair and pillows and a blanket, on the other side of The Bed, her face tear-stained and white with weariness. He would have chalked that up to a hallucination if he hadn't come to this morning to find her here.

This was certainly a new experience; the very first time

he'd ever awakened in The Bed after an injury to find that he wasn't alone.

"So, you were starting to explain just what Thomas Cadge has to do with all this when the phone rang," he prompted.

"Yeah, I wanted to hear this, too," FX said with interest.

She thought for a moment, then resumed the interrupted explanation. "Thomas is Chinthliss' older half-brother," she said. "Chinthliss says that while they have the same dragon-father, Thomas' mother was a human, one of the Sidhe fosterlings who was a very powerful Healer. Thomas used to feel very strongly against cross-species romance, partly because of all the trouble he had growing up. So when Chinthliss got involved with my mother, Thomas was against it from the very beginning, and did everything he could to break the romance up."

Tannim shook his head, puzzled. "All right, that much I've got. So why did he get involved now? And what the hell was he doing, pretending to be a crazy old blind guy?"

"That was part of his plan—you see, he got involved because he saw how unhappy Chinthliss was after Mother left him. He says he heard from some of his friends that Mother wasn't exactly full of cheer either, and he—reexamined his feelings." She fell silent for a moment. "He told me after we brought you back here that he felt at least partially responsible for their breakup, because of all the things he'd said to Chinthliss. He decided he was wrong, and he wanted to make it up to them. He loves Chinthliss; all he ever intended to do was to try to protect him from getting hurt. And whether or not he'll admit it, Chinthliss adores him, too."

Tannim nodded; he could understand that. Chinthliss had often remarked on how unfortunate it was that Tannim was an only child, how he missed out on a great deal by not having a brother. Tannim had never known, before now, that it was because Chinthliss himself had a big brother who watched out for him.

"So. Thomas decided that he was going to have to find

a very subtle, clever way to get Ako and his brother back together." Shar paused. "*He* is the reason we used to dream about each other."

Tannim blinked. "W—wait. You mean, since he couldn't get the two of *them* to talk to each other, he forced the issue by getting the two of us—what would you call it? Curious about each other? Involved?"

Shar shook her head, puzzled. "I'm not quite sure. I think his original intention was just to have us get glimpses of each others' lives, so we'd be sufficiently intrigued to see if we couldn't track each other down. He *certainly* didn't intend for us to have the kind of dreams we've been having since we discovered the opposite sex!" She laughed then, the first time he'd heard her laugh with no sign of strain in her voice. She had a beautiful laugh. "He was *very* embarassed when I came right out, described the dreams, and asked him if he was the cause!"

"I guess the only thing we can blame is our own subconsciouses for that." He chuckled—very carefully, more of a wheeze. Laughing hurt too much. "So, he figured that if *we* went looking for each other, Ako and Chinthliss would have to go along with it. And if we became friends, Ako and Chinthliss would be forced together, is that it?"

"Pretty much. Then things got out of hand." She licked her lips and stared at the wall for a moment in thought. "He wasn't prepared for Charcoal molding me into your opposite number."

Tannim sipped his Gatorade. "So what did he do?"

"He said he worked with it, keeping an eye on me through my air elementals. He figured he could get things back on track when I broke away from my father, but then I made alliances with the Unseleighe, and that was almost as bad. The *last* thing he wanted me to do was—well, what I did, kidnapping the Mustang. He knew you were going to come after it as well as I did. That was when he decided he'd better get involved directly, disguised as Thomas Cadge." She shrugged. "He freed the real Thomas Cadge, took his clothes and his cart and all, and folded so many disguise-shields on himself I didn't have a clue, and neither did you. He said he didn't know what he was going to do, he just knew that if he didn't come along, we'd probably get caught again, and Ako and Chinthliss would never reconcile and never forgive him."

"Well, that's where I came in," Fox said lightly. "Shar, since you don't need me to talk to to keep you awake, I've got a date with a pretty lady fox." He winked at Tannim. "Glad I'm seeing you on this side of the spirit-world, buddy."

With a *pop*, FX vanished, leaving his glowing "FX" hanging in the air for a moment, like the grin on the Cheshire Cat.

"Huh. That's Fox all over. Vixen chasing." He finished the Gatorade and put the empty glass down. "So that's what Thomas Cadge was all about. I wish he'd pulled his rescue a little sooner." He tried to say it lightly, to make a joke out of it, but it came out badly. The implications hung heavily in the air, and he flashed on the talon penetrating his chest again . . . .

He shivered, and caught a pain-filled breath. How long before he'd stop seeing that in instant replay?

Shar bit her lip. "I saw him sneaking out of the car. I thought he was the one who had led Charcoal to us in the first place when I saw that. Then, when I realized what he really was, I was almost as mad at him for not showing up sooner, too. For what it's worth—he demonstrated draconic shape-changing to me, and since he's half-human, it takes a *lot* longer for him to go from human to dragon than it does to do the reverse. Chinthliss told me that if the dragon is interrupted halfway through, it kills him. He feels really awful, Tannim. As badly as you'd like him to feel, I think. The only way he'd feel worse is if—if you weren't all right."

"Oh." Tannim digested this, and to buy himself a little time to think, picked up the audio controls and triggered the CD player. He didn't remember what he'd left in there, but it would probably help lighten the mood a little—

But the first selection hit him between the eyes and left him stunned. "I'll Find My Way Home," by Jon Anderson and Vangelis.

Home. He'd thought he'd lost his home forever; that he didn't fit in the old one, and hadn't found a new one. Shar had never *had* one. What was it that Thomas had said—something about not being able to go back to your childhood home because you outgrew it? And that part of being an adult was building your *own* home?

And building it meant finding someone to share it. Home wasn't really more than a place to live if it meant being alone.

So why did this room feel so much like a home?

"Ah—are Chinthliss and your mother—getting along?" he asked carefully.

She smiled, and it was clear that she approved of what was going on. "As a matter of fact, I think they're doing just fine. Mother confessed that she was stalling him to let me get you out of the mess on my own, but by then, Chinthliss was so grateful for the way she'd spent herself for you that if she'd confessed to murdering his parents and sleeping with Madoc Skean, he'd have forgiven her." Her green eyes softened, and her smile softened with them. "He really cares a great deal for you, you know," she said quietly. "He could *be* your father; he loves you that much."

Another revelation that left him a little stunned. "I think maybe you're exaggerating a little."

But she shook her head. "No. No, I don't think so. I watched him with you here; I listened to him browbeating the Healers, swearing he'd search through every domain Underhill if he had to, in order to find the best for you. He nearly did that, too—he's going to owe a lot of people a lot of favors for a long, long time."

"Oh, hell," Tannim muttered numbly. "He's never going to forgive me for that—he *hates* owing people—"

But she leaned over and placed both her hands on his. "He *doesn't care.* Didn't you hear what FX said? You nearly died, not just Underhill, but three more times after we brought you here."

"I did?" Some of those confused memories began to make appalling sense . . . .

"You have no idea how much damage Charcoal did to you," she said soberly, the color draining from her face. "Mother thought that the talon missed your heart—it didn't. Thank the Ancestors there were Healers *here* when—" She shook her head. "I can't talk about it. I thought Chinthliss was going to go mad, or I would. Fox was the only one who stayed calm. He was always here, the least powerful and the most hopeful, when we were feeling like hope was lost."

He took a slow, careful breath. "So what's the real damage?" he asked. He didn't want to know—and he did. Hell, he had to know; he was going to have to live with it for the rest of his life.

"The permanent damage is in your left lung and your heart," she said bluntly. "You've lost the bottom lobe of that lung. The rest—broken ribs, torn muscles, internal damage—is either healed or is going to heal." She blinked, and her eyes glistened suspiciously. "You're going to have to be careful. It's always going to hurt when you really exert yourself, like a stitch in the side, only worse. That's the best they could do, and Chinthliss would have sold himself into slavery to make you well."

Then she added in a very quiet voice, "So would I."

There it was, out in the open.

"You were here the whole time?" he asked softly.

She nodded. "I never left. I couldn't. When I thought you were—when Charcoal—" Her voice faltered and died. "Fox kept me company. I never saw much of the lesser *kitsune* before this. He's a lot deeper than he lets on. He couldn't do anything physical on this side of the Hill, but he watched you for me when I just couldn't keep my eyes open anymore."

So the "memories" were real . . . .

He thought very carefully about his next words, picking

them with utter precision before he spoke them. "You're probably the most unique lady I've ever known, Shar. It's kind of funny—Charcoal tried to make you into my opposite, and failed. But you wound up becoming my—complement. Or else I became yours."

She licked her lips nervously and nodded, clearly listening very carefully to what he was saying.

"What I'm trying to say is that we went through a pretty wretched experience together and I *think* we make a good team." He grinned, just a little. "And, dreams aside, even though we haven't known each other very long, I *think* we know each other pretty well." His grin faded as he turned his hands over and caught both of hers. "What I'm trying to say is that I would really, really like it, Shar, if you would decide to stay here. With me. Maybe we can make this place into a home together. If you'd do that—every bit of this will have been worth it to me."

She stared at him, and her hands trembled in his. He bit his lip. "The three best words on this earth are 'I love you.' Would you believe me if I used them now?"

She blinked rapidly, and nodded.

"I love you, Shar," he said softly. "I really do. I gotta be crazy, lady, but I do."

"I—I guess we both are." She smiled tremulously. "What a pair we are! A half-*kitsune*, half-dragon, and a human racer-mage! If Thomas hadn't changed his mind, he'd be having a litter of kittens. I—" Her voice broke. "Tannim, I love you."

He looked into her eyes for a long time, then gently lifted one hand and kissed the back of it. "I'm afraid that's the best I can manage at the moment—" he said with a rueful chuckle. "You're not getting much of a lover right now."

"You'll just have to make it up to me later," she replied, regaining some of the mischievous sparkle he remembered from dreams. "And you'll have to remember, I *am* a *kitsune*—half, anyway. I won't be tied down. I won't be Suzie Homemaker."

"I never thought you would," he replied, with growing content. "There's a lot more to life than picking out drapes."

She looked at him for a long time, a penetrating stare that weighed and measured the truth of everything he had said and done. He just smiled, knowing that she would find he meant exactly what he had said.

Finally, she returned his smile and moved forward, arranging herself very carefully against—not *on*—his shoulder. He managed to get an arm around her without hurting himself.

He closed his eyes, savoring the moment, and realized that it was this that he had been looking for, without knowing what it was he had been in search of. Somehow, through pain and fear and long loneliness, they had found their way home.

Together.

Tannim held her, lovingly, as they drifted off to sleep. They had a lot of new dreams to catch up on.